. . .

354440

PB EVA

Evans,

Longar

sweet

RY 2/13.

D0171854

Jessica

onto hi:

Long

tendrils

throb w

"Lord above, woman," Longarm gasped. "What fine tricks Myobu has taught you."

"There are no tricks, silly," Jessica laughed. "The geisha's art lies not in playing tricks, but in knowing how to surrender . . ."

. . . from *Lone Star on the Treachery Trail*

"Ki . . . Ki . . ." Daphne cried, while her naked flesh began to tingle with renewed excitement.

Then she suddenly screamed, freezing rigid. Ki twisted his head sideways to see what had shocked her into mental terror.

"I thought I heard that squawk of yours," Volpes snarled.

"I—I'm sorry," she whined. "I'll never do—"

"You're right, you won't!" Volpes loomed menacingly over them. He pivoted, and drew his pistol as Ki flew into action.

LONGARM
AND LONE STAR

SWEET REVENGE

TABOR EVANS
AND **WESLEY ELLIS**

Thompson-Nicola Regional District
Library System
300 - 465 VICTORIA STREET
KAMLOOPS, B.C.   V2C 2A9

JOVE BOOKS, NEW YORK

THE BERKLEY PUBLISHING GROUP
Published by the Penguin Group
Penguin Group (USA) Inc.
375 Hudson Street, New York, New York 10014, USA

Penguin Group (Canada), 90 Eglinton Avenue East, Suite 700, Toronto, Ontario M4P 2Y3, Canada
(a division of Pearson Penguin Canada Inc.) • Penguin Books Ltd., 80 Strand, London WC2R 0RL,
England • Penguin Group Ireland, 25 St. Stephen's Green, Dublin 2, Ireland (a division of Penguin
Books Ltd.) • Penguin Group (Australia), 250 Camberwell Road, Camberwell, Victoria 3124, Australia
(a division of Pearson Australia Group Pty. Ltd.) • Penguin Books India Pvt. Ltd., 11 Community
Centre, Panchsheel Park, New Delhi—110 017, India • Penguin Group (NZ), 67 Apollo Drive,
Rosedale, Auckland 0632, New Zealand (a division of Pearson New Zealand Ltd.) • Penguin Books
(South Africa) (Pty.) Ltd., 24 Sturdee Avenue, Rosebank, Johannesburg 2196, South Africa

Penguin Books Ltd., Registered Offices: 80 Strand, London WC2R 0RL, England

This is a work of fiction. Names, characters, places, and incidents either are the product of the author's
imagination or are used fictitiously, and any resemblance to actual persons, living or dead, business
establishments, events, or locales is entirely coincidental.

LONGARM AND LONE STAR: SWEET REVENGE

A Jove Book / published by arrangement with the authors

PUBLISHING HISTORY
Jove edition / January 2013

Copyright © 2012 by Penguin Group (USA) Inc.
Cover illustration by Milo Sinovcic.
Longarm and the Lone Star Legend copyright © 1982 by Jove Publications, Inc.
Lone Star on the Treachery Trail copyright © 1982 by Jove Publications, Inc.

All rights reserved.
No part of this book may be reproduced, scanned, or distributed in any printed or
electronic form without permission. Please do not participate in or encourage piracy of
copyrighted materials in violation of the author's rights. Purchase only authorized editions.
For information, address: The Berkley Publishing Group,
a division of Penguin Group (USA) Inc.,
375 Hudson Street, New York, New York 10014.

ISBN: 978-0-515-15352-1

JOVE®
Jove Books are published by The Berkley Publishing Group,
a division of Penguin Group (USA) Inc.,
375 Hudson Street, New York, New York 10014.
JOVE® is a registered trademark of Penguin Group (USA) Inc.
The "J" design is a trademark of Penguin Group (USA) Inc.

PRINTED IN THE UNITED STATES OF AMERICA

10 9 8 7 6 5 4 3 2 1

If you purchased this book without a cover, you should be aware that this book is
stolen property. It was reported as "unsold and destroyed" to the publisher, and neither the
author nor the publisher has received any payment for this "stripped book."

ALWAYS LEARNING   **PEARSON**

3 5444 00124523 1

CONTENTS

Longarm
and the
Lone Star Legend

TABOR EVANS

Chapter 1

It was nine-thirty in the morning on a gray day in Denver, and Longarm, his gunmetal dark eyes bleary, was wondering just how many fried eggs and slices of ham he was going to have to watch Billy Vail eat before the man explained why the hell they were having breakfast together. Not that Longarm and his boss, the Chief United States Marshal of the First District Court of Colorado, weren't friends, but Billy's usual style was to summon his deputies to his Federal Courthouse office up on Capitol Hill, growl out his orders, and then send his men off with a boot in the ass.

But not this morning. This morning, Vail's pale-faced young clerk, Henry, had left his typewriter in the front room of the marshal's office long enough to skitter his way across Cherry Creek, over to the unfashionable part of town, to Longarm's rooming house. The knock on Longarm's door had brought the lawman awake, his big right hand finding his double-action Colt .44 in its place beneath his pillow. His groggy-sounding "Who is it?" nicely covered the sharp double click of the Colt's hammer being pulled back.

Henry had identified himself and called out Vail's invitation through the room's closed door. Longarm had eased down the Colt's hammer as he told the clerk that he'd meet Marshal Vail presently, and then swung his six-foot, four-inch frame up and out of bed.

He'd stared into the old mirror above the dressing table, viewing his reflection in between the black spots where the silvery stuff had been scraped off the glass over the years. His longhorn mustache and close-cropped hair, both the brown, lustrous color of well-oiled saddle leather, had been tended to just yesterday by a barber over on Colfax Avenue, so Longarm had figured he could get through the day without a shave. Over on the washstand, a bar of soap floated in a china basin three-quarters filled with tepid water. Having decided that being able to see the basin's cracked bottom vouched well enough for the purity of the water, he'd frothed up some suds, dipped a washrag into them, and scrubbed himself down. The friction of the rough cotton against the hide of his lean, muscular body had soon banished the last remnants of the previous evening's tour of Larimer Street's saloon row.

So much for the outer man, Longarm had thought. He'd picked up the bottle of Maryland rye he kept by the bed, pulled the cork with his teeth, and aimed the bottom of the bottle toward the grimy plaster of the ceiling. One big swallow later, with the rye stoking a fire in his belly, Longarm had felt ready to face the day.

He'd dressed quickly, shrugging on a clean gray flannel shirt, fumbling his shoestring tie into place, and tugging on his cotton longjohns and skintight brown tweed pants. After hauling on a pair of woolen socks and stomping his feet against the threadbare carpet of his room to get his low-heeled stovepipe boots on snugly, he'd turned his attention to the important parts of his wardrobe. His gunbelt was a cross-draw rig, and he wore it high, just above his narrow hip bones. Retrieving his Colt Model T .44-40 from where he'd left it on the bed, Longarm had slipped the six-gun, butt forward, into the waxed and heat-hardened holster on his left hip. He'd positioned himself in front of that tarnished mirror, and had then reached across his belt buckle with his right hand, drawing the weapon in a whip-fast, rock-steady, single motion. Yep, the gun's polished walnut grips were just where they ought to be . . .

Longarm had next turned his attention to the Colt itself. He'd cleaned and oiled the weapon and then checked all five of its cartridges—only a fool neglected to let the firing pin ride safely on an empty chamber—late last night, before turning in. Lucky for Marshal Vail that he had, Longarm had thought to himself with a grin. It could've been the President of these United States, Rutherford B. Hayes himself, waiting breakfast for him—Longarm *never* started the day without first seeing to his revolver. He'd paid his respects to the grave markers of too many fellow lawmen *ever* to neglect the main tool of his trade.

The Colt had a barrel cut down to five inches, eliminating the front blade sight as well, and good riddance to it—a front sight could cost a man a precious instant of drawing time if it snagged the lip of an open-toed holster. A handgun was for close-in work. If a man needed to sight-aim, he'd best turn the job over to Mr. Winchester's saddle gun.

Returning his Colt to its place on his hip, Longarm had then put on a vest cut from the same brown tweed as his pants. Next came his ace in the hole. He'd scooped up his Ingersoll pocket watch on its long, gold-washed chain. The other end of the chain was clipped to a ring in the butt of a double-barreled .44 derringer. The watch had gone into the left breast pocket of his vest. The derringer—that ace—had gone into the right. As always, the gold-washed chain draped between the two, like a wide, innocent smile.

He'd slipped into his brown frock coat, patting the pockets to be sure they held some spare .44 cartridges, his wallet—inside of which was pinned his silver-plated federal badge—a pair of handcuffs, and a bundle of waterproofed matches. On the way out of his digs he'd grabbed his snuff-brown Stetson from its nail on the wall. After locking his door, he'd pulled out one of the matches and broken off a piece of matchstick, then wedged it into the crack between the door and the jamb.

Longarm considered himself a generous man. He liked to give surprises, not receive them. If the match splinter had been dislodged when he returned, he'd know somebody had been in the room. Or was *still* in it, waiting for him.

He'd crossed the little sandy wash of Cherry Creek, leaving the cinder path behind as he headed up Colfax Avenue, his boots clicking on the brown sandstone sidewalks they'd installed here on the better side of the city. Up ahead, the gold dome of the Colorado State Capitol glittered against the overcast sky like a fine piece of jewelry nested in folds of gray flannel.

Nodding good morning to the Front Range of the Rockies, fifteen miles to the west, but looking like they were close enough to topple over and crush a man, Longarm had begun to turn into the Federal Courthouse before he'd remembered that Marshal Vail wasn't in his office upstairs, but was waiting for his deputy down the block, in Hodder's Café.

Breakfast had proceeded at a leisurely and—for Marshal Vail—very subdued pace. The big-gutted, red-faced, balding marshal was normally about as quiet and easygoing as a Kansas twister. This morning, or at least so far, all Billy did was make dumb small talk.

But something was up. Longarm had sensed it. He'd been a lawman too long not to know when a man had something on his mind but wasn't yet ready to speak it plain. The café was still crowded, so Longarm had figured that Billy was waiting until these stinkwater dudes had drained their teacups, gathered up their legal briefs, and then wandered off to do battle along the marble corridors of the State House and the Federal Court.

At about nine-thirty, the large group sitting at the table just to the right of Longarm and Vail had lit up their cigars and pipes, paid their check, and left. Vail had watched them go as if they were the James gang on their way to the nearest bank.

Longarm leaned back in his chair and tucked the end of a cheroot into the corner of his mouth. He didn't light it, and not just because Billy was still working on his *second* plate of ham and eggs. Longarm had been trying to quit the damned tobacco habit for a long time, and his latest ploy was a vow not to light up a smoke before noon.

The waitress, a pretty little redhead whose sky-blue eyes had been sending smoke signals Longarm's way since he'd come in, came around to their table to refill their coffee cups. As she passed behind Longarm's chair, her cool fingers caressed the back of his neck. Not a word passed between them, and then Longarm was watching her walk away, her shapely behind doing a soul-stirring, rhythmic dance beneath the snug expanse of her skirt, which was stretched even tighter by the big, puffy bow of her apron . . .

"Why don't you ask her if she's on the menu?" Vail grumbled as he pushed his cleaned-off plate away.

"Chief, that line stopped getting women when you were still young enough to want them," Longarm drawled, knowing that Vail could take a joke. The marshal had long ago been roped and branded by a fine woman. Like most lawmen smart enough to survive, Vail had waited until he'd taken a desk job before taking a bride.

Vail signaled for more coffee and the check. "I don't want us to be disturbed while we talk," he told the pretty waitress. Longarm breathed a sigh of relief when Vail paid for the meal. Fifty-five cents for two breakfasts was robbery, even if this eatery was a Capitol Hill hangout! He'd not had a raise since '78, and everybody was saying that 1880s' inflation was going to be the worst ever.

Longarm eyed Vail, wondering if now was a good time to bring up the question of his raise. It was funny how a man might be able to measure his opponent when it came to a fight, and yet be as skittery as a mustang when it came to jawing about money matters.

"You're most likely wondering why I didn't want to talk to you in my office," Vail began once the waitress had scooted off with their money, giving them both a big smile of thanks for their generous tip.

"It had crossed my mind," Longarm replied, chewing on his cold cheroot, trying to keep his mind off that waitress and on what Billy Vail was saying. She'd settled down at a table on the far side of the now nearly empty dining room, taking a break now that the morning rush was over. She was counting up her tip money as she sipped at her own mug of coffee. Every time she leaned forward over her sums, her fine, full breasts strained the buttons of her bodice, threatening to pop over the demure white piping of her uniform as if they too wanted to witness the count.

"Fact is, I've been issued orders from the Justice Department not to let anyone but the deputy I'm assigning hear about this case," Vail quietly explained. "I've sent you out to investigate murders before, but this time I've got something a mite rarer for you, Longarm." Vail took a deep breath and looked his deputy square in the eye. "This time I'm sending you out to unravel an assassination. You remember the killing of Alex Starbuck?"

"Hell, everybody remembers the Starbuck shooting," Longarm said. "He was one of the wealthiest, most powerful cattlemen in Texas. But why all the secrecy? Usually we're either in a case or we're not, depending on whether any federal laws have been broken. What's Justice's angle on this one?"

"A lot of angles," Vail muttered into his coffee. "But the one that scares me is that we've been *unofficially* ordered in." He sighed. "Maybe I'd better start from the beginning. At the time of his death, Starbuck was in his late fifties." Vail reached down for a manila folder that had evidently been propped on his lap throughout breakfast. He opened it and removed from it a photograph, which he handed across to Longarm. "Got this sent to me from San Francisco. Big newspaper there had it in the files."

It was a well-detailed, full-front, formal pose, showing a tall, barrel-chested man with a full head of gray hair. The man was dressed in a fine suit, obviously custom-tailored, and probably from one of the shops in San Francisco. Once, while on a case that had taken him to the West Coast some years before, Longarm had visited such a shop. Even then, a suit like that worn by Starbuck in the photograph would have cost Longarm half a year's salary. He flipped the photograph over. "According to the date written here, this was run pretty recent. Whatever they were writing about him, it wasn't his obituary. How did a Texas cattleman rate a picture in a San Francisco newspaper morgue?"

Vail smiled. "You ain't been reading the financial pages."

"Where you've been sending me, there's no newspapers. I did run across one of those telephone contraptions a while back, in the Sand Hills . . ."

"Well, if you did read a paper once in a while, you'd know that cattle were the least of Starbuck's fortune, and the most recent addition to it," Vail replied, tapping the manila folder. "He got into beef just in time to reap the profits of the bad harvests and political troubles in Europe. He made his real fortune back in the fifties. Starbuck happened to be one of the sailors on Perry's fleet, when the commodore used his gunboats to convince the Japans to open up their ports to the United States. Hell, that was around '50, I'd reckon—"

"It was 1853 to '54, Chief," Longarm grinned from behind his cheroot. "I read me a book about it once that some fellow wrote," he added in an attempt to damp down Vail's slow burn.

"Anyway," the glowering marshal continued, "Starbuck might have been just another sailor boy, but he saw his opportunity. As soon as he was discharged back home, he gathered up every penny he could borrow and got himself passage back to the Orient. He stayed there for a while, learning the language and such, and then returned to San Francisco with a sizable piece of the Japans' import-and-export trade in his pocket."

Longarm nodded ruefully. "Then he was in the right place at the right time. San Francisco's harbors were just being dredged for foreign trade, and the transcontinental railroad was getting itself into one piece to carry his goods to the East."

"Today, the Starbuck empire stretches all across the country," Vail agreed. "But we ain't here to jaw about the man's good luck. What we're concerned with is the one instant when he was in the *wrong* place at the *wrong* time."

"Starbuck was murdered in Texas, right?"

"Right."

"Well, Texas is a state," Longarm said. "One of the thirty-eight. They got all kinds of solid law down there. One more lawman shoves his badge into Texas, the state, big as it is, is going to sink like an overloaded rowboat. And I still don't understand what all the secrecy's about. It sure as hell ain't a secret that Starbuck's dead—"

"Keep quiet and let me get there," Vail ordered. "First off, there's no local law big enough to investigate Starbuck's death. Hell, Starbuck *was* the law in his part of North-Central Texas. His hands did a damn fine job of keeping things peaceable, from what I've been told. The governor is a sissy who spends most of his time in Washington, sucking up to the federal politicos. Word is, *he's* got his eye on a Senate seat. That must have been all right with Starbuck, as he was the one who paid for the governor's election."

"I'm starting to get the idea," Longarm drawled.

"Then get this. President Hayes has personally taken an

interest in this case. The worry is that without Starbuck's restraining influence on the area, vigilante groups will form, and then it'll only be a matter of time before range wars break out as the various groups start shooting each other up for killing Starbuck."

"Hell, Billy, I didn't think any man *but* the President was so all-fired important."

"Starbuck was also the head of the Cattlemen's Association. It was his money that allowed his neighbors to build up their own herds. Starbuck lent them that money to bring stability to the state. His death has shaken Texas's stability. His killers have got to be brought to justice."

"And that's where I come in," Longarm nodded.

"Wrong," Vail spat. "That's where the army comes in."

"The army!" Longarm groaned. "They can't do this sort of snooping-around work. Everybody knows that the army's method of smoking out a rat is to burn down the whole barn!"

Vail shrugged. "Everybody but President Hayes, it seems. The various spreads in that part of Texas are about to start their big roundup, driving their combined herds to the railhead. They'll fatten those steers up in the feed pens of Kansas and Nebraska, but they breed 'em and birth 'em in Texas. The nation needs that beef, and President Hayes has promised millions of pounds of it to England and the rest of Europe. The President aims to keep his promise to those countries, and it's his feeling that what Texas needs is a good dose of martial law to keep things quieted down."

"How do we come into it?" Longarm asked.

"Secretly. I told you that the governor has friends in Washington. He's afraid that flooding the state with soldiers might make him unpopular, come the Senate elections."

"Makes sense," Longarm mused. "If the army comes into the proud Lone Star State, the governor's career would be finished. He'd be out on his ass."

"Now the Justice Department wants the credit for solving this case, so between Justice and the governor's friends, the President's orders to the army have gotten 'lost.' For the time being, at any rate. You've got a week, Custis, maybe a day or so more, but not much more," Vail warned. "If you can wrap it up by then, we'll both of us have earned ourselves a pat on the back from Justice. If you fail, it'll likely mean our jobs."

"You sure about that, Billy?" Longarm asked softly. "Damn, that don't hardly seem fair—"

"I'm sure."

Longarm looked into Vail's seamed, care-worn face, and saw that he was. He himself would get along just fine if he lost his badge. He was still on the friendly side of forty. But Vail had spent his entire life as a lawman, and was counting on his pension to support him and his wife in their old age. Damn—It was always the good and true men, men who had ridden out their lives in the cause of the law, men like Billy Vail, who had to suffer the consequences for the dumb actions of a bunch of politicos who'd ruined more lives with a stroke of their pens than any outlaw *ever* had with a six-gun.

"I drew up all your papers and travel vouchers myself," Vail was explaining. "I didn't want that rules-and-regulations clerk of mine controlling the case records on this one. I picked you because you keep that badge of yours pinned in your wallet, and flash it only when you have to. You know how to be . . . dis-*creet*—" Vail blushed—"and, Jesus, that's what I need this time around. If word gets back to Hayes before you're ready to make an arrest—"

"First I've got to find the killer, and *then* I've got to find a federal angle, else all I can do is point my finger for the local law—"

"I know that!" Vail snarled. "I was making arrests when you were still wearing short pants—"

"Sorry, Chief." Longarm grinned. "Well, reckon I've got me a cattle baron's murder to solve."

"Assassination."

"Now there you go throwing that word around again, Chief." Longarm glanced at the pendulum clock hanging just above the blackboard that announced the day's blue plate specials. He sighed and placed his still-unlit cheroot into the ashtray, where he could eye it wistfully. Still two hours before noon. "What makes you so all-fired sure Starbuck wasn't cut down by a spurned woman, or an envious neighbor whose loan was coming due, or maybe a passing rustler or two?"

"Because Alex Starbuck had seven rounds in him, and from the looks of the spot where he'd been ambushed, at least thirty rounds had been fired." Vail's features softened with joy over the fact that he'd been able to tell Longarm something the man hadn't already known. "The Texas officials put a lid on any of this going out over the telegraph lines, again at the behest of the President. At least fifteen men had to have been involved in the ambush, and they'd been lying in wait for Starbuck to pass."

"I guess he never knew what hit him," Longarm mused as he glanced down at Starbuck's photograph.

"Guess again," Vail said. "He lived for a couple of hours afterward. Tough old buzzard."

Longarm didn't answer, but just stared down at the photograph. The print was sharp enough for him to make out Starbuck's characteristics—the sorts of things an experienced lawman could tell about a man from glancing at him. Longarm could tell that Starbuck was no greenhorn. Despite his fine clothes, he had the hard, callused-looking hands of a man who had roped his share of cattle and thumbed back his share of Colt hammers. Longarm could only wonder: What sort of soul was this who had conquered the Japans, built up an empire, and then, as dessert, tamed Texas until it had trotted at his feet like a hound at heel?

"Starbuck's daughter—her name is Jessica—was the only one at her father's bedside when he died. Maybe she'll know something. Starbuck's wife passed away long ago. Jessica is the only heir. It all belongs to her now—lock, stock, and barrel."

"Maybe *she* killed him." Longarm winked and reached into his pocket and came out with a match, which he struck against the table. "Her and her fifteen boyfriends." He brought the flaring tip of the match up to his cheroot, and puffed it alight.

"Well, get on to Texas and find out, dammit," Vail growled.

"On my way." Longarm smiled, grateful that Vail's usual nasty disposition was coming back. It meant the old boy was growing less worried.

"By the way, I thought you'd told me that you weren't going to smoke those two-for-a-nickel stinkweeds of yours until noontime," Vail taunted as his deputy rose from the table. "Ain't got the willpower, is that it, old son?"

"Sure I do, Billy." Longarm exhaled a great stream of blue smoke, the expression on his face blissful. "I just figured I ought to commemorate the event. It's not every day a deputy marshal gets to investigate an *assassination*."

Longarm left the café and swung around the side of the building to the alleyway behind it. Once he'd passed the long rear expanse of the courthouse building, he could save himself some time by shortcutting to yet another alley that would lead him to the livery stable, where he could collect his McClellan saddle and Mexican bridle. His plan was to gather up his gear, then haul it along to the railway station, which was just about halfway between the stable and his rooming house. Longarm's years as a deputy marshal had taught him the railroads' schedules. He knew he had little more than an hour before the Kansas Pacific's local huffed its way out of Denver toward Pueblo, the site of his first transfer—that was, if he wanted to leave today, and he did. He had just about a week, and ahead of him were several train changes and a few days of travel by rail until he reached his jumping-off point.

The baggage clerk would watch his gear while Longarm went back to his rooming house to get his saddlebags, bedroll, and Winchester. He'd be back at the station, waiting for his train, in plenty of time. All of his travel papers were already tucked away in his frock coat, along with his authorization to borrow an army mount. He'd pick up the horse at an army remount station located on the New Mexico side of the border. It would cost the Justice Department a bit more for Longarm to transport the mount via the railroad, but that was better than sparking curiosity inside Texas by flashing his badge and papers at some Ranger post.

Be discreet, Vail had warned him. Well, Texas Rangers were fine men, but they considered any business in Texas *their* business.

He could ride the railroad all the way to Sarah, one of the newest cow towns in that region. Starbuck had built the town, persuaded the railroad to run a spur into it, and contracted with cattle buyers in the East to have holding pens built. Sarah was the place where the Old West's cattle drive jumped into the next century, where drovers wearing chaps came in from the range to turn their cows over to men wearing ties, who kept their herds in ledger books. Sarah was the site upon which Alex Starbuck had built his empire.

Overhead, the sun had poked holes through the fuzzy gray blanket of clouds, so that the sky now looked like an old bedroll that had been worn out by hard use on the trail. It was just a little after ten, but the air was already stifling and still. It was going to be a true Denver dog day.

But it wasn't the heat that was making Longarm feel uncomfortable; it wasn't the breakfast in his belly that was causing that flutter in the pit of his stomach.

Longarm continued on his way down the deserted alley. He ambled—quick, but easy—his boots making hardly a sound on the hard-packed dirt beneath them. He was channeling all of his awareness into his sense of hearing now, and any sound he himself made might just muffle the crucial sound.

As he passed a clapboard building, the front of which housed a stationery store, a crow loitering in the building's eaves squawked in outrage over being disturbed. A covert glance told Longarm that the crow was no longer watching him but had focused its beady, sideways glare on the alleyway behind him.

The crow squawked again, and as it did, Longarm used the distraction to casually brush back the left side of his frock coat, clearing the butt of his Colt. But he kept on walking, resisting the urge to look back over his shoulder.

The crow had been confirmation, but Longarm had already known he was being followed—and had been, since he'd left the café. The real question was by whom. And why?

The end of the alley loomed before him. When he cut over, he'd only have a short stretch of the second alley to go before he reached the street, where there would be people, where the stable was located. If his shadow was planning on doing some shooting, now was the time.

Still, Longarm kept on walking, not looking back, trusting instincts born of long years at this sort of work to get him through. It just didn't feel like a gunplay situation to him, and

Longarm didn't want to be the one to provoke gunplay by spooking his tail. For one thing, Vail would hit the roof if his deputy had to spend the rest of his morning filling out papers on a corpse, thereby missing his train.

That he would be the one standing over a corpse, and not the corpse himself, Longarm had no doubts. He knew that he could take whoever it was. Hell, if the fellow was twice as good with a gun as he was at trying to follow somebody inconspicuously, he'd still be tenderfoot-lousy.

The end of the second alley loomed before him. Longarm concentrated, ears straining for the faint metallic click of gun mechanism, which would be all the warning he'd have before it was time to get out of a bullet's path. Then he was out of the alley.

The tail hung back as Longarm crossed the street, dodging the weekday traffic as he did so. Inside the livery stable it was dark and still cool, the air fragrant with the honest, pleasant smell of oiled leather and healthy horseflesh. Several horses whickered in their stalls as he walked by them to the rear of the building and the storage shelves.

"Morning, Deputy Long," the stable boy beamed. He was a gangling fourteen-year-old, looking like a scarecrow in his baggy union-suit shirt and too-short, obviously hand-me-down britches.

"Morning, son, fetch me my gear, would you? I've got a train to catch." Longarm flipped the boy a shiny dime, which the youngster caught even as he headed off to do the deputy's bidding.

"Take a look at what we got in stall six, Deputy," the boy enthused as he wrestled down Longarm's McClellan saddle from its place on the wall.

Longarm did so and whistled softly in appreciation at one of the finest specimens of Virginia walking horse that he'd ever seen. "Mighty fine, boy." He reached out to lift the chin of the horse, watching the animal's muscles tremble with life beneath the sleek dappled gray of its hide. "Whose stallion is this?"

"Judge Bing had him shipped in," the boy answered, lugging Longarm's saddle to a sawhorse just a few feet away from where the lawman was standing. He set the McClellan across the sawhorse and then paused before going back for the bridle.

"The judge already has himself a few fine mares, and means to get into the breeding business. He'll be taking this fella home tonight." The boy gazed with undisguised admiration at the horse. "Wouldn't you like to call him your own, sir?"

Longarm smiled. "That I would, son."

Like most working men in the West, Longarm had never owned a horse. It was a hell of lot cheaper—even if the government didn't pick up your expenses—to take the train to where you wanted to go, and rent a horse when you got there. "Hope that fool judge has more sense than to try and ride this fellow home."

The boy giggled as he headed back to the rear of the stable. "Wouldn't that be something?" he called over his shoulder. "That old judge holding on for dear life, his black robes flapping, while his fine stallion does it to the milkman's old mare—"

The stallion gave a nervous whinny, its massive head bobbing up and down as its eyes showed white and rolled toward the stable's front doors. The other mounts—geldings all—seemed undisturbed, but something was spooking the stallion. Longarm remembered his unseen follower.

He walked to the rear of the stable. "Boy, I want you to run an errand for me," he began. "Get on to my rooming house, and tell my landlady that I said to let you into my room to pick up my saddlebags, bedroll, and rifle. I keep that stuff all packed up and ready to go. Bring it all back here for me, all right?"

"Gee, Deputy . . . I don't know, sir. I'm supposed to watch over that stallion—"

"You git," Longarm ordered good-naturedly, handing over some more change. "Reckon that horse can't have a better guard than a federal marshal. I aim to wait right here for you."

"That's fine, then," the boy laughed, relieved that he didn't have to give up the money.

Longarm gave the boy his address. "Hold on," he called thoughtfully as the boy headed toward the front doors. "You go out the back way, son, through the corral. And shut those two old doors behind you as you go."

The boy peered up at Longarm's face. "Sir? Is there something up?"

"Go on now," Longarm said absently. "And if you should stop off for a soda on the way, I don't aim to tattle to your boss."

The stable boy ran off. Longarm waited until he was sure the kid was well away, and then began to make his way silently toward the front of the stable. The stallion was pawing the ground, huffing and snorting, as if agreeing with Longarm that the tail was hiding behind the front stable door, which was still swung closed.

Longarm considered climbing up into the hayloft, the better to get the drop on his adversary, but decided against it. It was a hot day, and this fellow's bumbling attempts at trailing him had put Longarm in a bad enough mood as it was.

Longarm leaned against the tall sawhorse that held his saddle and waited, watching. The door was nothing but a bunch of old boards nailed to a frame. Sunlight streamed in through the various chinks and knotholes. Whoever it was on the other side, creeping along to the door's edge, standing between the sun and those chinks, he was evidently too dumb to realize that Longarm could chart his progress by the way his form passed from chink to chink, blocking one sunbeam after another.

As the tail's fingers curled around the door's edge, Longarm sprang forward, locking his big hand about the other's wrist. He gave one solid yank, and almost followed the trajectory of his own arm as his adversary came flying in to tumble onto the stable floor. The jasper was sure a lightweight . . .

"Owww!" bawled the mysterious form, in a high, unmistakably feminine voice.

"I'll be damned." Longarm kicked open the stable door to let the sunlight flood in. Sprawled across the floor, with her skirts up around her thighs, was the waitress from the café!

"My God, Deputy," she pouted, her fingers gingerly rubbing her wrist. "I think you came awfully close to breaking my arm." She extended both arms to him. "Help me up!"

Longarm did as he was told. Placing a hand on each side of her slender waist, he picked her up, setting her on her feet. "Sorry about hurting you. But how was I to know it was you stalking after me like the wolf after the lamb?"

"I might have been doing the stalking, but I surely hope you've got that wolf-and-lamb stuff backward, Deputy," she laughed.

"Never mind. What *are* you doing following me?" Longarm asked sternly. He tried to keep his eyes on her face, but as pretty as it was, with her big blue eyes blinking at him as wide and seemingly innocent as a newborn babe's, his own eyes kept wandering back to her bodice. Her breasts were rising and falling, obviously over the excitement of being hauled into the stable.

"Well, answer me!" Longarm demanded, but the waitress just smiled, and took a step closer.

"It's a long story. I'm sort of new in Denver. I only arrived here, from back East, a few weeks ago. I don't hardly know *anyone*," she complained, brushing a tendril of her copper-colored hair off of her face. The tight bun in which she had been wearing it had come loose during her tumble. Now wisps of her hair hung down, the strands clinging to the hot, moist nape of her neck. "Not knowing anyone really doesn't bother me, because that just means I get to save more of my salary. I intend to open up a dress shop in just a little while."

"That don't explain why you were following me."

"Hush. I'm getting to that. You see, Deputy, coming out West, leaving my parents, was a big step into a new way of life. So when I saw you in the café—and I *knew* you saw me—um, well, I have a couple of hours before it'll get busy again, and so, well, I decided to come meet you and—" Here she blushed, cat-grinning at the same time, her bright white teeth flashing like a bunch of daisies in a field of pink rose blossoms. "What can I say, Deputy? A girl only lives once. This is sort of like moving West. I thought maybe you and I could—"

Now it was Longarm's turn to grin. He thought about scolding her for trailing him, about pointing out to her that those who wanted to stay healthy ought to make it a habit to approach both lawmen *and* outlaws from the front, but somehow this didn't seem like the right time.

"My name's Maggie Henders," she said, and then waited. "And you're Deputy . . . uh . . . ?"

But Longarm seemed not to have heard her. He was still watching her breasts. Maggie smiled knowingly, as if she'd witnessed such reactions on the part of men before. "I should point out that while this *is* my first time out West," she continued demurely, "This will *not* be my first time, um, you know . . ."

Longarm just had to chuckle. Something about this young

lady made a man feel like it was springtime. "Custis Long, ma'am. At your service."

"Oh, I hope you are." Maggie's eyes glinted merrily.

"Well, now, Maggie, we've got ourselves a little problem on that score." Longarm sighed, thinking that she was a fine woman, and certainly an experienced one who knew what she wanted and how to handle it after it was given. "I've got a train to catch in about one hour, and that means there's no time to get to my rooming house between now and then."

"Well, what about right here?" Maggie challenged. "We're alone, and there's piles of nice, soft hay in the loft." She took another step closer and slid her hands around his waist, her palms caressing his buttocks beneath the tightly stretched tweed of his britches.

Brazen as she was, Longarm could feel her trembling as he pulled her to himself and found her lips with his own. Their tongues did a fine mating dance, and Longarm felt as if the crotch of his pants had suddenly shrunk in size as Maggie rubbed herself against him. He noticed that she was still wearing her waitress's apron.

"Oh, *let's*, Deputy Long," she breathed, pecking moist kisses up the curve of his jaw while fingering the solid bulge behind his fly.

Longarm thought about it and then decided, Why not? The stable boy was gone, and he'd told the kid to take his time.

"Folks generally call me Longarm, Maggie."

"Well, *I* won't," she teased. "Not until you prove it."

Longarm untangled himself from her grasp long enough to hurry to the stable door and swing it halfway closed. The light that filtered in made the stable's interior agreeably dim.

"Is this your saddle?" Maggie asked, running her fingers along the smooth leather curve of the McClellan. She'd already begun to get undressed, the two halves of her unbuttoned bodice parting like curtains before the proud swell of her fine round breasts. As Longarm feasted his eyes, her nipples stiffened to attention. "But Deputy"—she frowned, a look of puzzlement suffusing her lovely features as she stroked the front part of the saddle—"where's the—the *thing?*"

Longarm had already taken off his coat and gunbelt, and

was unbuttoning his shirt, which he would keep on, along with his loosened vest. That way his derringer would remain within easy reach. It was one thing to be a fool in love, quite another to be a loving fool . . . "You mean the saddle horn, Maggie? This here's a McClellan saddle. It doesn't have a horn." He kicked off his boots.

Maggie winced at the thought of a male crotch sliding along that saddle. "If there's no horn, how do you protect your . . . *things*? she asked wide-eyed as Longarm peeled off his pants. "Oh, I hope they're *all right*," she whimpered as he kicked off his longjohns. "Oh, they *are!*"

Longarm laughed as he gathered her up in his arms for another kiss. She was still wearing her skirt and apron, but she placed a hand under each of her breasts and lifted them for Longarm's approval, as if she were right now fulfilling her waitress's role, presenting two sumptuous globes of fruit.

"Deputy, I know just how I want to do it," she giggled. "Oh, you'll think me shameless!" She reached behind her to unhook her skirt, then wiggled out of it, the pert, round cheeks of her bottom finally bouncing free and bare. She skipped over to the saddle and stood on tiptoe to drape herself belly-down across it. "I'll keep my apron on to protect my belly from all these nasty brass fittings, Deputy Longar—Oops! I almost said it." She licked her lips. "But you haven't made me yet!" With that she lowered her head and raised her bottom in invitation.

Though Longarm did fleetingly wonder if she'd left her underwear back East, along with her folks, he couldn't remember when he'd gazed at a finer sight. Her long legs and full, soft buttocks were a lovely white and pink against the brown leather of the saddle. And above it all was the crisp white bow of her apron, its knot resting right at the small of her back, just an inch above where her buttocks began their soft, full swell. It reminded him of the twitching, white cotton-ball tail of a female bunny in heat.

As he rushed toward her, she parted her legs and arched her back, tilting her hips in order to draw him in. He toyed his rigid member along the crevice between her thighs. "Lord, are you wet," he laughed. "Good thing you're wearing that apron, Maggie, else you'd be soaking my saddle!"

"Soak *mine!*" she bawled like a cat, and before she could

say another word, Longarm slid into her to the hilt, with-drawing slowly and then sliding back to set an easy, slick, incredibly pleasurable rhythm, like that which a cow pony might set as it loped along the prairie. Like that cow pony, Longarm knew that this was a pace he could easily keep up for a long, long time.

Maggie's cat-bawling had now become something that sounded more like a coyote howling at the moon. As she wiggled and twitched to meet his thrusts, she slipped forward across the saddle, so that her toes left the ground. She was helpless now, draped across the expanse of leather as if she were a set of saddlebags. Longarm gripped each side of her hips and impaled her again and again, each thrust making her yelp and kick her legs uselessly and wave her arms in the air, until he began to worry that someone outside the stable might think a murder was taking place.

Her hips, beneath Longarm's fingers, began to rock and buck, while her juices gushed out of her, rolling down the sides of her legs in beaded trails. "Oh, God!" she sobbed, arching her back. "Oh Deputy, I'm dying—"

"What's my name?" he teased, quickening his pace, driving her to her climax with short, sharp strokes.

"Ahhh! Longarm!" she sang. "Longarm! *L-o-n-g-a-r-mmm!*"

All tension left her as she collapsed limply across the saddle to shudder through orgasm after orgasm. Longarm, his muscles corded, threw back his head to growl his pleasure as he spent himself deep inside her.

As he withdrew, she shimmied off the saddle to spin around, throwing her arms about his neck as she locked her legs about his waist. Longarm felt the wonderful wetness of her center pressing against him as she kissed him over and over, murmuring endearments.

"Best that we start getting dressed," Longarm said gently.

"Oh . . . can't we *again?*"

"We *can*, but we *won't*," Longarm laughed, rubbing her bottom. "Maggie, we can't expect to keep this stable to ourselves forever, you know, and I've got a train to catch."

"But we can when you come back, right?" Maggie asked earnestly.

"I promise, ma'am."

Nodding happily, Maggie let go of him and began to gather up her clothes. Suddenly she stopped and, pointing at one of the stalls, called out delightedly, "Oh, darling! Look at the boy horse!"

Longarm whirled to look at the stallion, and then began to roar with laughter. The big gray walker was reared up on its hind legs, its nostrils flared, and its total, equine attention transfixed by Maggie's delectable form. *No wonder*, Longarm thought. No wonder the stallion, of all the mounts in the stable, was the one to become agitated by the approach of the mystery adversary! All the other mounts were geldings. But the big Virginia walker was a stud, and on this warm, still day, he'd focused on what it took Longarm longer to get to: a female in heat!

"Ohhh," Maggie sighed as she stood with her legs apart, absently stroking the tousled wet fur between her legs. "Look at *his* thing . . ."

Still laughing, Longarm walked over to her and slid his arm around her shoulder. The stallion's long, slender member stood out, a trembling, bobbing rob. "Yes, ma'am, Maggie," he mused. "Just look at it. It sort of makes a man stop and think . . ."

Maggie spun around to gaze up at him with adoration in her eyes. "Some men, maybe. But not you, Longarm . . ."

He scooped her up under one arm and headed for the ladder that led up to the hayloft. As Maggie giggled with delight, and squealed with certain knowledge of the joy to come, Longarm thought: *What the hell, that old local to Pueblo is always late!*

Chapter 2

Longarm stretched out as best he could across the red plush seat toward the rear of the Texas & Pacific passenger coach. The train was crowded, but there were plenty of cars. Even if there hadn't been, Longarm would most likely have kept his Stetson tipped over his eyes. He was in no mood for company. Trains had been his entire world for the last forty-eight hours, and he was feeling ornery as hell. Well, all he had to do now was get through the night. They were scheduled to reach Grassy Bow, a jerkwater town in New Mexico where the army remount Station was located, in a few hours. He'd pick up his horse, and then, by tomorrow afternoon, they'd be at Sarah, Texas.

Longarm felt himself drifting off into a doze. He wasn't worried about being disturbed, since folks tended not to trouble fellows wearing double-action Colts. As he drifted toward sleep, his mind returned—as any man's would—to that last time with Maggie, up in the hayloft. Besides, thinking about Maggie might just serve to take his mind off the stale sandwiches he'd eaten for dinner, peddled to its captive clients by the railroad.

"Tickets! Tickets!" droned the old conductor as he stumbled down the swaying aisle. He was dressed in his regulation blue suit and cap, with its black, duck-bill visor. This train made more stops than an old hound had fleas, and an eternity ago, when Longarm had first boarded, the conductor had grumped about how impossible it was to keep track of who had paid their fare and who had not. "Hope you stay settled in one place," the conductor had muttered as he punched Longarm's federal vouchers. He'd made it sound as if asking a man not to get out of his seat for more than a day and a night were the most reasonable thing in the world.

Longarm had figured that the conductor probably considered him a sort of fellow civil servant. What a railroad man thought he had in common with a deputy marshal was beyond Longarm, but the old conductor had insisted on talking shop, complaining about the fact that he was the only conductor on board, and there were just too many folks riding the trains these days . . .

Fortunately the old codger had been too busy tracking down fare evaders to chew the rest of Longarm's ear off during the journey.

Now Longarm lifted his hat just long enough to watch the conductor disappear through the door at the front of the car, which led out to the open platform between this coach and the rear of the next. *Crazy old coot*, he thought, and then lowered his hatbrim, letting the murmuring drone of the other passengers conversing among themselves send him back into his reverie.

The rocking and swaying of the train on its track reminded him of the rocking and swaying he and Maggie had done up in that loft. They'd had a fine time together, but Longarm had to admit to himself that the best memory he would take from the experience came after their loving was over, and they'd descended back down to the stable floor. Longarm had dressed quickly, and Maggie had dawdled, standing slightly spread-legged, still totally nude, so that her sassy rump and proud breasts were jutting out in all their glory. She'd been standing in front of that stallion's stall. She was so transfixed that she evidently didn't hear the squeak of the rear stable door, or the soft footsteps of the stable boy across the scattered hay.

"Deputy!" the boy had begun. "I've got your gear—*holy cow!*"

Maggie'd given a little scream as she whirled around to stare wide-eyed at the boy, whose own eyes were about the size of saucers. She'd blushed about the color of a strawberry from head to toe, as both Longarm and the boy had ample time to see, as she darted this way and that, gathering up her clothing, and finally dashing into an empty stall to get dressed.

Longarm had kept an eye on the boy. That little fellow had grown up about five years' worth in the time it had taken Maggie to find a place to hide. Longarm had pushed the youngster out of the stable, muttering something about giving a lady time to make herself presentable.

"Yes, sir, I understand," the boy had said, doing his best to keep the top half of his face respectful, even though his mouth had been wearing a shit-eating grin wider than he was tall.

Even now, on the train, the sight in his mind's eye made Longarm chuckle. Most likely that stable boy's interest in horses was about to shift over to another kind of filly!

The door just behind Longarm swung open, and the deputy, out of habit, turned his head to see who was entering the coach. It was another conductor, this one much younger than the other, although his face wore a three-days' growth of glossy black beard. *Now why didn't the old codger know about this fellow?* Longarm wondered.

"Hey, Conductor!" called a man sitting on the aisle two rows up from and opposite Longarm. He was a rough-hewn laborer of some sort, according to the story told by his clothes. He wore a ragged chambray shirt, bib overalls, and a straw hat. The man waved his ticket in the air, saying, "The other conductor didn't punch it."

"No time now," rasped the conductor. "Get the other fellow to do it."

But the man in the straw hat wasn't taking no for an answer. He reached out to grasp the conductor's coattails. "Punch my ticket!" he demanded.

The conductor pulled away, nervously smoothing his jacket. "Shut up afore I punch *you*," he snarled.

Up ahead, a matronly woman tried to ask, "What time will we—"

"Dunno," the conductor cut her off. "Pretty soon."

Straw Hat, meanwhile, had been looking to his neighbors for sympathy. "Didn't punch my ticket," he moped to Longarm.

"Well, old son, I'd say he's a pretty strange bird to be a railway man."

"Ignorant sumbitch," Straw Hat agreed.

And he's no damned conductor, Longarm thought. The uniform was correct, right down to the man's black shoes, but a uniform was easy enough to fake. It was what was *under* the uniform that gave this man away. Even before the fellow in the straw hat had inadvertently lifted the conductor's coattails to reveal the snout of a protruding weapon, Longarm had spotted the bulk of iron hanging from beneath the fellow's armpit. The conductor's suit jacket had fit him funny, and that was clue enough for a lawman.

Longarm waited until the conductor had disappeared through the front door of the car before quietly sliding out of his seat to follow. Even granted that the railroad had decided to arm their employees, no conductor would dare risk his job by walking around with several days' worth of scruffy beard. The railroad had a separate washroom where employees could shave. Most passengers, of course, did not bother.

As Longarm trailed the conductor, hanging back about a car's length so as not to be observed, he pulled out his wallet to remove his badge so that he could pin it to his lapel. Something nasty was about to occur, and since the other fellow was cloaked in the authority of the railroad, Longarm wanted all trigger-happy bystanders to realize that *he* was the law.

He caught up to his quarry in the next car. Standing as solidly as he could in the swaying coach, Longarm called out to the man's back, "Federal Marshal! Stop where you are!" Even as he spoke, Longarm saw the phony conductor—now there was no doubt that the man was bogus; a real conductor would have obeyed the order—unbutton his jacket and begin to spin around.

Dumb bastard is going to draw, Longarm groaned inwardly, even as his Colt found its way into his own hand.

But the conductor did not draw. Instead, in the fraction of the time pulling a handgun would take, he swung up from out of his unbuttoned jacket a sawed-off, double-barreled shotgun, suspended from his right shoulder by some sort of leather loop.

Longarm did not fire, but instead hurled himself facedown in the aisle. He stayed there, praying that the man would not fire his awesome weapon, but instead make a break for it, as all around Longarm, the coach's passengers erupted into screams. They began to rise out of their seats. Exactly the worst thing they could do, Longarm mourned.

Fortunately the phony conductor held off pulling his dual triggers, instead choosing to back-pedal his way down the aisle and out through the end door. Longarm, breathing a sigh of relief, sprang to his feet to continue the pursuit. It had not been concern for his own personal safety that had kept him from shooting that bastard, but rather concern for the safety of the other passengers. A sawed-off shotgun was the evillest weapon on the face of the earth. It was totally unsuited for killing any sort of critter except the human kind. A blast from that shotgun would have killed or maimed half a dozen of the passengers crowded into seats between the conductor and Longarm.

As Longarm raced through the coach door and onto the platform, he saw the man raise his shotgun to fire right through the next coach's door. As the blast thundered, punching through the door's windowpane, so that shards of glass were now added to the cloud of twelve-gauge shot coming his way, Longarm swung out and off the train's platform, so that he was hanging on only by the grip of his left hand's fingers on a grab-iron, and the leverage provided by his boot tips dancing on a greasy bolt overhanging the platform's flooring. He fought to regain the relative safety of the narrow space in between the cars, almost losing his Colt in the process, while all the while the hot, dry New Mexico wind buffeted him.

"One barrel down and one to go," Longarm muttered to himself as he pushed through into the next car, trying to get past the confused, milling passengers blocking the aisle. He could see the blue expanse of the phony conductor's back disappearing through the far door. This was getting serious. It was only a matter of time before his quarry ran into the real conductor, and that old coot was just rambunctious enough to try and *argue* with a double-barreled sawed-off. And there was the little question of the whereabouts of the rest of the outlaw gang. Nobody tried to hold up a train all by his lonesome . . .

As Longarm hurried along, his eyes flicked from right to left, searching the parallel rows of seats, trying to guess which of the passengers was planning on rising up as soon as Longarm had passed, in order to blast his back. But no one did rise up, and Longarm began to understand what had been the phony conductor's plan.

Entering the next car, Longarm saw his adversary waiting for him. The man was braced at the far end, but he was still close enough for his shotgun to do its dirty work, either to Longarm or the people caught in the middle between them.

"Thought so, old son," Longarm called. "Thought you were about out of time to play around with me."

"You—you're the one out of time, Marshal," the outlaw excitedly shouted back. "Throw down yer pistol!"

Between them, one of the passengers began to rise, his movement attracting the snout of the shotgun. "Get back down!" Longarm commanded, and the passenger, looking into the twin stare of the shotgun's barrel, and suddenly thinking better of his initial impulse towards heroics, obeyed.

Time for a bluff, Longarm thought. "See here now, we both got guns in our hands," he began.

"Yeah, but mine's bigger than yours," the phony conductor leered. "You shoot me, Marshal, and this here scattergun of mine is gonna take a lot of these citizens with me."

So much for bluffing. "Throw it down or I'll shoot you where you stand!" Longarm growled. At that moment the door behind the outlaw began to open.

Feeling the wind on his neck, the man with the shotgun began to turn, but then paused in mid-movement, stuck in between the two distractions the way a mule can get paralyzed between equidistant piles of hay. The outlaw's head swiveled desperately from Longarm to whatever was coming in behind him, and in the couple of seconds it took for all of this to go on, two more things happened: there was a sharp report, the sound like that of a dry twig being snapped in two, and the outlaw slapped at the back of his neck, as if he'd been beestung. The squat shotgun rose up a few inches—

—and a few inches were all Longarm needed. In one movement he swung up his .44 and fired, the round taking the outlaw just above the ear, lifting the top of his head beneath its cap in a spray of red mist as the car erupted into shouts and screams.

The outlaw tottered on his feet, the shotgun slipping from his grasp to swing like a pendulum from its shoulder loop. Then he fell to the floor, revealing behind him the tiny form of the real conductor. The old codger was dancing in place like a randy rooster. Gripped in his right hand was a small pistol.

"We got him, Deputy! We surely did!" he crowed as Longarm walked up the aisle, ignoring the panicked queries of the passengers.

"That we did, friend," Longarm calmly agreed. He reached out for the conductor's weapon, and then examined it. It was a diminutive .25-caliber Smith & Wesson revolver. It had tape holding its grips to its butt, and deep nicks and scratches along the cylinder and barrel. It looked as if it had hammered more nails than bullets.

"Bought me that there belly-gun in a pawnshop," the conductor winked. "Did it when they transferred me to this here New Mexico-Texas run. Outlaws, boy! I knew there'd be outlaws, and I was right! Shot this one dead, I did!"

Longarm decided not to spoil the old man's fun by reminding him that the outlaw most likely could have picked that little bitty .25 slug out of his neck like it was a thorn, and that it was the man-sized piece of lead from his own .44 that had settled the train robber's hash. "You see any other suspicious-looking passengers along the way you came, Conductor?"

"Not a soul, Deputy." He removed his cap to scratch at the gray wisps of hair plastered across his bald dome. "That's a good point, though. Did this hombre expect to hold up my train all by hisself?"

"Not hardly," Longarm muttered. "Reckon he was aiming to use his conductor's suit to bluster his way into the locomotive crew's area. Then, once his gang started riding alongside the engine, he'd force the crew to stop the train. Don't imagine most men would say no to that shotgun of his."

"You mean we're going to be ambushed?" the conductor asked as Longarm handed back his little gun.

"Let's get this fellow out of sight of the ladies," Longarm suggested. "Then you and I will talk."

Two male passengers volunteered their services, and the corpse was hoisted up. As Longarm held open the coach door, the conductor said, "Throw him off the side, boys!"

"No!" Longarm said. "We'll put him in the baggage car, and leave him at the remount station in Grassy Bow. I figure that's the closest thing there is to authority in this part of New Mexico Territory."

"Damn, I forgot!" the conductor said. "The reward! You reckon there is one, Deputy?"

"If there is, it's all yours," Longarm said, "Federal lawmen ain't allowed to accept rewards."

In the baggage car, Longarm thanked the two men who'd helped, and waited until they'd left before asking the conductor to help him strip the suit jacket off the dead man's body. He explained that since the outlaw had been making his move when he died, the rest of the gang could not be far away.

As Longarm stripped off his own frock coat and replaced it with the regulation blue suit jacket, the old conductor beamed. "I get it! You're planning on taking this hombre's place!"

Longarm nodded. "It's getting dark. If we don't nab these fellows, they'll just try this stunt again. I'm hoping that being all nervous about the holdup, the gang will see what they're expecting to see. In the dark, with this man's outfit on, I ought to be able to fool them long enough to get the drop on them."

"What do you want me to do?" the conductor asked.

"Lend me your cap. The one this poor soul was wearing is a mite messy." He reached into the pocket of his folded frock coat and came out with a fresh cartridge to replace the one he'd fired. "And make sure you keep the passengers from lending a hand. Should shooting start, my two advantages will be the darkness and the fact that everything in front of me is fair game."

Patting the suit jacket's pocket, Longarm found spare shells for the shotgun. He loaded the spent barrel of the weapon, pulled off its rawhide shoulder loop, and headed for the loco-motive. His badge was back in its usual place, pinned inside the fold of his wallet, which itself was tucked into his hip pocket. Not that he seriously expected that he'd have to show it. The gang would either give up when he said he was a law-man, or they'd start shooting. No, the only men who might want a look at his symbol of authority were the locomotive crew.

He spent a nervous quarter of an hour with them, the noise of the engine precluding any attempt at conversation as the four pairs of eyes—Longarm's, the engineer's, the brakeman's, and the stoker's—scanned the rapidly darkening, rugged terrain.

It was Longarm who spotted the three horsemen atop a low, mesquite-studded butte, their forms silhouetted against the last glimmer of a sun that had long since dropped below the horizon.

The horsemen seemed only to be watching the progress of the train. Longarm wondered fleetingly if he was supposed to send them some signal that he was in control, perhaps a series of toots from the locomotive's whistle. Well, better no signal than the *wrong* one; that way, the gang might just figure their man on board had forgotten.

"Brakeman! Now!" Longarm commanded. The crewman pulled his levers, and the world around them erupted into sparks and one long, banshee-like scream as locked metal wheels filed shavings off the tracks. Its boiler-head bleeding steam, the big locomotive's pistons slowed until they were barely moving. The train jolted several times, then came to a stop.

Longarm watched the three riders spur their horses down the treacherous incline of the butte. As they reached the level prairie they broke into a full gallop toward the stalled train.

One of the riders was leading a saddled horse, obviously the mount that their confederate aboard the train was to use for his getaway. This rider came toward the locomotive, while the other two rode toward the baggage and mail car in the center of the train. Longarm realized he had to take out this first outlaw, then get the other two before they discovered their comrade's corpse—or else the jig would be up. Fortunately the baggage car was unattended, so no unarmed clerk would have to absorb the outlaws' wrath.

"Get your hands up!" Longarm hissed to the crew as the rider reined up beside the locomotive.

"How'd it go, Walt?" the rider asked, his own gun out.

"Fine," Longarm said, doing his best to approximate the raspy voice of the late Walt. He had his conductor's hat pulled low, and tried to keep to the shadows of the engine's interior.

The rider dismounted and reached up with his free hand for his comrade to give him some help in climbing up onto the locomotive's platform. Longarm reached out a hand and helped pull the outlaw up, at the same time slamming the butt of his shotgun into the man's face. Knocked cold, the outlaw fell back to sprawl motionless in the dust. Longarm jumped down to

retrieve the fallen man's gun. It was a big old Colt Dragoon
rechambered to take brass cartridges. Tossing the hogleg to the
first pair of hands that appeared over the side of the engine,
Longarm whispered, "Watch him, and if he comes to, keep
him quiet, but don't kill him. He's unarmed."

That done, Longarm began to run in a low crouch along the
length of the train, toward the baggage car. The old conductor
was doing his job well, maybe too well. The passengers were
acting as unconcerned as if this were a scheduled stop. With
any luck it would all be over before the remaining pair realized
something was fishy.

Longarm heard the squeak of the baggage car's side door
sliding open. He ran faster. He *had* to get the drop on them
before the two found that body. As he ran, he snapped back
both hammers of the stubby shotgun.

The rider who was still mounted twisted in his saddle,
bringing his handgun around to point in Longarm's direction.
Longarm quickly straightened up, holding his shotgun to port,
relying on his outline in the darkness to fool the outlaw.

The outlaw lowered his pistol. "I told you to stay up front,"
he shouted angrily. "And you screwed up on the whistle signal
we'd agreed on. What's wrong with you, Walt?" he demanded.

The other outlaw appeared in the baggage car's open side
door, his own gun in his hand. "Walt's in here dead!" he cried.

Longarm muttered a curse under his breath. It was too late
to give these fellows fair warning, as he was expected to do.
He just pointed the shotgun toward the car's open doorway and
let fly with both barrels, blasting the outlaw back into the darkness of the car's interior.

"What the hell?" the mounted gang member swore as he
shot fast three times, his gun erupting flame, his three slugs
kicking up dirt where Longarm had been standing. Dropping
the empty shotgun, Longarm had crabbed sideways, drawing
his Colt as he did so. As the mounted man tried to get a bead
on him, Longarm fired twice. The outlaw fell backward out of
the saddle as his horse bucked in fear. He landed heavily on
the ground and lay still.

Longarm checked him. Both of his rounds had taken the
man in the chest. He was dead. Boosting himself into the baggage car, Longarm struck a match to check on the other one.

The shotgun hadn't left much to check. Longarm flicked out the match and jumped to the ground to get away from the grisly remains, and to get a breath of fresh air. He felt a little weak-kneed now that it was over—

A deep boom came from the front of the train. Longarm had heard that boom a lot fifteen years ago, during the War. It was the sound made by an older-model sidearm—like a Colt Dragoon, for instance.

Longarm repeated his run in reverse, going toward the engine. When he got there he saw, by the flickering light of a lantern, the brakeman holding the outlaw's smoking Dragoon in both of his trembling, white-knuckled hands. His face was pale and a trifle green around the edges.

"I had to, Marshal!" the young man wailed. "When he came to, I told him to lay still, like you said, but he just laughed at me. He got to his feet and went for that rifle there on his saddle!"

The other crew members nodded in agreement, and Longarm glanced at the body stretched out on the ground, a hole a half-inch across in the center of the man's back. The outlaw's horse was just a few steps away; obviously it had shied at the sound of the shot. As if in mute testimony to the brakeman's story, the outlaw's saddle gun, an old Henry repeater, was hanging half out of its boot.

"You ain't gonna arrest me, are you, Marshal?" the brakeman asked fearfully. "I didn't want to shoot—"

"Quiet now," Longarm soothed as he holstered his Colt. "You had no choice, old son. You surely did the right thing."

The brakeman looked down at his hands, and as if surprised that he still held the revolver, he quickly tossed it to the ground. "I never killed anyone or anything before, Marshal. I was too young for the War, and—" He clamped both hands over his mouth and scrambled down from the locomotive platform. Falling to his knees, he vomited in the dust.

A crowd of passengers, led by the conductor, had gathered around the scene. "Anybody have a flask or bottle on them?" Longarm called. "This boy could surely use a drink."

One of the men approached the sobbing brakeman. From his hip pocket he pulled a silver flask. "Drink up, boy," he ordered softly. "No sense carrying on like *you* was the dead one."

"Well, it all happened like you said it would," the conductor told Longarm. "How'd you figure it so neatly? This sorta thing old hat to you?"

Longarm laughed. He patted the pockets of his coat for a cheroot, realized he was still wearing the phony conductor's garb, and stripped the garment off, letting it fall to the ground.

"Like I told you before," he began, "it wasn't likely that the fellow with the shotgun was going to try and keep watch over the crew for too long." He pulled the stub of a cheroot out of his vest pocket and fired it up. "And they had to make their move this side of the New Mexico-Texas border. New Mexico being only a territory, there's no real law to chase after them."

"Except for that army remount station at Grassy Bow," the conductor pointed out.

"Right, but that meant they had to make their move now, before we reached that station. We're still an hour or so away. Robbing a train in the army's backyard would've just about guaranteed them a cavalry troop riding up their asses."

The old conductor cackled with laughter. "Sure as hell wasn't their lucky day when *you* boarded, Deputy—what is your name, son?"

"Custis Long. Folks call me Longarm. See here, Conductor. You got your train back now. See that these bodies and horses are loaded up. We've got to drop 'em off at the remount station."

"Yessir!" Chuckling to himself, the spry old conductor snatched up the lantern and began waving it in the air as he walked the length of the train, calling out, "All aboard! Let's go, folks! We're behind schedule! All aboard!"

Longarm was the first to obey the conductor's command.

Chapter 3

That night, while Longarm slept, his train crossed the border into Texas. It paralleled the Rio Grande for some forty-odd miles before veering east to cross the Pecos River and then slice through the baked brown crust of the Llano Estacado, the Staked Plains.

A few hours after dawn, the train began its descent into the north-central plains, crossing the Colorado River. The mesquite, yucca, and their brother cacti gave way to buffalo grass and little bluestem. The buttes turned into hills, and then even softer hills, and then woodlots of pecan, walnut, and hickory, lorded over by massive oaks. And carpeting the thickly grassed prairie everywhere was a dusting of wildflowers—bluebonnet, just now giving way in early summer to asters, daisies, and goldenrod.

But most important, as the train made its way from the Staked Plains to the north-central prairie region, the mountain sheep and mule deer, the jaguarundi and bobcat, gave way to cattle. Magnificent herds of steers basked in the warm sunshine of the Lone Star State—the cow nursery of the world.

Longarm had spent time in many cow towns in his day, but none had prepared him for Alex Starbuck's cow town of Sarah. Once the train had pulled into the station, he'd led the chestnut gelding he'd borrowed from the army remount station to a quiet place alongside the now-empty cattle pens and loading ramps. His gear—saddle and bridle, saddlebags and bedroll—had been carried for him by a pair of boys, just two of the multitude of young scamps who made pocket change by transporting baggage from station to hotel. The only thing Longarm carried was his Winchester. He didn't believe in letting others handle his firearms if he could help it.

Last night, for example, the old conductor had offered to clean Longarm's Colt for him. Longarm had politely thanked the man, but informed him that that was the sort of job he always did himself. As he'd tended to his weapon, using kerosene, a small brush, a soft rag, and then sperm oil for lubrication, all of which Longarm carried in a kit in his saddlebags, he'd had to suffer the curious looks of just about every passenger on the train, every one of whom just sort of happened to stroll by his seat. Never for the life of him could Longarm figure out the fascination of his fellow man for those who had the misfortune of having to kill others. Blessedly, things quieted down once they'd left Grassy Bow. Longarm had filled out a few forms for the army detailing the events that had led up to the triple shooting, sympathized with the old conductor when it was learned that there was no reward for this particular gang, and arranged to borrow his mount.

His gelding was a good one. A veteran of several shooting campaigns, the animal was not in the least fazed by the tumult of the station. Once his horse was saddled, his bags in place, and his Winchester tucked into its boot, Longarm rode the short distance to Sarah's main street.

Longarm liked to get the lay of a good-sized town, which Sarah was, before he began an investigation. Sarah's wide, regularly sprinkled Main Street had several general stores, a bakery, two gunsmiths, a bank, a telegraph office, and—obviously the showplace of the town—a magnificent, brightly painted, three-story mansion. Above the wide, golden-oak double doors, there hung a sign painted in gilt script that read: SARAH TOWN-SHIP CATTLEMEN'S ASSOCIATION.

As Longarm walked his horse along the avenue, he saw raised wooden sidewalks on both sides of the street. Clustered together were several saloons and cafes, and next door to them, as if keeping watch like a stern parent, was a combination jail and office labeled TOWN MARSHAL. On the saloon side of Main Street, the buildings were more ramshackle, and were mostly devoted to the day-to-day business of tending to cowboys and their mounts. A few blocks down along this side of town, the railway holding pens and ramps began. Nearby he saw canvas tents being erected by workmen.

Walking his mount around to the residential neighborhood behind the Cattlemen's building, Longarm explored rows of brightly painted clapboard houses, each with a picket fence, and many with gardens, and trees planted in horse-trough-sized planters. Here there were two schools—a primary and a secondary one—and a fine church. The golden bell in its tall steeple gleamed against the deep blue, cloud-studded sky.

Longarm rode up to the one hotel in town, around the corner from Main Street, and tied his horse to a hitch rail in front. Inside, he inquired about a room. The clerk, dressed in a blue velvet suit, despite the eighty-degree heat, was polite but adamant.

"We can lodge you just for tonight, Mr."—the clerk spun the register around to read Longarm's scrawl—"Mr. Long. Beginning tomorrow, we're completely booked up. Lots of folk from the East are arriving for the round-up, you see."

Longarm nodded, sighing. "I didn't notice another hotel. I don't suppose there are any?"

"I'm afraid not," the clerk sniffed. "You might try Canvas Town—"

"Where?" Long asked.

"Oh, that's our area out by the railway spur. Every round-up, tents are set up to house and entertain the hands who sign up temporarily at the various cattle outfits hereabouts. Check at the Cattlemen's Association. You'll find bulletin boards there that carry announcements concerning who's hiring and who is not." The clerk's brow furrowed beneath the slicked-back thatch of his hair. "You are in town to work as a hand, I presume?"

"Exactly right." Longarm nodded, thinking that this clerk was indeed an imbecile to imagine that a man dressed the way he was even faintly resembled a working cowboy. "You certainly are a fine judge of character," he added.

"Thank you," the clerk replied, beaming. "It comes with the job."

"I know what you mean. Say, I've got a horse out front. Can you recommend a good stable?"

"Oh, we have our own stable," the clerk said. "For an extra charge, we'll care for your horse."

"Good enough," Longarm said.

"But you must be out by noon," the clerk reminded him.

"Actually, I'll be out very early in the morning," Longarm told him. "Why don't I pay now?"

"That'll be three-fifty, including the stable charge," the clerk replied, and in answer to Longarm's wince of surprise, he added, "Tomorrow it goes up to five dollars." He said it like a boast. "Do you have any luggage?"

"Just my saddlebags," Longarm said. "Send a boy around for my horse, would you?"

"Right away," the clerk said. "Here's your key."

Longarm took it and went outside to fetch his bags and rifle. The clerk eyed the Winchester as Longarm reentered the hotel, but said nothing.

After stashing his property in his room, Longarm went back downstairs and out to visit the town marshal's office. It was fast becoming early evening, but Longarm wanted to gather whatever information he could, so as to be able to start out bright and early the next day.

He had to cool his heels awhile outside the marshal's office. Several deputies were receiving some instructions before beginning their rounds of the town. Longarm knew he had to reveal his identity as deputy U.S. marshal to Sarah's chief law officer, but he'd prefer that the several deputies not know who he really was. There was most likely a small newspaper office stashed away somewhere in Sarah. A loose-lipped local deputy would be all it would take for the news of Longarm's arrival to make town headlines. After that it would only be a matter of time before word got back to those officials in the nation's capital who were in charge of the case.

Once the deputies had left, Longarm entered the marshal's office. The marshal, a big-bellied man—what was it about desks and bellies that seemed to go hand in hand?—had his head down and his eyes fixed on a report written on yellow paper.

"Be with you in a minute," he grumbled, his voice a Texas version of Billy Vail's.

Longarm used the time to look around the office. A door to the rear, just behind the marshal's desk, led to the cells. Along one wall was a rack of rifles and shotguns, all securely locked in place by a length of chain threaded through their trigger guards. On the opposite wall hung a motley assortment of wanted flyers, from the federal government and neighboring states, as well as from private organizations like the Pinkertons. Several straight-backed chairs stood scattered about, but Longarm, who had done more than his share of sitting during the trip, preferred to stand. As the marshal tended to his desk work, Longarm read over the duty roster that told which deputies were supposed to be on patrol, and where.

"What can I do for you?" the marshal finally asked.

When Longarm turned to face him, he saw with some satisfaction that the town marshal was staring at him with narrowed eyes. Unlike the hotel clerk, the lawman probably knew how to judge a man.

"My name's Custis Long, and I'm a deputy U.S. marshal, working out of Denver," Longarm explained, pulling out his wallet and flipping it open to show his badge.

"My name's Farley. Pleased to meet you, Deputy," the town marshal said, standing up to shake hands. "Guess I know why you're here," he said shrewdly. "Though I'd thought the army was going to handle this."

"Well, sir, I was passing through the region, and got sidetracked to take a look-see around," Longarm fibbed. "Incidentally, I'd appreciate it if you kept my job to yourself. I can work easier that way."

Farley nodded. "Whatever you say. Grab a chair and tell me what I can do to help."

"First off, I'd like to know the results of your investigation of Starbuck's murder," Longarm said, turning a chair around and straddling it horse-style, folding his arms on top of the back rest. "If you've got any reports I could borrow to read—"

Farley cut him off gruffly. "No reports."

"Why not?" Longarm asked, surprised.

"Damn it, you're federal, Long, so you ought to know that my jurisdiction ends at the town limits. The shooting took place on Starbuck's spread. That makes it a job for the Rangers."

"I understand, Marshal," Longarm said quietly, as Vail's

words echoed in his mind. *This case is too big for any local law* . . . Any law officer who stuck his neck out by getting involved in something as serious as the Starbuck assassination risked having his head cut off for incompetence if he failed to find the culprits. It made perfect sense that Farley was less than anxious to involve himself with a hot-potato case like this one.

"Don't get me wrong, Marshal," Longarm continued, "but the Rangers—and they're good boys—are better suited for stomping a range war or shooting it up man-to-man with a bunch of cow thieves. Investigations ain't their meat."

"My jurisdiction ends at the town limits," Farley repeated stubbornly.

"Yes, sir," Longarm said wearily. "How do I get to where it happened?"

"That's easy," Farley said, obviously relieved. "Just take Main Street out of town past the Cattlemen's building. It becomes a trail that cuts across a creek a few times. That's Goat Creek. It, along with Goat Lake, is fed by an underground spring hereabouts. Anyway, you just follow that trail for about two hours. You'll see a number of cutoffs that lead to various spreads, but stay on the main trail. Eventually you'll hit a granite outcropping, and alongside it a wooded rise. You're on Starbuck property at that point, and you're also where it happened. Mr. Starbuck was riding past that outcropping when they all fired down on him."

"You really believe fifteen men shot him up, Marshal?" Longarm asked skeptically.

"See for yourself, Deputy," Farley muttered. "Everybody else in Sarah has. Place has become a regular sightseeing spot. Reckon they'll run tours out to it once the Easterners start arriving tomorrow," he added in disgust.

"You haven't answered my question," Longarm persisted. "What's your opinion? From one lawman to another."

Farley shrugged. "Starbuck lived big his whole life. It makes some kind of sense to me he would *die* big as well." The marshal shrugged. "Hell, Long, hand me a guitar and maybe I'll write a ballad about it," he chuckled.

"Sarah's a strange name for a Texas cow town," Longarm said, to change the subject.

"That was the name of Starbuck's wife. She died long ago,

over in Europe it was. Alex Starbuck built this town. Figure he had the right to name it what he wanted." Farley tugged a pocket watch out of his pants and glanced at it. "I'm due somewhere, Deputy. Anything else I can help you with?"

"Just one thing," Longarm said, getting to his feet. "Point me toward a place to fill my belly."

"Best grub in town is at Leda's," Farley smiled. "Two doors down from the Union Saloon," He rose. "I'll walk you down since I'm going that way."

"Thanks just the same, Marshal," Longarm said. "But I'd just as soon not attract attention by being seen with you."

"I get it," Farley replied with a wink. "Go on, then. Don't worry, My lips are sealed."

Longarm thanked him and left the office, strolling down the block past the Union Saloon, to a small café with LEDA's painted across the window. Inside, he had a decent, uneventful meal of steak and eggs, despite the fact that beef was the most expensive thing on the menu. It made Longarm smile. No cattleman liked the taste of his own beef—not when that very slab, shipped on the hoof to the East, could put dollars in his pocket.

After dinner, Longarm stopped at one of the saloons and bought a bottle of Maryland rye, which he took with him back to the hotel. Once in his room, he undressed, and after scattering a few balled-up sheets of the hotel's stationery between his double-locked door and his bed, to give him some advance warning should an unannounced visitor try to enter, he stretched out upon the crisp, fresh sheets of the fine four-poster, and took a few sips off the top of his bottle.

Five minutes later, Longarm was sound asleep. Maryland rye was not as sweet as a mother's lullaby, but for Longarm it worked just as fine.

Chapter 4

Dawn's first flush broke pink, as radiant as a pleased woman's blush, before that rosy glow bled down into the pearly gray that marked the real start of the day. Longarm walked silently down the stairs, so as not to disturb the other guests. The hotel seemed to rise and fall with the rhythmic breathing of so many sleeping people.

His saddlebags over his shoulder, and his Winchester in the crook of his arm, Longarm stopped off at the desk to hand his key to the weary night clerk who was about to go off duty. Then he left the lobby and walked around the side of the hotel to the stables.

The young kid who was supposed to keep watch over the mounts was sleeping curled up on a bale of hay. That was fine with Longarm. He'd rather saddle his own horse anyway. Saddling your own horse was like buying somebody a drink: it broke the ice between two old boys who wanted to be friends.

The stable boy stirred in his sleep behind Longarm as the tall deputy finished fitting his Mexican bridle into place over his gelding's nose. As Longarm tied his saddlebags to the brass fittings of his saddle and slid his Winchester into its boot, the boy woke up.

"Sorry, mister," the kid yawned, rubbing his eyes. "I was supposed to do that for you."

"No problem." Longarm handed him a nickel just so the kid

wouldn't feel bad, and began to lead his mount out past the stable doors.

"If you wait a bit, mister, there's coffee," the boy called after him. "The pot's all ready to go on the stove. I've just got to start the fire."

"No thanks, I'm in a hurry," Longarm replied. A hot mug of black coffee would have been just the thing to wash out of his bones the last syrupy remnants of sleep, but Longarm was concerned over Farley's remark that the site of Starbuck's shooting had become a tourist attraction. If that was true, Longarm wanted to get there nice and early, so he'd have an hour or so to poke about the site undisturbed.

Longarm kept his gelding to an easy trot during the ride out. It was going to be a warm, sunny day, and since Longarm had no idea where he and the horse were going to spend that evening—except that he knew for sure that Canvas Town was out of the question—he did not want the horse exhausting itself. He didn't mind the possibility of camping out for the night, and in fact he sort of relished the idea. He had dried beef, flour, coffee, and salt, to go with a compact little cook set in one side of his saddlebags, and he had his bottle of Maryland rye. There was plenty of water from old Goat Creek available for both him and his mount, and he figured the gelding could make it through the night without starving by grazing on the fine grass that covered the prairie in a thick carpet.

During the couple of hours it took to reach the site, passing the cutoffs Farley had warned him about, and splashing through the creek as it cut across the trail, Longarm actually began to look forward to a night under the stars. The groundcloth wrapped about his bedroll was all the shelter he'd need for the coming warm, rainless night.

The ground all around the granite outcropping had been stamped down by the hooves of countless horses and the iron rims of buckboard and wagon wheels. Farley had been right. The place looked as if everybody in Sarah had taken a ride out to the spot where Alex Starbuck had met his end.

Longarm dismounted, merely dropping his horse's reins to the ground. The army mount had been trained to stay in place when its reins trailed.

"Well, fellow," he told the horse, "maybe this ride out was

a waste of time after all." Longarm stood with his hands on his hips and shook his head. The place was as dirty as a street gutter back in Denver.

Cigar butts and chewed-up, dried-out plugs of tobacco littered the ground around the boulders, while candy wrappers had been jammed into the crevices and fissures veining the rocks. Over on a flat surface of granite, some cowpoke had chiseled an endearment to his sweetheart.

But there was one piece of evidence that no amount of gruesome touristing could erase or deface. Longarm ran his fingers across the wide swath of nicks and scratches gouged out of the boulders by the hail of bullets that had ended Starbuck's life. From their number, it did seem that the assassination had been the work of a small army of bush-whackers. By studying the angle of the scratches, he tried to determine the direction from which the deadly fusillade had come. He tilted his hat to one side and laid his cheek against a boulder, sighting along one especially deep gouge.

He found himself looking at a high, wooded rise a little distance from the outcropping. He straightened up and squared his hat on his head, pondering. There was no sense in looking for rounds that might have ricocheted off the rocks. Any such bits of lead would long since have been taken as souvenirs by the local folk. But it would be a long, hard, sweaty climb to the top of that hill. Longarm couldn't be sure, but he'd lay fair odds that no sightseers had troubled to haul their asses up that slope on the off-chance of finding a few cartridge cases. Farley and his deputies might have thought of doing that, if they'd bothered to ride out and take a look around, but they hadn't.

As the first lawman to poke around the scene, Longarm figured he had a good chance of finding a slug casing—or a bunch of them, assuming that a number of men had participated in the ambush. Of course, there was always the chance that the murderers had cleaned up after themselves, but remembering to do something like that took cool logic, and such things usually fled a fellow's mind after he'd murdered a man.

Yep, it was time to climb, Longarm decided grimly. "Don't go running off to do anything interesting without me," he told the gelding as he untied the flap of his saddlebag, extracting a pair of leather gloves to protect his hands during the climb.

The gelding tossed its head and then lowered it to resume its stoic stance, as if Longarm's unneeded admonition had hurt its feelings.

It took Longarm a half hour to reach the top of the rise. He'd left his frock coat down below, but he'd nevertheless soaked through his shirt and vest as he threaded his way through clumps of post-oak and blackjack, and scrambled on all fours over wide belts of crumbly sandstone and slick marble. Finally he reached the top, which was a surprisingly pleasant area, thick with soil and studded with dense groves of hickory. There was brush everywhere and—thankfully—a cool gurgle of pure water slithering out from between two boulders, so that Longarm could slake his thirst and douse his sweaty head.

Refreshed, Longarm began his search for those shell casings. He sighted down at the granite outcropping, using his own gelding to give him some perspective. It was just about a hundred yards to where Starbuck would have been, certainly an easy enough shot for a band of men armed with rifles. Longarm was surprised that so many of the rounds they'd fired had gone off target . . .

He kept his eyes fixed on the ground as he ambled from one side of the likely ambush area to the other. Grasshoppers fiddled away, playing their sleep-inducing song, and from somewhere in the trees a mockingbird lived up to its name, its callous laugh seeming to suggest that anyone who would bother to come up here without the help of a set of wings was a damned fool . . .

And then Longarm found the shell casings. Except that what he found was just plain, damned crazy.

There, within a two-foot radius, were some thirty shell casings, almost as if they'd been piled up, neat as you please! Longarm bent to pick one up. He examined it, and then another, and a third. All were small caliber, .25s, and all had—

Longarm was startled by the dull, thudding rush of a pair of warblers taking off from a stand of brush. He turned his attention back to the cartridge casings as some small part of his mind registered the fact that the grasshoppers had suddenly grown quiet . . .

He threw himself to the ground as the report of a handgun echoed. The round ricocheted off a rock, which would have been spared its wound by Longarm's head if he'd been a fraction of a second slower in reading the warning given him by the birds and bugs.

The rocks had distorted the sound of that gun, so that Longarm didn't know where his attacker was firing from. He hauled himself to his feet, his Colt in his hand, but still feeling as naked as a newborn babe, standing out in the open, with his ambusher hidden from view.

Another shot thwacked into the rock just behind Longarm, flecks of granite stinging his cheek. Then, out of the corner of his eye, to his left, he saw movement: a man's hatless figure dashing from one stand of trees to the next.

Longarm snapped off a shot in the fellow's direction, not really expecting to hit anything, but simply to let his adversary know he was mad. He began to move in that direction, thinking that as fast as that man had been, he had gotten a good look at him. The man had not been holding or wearing a gun—

Damn decoy, and I've fallen for it, Longarm chided himself, even as he heard the noise and twisted his head to his right, in time to see a blue-denim-clad blur streaking toward him. Before Longarm could bring his gun around, the blur rammed into the backs of his knees, sweeping his feet out from under him. Longarm fell hard. His Colt went clattering off somewhere.

He was flat on his back when the blue-denim man sat squarely on his stomach. Longarm bucked him off, but not before realizing that the fellow he was bucking was a *her*—he'd had enough womanly bottoms straddling his belly to know another when he felt it.

"Just hold on," Longarm managed to shout as he rose to his feet, but not before the *other* one, the hatless, gunless man, came at him. Longarm brought up his fists to meet the attacker, but was totally unprepared for what happened next. The fellow jumped about five feet off the ground to snap out a barefooted kick at Longarm's head!

Whip-fast as Longarm's reflexes were, the kick still grazed the side of his skull. He fell back, dazed, but awake enough to jam his boots into the other fellow's rock-hard stomach as the man dove toward him. Longarm kept his knees locked as he jackknifed his legs, sending the man sailing past. He was pleased with this old-as-the-Virginia-hills "wrassling" move, but disappointed at the way his attacker managed to land as lightly as a robin on the soles of his feet. The girl, meanwhile, was crawling rapidly on all fours toward the revolver that had fallen out of her holster.

These two might just manage to kill him, Longarm realized, before he even got a chance to arrest them. He reached into his vest pocket and came out with his brass-plated, double-barreled, .44 derringer. He thumbed back the hammer of the little gun, the metallic click freezing both of his attackers.

"Just hold it, you two," Longarm muttered as he scooted around on his butt to lean back against a rock, in that way managing to get his wind back while keeping them both within his field of fire.

"Do you plan to murder me the way you did my father?" the girl spat.

"Jessica Starbuck," Longarm said, smiling. "Pleased to meet you." And he was. Lord, she was lovely! She'd straightened up to stand with her hands on her hips. Her angry green eyes flashed daggers Longarm's way. Her hat had fallen off during the struggle, to reveal a tawny mane of honey-blond hair, glinting with a hint of copper beneath the strong Texas sun. She was in her twenties. She was long-legged and had high, full breasts, a slender waist accented by the gunbelt she wore, and a firm, pleasantly rounded bottom. None of her figure was in the least hidden by her tight denim jeans and wrangler's jacket. The clothes fit her like a second skin. "Miss Starbuck, you've got things a mite backward," Longarm continued. "I'm not one of your father's murderers. I'm the law."

"The hell you are!" she snarled.

"Easy, Jessie," soothed the fellow with her. "There is time. We will listen to what he has to say."

Longarm glanced the man's way. He'd been standing so rock-still that Longarm had almost forgotten he was there. *Probably what he wanted me to do,* Longarm scolded himself. "My name is Custis Long. I'm a deputy U.S. marshal, working out of Denver. I've been assigned to investigate your father's death, ma'am."

"How do I know that?" Jessica asked skeptically. "I don't see your badge."

"Damn," Longarm swore. "My damned badge is in my damned wallet, which is in my damned coat, which is down with my damned horse."

"What were you doing up here?" she demanded.

"Just one minute, ma'am," Longarm said, his temper rising. "I'm the one holding the damned gun, so I'll ask the damned questions." He cooled down as he saw a glint of laughter in the girl's eyes, and before he knew it he found himself grinning back at her. "Sorry to lose my temper, but I tend not to take kindly to being ambushed."

"What do you think, Ki?" Jessica asked her companion.

The man shrugged. "He has the gun, what need would he have to lie? He could have killed us by now, if that was his purpose."

"Thank you, Ki," Longarm laughed, getting to his feet. "Strange name, but then you're sort of a strange fellow, ain't you?" Longarm trailed off, examining the man. He was around thirty, and tall; about six foot two, Longarm estimated. The man had brown eyes and thick, straight, blue-black hair, worn longish just past the tops of his ears. He was dressed in well-broken-in, well-fitting denim jeans, a blousy, pullover collarless shirt of cotton twill, and a loose, many-pocketed leather vest. Longarm peered at his face. It was a white man's face, except for the eyes, which were almond shaped. *He's half Oriental*, Longarm told himself. He looked down at the man's feet. "You don't seem to be in the habit of wearing shoes or boots, Ki," he remarked.

"My feet are quite tough," the man said in a calm voice.

"I know they're tough, old son," Longarm said. "And you ought to *know* that I know. You seem to disremember the fact that you were scraping one up alongside my skull a few minutes ago."

This time Jessica Starbuck laughed out loud, the sound rich and throaty. "Oh, I hope he really *is* a marshal, Ki," she drawled. "I hope he really hasn't anything to do with my father's death. It'd be a shame to have to kill him."

"I guess that's a compliment," Longarm acknowledged dryly. "Now that we're all being friendly, I think I'll put my little pacifier away." He uncocked the derringer and slipped it back into his vest pocket. "Now what say you pick up your gun, and holster it, Miss Starbuck. I'll do the same with mine, and Ki here can keep his damned feet on the ground where they belong."

"Folks hereabouts call me Jessie," she said as she bent to retrieve her gun. "Friends do, anyway." She eyed Longarm speculatively.

"Folks tend to call me Longarm," he said. "And I reckon we three best be friends if we're going to get to the bottom of who it was murdered your daddy."

Chapter 5

"Just what were you two doing up here?" Longarm asked again, once he and Jessica Starbuck had gathered up their revolvers under the watchful eyes of Ki, and had walked a short distance to sit under the shade of a hardwood tree.

"Marshal Farley rode out late last night to let me know that a fellow had stopped by his office to ask about what was known concerning my father's murder," she began.

"I told him I was a federal deputy," Longarm said, frowning. "And I showed him my badge."

"He mentioned that, of course," Ki interrupted. "But it is nothing to say one represents the law, and badges can be easily forged. We wished to watch your actions. A man's actions, when he thinks he is alone, are much more revealing than his words or credentials."

"I trust my actions have convinced you," Longarm said. "I've been assigned to this case sort of on the sly. It won't help me find Alex Starbuck's killers if everybody in Sarah knows a federal lawman is on the job."

"You mustn't blame Marshal Farley, Longarm," Jessica said. "He was a good friend of my father's. And telling *us* who you are doesn't mean everyone in Sarah will know. Your real identity is safe with us." As she spoke, she shrugged off her denim jacket. "Today's going to be a hot one . . ."

Longarm tried not to stare. She was wearing a pearl-colored, thin silk blouse, with nothing at all on underneath it. Her nipples were tantalizingly visible through the sheer material.

Making an effort to maintain his composure, he said, "Yes, ma'am, it seems as though it's going to be hot indeed." He longed for his frock coat, and for the sun to be directly overhead, signaling noon. That way he could banish the randy thoughts he was having by tucking a cheroot between his lips.

As if she could read Longarm's mind, Jessie pulled her revolver out of its holster, but only to extract the spent shells. Longarm peered at the handgun with surprise, which Jessica evidently noticed. She handed him the weapon, saying, "My father taught me how to shoot. He used a double-action .44, the Colt Model T. Just like yours, unless I miss my guess."

"I'm impressed," Longarm admitted. "Not many females know their way around either firearms or horseflesh."

"I'm a special sort of female, a Starbuck," Jessie explained. Her bewitching green eyes sparkled, but there was also something straight-on, no-nonsense serious about the way she said it. "Anyway, the .44's recoil was just a hair too strong for my hand. During one of his business trips back East, my father visited the Colt factory in Connecticut. He commissioned that weapon as a gift for my eighteenth birthday. It's bored and chambered for .38 shells, but mounted on a .44 frame. The recoil's been reduced to the point where I could squeeze off all five of my pistol's rounds—and accurately too—before my father could fire his own .44 three times."

Longarm was silent as he examined the weapon. Her gun was indeed a double-action Colt, finished blue-gray, with grips of polished peachwood. *What money won't buy*, he thought to himself. As far as Longarm was concerned, the jury was still out on Jessie Starbuck. Her daddy had bought her this toy. Longarm hoped her daddy had taught her how dangerous it was, and how one had to be responsible with it. She'd shot at him twice before even knowing who he was. True, she hadn't hit him, but was that because she hadn't *wanted* to, or hadn't been *able* to?

"Isn't it beautiful?" Jessica asked. "The color reminds me of the Texas sky at dawn."

"Just like a woman to go prattling on about how pretty a handgun is," Longarm chuckled, handing back the revolver.

"There is nothing foolish about seeing beauty in an exquisite weapon," Ki said suddenly. He tossed his head to flip back the glossy mane of his ink-colored hair. His almond eyes traveled from Jessica's form to Longarm's face. "What is foolish is to ogle obvious beauty, forgetting one's manners in the process." Though his expression was impassive, there was a hint of warning in his tone.

"Uh, yeah," Longarm muttered, thinking, *Careful! Jessie might be this fellow's woman* . . . He didn't cotton to muscling in on another fellow's claim. "I notice you ain't armed."

"I don't often carry a gun."

"Mighty dangerous, lying in wait for murderers with no weapons—"

"I said I did not carry a gun," Ki corrected him. "I did not say I was weaponless."

"What clue had you found when we made our move on you, Longarm?" Jessie asked.

"You mean when you almost *killed* me, young lady," Longarm said sternly.

"Oh, Marshal, if I'd wanted to kill you, I would have," Jessie announced. "I don't miss unless I want to." She patted the revolver resting in its holster of cordovan leather. She wore it riding high, just behind the shapely curve of her right hip. "I don't often strap this on," she said. "I don't think it's right for a woman to go strutting around wearing a gun. That can cause needless trouble. But when I do pull a gun, I know how to use it."

"Yes, ma'am," Longarm said. "Reckon you just wanted to distract me so as to take me alive, which you did. I have to give you that, though I got myself out of it. But the fact remains that you came up here fully intending to administer justice to a man you thought had something to do with your daddy's murder."

"What's wrong with punishing the men who killed my father?" Jessica asked, eyes flashing.

"The *law* will punish them. And *I* represent the law," Longarm cut her off; his own steely gaze flashing fiercely. "Vigilante justice is worse than no justice at all. Now I know this here part of Texas is considered Starbuck country, but it's also federal country. As a federal lawman, I'm telling you that if you try to take the law into your own hands again, I'll punish you, and I don't mean by taking you across my knee, which I'm starting to think you need, young lady. I'm talking about taking you off to jail. Is that clear?"

"Get hold of yourself, Longarm," Ki growled.

"You get hold of yourself, old son," Longarm snapped back. "You're so all-fired keen about seeing beauty, try and see authority when it's staring you in the face."

Ki nodded. "You are correct, Marshal. I accept your admonition."

"And you?" Longarm turned his gaze on Jessica. "Is what I said clear to you?"

"Yes, sir," she pouted.

"Fine. Now maybe we really can be friends," Longarm said, softening his tone.

"What was it you found back there, Marshal?" Jessica asked again. "You can tell us now that the smoke has cleared, so to speak."

"Shell casings, Jessie." Longarm climbed to his feet. "Come along, you two, and I'll show you."

He led them to the pile of casings he'd found earlier, before all the excitement had started. Jessica picked one up and held it to the sun.

"These are .25-caliber casings," she sighed. "My father had .25-caliber rounds in him."

"I was going to ask if you knew that," Longarm said uneasily. "At first I thought these had been left by a hunter. Odd as hell, this low-powered a round being used to ambush a man."

"That's what I thought," Jessie said. "But it's true. After my father died, I removed the seven bullets in him myself."

"That must have been hard on you," Longarm remarked, surprised.

"Hard or not, it had to be done," Jessie answered quietly. "I didn't trust the doctor in Sarah to do it. Oh, he's a fine physician, but an old-fashioned man. I was afraid he wouldn't tell me what he'd found." She nodded meaningfully at Longarm. "Like most of his sex, he has no idea what a good woman is capable of."

"Not me," Longarm replied quickly. "I remember the capabilities of every good woman I've had the good fortune to know." He noted with satisfaction the blush he'd brought to

Jessica's lovely features, as he knelt down to gather up the pile of shell casings.

"Did you group them all together like that, Longarm?" Ki asked.

"No sir. You thinking what I'm thinking?"

"That one, or perhaps two rifles, did all the shooting?" Ki shrugged.

"That can't be," Jessica broke in. "Willie said he heard all the shots fired in just a few seconds."

"Who's Willie?" Longarm squinted up at her. "You mean there was a witness?"

"Sort of," Jessica said slowly. "He didn't exactly see anything. Willie's an old hand at my spread, Longarm. He and my father were good friends from the old days, when I was just a little girl. My father and Willie would go riding together. Willie doesn't have any duties except during the roundup, when he acts as cook; he's sort of on pension at the Circle Star outfit. That's our brand. Anyway, he and my father were together the day it happened. Willie was off chasing a stray calf when he heard the shooting. He said it sounded like a string of firecrackers going off on the Fourth of July. He said it only took him a few moments to ride to my father, and by then the shooting was over." Jessie shook her head, perplexed. "There's no way one or two men could have levered off thirty-odd-rounds in that short a time."

"There's something purely crazy going on here," Longarm mused. He lined up three of the cartridge casings between his thumb and forefinger, holding them up for examination by Jessie and Ki. "See it?" he asked.

"A long scratch running along each one," Ki said. "The scratch is identical on these three. Are they all like these?"

"Every one that I've found," Longarm said. "Yes, there's something crazy going on, all right. Reckon I'd better have a talk with your Willie. How far is your spread from here?"

"About three hours' ride," Jessie answered.

"Five hours, all told, from town!" Longarm exclaimed.

"Yep," Jessie said proudly. "We're just at where my land starts, right now. A soul could ride for two days and not leave Starbuck land."

"Texas and Texans." Longarm grinned. "Would you mind

if I camped out on some of this here Starbuck land? It would kill a day to ride back and forth between your spread and Sarah."

"Marshal Farley said you were staying at the hotel."

"Only last night. They don't have a room for me as of today. They're all booked up because of the roundup."

"Well," Jessica smiled. "You are certainly not going to sleep outside. You'll stay with us." She winked. "That's Texas hospitality."

"I'm obliged," Longarm said. "Where are your horses?"

"Down below, on the other side of this rise," Ki answered. "We'll travel down to get them, and then ride around to meet you by the outcropping." Ki paused to lock Longarm's eyes with his own. "You have some theory about what has taken place here, do you not, Longarm?"

Longarm ran a finger along both sides of his longhorn moustache. "Friend, the first thing a lawman learns is to keep his mind open to all sorts of theories, meanwhile collecting the facts. Then you fit your theory and the facts together, and if the two halves balance, you just may have an answer."

Ki grinned. "A warrior once said, 'To open one's mouth indiscriminately brings shame.'"

Longarm shrugged. "I just believe in eating the apple one bite at a time."

"Longarm! You are a poet!" Ki's strong, even teeth flashed white as he roared with laughter.

"Don't know about that, old son," Longarm smiled. "But I do think you and I are finally starting to understand each other."

Chapter 6

It was past noon before the trio reached the Starbuck spread, so Longarm took advantage of the hour to light up his first blessedly sweet cheroot of the day. He offered one to Ki, who politely refused. Despite Jessie's smile, Longarm decided that it wouldn't have been proper to offer one to a lady, even if she was packing a .38.

During the ride, they passed small herds of cattle tended by Circle Star hands. To a man, the cowboys touched their hats and called out, "Morning, Miss Jessie," as she rode past.

Longarm was impressed. He himself had spent some years as a hand, and he knew that unless cowboys truly respected a person, they could be taciturn to the point of rudeness, even if that person was paying the bills. These hands were clearly experienced men who could write their own tickets with any outfit. The fact that they addressed Jessica Starbuck with the respect usually reserved for a foreman said a great deal about the way she managed her outfit.

Longarm was even more impressed when he caught his first glimpse of the Starbuck house—or *mansion*, rather. It was built of stone, with the main, middle section looking to be three stories tall. One-story wings jutted out from either side. There was a bunkhouse for the hands, and a stable nearby. Trees were plentiful, lending a cool, shady feel to the home spread.

As Jessie and Ki rode up to the veranda of the house, a

young boy in denims appeared. He was one of the green hands fulfilling his apprenticeship by working for the spread's boss wrangler, the experienced ranch veteran who was in charge of the outfit's stable of horses. The boy gathered up the reins of Jessie's and Ki's mounts, and then looked inquiringly at Longarm's.

"See that this man's horse is well cared for," Jessica ordered. "He'll be staying with us for a spell."

A shape detached itself from the shadows beneath the veranda to reveal itself as a huge, hulking man, standing at least as tall as Longarm, but outweighing the deputy by at least twenty pounds. None of that extra weight looked like fat, either. He was dressed in a suit, complete with a string tie in place down the front of his grimy white shirt. "Hold it, boy!" the man snapped out at the young wrangler, countermanding Jessica's orders. "Just who is staying with us, Miss Jessie?"

"This doesn't concern you, Higgins," Jessica said.

"As foreman of there here outfit, I guess it'll be me who decides what concerns me or not. With all due respect, Miss Jessie." He grinned, his smile yellow-toothed and resembling that of a grizzly just before it cracks open a beehive. He ambled over to Longarm's horse, patting its flanks as he looked the gelding over. "Fine animal. Don't often see a hand with his own mount." He turned to stare at Longarm. "You signing on as a hand, boy?"

"I'm signing on to dig your grave if you call me 'boy' again," Longarm told him. There was the sound of guffaws swiftly choked off. Four more men stepped out from the interior darkness of the veranda to lean against the railing.

Longarm looked them over. They were wearing expensive Stetsons and shiny Justin boots, though the rest of their clothes were broken down and dusty. Their gunbelts were cracked and scuffed, cinched tightly about their waists. Longarm didn't have to examine their weapons to know that they'd be single-action weapons, working hands' weapons—not the kind of guns that man-killers carried. They were a wolf pack following their big bad he-wolf, Higgins. They could be troublesome when drunk, all of them against one man in the dark, but they were nothing but wind when stared down in broad daylight.

Higgins, however, glancing back at them, did not appear sorry to see them. "You son of a bitch," he said to Longarm.

"Easy, boss," one of the men on the veranda warned.

"Shut up, Ray," Higgins glowered back over his shoulder. He looked back at Longarm. "I called you a son of a bitch."

"Now that ain't much better than 'boy,'" Longarm drawled. "Try again, else I'll have to fetch me a shovel."

Higgins flushed red. He whipped off his Stetson to wipe at the sweat dewing his brow. He was bald. His hatband had pressed a red ridge across his ivory pate. "You get your horse," he snarled, "and ride off this spread."

"Whether I stay or go is up to Jessica," Longarm explained. "That's *Miss Jessie* to you," he added.

Higgins unbuttoned his suit jacket.

"Easy, old son," Longarm cautioned. "I can see you're carrying your gun in a shoulder rig. You ought to realize there's damn little chance you can outdraw me."

Higgins, his hand hovering in midair, seemed to think that what Longarm had said was good advice.

"This has gone far enough, Higgins," Jessica fumed. "Now get back to work."

"Your daddy made me foreman, and it's my job to take care of you," Higgins argued.

"Your job is to take care of this spread, period," Jessica said.

"Now don't go getting all riled, Miss Jessie." Higgins winked slyly. "You know I only got your best interest at heart."

More men have their eyes on this filly than Texas has cows, Longarm thought to himself. Plain as day, Higgins saw himself as Jessica's beau, regardless of how Jessica saw it.

"Just get back to work," Jessie said disgustedly.

"First I'll take his gun," Higgins replied, pointing at Longarm. "I'm doing it for you, Miss Jessie. With your daddy being shot dead and all, we can't have no strangers being around you armed."

"Higgins, I'm warning you—" Jessica began, but Higgins waved her aside as he strode down the steps of the veranda.

"Hush now, girl. Your daddy would want me to do this." He advanced upon Longarm, his hand outstretched. "Give me your gun, boy. Else you'll have to outshoot me *and* the four behind me."

Longarm prepared himself for trouble, but just then Ki glided between the deputy and the burly foreman.

"Miss Jessica has given you an order, Higgins," the unarmed man said in his soft voice.

"Get out of my way!"

Ki was now less than a yard away from the foreman. He seemed dwarfed by Higgins's hulking form. "You are not being polite to our guest, Higgins."

"Now that Mr. Starbuck is dead, maybe there's no room for you on this spread," Higgins snarled. "What do you think, boys?" he called over his shoulder.

"Get rid of him, boss," one of the men called.

"Bust his hole," another chortled.

"That tears it." Higgins grinned. "Run along, Chinaman—"

Before he could say another word, Ki struck with a round-house kick. His torso bent sideways as his leg came around straight and true, his foot catching Higgins beneath the chin.

The foreman rose about six inches in the air, and then fell, to land hard on his butt. By then, Ki was back in a relaxed, standing position. The whole kick and return had taken less time than a rattlesnake takes to strike.

"I am of Japanese ancestry, not Chinese, Higgins," Ki said, staring down at the foreman. "But you needn't grovel in the dirt. Merely apologize."

Higgins lumbered to his feet. He was swearing and spitting in rage. He tugged out from beneath his jacket a blued steel Peacemaker. But before he could even thumb back the hammer on the single-action weapon, Ki moved in fast. He swatted Higgins's gun with the edge of his right hand. The Peacemaker went flying off in the direction of the Texas Panhandle as Higgins yelped in surprise and clasped his wrist.

"Shoot the yellow chink!" Higgins shouted in frustration to his men.

Longarm quickly moved toward the veranda, drawing his Colt as he did so. "Let's all stay out of this, boys. What do you say?"

The four men stared at Longarm's Colt. They noticed that its barrel had been cut down to five inches, and that it lacked a front sight. They looked at the cross-draw rig, and then back at the gun trained rock-steady upon them. "He's a gunslick, we can't do nothing!" one of them said. Gradually they lifted their hands toward the pitched roof of the veranda.

"Then I'll kill you myself, chink. With my bare hands," Higgins huffed, now truly resembling a grizzly. He moved warily around Ki, who stood motionless, not even bothering to turn as Higgins attacked from behind.

As the foreman looped both brawny arms around Ki's neck, the smaller man thrust his elbow into the other's solar plexus. Higgins gasped in pain, his arms going limp, now encompassing nothing but thin air. Ki slammed his elbow into Higgins's ribs, and the foreman staggered like a poleaxed steer. Ki swept Higgins's boots out from under the heavy man, using only his own bare foot, but that foot was like a broom sweeping away litter. Higgins landed on his knees, and then toppled all the way to the ground. He rolled over on his back, his breath coming in agonized rasps as he clutched at his chest and side.

Light as a feather, Ki knelt beside him. With one hand he tilted Higgins's chin to expose the foreman's throat. "If I struck here," he said, his finger gently tracing Higgins's Adam's apple, "you would choke to death on your own crushed throat."

"Please . . ." Higgins gasped, his eyes rolling white. Ki's rigid grip had arced his neck back at an impossible angle. Higgins resembled—in more ways than one—a chicken with its neck stretched across the chopping block.

"Or here," Ki continued, ignoring Higgins's plea. He touched the foreman's nose. "If I struck here, shards of bone would drive themselves into your pig's brain. Your life would bleed out of your ears into the dust—"

"Ki," Jessica called. "Don't. Let him go."

After a moment, Ki smiled and nodded. "Higgins, am I Chinese?"

"No . . ."

"What am I, Higgins?"

"Japanese . . ." the foreman gurgled, and then moaned.

"*Half* Japanese," Ki remarked. "But close enough, Higgins, close enough." He rose to his feet without apparent effort, as if he were a puppet wafted into the air by strings attached to his head and shoulders. "The mistress of this ranch gives you back your life, Higgins. *I* give it back to you. Take it now, and flee with it." Ki paused a moment, waiting, as Higgins stared up at him, paralyzed, a bird bewitched by a serpent.

"You are fired," Ki said.

Wincing in pain, Higgins tottered up onto his feet, and stumbled off toward the bunk house.

Ki turned to the four men held at bay by Longarm. "You are all fired as well," he announced. "Get off Circle Star land." Silently, the four began to do as they were told. Ki watched them shuffle off in the direction Higgins had taken.

Longarm holstered his Colt as he stared at Ki. "That was something . . ."

Ki smiled. He flipped back the blue-black shock of hair that had fallen across his forehead, and stood with his powerful hands resting on his narrow hips. "He called me Chinese. That was an insult."

"Absolutely," Longarm said.

"The Chinese and the Japanese do not mix."

"Don't mix," Longarm agreed adamantly.

"Oil and water," Ki added.

Longarm gazed at the man's slender form. "You didn't hardly work up a sweat with that big bruiser, did you?"

"Hardly," Ki agreed.

"If there had been maybe a half-dozen more of him against you," Longarm said thoughtfully, "it wouldn't have made all that much difference, would it?"

Ki shrugged. "Not much difference at all."

"How?" asked Longarm. "I mean, you never even made a fist."

"It is called *te*," Ki interrupted. "In your language the word roughly translates as 'hand.' Long ago, in a faraway land known as Okinawa—"

"That's a chain of islands off the Japanese mainland," Longarm remarked.

"Longarm!" Ki laughed. "That is twice today you have delighted me! The Okinawans were conquered by my own people, the Japanese, and as their overlords, my ancestors forbade the Okinawans the honor of owning weapons. The Okinawans are a proud people. To have the ability to defend themselves they developed the art of *te*—empty-hand fighting, in which one's body becomes the ultimate weapon."

"Is that what you meant before, up on the rise, when I asked if you were unarmed, and you said you had weapons?"

"To a degree," Ki smiled. "But I am armed in ways other than *te* . . ." Turning his gaze toward the stables, he added, "We will speak of that another time, my friend. I wish to make sure that Higgins and his followers indeed leave as ordered."

Longarm watched Ki stride away. "Quite a strange bird, that one . . ."

"That's an interesting way to put it," Jessica smiled.

"He seems mighty devoted to you."

"It's a long story," Jessica walked to Longarm's side. "Thank you for helping. I mean keeping those others out of it."

Longarm shrugged. "I wanted to keep it a fair fight. 'Course, that was before I knew that Ki could beat up the whole damn bunkhouse if he had a mind to. Sorry about causing you the trouble in the first place. It looks as if my arriving here has cost you your foreman and a bunch of hands. And at roundup time, as well . . ."

"Things were coming to a head anyway, Longarm," Jessie said. "Higgins was one of our top hands. A few weeks before my father was killed, he made Higgins foreman. I guess you know that on a spread of this size, the foreman's job is pretty much taken up with desk work, with balancing the books. Higgins was good at it. He took to wearing suits, like my father. Like a businessman. He got rid of his gunbelt and took to that shoulder-holster rig, thinking it was more dignified. Now don't get me wrong," Jessie added, her pretty green eyes serious. "There's nothing wrong with a man wanting to improve his station in life. That's what this country and Texas are all about. It's just that once my father was gone, Higgins started to think *I* came along with his job. That somehow the fact that he was foreman made him the man I'm supposed to marry. Why it all came to a head with your arrival is beyond me."

"I could see that he considered you a stray heifer ripe for his brand," Longarm mused.

"Painful analogy." Jessica rubbed at the seat of her jeans and pretended to wince. "But apt, nonetheless."

"Forgive an old cattleman, ma'am," Longarm smiled, his eyes dancing merrily.

"You're forgiven," Jessica answered. "But I must say, Deputy, you can't know very much about women if you think the way into their hearts is with a branding iron." She took his arm and led him up the steps, across the veranda, and into the house.

"A man has no business trying to brand a woman as his own," Longarm agreed thoughtfully. "Though a red-hot poker does have its place," he chuckled.

"It does indeed," Jessica laughed with abandon, and Longarm thought that unless he was careful, he'd have to add his own name to Jessica Starbuck's list of admiring beaus.

Chapter 7

That night, Longarm, asleep, tossed and turned in his bed. It wasn't his fault the Springfield had jammed. There was just too much mud. Too much blood.

At Shiloh!

The Springfield had jammed! Custis Long's panic grew by the moment. He was defenseless against the enemy marching upon him.

Against the boy marching upon him! The bullet hole Custis Long had just put into the boy's chest seemed to have no effect. How could that be? The boy was only fourteen or so. A .51 was way too much bullet for such a skinny stripling . . . but the bullet hole just glistened there on the boy's chest like some ghastly boutonniere of flesh. The boy wore it proudly. He'd take it home to show his mama, his papa, his girl. The boy was leering and laughing as he fixed his bayonet and broke into a dog-trot charge directly at his murderer . . .

His murderer, Custis Long, brought his useless Springfield up like a club. As he prepared to repel the attack, he felt the rifle crumble into dust, spilling across his now-empty hands.

The boy laughed. The boy's chest wound laughed. It said, *"He's a gunslick, but he can't do nothing!"*

Custis Long's panic was greater than the whole muddy field, greater than the entire limbo that was Shiloh. Amid dying men's cries, the sky became a huge chest wound, ragged and burning, blood-crimson wet, urine-yellow, urine-stinking . . .

Custis Long stood frozen in place, waiting for the keen edge of the boy's bayonet. All around, the Springfields and Spencer rifles chewed their bites out of men. All around, a *new* sort of gunfire emerged. The sound was like a string of firecrackers going off in quick succession. The sound signaled a change in the odds. The sound changed the battlefield from limbo, where, after all, there was some hope of redemption, into *hell*—where there was no hope at all . . .

Longarm woke up and came to his senses a split second before he began to fire his Colt into the dark corners of the room. He was slick with sweat, disoriented; despite the room's open windows he felt suffocated. A moonbeam, a softly glowing shaft of light, angled into the room. Longarm's eyes focused on it in desperation.

The Starbuck spread, he realized. In a bedroom in the Starbuck house. It had been a dream, but what a dream!

With shaking fingers Longarm struck a match, one of the bundle lying on the bedside table, and held the flame to the wick of the kerosene lamp. The flickering light banished the last of the nightmare from the room, but not from Longarm's mind. The damp bedsheets were wound around his legs like swamp grass. He kicked his way free and got out of bed, to pad across the room to where his saddlebags were draped across a chair back. He extracted his bottle of Maryland rye and took a healthy swallow. And then another swallow.

And then a third swallow. For the boy.

Longarm's nightmare had stacked the deck against him. Hell, the war was fifteen years ago. He'd just been a boy himself at Shiloh, where he'd killed for the first time. That time he'd killed the boy—he was no gunslick back then . . .

It had been just one boy—himself—against another. That damned fool kid had shouted some brave nonsense as he'd charged into the sights of that other youngster's Springfield. Longarm still remembered the impact of the rifle's butt against his shoulder as the Springfield spat blue smoke and gray lead the boy's way.

"Kid must of thought he was going to live forever," Longarm

muttered out loud to break the oppressive silence in the room. "Well, he found out how short 'forever' could be."

Longarm stretched out on the bed to let the fragments of the dream drift back to him. Nightmares had a way of shuffling—as well as stacking—a deck. Nightmares shuffled time, for example. In his dream, that firecracker sound filled the air at Shiloh, but Longarm knew he hadn't actually heard the unique, chattering noise of a Gatling gun until just after the War, when the carpetbaggers flooded into the South, and the Union Army was ramming through the once-Confederate states, hunting down the scattered bands of defiant, bitter rebels who refused to pledge their allegiance to the Stars and Stripes. And so they were branded outlaws, and hunted down—one way or another . . .

The big, carriage-mounted Gatlings were often used by the Union Army to intimidate those stubborn rebels who would not surrender, and execute the ones considered too damned ornery to tame. It seemed to Longarm that just such a weapon had been used to murder Alex Starbuck.

But how?

But Alex Starbuck was riddled with .25-caliber bullets, and shot at from a high rocky crest, a crest from which the ambushers had managed to escape—with their weapon—within minutes. No Gatling had that sort of mobility, and no Gatling was chambered for .25s. And yet it had happened, somehow. Happened to Alex Starbuck the way it had happened to so many poor, bullet-riddled bastards just after the War . . .

Longarm sighed to himself. It was bad to have the War and its aftermath on one's mind. Well, by morning's light he'd go to talk to Willie, the old hand now turned cook, who was with Alex Starbuck the day he was murdered. *It sounded like a string of firecrackers going off on the Fourth of July*, Willie had told Jessica. Chances were, old Willie knew something about Gatling guns. Chances were, old Willie had what he'd witnessed just after the War on his mind, as well . . .

It was just too hot in the bedroom. Longarm needed air. He slipped on his trousers, scooped up his bottle, and left the room on the second floor of the house.

Though this part of the house was three stories high, there were only two floors. The second-floor bedrooms opened out to a corridor, one side of which was a railed balcony that overlooked a huge combination dining and living room. The dark-stained roof rafters soared above this room, which had polished wood floors, and a magnificent slate fireplace. Comfortable furniture was arranged about the room, and off to one side, in a generous space of its own, there stood a massive mahogany dining room set. At this table Longarm, along with Jessie and Ki, had earlier eaten a delicious dinner, prepared and served by an elderly, diminutive Oriental woman—a Japanese, Longarm was quite sure.

The big room was dark now, except for the moonlight filtering in through a brace of curtained bay windows. The idea of wandering alone through someone's house did not appeal to Longarm. He was about to return to his own room when his sharp eyes caught a flicker of movement by the fireplace. He strained to see in the dim light, and called out softly, "Is there someone there?"

"Longarm?" Jessie called back. "What are you doing awake?"

"Same as you, I guess," Longarm laughed.

"Quiet," she scolded. "You'll wake the others."

Longarm walked to the end of the corridor and felt his way down the steps, his bare feet silent against the sturdy wood planks. As he reached the ground floor, he squinted against the bright flash of a match as Jessica lit a candle on the mantelpiece. The tiny flame dimly illuminated the portrait mounted above the fireplace. It was of a lovely, red-haired woman dressed in a green gown. The dress's hue exactly matched the woman's emerald eyes.

Although he had noticed the large portrait earlier in the evening, he had not had the opportunity to comment upon it. As he approached the soft circle of steady light thrown by the candle, Jessica saw that his eyes were fixed on the painting.

"That's my mother," she said proudly. "She died when I was very young."

"I'm sorry," Longarm said. He did not mention that the file Billy Vail had given him back in Denver had such information between its covers.

"Some say that death is just awakening from the dream that is life," Jessica murmured.

"Did Ki teach you that?" Longarm asked, thinking of boys killed in wars, and of dreams of such boys.

"No," Jessica smiled, turning from the portrait, to face Long-arm. "My father taught me that."

So close to her now, close enough to breathe in the fragrance of her hair, Longarm could see that she had been weeping. Her eyes were red-rimmed, her cheeks tear-stained. Tears had also stained the front of the long robe she was wearing. The robe was of sheerest silk, colored pale lavender. Her feet, beneath the hem of the robe, were bare. Was she bare as well, beneath the robe?

Jessica gestured toward Longarm's hand. "What have you got there?"

He looked down in surprise. He had forgotten he was hold-ing the bottle of Maryland rye. He held it up to the candle's light so that the amber whiskey's color would please her. "Take a drink," he coaxed, "and tell me why you were crying."

"It's nothing . . ." she began tentatively, and then stopped to shake her head, as if at the foolishness of such a statement. "If it's nothing, then why am I crying over it, I know, I know . . ."

Longarm chuckled. "Took the words right out of my mouth. Look, problems can be solved." His head was full of what he was sure was worrying her. She'd lost her foreman and a bunch of hands. The roundup was coming, and the running of such a huge spread had to be the cause of her anxiousness. "If you'd like, tomorrow we can ride into Sarah together, to see who's available to be hired. If you think about it, one of your top hands right here might be able to handle the job."

"You're very kind to be concerned," Jessica said. Before the fireplace was a fur throw rug in front of a sofa. She sat on the sofa with her back against the armrest and her legs curled beneath her. Patting the sofa, she said, "Sit down and give me your bottle. I think I will have a drink." She tilted the bottle, taking tiny sips from it, as she explained that she'd already appointed one of her hands as foreman, and that the Circle Star had more than enough men to handle the roundup. "My father taught me to shoot and ride and rope, Longarm, but he didn't neglect my brain. Maybe it was because he'd always wanted a son, I don't know . . . Anyway, I know all about how the cattle business works, as well as all the other businesses my father owned, which I've inherited. I fully intend to run them all myself," she trailed off. "Someday . . ." She stared at the fireplace, cold and empty as a mineshaft. "I wish it were fall. I could do with a roaring fire. I could do with being able to gaze into the flames."

"Why were you crying?" Longarm persisted. "Why must you wait to take control of your father's empire?"

Jessica looked at him. "I have to answer your questions with some of my own, but be patient and answer me honestly, and you'll find out what you want to know. Longarm, suppose you capture the men who killed my father—what happens then?"

Longarm shrugged. "They'll stand trial, of course."

"And if duly convicted they will be hanged." Jessica nodded. "But what if they were merely the muscles that pulled the triggers? What if the brain that ordered them to do the deed belonged to someone else?"

"You folks in Texas sure have a funny way of talking," Longarm muttered. He reached for the bottle and took a swig. "Reckon what you're asking is, what if this gang has a boss that sent them out to do their dirty deed? If that's the case, I'll arrest the boss as well, if I can dig up the proof that links him to the gang."

"And what if that boss has yet another boss? A boss far away? What if *that* boss can't be touched?" Her smile was warm. "Not even by a federal lawman?"

"I think you've got more than a 'what if' situation on your pretty little mind," Longarm said. "What you're talking about is a conspiracy."

"What's on my mind, Mr. Longarm of the law, is not at all a conspiracy, but a *war*. A war in which my father was a casualty." She paused. "And not the first."

"Tell me why you were crying, Jessie."

"Because they think that killing my father has ended the war. It hasn't, Longarm." She stared into his eyes, her expression in the candlelight both fierce and beautiful. "I'm crying because I've got to prove to them that the war isn't over, and that means I've got to do some things—live my life—in a way I'd never planned, in a way I don't really want. It means I've got to fight, and kill, even though those things are *not* what women are meant for."

"What are women meant for?" Longarm asked.

"For love," Jessica whispered, her eyes now bright, liquid,

emerald-hued as her mother's. "But before I can love," Jessica finished, "I must hate."

Longarm was silent, pondering what he'd been told. Finally he said, "Two things are on my mind. Number one, I'm sorry for saying that your mind was pretty and little. That just sort of slipped out. Your mind is certainly not little. The second thing on my mind is"—he grinned—"I haven't got the slightest idea what you're talking about. Why don't we eat this apple—"

"—one bite at a time!" Jessie chimed in before giving vent to her rich laugh. "Oh, Longarm"—she reached out to squeeze his hand—"I'm glad you're here. I might have gone insane if you hadn't showed up."

"Well, you going to start from the beginning?"

"From the beginning," Jessie declared. "From the first bite of the apple."

"Whoa now . . ." Longarm chuckled. "That's a little *too* far back. As I recollect it, that was Eve who took that bite."

Jessica Starbuck didn't laugh. "That's true. That first bite out of the apple came about because of temptation. Temptation brought about the start of the trade wars between my father and his enemies."

"I assume the start of your father's troubles was in the Japans?" Longarm asked.

Jessie nodded as she rose to fetch two glasses from a sideboard. "Would you prefer brandy to your bottle of rye?"

"This here suits me fine, thank you."

"I'll stick with the rye as well," she said, and then continued to tell her story as she returned to the sofa. "You have to try and picture what the Japanese were like when Commodore Perry's fleet sailed into their harbor. The Japanese had kept all Western influence out of their country for two hundred years. Two hundred! Think about it, Longarm. They'd conquered the Okinawans, as Ki told you. But he neglected to mention that they were, for all practical purposes, the overlords of the Chinese as well. They were the masters of their part of the world, and they thought that because the rest of the world was beneath their interest, their paradise would be left undisturbed."

"Paradise for the Japanese, maybe," Longarm pointed out. "But not so wonderful for the Okinawans and Chinese under the Japanese thumb."

"Spoken like an American." Jessica grinned. "Like a lawman. But that's how it was, at least, for the Japanese. Then America steamed up to their front door. My father was just a sailor, but he saw his chance, and fate was kind to him. By the time he'd returned to our own West Coast, and convinced enough wealthy businessmen to lend him the money he needed to buy up import and export rights, the civil war in the Japans was in full swing."

"I reckon there were fellows in the Japans who were all for tossing us foreigners out on our ears. Those Japanese fellows were most likely the fat cats. They had things sewed up nice and neat. Then along comes America and Europe, wanting a piece of the pie."

"A samurai—that's a warrior, a man a lot like you, Longarm—once said, 'If you understand on situation, you understand all.' You've proven him right. The Japanese civil war was fought by a group of conservative men who had everything to lose if the traditional order of things was changed. To be fair, they were also concerned about losing their heritage." She paused. "Heritage is very important to the Japanese. To the samurai, especially," she added sorrowfully.

"But the old order lost, as it did in our country's Civil War?" Longarm interjected.

"Yes, the Shogunate was overthrown by an alliance of progressive-minded lords and samurai fighting under the banner of the young Emperor Meiji. A city called Edo became the nation's new capital, and was renamed Tokyo to commemorate the nation's change."

"And your father rode the Japans like a man rides and breaks a bucking horse."

Jessica stared into her glass. She had drunk too much. The whiskey had loosened her resolve, allowing the memories she'd kept locked away to rise. She remembered her father when he was young and strong. In her heart she saw him the way he must have been during that wonderful time when his thick blond hair had blown in the wet winds coming off Tokyo Bay. Her father had brought her fine silk kimonos and painted fans like jewels—trappings more exquisite than any princess's adornment pictured in the storybooks of her childhood. He had told her about houses built of paper, and about warriors who made fierce faces and crowed like ogres as their glittering blades flashed through the clear blue sky like lightning bolts. Since her father's death she had banished the memories of the way he had held his small daughter upon his knee, regaling her with tales that allowed her to see and smell the pink cherry blossoms falling like snow-flakes, and taste the sweet plum wine . . .

"Jessie?" Longarm whispered. "If it hurts you to talk about it, let's not." He poured himself more rye. "Memories can hurt."

She shook herself. "My father *did* ride and break the Japans," she began again. "He branded his presence onto that land the way a hot iron sears the hide of a steer, or an artist's brush sweeps across white canvas." She glanced at her mother's portrait. "During that time, while back in America, he met my mother and they married. I was born in San Francisco. That's where the original Starbuck office was established. Things went very well. Not only for my father, but for other American and European businessmen. The British built miles of railroad in the Japans. The French and Germans had a fair share of commerce as well."

"There's no such thing as a fair share when you're talking business and commerce," Longarm said. "Two men might be working their claims on opposite sides of a mountain, all of a sudden one figures half a mountain isn't nearly enough, he wants the whole pile of rock for himself."

"And he'll try and take the whole mountain if he thinks he can get away with it," Jessie agreed. "The trouble began in the late sixties. The depression of the seventies was just beginning, and money was growing tight. My father was overextended. The men who had lent him money were beginning to feel the pinch so many Americans would soon feel. He and my mother were in danger of losing everything for which they had worked so hard."

"Of losing what they were trying to build for you?" Longarm asked.

"Yes." Jessie blushed. "Of course my future was weighing heavily upon their minds. Remember, I told you that like Adam and Eve in the Garden of Eden, my father's troubles began with temptation? Well, in those days he owned no clipper ships of his own, but leased ships from others. A group of European businessmen, Prussians, approached him with an offer. They were willing to sublease from my father all of his ships, at a price three times what he had been paying. The profit was enough to get him out of his immediate money problems. He accepted the Prussians' offer." Jessica's voice began to tremble. "There was, of course, good reason for the Prussians to be willing to pay my father so much. Their cargo was very precious. The Europeans were shipping slaves to America, Longarm. Chinese slaves, stolen from their homeland by the Prussians with the help of certain Japanese warlords."

"Your father knew what he was contributing to?" Longarm asked.

"Of course not. The manifests the Prussians supplied my father with listed the cargo as bolts of silk and other goods. Once he found out what was going on upon his ships he put a stop to it, but oriental philosophy says that a man is not excused from blame because he is ignorant of his part in some wrongdoing." She looked away.

"Well, my philosophy says you can't right a wrong till you know about it," Longarm scolded. "Your father did no more business with them, right?"

"He tried not to, Longarm, but once the Prussians had their claws into him they refused to let him go. They needed my father's cooperation to establish themselves in America. They considered our country ripe for the taking, and they believed in taking what they could. That's what you've got to understand about these men," she pleaded, her voice grown strong and intense. "They believe that a few men are destined to rule all men. They dismiss as foolishness the idea that men are created equal. They want to rule the world as they've ruled parts of Europe for so long, and they will do anything to get what they want!"

"Like murdering your father, Jessie? Or having him murdered?"

She smiled grimly. "One bite at a time, Longarm, remember? When my father refused their advances upon his business, they began to strike at his interests in the Orient. Old friends of his were at first coerced, and then, if they refused to listen out of loyalty to my father, they or members of their families

were killed. My father, meanwhile, had branched out into
Europe, and began to give as good as he got," Jessie added
proudly. "Ships were hijacked on both sides. Private armies
sprang up. Trade wars uncondoned by any government, but just
as bloody as those between countries, were waged. The battles
were fought with violence, paid for and protected with money.
Nobody interfered. Nobody could. Nobody dared. Money bought
silence. Men fought and died and the world was none the wiser.
It might have gone on like that forever, just another expense to
add to the profit-and-loss sheets, the lives of a lost crew memo-
rialized by a few ink marks in a ledger." She paused. "My father
has done many wonderful things, Longarm. But please understand that what I've told you about him tonight is not something
I'm proud of."

"Men make mistakes in their lives, like I told you, Jessie,"
Longarm said quietly. "If your father did some bad things, so
be it. He's dead now. I reckon that ledger you were speaking
of shows he had more marks on the credit side of the page."
He longed for a smoke, but he dared not leave the room to get
one, thinking that if he left Jessie's side, the spell would be
broken and she would pull back into the shell she'd built around
herself in order to survive. "You said the war, the sea and land
battles, the hijackings between the two sides *might* have gone
on forever. What happened?"

"I now know that in a war, everyone is fair game," she said
bitterly. "My father didn't understand that, but then he'd had
little experience in such matters. For the Europeans it was old
hat. They bided their time, waiting for the proper moment to
strike. It came when my parents voyaged to Europe on business
and for a holiday. I was too young to make the journey with
them, of course. The authorities there said it was an accident,
and my father, for all of his power, was far from home. He
could not make them change their ruling. My father and mother
were crossing a street. A carriage came from around a corner.
Supposedly it was out of control. It careened into their path—
four maddened horses dragging behind them steel-rimmed
wheels. My father suffered minor injuries, but my mother . . ."
Jessica looked at Longarm and smiled sadly. "Thinking about
it, it seems so naive of my parents to have traveled into the
lion's den, so to speak. But in those days—and even until the

day he died—my father was a curious mixture of shrewdness and innocence. And back then, when it had happened, the idea of rivals striking at one's immediate family—well, even if my father had *wanted* to live his life in a fortress, my mother would not have allowed it." Jessie looked up at the portrait above the fireplace. She gazed at the women whose spirit seemed to live in her own green eyes. "My mother was not the sort of woman who would allow herself to be caged."

"Her murderers went unpunished?"

"You don't—*didn't* know my father if you can ask that," Jessie declared. "The actual assassins, the men who did the deed for money, were beneath my father's notice. He found out which of his Prussian enemies had ordered the attempt. The man who'd hatched the plot, a count, had a son, a young man in his twenties, who would fall heir to his father's holdings and power. The boy was a fop, a lover of high society and nightlife. On the eve of his sailing back to America, my father, all alone, trailed the young man until he came upon him on a secluded street. With his bare hands he snapped the boy's neck, leaving the body in the gutter. Several days later, as the count mourned his loss, a package came to him via courier. It was the boy's handkerchief, embroidered with his family's crest. Tucked inside the cloth was my father's business card. On it he had written, 'With my compliments'—"

"Sweet Jesus," Longarm murmured, when he could find his voice.

"There was an uproar, of course," Jessie continued. "The count demanded justice." She laughed. "But by then my father was back in America. Back in *his* territory. The shoe was on the other foot. The death of the count's son went unavenged."

"But surely not for long?" Longarm began.

"Yes," she nodded. "Things calmed down. Maybe the shock of my father losing his wife and one of his enemies losing his son spoiled their taste for further violence. In any event, there were fewer battles. Business interests on both sides enjoyed undisturbed prosperity. Things remained that way up until the day they'd finished what they'd started on those European streets. Up until the day they murdered my father, here on his own ranch." Jessie tilted the bottle, pouring the last inch of rye into her glass. "We've drunk it all, I'm sorry . . ."

Longarm smiled and shook his head. "This was thirsty talk, woman." He thought about things for a moment, then said, "How do you know that your father's murder had anything to do with what you've told me? I don't mean to be unfeeling, but what proof do you have linking his European enemies to the shooting?"

Jessica stared at Longarm, her eyes narrowed and her lips pursed, as if she were evaluating him and, at the same time, weighing an important decision. She rose from the sofa. Longarm saw the outline of her long, lithe body traced by the shimmering silk as she reached out to take his hand. "Come with me. I'm going to show you something." She held his eyes with her own. "Because I trust you."

She lit another candle, and by its light they walked down a hallway to a room that turned out to be Alex Starbuck's study. Fine leather-upholstered armchairs and sofas furnished the big room. The walls were lined with book-laden shelves and glass-windowed cabinets of gleaming, expensive firearms. In the air was the cherry scent of aromatic pipe tobacco. Longarm didn't have to ask to know that the humidor would be regularly replaced to keep that scent fresh and strong. This was Alex Starbuck's room. It always would be, while this house stood . . .

Jessica went to a shelf and removed a leatherbound volume. Wedged in its pages was a small key. This she took to an old, scarred, and battered oak desk. Its massive bulk dominated the room.

"This white elephant was the first desk my father owned," she said fondly. "He bought it secondhand, when he'd just started out. Then, it was all he could afford. He never used another. It was shipped here from San Francisco when we moved to Texas." She took a small, black leatherbound notebook out of the opened drawer. "With the exceptions of the circumstances surrounding my mother's death, and the fact that my father knew what sort of cargo the Europeans wanted to ship in his clippers, the history of my father's business was known to me since my adolescence. My father felt I had to understand its birthing if I was someday to run the empire. While on his deathbed, he told me about the slaves, about my mother, and about this book."

She handed it to Longarm. Inside, written in a careful hand, were a series of names and places. Beneath each heading, cryptic notes detailed that individual's business or position in government.

"After my father had returned from Europe, he waited for his enemies to retaliate. He hired private detectives on both sides of the Atlantic to ferret out the links between his enemies in Europe and their minions in this country. He wanted plenty of targets, you see, and he wanted his enemies to know that he was collecting such potential targets. This was the only way he had to protect me. It was his hope that his enemies would think twice about striking at his child if they knew that Alex Starbuck had tracked down their children, as well as their vital interests—both legal and illegal—in America."

"These European folks have illegal operations in America?" Longarm asked sharply.

"Through blackmail alone they own lawmen, congressmen, business tycoons—" She stopped, and grinned from ear to ear. Holding out her hand, she said, "Give it back, Mr. Longarm of the law."

Like a cat watching a canary get locked up in its cage, Longarm watched the black book get locked back up in its drawer. "Reckon I would need a court order to confiscate that juicy little diary." He was joking, but his tone was rueful.

"Reckon you would, Marshal," Jessie mimicked, giving his bare belly a playful poke. "But don't you see? Even if you did have the book, it would be useless to you. The men and women in it are above the law."

"Nobody's above the law. I told you that once." Longarm growled. He'd have been growing hot under the collar, if he'd been wearing one.

"Damn it, Marshal," she argued, "in many cases, the folks I'm going to track down *write* the laws!"

Longarm stood silent, his hands on his hips. "You can't be judge and jury all by yourself. It doesn't matter what your father did in Europe—"

"It does matter!" Jessie insisted. "It was the only thing he could do. Answer me truthfully. How long would you be a federal marshal, how long would your superior back in Denver keep his badge, if you started sniffing around the tracks of a crooked congressman?" She gave him a second to ponder that, then said, "Come on, Longarm, let's get ourselves a nightcap."

Back on the sofa by the fireplace, with snifters of brandy before them, Longarm added, "What you do concerning that book of names is none of my concern. But remember that I've warned you once that while I'm investigating the murder of your father, you're to stay out of the way and let *me* do the dirty work."

"And I've said that your point was clear to me."

"Fine," Longarm said. "How do you know those names in that book are even current?"

"Well, as I told you, there was no retaliation from abroad, so my father was content to let things rest. Losing my mother tore a whole lot out of him—out of his spirit, and he had me to contend with. Anyway, he kept his detectives on the case through the years. Up until his death he kept crossing out those who had died, adding in those newly recruited. I've kept the investigators on the payroll. Now their reports will come to me."

Longarm nodded. He yawned and stretched. It was late, and his body was thick with sleep, but his mind was wide awake. He needed sleep, knew he ought to get some, for tomorrow promised a hard day of riding to find Willie, the only witness to the Starbuck shooting. The old hand was acting as cook for a bunch of Circle Star hands rounding up a distant herd on Starbuck land.

"What's wrong?" Jessica suddenly asked.

"Who said anything's wrong?" he smiled.

"You did," she said. "You told me something was wrong in the way your voice sounded when you called down to me from the second floor. Your eyes told me something was wrong when I first looked into them tonight. You've no shirt on, so I could see the tension in your body." She smiled warmly. "You see, Longarm? You're telling me something is wrong in every way possible, without actually using words."

He shook his head in wonder. "Damn, woman. What a lawman you'd have made."

Jessie slid off the sofa to kneel on the soft fur rug in front of the fireplace. "Come, lie down on your stomach, here, on the rug. Let's see if I can rub the tension out of your shoulders."

Jessica, beside him, ran her fingers along the taut cords of his neck. With a feathery touch, she first stroked, then gently kneaded the thick masses of muscle and sinew padding his shoulders and upper arms. "Relax," she crooned, bending to him so that her lips were just inches away from the shell of his ear.

Longarm tried, but it was no use. A new worry was nagging at him . . .

Jessica sat back crosslegged. "You're too strong for me," she scolded lightly. "Your muscles are too developed for me to force them to relax." She raised one leg and bent it at the knee. The gown fell open, revealing the splendid curve of her thigh and calf.

Longarm colored, but her beauty was such that he could not look away. *If only . . .*

Sensing his unease, Jessica covered up. "Have I offended you?" she asked.

"No, ma'am," he said forcefully. "Hardly that. I think you're lovely, and what I'd most like to do is slide that silk thing off you and start rubbing the tension out of you. It's just that—"

"What?" Jessica demanded.

"It just doesn't seem right." He glanced up at the portrait above the fireplace. "I mean, with your mother looking down on us and all."

Jessica laughed in delight. "You really are a samurai! Gallant, and a gentleman to the very core!"

"I don't see what's so funny," Longarm said, disgruntled. "Just because a man has a sense of what's right and wrong—"

"Hush," she giggled, pressing her finger to his lips, and then, as if to make sure he obeyed, she pecked a cool, delicious kiss against his mouth. "Lie back down. On your stomach. That's an order," she said sternly.

Longarm obeyed, somehow not at all surprised by the fact that Jessie was unbuttoning his trousers and then peeling them down over his buttocks, past his thighs, and then off. He heard a soft rustling sound, and turned his head to see the silken gown fall to the floor, the folds dropping in on themselves so that the garment resembled a stream of plum-colored liquid splashing down. When he tried to look at Jessica, she placed a hand on either side of his head, her palms acting like blinders.

"No, you're not to look at me. Not until I give you permission," she teased. "You must lie on your stomach with your eyes closed while I massage your back. Just relax and listen to what I have to tell you."

Longarm felt his erection grow rock hard, and his heart begin to pound, as Jessica straddled him. She gave her bottom a little shake as she settled down on the small of his back, light as a butterfly. As her fingers began to do their dance down along his shoulders and spine, Longarm became mad with passion. Her trick of touching him without letting him see her had a way of driving a man loco! Where had she ever learned such a wonderful love-game?

"I've told you that my parents were unusual people," Jessica said. "Part of that came from their love of the Orient. They had always planned to retire in the Japans someday, but after my mother was killed, my father knew that to return there without her would be much too painful. What he decided to do was bring a bit of the Japans to America. Instead of hiring an American woman to be the ranch's housekeeper and my nanny, he arranged for Myobu to come to our country, and to take over those duties."

Longarm thought of the small old woman, so graceful and polite, who had prepared and served the fine dinner earlier in the evening. "Did your father know her?" he asked.

"In a manner of speaking," Jessica laughed. "Longarm, do you know what a geisha is?"

Longarm chose his words carefully. "Reckon you might describe one as a very high-priced, uh, lady of the night."

"A courtesan, to be sure," Jessie agreed in amusement, "but please understand that things in the Orient are not the same as they are in America. In the Japans, body and soul are not considered two separate things. Here, women are hired by men to tend only to their physical cravings. In the Japans, geishas cater to men's bodies, but also to their souls. The word geisha best translates as 'artist.' She is trained from childhood to be skilled in music, art, and literature, the preparation and serving of fine food, and finally, if she has proven herself worthy, she is taught the skills and abilities that are the keys to a man's soul. A geisha is not only an artist, but also a sort of priestess. Through her body, a man can experience enlightenment. For the brief time a man spends with a geisha, he is one with the universe. This frees the geisha's soul, as well."

"And Myobu was such an . . . artist?" Longarm marveled.

"Many years ago, she was one of the most famous geishas in the Japans," Jessie told him. "She had an honored place in the Emperor's court. She was one of the most powerful women in that nation."

"Do geishas become rich?"

"Oh, yes," Jessica said, her fingers rubbing the last drops of tension out of Longarm's body. "And along with monetary wealth comes public respect, and a high, honored place in society."

"Then forgive me for saying so," Longarm frowned, "but it strikes me as powerful sad that such a woman has to end her life as a housekeeper, happy as she is here, I'm sure . . ."

"Oh, she didn't *have* to, Longarm," Jessie explained. "She still has her wealth, most of it transferred to this country. She could live well, anywhere in the world."

"Then why did she choose to become a housekeeper and nanny for a Texas tycoon and his daughter?"

"During the time he was in the Japans, long before he met my mother, Myobu was my father's geisha. During their time together, she guided my father as he melded his mind and spirit into what we in this country call our soul, and then she guided him through the process in which the soul and physical body become one. That is enlightenment. In addition, Myobu, who already had extensive business holdings, taught my father much that was to help him later on, while building his own business in his own country."

"I still don't understand," Longarm interrupted. "If all that's so, why did she consent to work for him?"

"After my mother was killed, my father wrote to Myobu. She was older, and her time of being an active geisha was coming to an end. In the Japans, it is traditional for such an older woman to open a *ryu*, a school in which worthy young girls are initiated and then taught the various aspects of becoming geishas. My father explained to Myobu that he would never again marry, which meant that I was to be the sole heir to all of his holdings. Accordingly he wanted me to have the benefit of the finest education in the world. That meant tutors and, later on, university schooling, but it also meant that from childhood on, I was to have that special guidance that would allow my soul to blossom, and later to join together with my body—guidance and training that would prepare me for the awesome responsibility of ruling the Starbuck empire. Myobu considered herself my father's mentor. When his request came to her, she considered it her destiny, her *karma*, to accept. She had favored the father who built the empire, thereby beginning the circle. Now she would train the daughter who would complete the circle. The chance to do such a thing, the honor to do such a thing, could only come to a geisha as fine as Myobu."

"But to do the cooking and cleaning . . ." Longarm shook his head, perplexed.

"Don't you try to look at me yet," Jessica warned him as she slid down to straddle his thighs. Gently she caressed his lower back, her touch now sending velvety pulses of pleasure through his body. How he longed to turn her over and kiss her! But he didn't move.

"A true geisha will cook and clean as expertly as she will play an instrument or manage her business affairs," Jessica was murmuring. "She doesn't concern herself with the relative status of a task. All tasks that are honestly performed will bring honor. A geisha is an artist, and life is her art form."

"Earlier you told me that women weren't meant for hate but for love—" Longarm started to say, but Jessica cut him off.

"I've been given a very different, special sort of destiny. There is the art of negotiating one's way through the world, and the art of loving one's way through it. In these two aspects of life, Myobu has trained me well. I am a geisha." She slid off his legs, her hands now guiding him over onto his back so that he could see her.

Longarm gazed at her lovely features, suffused with passion. By the flickering candle glow he watched the nipples of her full, lush breasts tighten, as if they could actually feel his eyes' loving caress.

He reached out for her, his fingers gently locking about her arms, and pulled her down upon him. As she let herself fall, she dipped her head so that her shimmering tresses brushed across his chest. The touch was like fire, but a pleasurable fire. The gold-and-red tendrils of her hair sparked desire so strong it made Longarm throb with anticipation.

As they kissed, Jessica pressed her soft, flat belly against his erection, blanketing it with sweet warmth. She slid up to lock and squeeze his member between her thighs, allowing him to touch and tease her center, but never quite enter. She planted a hand on either side of him to support herself, and stretched and arched her back, catlike, brushing her pubic hair against him again and again. Her teasing forced him to grow harder, to swell and swell.

"Do you feel what is happening?" Jessica breathed into his ear between long, wet kisses. "Do you feel it?"

Longarm felt himself grow dizzy. Up above, their tongues were intertwined, and down below, his erection was kissing the moist folds between her thighs. Between one kiss and the next, Longarm rolled over onto his side. He pulled Jessie in tight against him, and buried his face in her mass of fragrant hair, his palm gliding the length of her curled body. Her skin was far softer than even the silk robe she had worn. His fingers rode up the curve of her hip, to cup and stroke the hemispheres of her buttocks.

"Lord above, woman," Longarm gasped. "What fine tricks Myobu has taught you."

"There are no tricks, silly," Jessica laughed. She watched his face as she licked and lightly bit his nipples. Her fingers stroked his erection and cupped his scrotum, making him moan. "The geisha's art lies not in knowing how to play tricks, but in knowing how to surrender."

Longarm buried his face in the warm valley between her breasts. He inhaled her woman scent. He flicked his tongue around and around the dark rosettes of her breasts. Quickly he moved from one to the other, at first licking and sucking, and then using his teeth to barely rake her swollen nipples, until her pleasured purr rose to a sob of joy.

Jessica's legs parted then, and as she rolled over onto her back, she drew him into her. They moved flesh against flesh, sliding and rocking together against the soft fur of the rug. Longarm kept her cradled in his arms as he swung his hips up and then plunged down, each thrust seeming to take him deeper and deeper. It went on like this for long minutes. All barriers between them now fell. Neither had any thoughts, but lived only in those parts of their bodies that touched. Those were the only parts that mattered.

Longarm slowed his movements each time he felt his orgasm growing near. Jessica rubbed her bottom against the rug as her inner muscles squeezed against him. Finally, moaning uncontrollably, she dug her fingers into Longarm's buttocks and pressed him in to the hilt, all the while gyrating her hips in an endless circle. Helpless in that luscious embrace, Longarm felt his orgasm build and build until it burst forth. At that moment, Jessica locked her mouth to his as she came, so that their love-cries were exchanged as their kisses had been.

Longarm stayed nested inside her as they talked, punctuating each exchange with kisses. Soon her silken, rippling contractions brought him blossoming forth, newly hard, and more ravenous for her than he had been before. This time their love-making was slow and playful—after all, now they were old friends. They exchanged gifts of love. Jessie gloated each time she was able to make him beg for mercy, for a moment's rest. This time when they came, Jessie threw her legs up around Longarm's back. His fire spread into and through her in ever-widening circles. Waves of rapture washed over her, her eyelids fluttered, and her mouth formed a perfect circle. She clutched at Longarm like a woman about to drown, and she didn't let go until he had carried her to their passion's limit.

They had only a few hours until dawn, so they went up the stairs to Jessica's bedroom, to sleep wrapped in each other's arms. As Longarm dropped off, while his lips nibbled absent-mindedly kisses across the nape of Jessie's neck, he thought of the diminutive, elderly Myobu, of her small round face, cracked and yellowed like ancient porcelain. He thought of her laugh, tinkling like wind chimes, and of her eyes flashing brightly, like those of a young girl's.

Listening to Jessica's soft, regular breathing, pressing his length against her, Longarm remembered what this woman in his arms had said about destiny, about *karma*. He wondered what was going through wise Myobu's mind tonight. How much did the frail geisha's soul know about what had gone on between this woman and him?

When Longarm finally slept, his dreams stayed far from the Shiloh battlefield, where death came too soon, to boys too young. Instead he dreamed of the Japans, and geishas, and women everywhere—women meant for love.

Chapter 8

Longarm awoke a few moments before dawn. He slipped from Jessica's embrace and padded silently to his own room, where he groomed and dressed himself for the day.

As he left the house and walked toward the stable, his Winchester in hand, he spied Ki sitting crosslegged on the ground, facing the rising sun. His back was ramrod straight and his hands were placed in his lap. He had his eyes half closed and was breathing in a deep, regular manner, almost the way a sleeper breathes.

Longarm knew instinctively not to disturb the man. It was some kind of praying that Ki was doing, or not praying exactly, but the sort of thing that goes on in church when the pastor calls for a moment's silence.

In the stable he found his gelding already saddled up and ready to go. The only other person awake was Ki, so Longarm wanted to thank him on the way out, but when he led his horse out of the stable, Ki was nowhere in sight.

It was full morning by the time Longarm reached the range area where Willie and the other hands were supposed to be. The hands had long since ridden out for the day, and Willie was stacking up the other men's bedrolls before he started the day's cooking chores.

The little fellow looked to be in his late sixties. He had a gray, close-cropped beard covering his chin and cheeks, maybe to make up in part for the lack of hair on his head. He was dressed in baggy jeans and a ragged flannel shirt. His boots were low-heeled, as befit a man who did more wagon-sitting and walking than riding. He wore no gunbelt, but an old Colt Peacemaker hung from its trigger guard on a nail pounded into the chuck box.

As Longarm rode up, Willie pulled a cloth cap out of the back pocket of his denims and perched it on his bald head.

"It's my cooking hat, and gives me something to wipe my hands on," he told Longarm by way of greeting. "Now who might you be?" Before Longarm could answer, the old cook turned his attention to stoking up a cookfire.

"Can you keep a secret, Uncle?" Longarm asked Willie's back. He dismounted and let the gelding's reins trail.

The cook straightened up, grimacing, and then spat into the fire. "Sonny, I forgot more secrets than you'll ever have the pleasure to tell. Now if you can get me a little drunk while you're telling me, I can surely forget what I heard." He looked hopefully at Longarm, his pale blue eyes twinkling.

"Damn, I don't have a bottle with me, Uncle," Longarm apologized.

"Shoot, then we'll have to drink mine," the cook said disgustedly. "And my name's Willie. You keep calling me 'Uncle,' folks gonna think I'm old, boy . . ." He rummaged around in the chuck box and came out with a bottle of bourbon. "I keep this about for cooking purposes, you understand." Willie winked at Longarm as he pulled the cork with his teeth. "Can't cook for shit unless I'm half sloshed." He gulped a big swallow, and handed the bottle to Longarm. "Now who the hell are you, boy? This here's Starbuck land. What are you doing here?"

Longarm took a tentative swallow of the bourbon, and liked what he tasted. "Willie, I was going to spin you a tall tale concerning the who and why of me, but I need your help, and if I'm asking for a man to help me, least I can do is tell him the God's honest."

"Well said, sonny." He kicked the last bedroll under the awning jutting out from the side of the chuckwagon, and looked back at the fire, which was sputtering and crackling now as the seasoned wood caught flame. A sudden, short breeze sent the smoke his way, and as he turned, coughing and swearing, rubbing at his eyes, he spied Longarm about to take another pull off the bourbon. "Here, sonny!" he cried, lunging for the bottle. "Don't drink too much, else you'll fry your brain!" He beamed a moony look at his quart, took a long drink, and then smacked his lips. "Now who the hell are you, boy?"

"I'm a deputy U.S. marshal, and my name's Custis Long. Folks generally call me Longarm. I'm here to look into Alex Starbuck's death. I'd appreciate it if that could stay between us, Willie."

The old-timer nodded sagely. "You be the fellow they call Longarm?"

"Yep," Longarm smiled.

"The lawman?"

"That'd be me."

"The *federal* lawman?"

"The very one." Longarm knew what was coming.

"Never heard a' ya!" Willie cackled. He slapped his thigh and hopped about, cackling like a chicken that just laid a turkey egg. "Ah, my, still as sharp as the day is long," he complimented himself as he wiped the tears from his eyes. "Reckon you want to talk to me about that fateful day. Yessir, many have, many have. You could say that I've become sort of a famous person in these parts as the man who knew Alex Starbuck best. I taught him what he knew about cattle, you see. He'd often said to me, 'Will'—he called me Will, you see—'Will, I owe everything I have to you—' "

"Care for a smoke?" Longarm asked. He'd hoped to wait the windstorm out patiently, but Willie showed no signs of blowing until next day's dawn.

Willie plucked the proffered cheroot out of Longarm's fingers. "Smoke it later," he explained, tucking it behind his ear. "No good, a fellow smoking while he cooks," he announced. "Ashes might get in the grub." He headed for the rear of the wagon, where the chuck box was firmly bolted into place against the tailgate. The box was about four feet tall and a yard wide, with its outer wall hinged at the base so that it could be swung down to form a sturdy work table supported by a leg. The leg was itself hinged so that it could be folded flat when the box was closed. "You want to ask me stuff, go right ahead, Longarm. But I gotta keep cooking while you talk. Some new hands came in last night from Sarah. We're signing on hands faster than I can make biscuits." He reached into the chuck box, rummaging around in the various partitions and shelves built into it, to come out with a small keg of sourdough, a sack of flour, and salt and baking soda.

"Can't get over Mr. Starbuck naming a cow town after his wife," Longarm said as he watched the cook work. "Cow town's a rough place to carry a woman's pretty name."

"You didn't know Alex, so you can say that, Longbow."

"Longarm."

"Right," Willie replied. He filled a large, pockmarked tin pan half full of flour, poured some of the sourdough batter into that and threw in some soda and salt. "Sonny, fetch me that skillet over yonder," he asked Longarm.

Longarm wandered over to where a black cast-iron skillet's handle was poking out from the rack of pots and pans beneath the wagon bed. He carried it over to Willie, who instructed Longarm to dribble some of the bacon grease it contained from the morning's meal into the batter.

"Like I said, you didn't know Alex, so you can say that." Willie began to knead the dough against the floured surface of his cook table. "Starbuck admired cowpokes. You see, he felt he had more in common with independent men than with rich ones. A honest hand makes his own way and answers to no one but his foreman, and if he and the foreman don't get along, he collects his pay and moves on. That's a hell of a lot better life than wearing a pinstriped suit and having a slack belly, breathing stale air, and getting a hump in your back from bending over your figuring—"

"I get it," Longarm cut him off.

"Anyway, we got fine schools in Sarah. And a church—not that I've ever been inside it," Willie cackled. "Fetch a Dutch oven and pour some of that bacon grease in it, will you? We got the railroad, and flowers and trees—*that's* Sarah too. There's a doctor and a dentist. In Sarah, kids will grow up healthy and knowing how to read. *That's* what Alex left for his wife."

Longarm watched the cook pinch off eggs of the dough and

place them in the greased Dutch oven. "I guess he loved his wife very much."

"You might say that, Longbow."

"Longarm."

"Right again, sonny, right again." He put a lid on the filled Dutch oven, and had Longarm set it in the summer sun, so that the biscuits would have time to rise before being baked on the fire. "Alex built an entire town to carry on Miss Sarah's memory. Beats a bunch of flowers at a stone grave marker. Flowers die, but a town goes on forever." He paused a moment to smile at Longarm, and then squinted up at the sun. "Guess I'd better start on the meat. Them peckerheads will be riding in for dinner soon enough. I tell you, boy, cooking three meals a day, it's surely just and fair that a cook gets paid better than the top hands."

"No argument there, Willie." Some of the worst meals he'd ever eaten had been chuckwagon prepared, Longarm remembered. But when well made, no fare on earth was tastier. "Where did Alex bury his wife?" he asked out of idle curiosity.

Willie shrugged. "No one knows. Alex took her back from that there Europe, and buried her himself, with a little help," he chuckled as he began slicing steaks from a haunch of beef hauled from the wagon's cool, dark interior. "Don't matter where Miss Sarah lies, the town's her monument." Willie set several skillets on the fire and began to fry the flour-dredged beef filets in hot fat. He put the biscuit-filled Dutch oven on the fire, and piled coals on its lid to create an even, baking heat. "Ain't you going to ask about where Alex himself is buried?" he asked as he prodded and poked the sizzling meat with a long, two-pronged fork.

"Reckon he's with his wife in some quiet, wooded grove." Longarm smiled. "I don't want to know where the graves are, Willie. I want to know about what you heard and saw that day Mr. Starbuck was shot and killed."

Willie was silent as he transferred all the cooked steaks to one skillet and moved it off the fire. He set a lid on the pan, to keep the meat warm and free of dust. When he finally looked at Longarm, there was suspicion and self-doubt in his pale blue eyes. "Don't rightly think I've the time to jaw with you anymore, sonny. I've got to make the gravy and un-crock the stewed fruit and—"

"You said the shooting sounded like a string of firecrackers going off," Longarm cut him off.

"And the other boys laughed at me. Said I was getting senile." He spat out the word like it was a piece of foul food. "They said I made it up to get free drinks. That I made up everything about me and Alex being trail partners."

"I believe you, Willie," Longarm said quietly, sincerely.

Willie squinted at him, trying to see if he was being joshed. When he spoke it was with an emotional, trembling voice. "All them others had me senile so many times, maybe I got to believing them. I don't want to talk about the day Alex was cut down. I'm afraid Miss Jessie will lose patience with me. Decide she's got no place for an old hand."

"You've got a home here till you die, Willie," Longarm assured the old man. "Miss Jessie herself told me so. She said you've got a pension here. She couldn't imagine running the place without you."

"Fine girl. What a fine girl," Willie muttered, turning back to his work table, so that Longarm could not see the film of tears glossing his eyes. "What a tussler she is!" he exclaimed in that hoarse tone of voice some men use when their feelings of love grow too strong. "Just like Alex. What a tussler!"

To get the conversation back on the right track, Longarm said, "You know, when I heard the firecracker remark of yours, it reminded me of a sort of shooting noise I'd once heard."

"Yeah?" Willie mused, his eyes growing shrewd. He carried a small sack of flour and a box of salt over to the fire. "Now where might that have been?" He poured the meat juices from all the skillets into one pan and threw in a handful of flour and a pinch of salt. This he stirred until it became a thick gravy.

"I heard it well over fifteen years ago, Willie. Now it don't matter if we were side by side during that time, or if we were facing each other. I've learned that it's best for a soul to disremember whether he rode for the blue or the gray." As he spoke he took a handful of the .25-caliber shell casings from his pocket and stood them on end, like a line of soldiers, along the edge of the work table.

Willie ambled over, attracted by what Longarm was doing.
He picked up two of the casings and compared them. "Same
damn gun fired them both, sonny. These two long scratches
prove that much."

"I know," Longarm said. "How many shots did you hear?"

" 'Bout thirty." After a moment's pause, Willie asked, "How
many did you find with that long scratch?"

"About thirty."

"Damn!" Willie gleefully slapped his thigh. He was almost
hopping up and down in excitement. Longarm had to remind
him that the gravy was going to burn if left untended much
longer.

After a moment's stirring of the thick sauce, the old man
put down his spoon and turned to face Longarm. "Sure as I
live and breathe, I'll never forget the first time I heard that
noise. I was a wild fella back then, hanging around with a bunch
of toughs who figured that despite the surrender, the War wasn't
nearly over yet, not for *us*. We raided Union outposts, way-
laid carpetbaggers—" Willie scowled, but good-naturedly.
"Never you mind where, and when, federal lawman. I guess
we thought we were small potatoes. We swaggered and bragged
about how we were making the bluecoats pay, but I don't
think we ever really thought the Union boys would bother to
get after us."

"The way they looked at it, they had to make examples,"
Longarm said.

"Well, they surely did make us into them examples, boy,"
Willie murmured sadly. "We was closing in on a supply wagon,
but it was a setup, an ambush. All of a sudden the canvas tent
on the wagon dropped, and this big old cannonlike thing began
chewing us up. It just kept on firing. It was like we had stepped
into a yellowjackets' nest. You know? The mean ones build
their nests in low bramble, or beneath hollow logs . . . I just
threw myself off of my horse and kissed that there grass like
it was a ten-dollar whore. The boys with me were jumping and
twitching just like beestung dogs, 'cept that it wasn't bugs tearing into them, it was lead. They were dancing in the air, dead
already, but so much lead was being pumped into them that it
was keeping them on their feet. The rounds that didn't hit flesh
chewed up the ground. Clods of earth and tufts of greenery

went flying. And all the while I was hugging the ground and shitting in my pants, I was listening to that string-of-firecrackers noise. It grew in my ears until it sounded loud as thunder. I knew I would never, *never* forget it."

"I never forgot what it sounded like either, Willie." Longarm's nod was doleful. "I never forgot what it could do to a line of good men."

The cook retrieved his bottle of bourbon. He took a swig and handed the bottle to Longarm. "You and yours, me and mine. Lot of good boys never made it past those awful years. A drink to them."

"To them," Longarm agreed. After the whiskey had begun its slow burn in the pit of his belly, Longarm asked, "Was it a Gatling gun you heard back during that raid? And on the day Starbuck was cut down?"

Willie sighed. "It was, sonny, but if we're agreed on that, it causes more problems than it solves. These here casings you gathered are .25 caliber. They've got more in common with a range hand's coyote gun. Hell, the Gatlings I saw after the War fired .42s. They looked like artillery. Weighed as much, too. They were big, heavy contraptions mounted on field carriages, and pulled along by teams of horses.

"Long-gun, I tell you true," the old cook admonished. "I was by Alex's side—at the very scene of the ambush—within seconds of the time they opened up on him. You climbed the rise to gather up these shells, so you know how steep it is. No way in the world ten men could carry a Gatling *down* such a slope, let alone *up* it in the first place. No way horses could haul it, either, not within the space of an hour, let alone moments."

"And even if we could figure out the way they got the gun up there," Longarm sighed, "we'd still have the fact that these here shells are .25s."

The cook said thoughtfully, "Be a real nightmare if they'd had a Gatling, say, small enough for one man to carry. That one man would be the equal of ten. Speaking of one man against ten, I've got a fine story for you. You're a lawman, you ought to appreciate a story about a good fight. You see, Alex and I were down by the Mexican border, and we ran into a gang of these here desperadoes. This goes back a few years, now—"

"Willie, save it for next time," Longarm said. "I'll bring a bottle of rye along with me, to keep our throats wet." He swept the row of shell casings into the palm of his hand, and slipped them into his coat pocket.

"Just as well," Willie said. "I got to lay out this here dinner for the boys."

"Remember, Willie," Longarm warned him as he mounted up, "this little talk we had, and my job in these parts, goes no further."

"I ain't gonna tell them peckerheads nothing," Willie cackled. "Why *should* I? I'm *senile*, for chrissakes." He turned back to his pots and pans, calling, "See you around, Longboat!"

"See you around," Longarm laughed, and rode off. After a mile, and just before he rode over the crest of a rise, he slowed his gelding and twisted in the saddle to look back at the camp. The hands were just riding in. Soon they'd be eating and laughing, and teasing Willie about the quality of his grub. After dinner the hands would return to their work, and then the few men left behind to day-herd could ride in for their midday meal. Willie would keep their food hot. He knew his job.

Longarm rode on, back toward the Starbuck spread. Jessie would be around, and he looked forward to seeing her. It was always hard to say goodbye to a fine woman, but bidding Jessie farewell when the time came was going to be the hardest yet. Longarm wondered if he even wanted to say goodbye. He only had a few days to get to the bottom of this case before the army came stomping in. Old Billy Vail was probably going crazy with worry back in Denver. Sending his boss a progress report over the telegraph wire was the way it usually worked, but this time around, Longarm didn't want to chance the Denver clerk intercepting it. He could send the wire directly to Vail's home, of course, but for now Longarm decided that he didn't have anything worth the cost of the wire to report anyway. According to Jessie and Willie, Alex Starbuck was murdered by Europeans with a weapon that didn't exist. Vail would not be pleased to hear that. He was a mite old-fashioned concerning murders, Billy Vail was; he liked his criminals to be one-hundred-percent American boys, just right for American courts of law. Billy was pretty much a meat-and-potatoes man when it came to murder weapons, as well. He'd take a six-gun or, in a pinch, a Winchester over a Gatling gun anytime.

The pocketful of shell casings jingled as Longarm rode. Their weight pressed against his side all the way back to the Starbuck spread.

Chapter 9

Longarm cut through a stand of tall pecan trees to come around to the wide, dusty trail that led to the Starbuck residence. About three hundred yards from the house, Longarm reined in his mount. In the front yard sat a brougham hitched to a two-horse team. There were other mounts around the closed buggy, and several men.

Longarm unstrapped one of his saddlebag flaps and poked around until he came up with a small brass spyglass. He extended the segments of the battered telescope, spat on and polished the scratched lenses, and, squinting one eye, peered through it at the scene. The brougham was displaying a flag. As Longarm watched, a breeze fluttered the square of cloth. It was the flag of Texas: on the left, a broad, vertical band of blue with a single white star in its center, on the right, two horizontal bars—white above, red below.

Longarm shifted the spyglass's narrow field of vision to the men around the brougham. There were three of them. One was obviously the buggy's driver, while the other two were escorts. They were mean, hard-looking men who appeared as if they needed both baths and shaves. The only things they didn't seem to need were more guns. They all wore two pistols holstered butt-forward in crisscross gun belts, and Winchesters were tucked into the saddle boots of the two mounts. One of the men had some sort of badge glittering on his chest. No matter. Longarm had run into men like these before, and knew that they were lax about everything but fighting. They were Texas Rangers.

Longarm kneed his gelding into a slow walk toward the bunkhouse and stables. The Rangers glanced his way, but Longarm knew that at this distance they could only assume he was one of the hands coming in early. At the stable he turned his mount over to the wrangler on duty, informing the kid that the horse would be needed later in the afternoon. Winchester in hand, Longarm walked around the back of the stables, by the corrals, to avoid any chance of being spotted by the Rangers. He had a good idea who the visitor to the Starbuck spread was. If he was right, there was no problem, although he would still want to keep from revealing himself to the Ranger escorts.

His plan was to rest up on one of the empty beds in the bunkhouse. There'd be cool, fresh water there, for washing as well as drinking. Longarm intended to ride into town for the evening and make a tour of the saloons. It had been his experience that the best thing a lawman undercover could do was to go trawling for information, and there were no more fertile fishing holes than the saloon row of a cow town in the middle of roundup fever.

He was about to enter the bunkhouse when he caught movement out of the corner of his eye. Some distance away he spotted Ki, partially hidden within the shadows of a grove of leafy hardwoods. Ki spotted him at the same time, and waved. Longarm strolled over.

"You're practicing archery, I see," Longarm said by way of greeting. "Funny-looking bow, though. It's crooked, ain't it?"

"Hello, Longarm," Ki said. "This is a Japanese bow."

Ki was shirtless, his torso filmed with sweat from the heat of the day. Longarm considered him very unusually built for a man who had been powerful enough to toss about the much larger Higgins during their fight. Ki's muscles were long and slender. His biceps bulged very little when he strung his bow. But lean of build as Ki was, and without an ounce of excess fat on him, the rippling pattern of his belly muscles and the cords of his shoulders showed clearly.

Longarm had to smile. If he were a betting man, he'd still have put his money on Higgins during that fight, and sure as hell, he'd have lost his cash. It was a simple fact that Ki looked skinny by Caucasian standards, which preached that there was no such thing as strength without bulk.

"Do you not wish to meet our esteemed governor?" Ki asked. He selected an arrow from the leather quiver by his feet, and fitted the notch to the string.

"Thought it was him. I spotted his flag on his buggy. Who else would rate three Texas Rangers as babysitters?" Longarm glanced overhead. The sunlight was filtering through the thick foliage of the grove. He tugged out his pocket watch. Eleven-thirty. Close enough. He took a cheroot from the breast pocket of his coat and lit up. "The governor come all the way from Austin to see Jessica?"

"More or less," Ki said. "He came by rail to address tonight's Cattlemen's Association meeting in Sarah. The meeting will be held late, after the day's work is done. A tally boss will be voted on. The various outfits are ready to combine their herds."

"Seems a mite unusual for a state governor to take an interest in something like picking a tally boss," Longarm remarked.

"There is more to it, of course. Alex Starbuck lent the cattlemen a great deal of money. He cared for their well-being in other ways, as well. Jessica is not the only individual in these parts who feels as if a father has been lost."

"So the governor is here to reassure them that all's well?"

"No." Ki seemed amused. He flipped his long hair out of his eyes and rested his bow, along with its notched arrow, against his hip. "If the governor did try to reassure them, who would believe? He has not brought the army, his only source of power, knowing full well that Texans would not be happy if he had done so. No, my friend. The governor is here to convince Jessica Starbuck that she must reassure her neighbors. As heir to her father's holdings, it is she who can extend the notes on the land, defer payments on the loans for cattle, and pledge the Circle Star hands to keeping the peace and protecting the big main herd."

"Will she do it?" Longarm asked. "Whatever it is the governor wants?"

"Of course!" Ki threw back his head and laughed heartily. "She will do so much more than he wants. The governor will be very surprised. He expects to comfort a trembling, frightened, frail female, to offer her a masculine shoulder on which she can cry. You see, he does not really know Jessica. The governor thinks that all that he had once owed to Alex Starbuck has been canceled out by the man's death. He is about to find out that Jessica controls the payment schedules to those debts of honor, as well." He swung his bow up into position.

Longarm looked the way Ki's arrow was pointing. One hundred yards away, a two-by-four post stood vertically planted in the bright sunshine. "You forgot to mount your target," he said. "And I still say that bow is lopsided." It was about five feet long, with several asymmetrical bends and curves in it. Ki gripped the bow a third of the way up from the bottom.

"All Japanese bows are shaped in this manner," Ki explained. "Although some are considerably longer." He pulled the notched arrow back to a point well behind his ear.

Longarm nodded silently, in respect. The strength it took to keep the bow flexed to that degree was clearly enormous, but Ki's arm and hand were rock-steady. "You still forgot to mount your target on that there post," he reminded the archer.

"That post *is* the target," Ki murmured absently. He turned his head as if he were shunning the distant two-by-four. He released the string, the twang of the hemp cord turning the bow a full one hundred and eighty degrees around in Ki's left hand. The bow was now pointing at the archer.

The method and style of Ki's shooting was so different from that of Indians, that Longarm forgot to watch the arrow's flight. When he thought to look, he saw that its head was firmly embedded in the two-by-four.

"How the hell did you manage to hit that itty-bitty stick without looking?" Longarm demanded.

"The arrow hit the target. All I did was prevent myself from getting in its way." Ki's soft voice was slightly slurred, and his dark brown, almond-shaped eyes were halfclosed. He resembled a man more than two sheets to the wind on fine whiskey, but there was nothing drunken about the way he selected another arrow from the quiver. "With the proper mind, or *zanshin*, Longarm, there is literally 'no way' I can miss even the smallest target. It is, as Westerners say, 'as easy as hitting the broad side of a barn.' "

"What kind of arrow is that you've got?" Longarm peered at the projectile's head. Instead of a point, or series of barbs, the arrowhead was a crescent-shaped wafer of steel. "May I look at it?"

Ki handed it over, warning, "Do not touch the edge. It is razor sharp. In my homeland, this sort of arrow is called the 'cleaver.' "

"What's it for?"

"For severing ropes or, say, the harness binding together a team of horses. In my own land, such an arrow was often used to cut down the enemy's battle flag, and in that way demoralize his forces." He took back his arrow, and notched it. In one smooth motion he raised his bow, drew the string back far past his ear, looked away from the target, and let the arrow fly. Without even watching it, he turned back to his quiver to select a third arrow.

Longarm, meanwhile, watched the 'cleaver' bury itself an inch or so beneath the first arrow. "Lord, the way you bend that bow, I'd think it would snap."

"A Japanese bow does not snap," Ki explained patiently. "Look." He turned the bow sideways, to show Longarm a light-colored sort of wood sandwiched between two layers of another kind. The layers were glued together, and wound at several points with a red-colored, silken thread. "This bow's core is held between two pieces of a wood called bamboo. The bamboo has been tempered by a special fire treatment. Its flexibility, lightness, and strength are unsurpassed by any bow devised by Americans."

It took Longarm a moment to figure out what Ki had meant by that last remark. "You mean by Indians, right?"

"I am an outsider," Ki shrugged. "Are not all people born here Americans?"

"It depends on who you ask, and how you look at it," Longarm said ruefully. "Someday maybe all folks will be considered just plain Americans. At least we can hope."

"You *should* hope," Ki said adamantly. "To remain strong, a nation must not divide itself. It is a bad thing to be an outsider in one's own nation." The arrow he was about to fire had a head as twisted as a corkscrew. "This is called the 'chewer.' It is designed to be fired into the midsection of the enemy so that it can rend and chew his bowels."

"Nice," Longarm said with a grimace. He watched as the arrow went whizzing on its way to join its brothers. "Seeing as you don't need to spend much time on aiming, do you mind if I ask you a couple of personal questions?"

Ki's eyes crinkled with amusement. "Actually, I have spent long years in aiming, without ever firing an arrow, but as to your questions, you may certainly ask."

"But you may not answer, that it?" Longarm finished for him. Ki did not answer, but only shrugged as he bent to his quiver. "Well, we'll cross that bridge when and if we come to it," Longarm decided. He flicked an inch of gray ash off the glowing tip of his cheroot. "I'm interested in why you're not up at the house with Jessie and the governor. Don't you care about what's being discussed? It could concern the future of this spread."

Ki sighed. "You know so little of me, Longarm. Be careful. In my homeland, ignorance is no excuse for compromising another man's honor."

"I'm just curious as to where you fit in. Are you Jessie's partner?"

Ki smiled at Longarm like a man looking at his dinner. "I *help* Jessie. I help her *accomplish* things."

"Ki, you're a man with a shitload of surprises up your sleeve. You've got all kinds of unusual weapons." Longarm dropped the stub of his cheroot to the dirt. Before he could grind it out with his boot, Ki did it for him, with the sole of his bare foot.

"Alex Starbuck was killed with an unusual weapon, was he not?" Ki asked.

"He was. That makes you a suspect, Ki." Longarm waited for the other man's response.

"In my homeland—" Ki began.

"We ain't in your homeland."

"In my homeland," Ki raised his voice to override Longarm's interruption, "a man who even *accidentally* brushes against another's blade must be prepared to pay for this dishonor with his life. But you do not even realize the dishonor you have done me."

"I'm still waiting for your answer, Ki." Longarm swept his coat from the butt of his Colt as Ki let his bow slide to the ground and shifted his weight onto the balls of his feet.

"Withdraw the question, Longarm, or I will kill you," Ki said matter-of-factly.

"Reckon we're at that bridge I mentioned a minute ago," Longarm said sadly.

"It is a very narrow and delicate bridge you bid us to travel," Ki whispered. "The bridge will only allow one of us to survive this journey."

Longarm watched Ki carefully. He'd seen this before, in Mexicans and Indians. They didn't bluster and fume the way a white man did when something got his dander up. They just got quieter and quieter. Maybe they would even smile. But finally there would come a moment—faster than the eye could see, faster than thought—and woe be unto the one who'd insulted or riled them . . .

Longarm decided it was time to defuse this situation, before things got past the point of no return. He brought his hands up to chest level, palms forward. "Easy, my friend," he said. "You don't have to answer my question. You already did. No guilty man who was smart would show that he was so upset at being accused. You got to realize it's my simple duty to pry into the business of anyone involved in any way with a crime."

For one measured moment, Ki stood silent, his eyes as if he were listening to distant sounds too faint for Longarm's ears. Then he smiled and relaxed. "We are not in my homeland. Your authority is the relevant point of this . . . discussion we are having. You are still my friend, Longarm."

"Glad to hear it," Longarm chuckled.

"I am not at the house because I am not concerned with wealth. I care only about Jessie's well-being."

"That I do believe, old son," Longarm interjected quietly.

"You must also realize that the agenda the governor has planned for today is, well, *known* to us. Jessica has been well trained in many aspects of business, but especially in the art of negotiating, an art the Japanese take very seriously.

"The governor will suggest that she give him power of attorney, that he sell off parts of her holdings. He will suggest that it is all too much for a young woman to comprehend. 'Don't you want to enjoy life?' he will ask. Jessica, meanwhile, will ponder what she has been taught, and do her best not to insult the governor by showing her boredom. They will dine together this evening, and then the governor will offer his protection as an escort to tonight's meeting. She will accept, of course, out of politeness, but she will have her horse towed along by one of the Rangers, so that she will be able to ride back with us."

"With *us?*" Longarm asked innocently. He tried hard to keep his amusement hidden.

Ki smiled to show that he understood the joke they were acting out. "Of course, *us!* Sarah has filled up with drifters and strangers working for the roundup. I know quite well that you must have planned to circulate around the town to see what you can learn. I intend to do the same."

"The governor isn't staying here?"

"Jessica could not bear that," Ki laughed. "He will stay at the hotel."

"That place didn't seem fancy enough to me to be fit for a governor," Longarm kidded.

"Oh, he will have a much nicer room than the one they gave you," Ki remarked innocently.

"How would you know? They let in folks *barefoot* in that place?"

Ki, his dark eyes sparkling, held up another arrow. "This is called 'death's song.' The bulb you see fitted just behind the head has a hole that catches the wind and, in that way, sings the last song the enemy will ever hear. Would you like to hear it?" he asked politely.

"Just a couple of opening stanzas," Longarm warned.

"Of course." Now Ki was grinning like a wolf. "In any event I advise you not to miss the Cattleman's meeting. It will be a treat to see Jessie . . ." His voice faded as he notched the arrow and let it fly.

Instantly the air around them was filled with a high, sharp keening sound. To Longarm it sounded like a combination of the world's biggest mosquito—one with murder on its mind— and a violin's strings being tortured to their breaking point. The arrow's pitch would have made a dog howl. The nightmare sound ended with an abrupt *thud!* as the 'death's song' found its target post.

Throughout the arrow's flight, Ki had stood as if mesmerized. "Once I heard that sound multiplied by several hundred. I was just a young boy, not yet in my teens. The army of archers were all accomplished masters of *yugamae*." In answer to Longarm's look of puzzlement, he added, "*Yugamae* is the term used to describe the correct etiquette with which to approach *kyu-jutsu*, the technique of bow and arrow. The battle taking place was one between rival warlords. The force for which the archers fought was badly outnumbered, so their warlord decided on the strategy of intimidation. He ordered his archers to being the technique of *inagashi*, the style of archery in which the bowman sustains a rapid rate of fire—fifteen arrows per man, let us say, accurately shot as fast as you could fire fifteen accurate rounds from your Winchester. As intimidation was the object of the attack, the 'death's song' was fired exclusively, with the exception of one 'cleaver' arrow, fired by the chief archer, to cut down the enemy's flag. Think of it, Longarm! The sky darkened by the hailstorm of so many arrows. The world was filled with the sound of 'death's song!' Now the warlord was careful to instruct his men not to hit any of the enemy, for if intimidation brings about anger in the adversary, it has failed in its purpose. No, all of the arrows landed in the same area to prove that the archers had the ability to control their weapons, but none of the arrows drew blood." Ki stared into Longarm's face to make sure he was understood. "They did not have to draw blood. At this warning chorus of 'death's song,' the enemy soldiers and warriors threw down their arms and clapped their hands over their ears in terror. Their warlord had no choice but to surrender to his opponent. His men had been intimidated. The battle was over, with not one drop of blood spilt, except for the vanquished warlord, of course, who committed *seppuku*. That is suicide, Longarm. It was the only way he could expunge his shame at being defeated."

"That's quite a story," Longarm said after a few moments.

They both stood silent for a while, until the vivid images the story had raised began to fade.

"Ki? Why did you come to America?" Longarm finally asked. "Did Starbuck send for you, the way he sent for Myobu?"

Ki looked at him sharply. "I was not sent for, but came here to seek my future. I stowed away on a clipper bound for San Francisco. Later I learned that the ship belonged to Alex Starbuck. It seemed to me to be an omen—I was to seek out and offer my services to the man upon whose ship I found transport. There were other reasons, of course. I felt that my *karma* was linked to those Americans who plucked their nourishment from my homeland. More about that I will not say . . . After some time in San Francisco, I found my way to Mr. Starbuck's offices. I was fifteen years old."

"And you actually got to see him?" Longarm asked, amazed. "You were just a boy, and you got past all of his clerks and assistants?"

"I had grown up in a house where English was spoken, so I had the language, though that would not have mattered, since Mr. Starbuck spoke fluent Japanese." Ki smiled faintly. "As for getting past his security provisions, I considered that to be my employment test. In any event, I offered him my services, and he accepted."

"What do you mean by 'services,' Ki?"

He shook his head. "Here the stream that is my story flows into the Starbuck River. I cannot tell the rest without Jessica's permission."

Longarm nodded. He did not want to strain their fragile friendship by revealing that Jessie had already told him her story. "You haven't mentioned why you decided to leave the Japans in the first place. You sound to me like a very homesick man."

Ki bowed. He placed his palms on his thighs and bent from the waist. It was a gesture of politeness, but not one of obsequiousness. During the entire maneuver he held Longarm's eyes with his own. "I mean you no disrespect, Longarm, but there are things I cannot discuss."

"Was it your father or mother who was Caucasian?"

"Forgive my silence, Longarm."

"I understand." Longarm looked away from the pain he saw in Ki's eyes. "Good enough." He picked up his Winchester and headed back toward the bunkhouse. "See you in town."

As Longarm walked away, Ki chose another arrow from his quiver and blindly notched it. He brought up the bow, pulled back the string, and fired. His eyes, blurred by tears, could not see the target, but his ears told him that he had hit it. His raging heart had not ruined his aim.

Ki nodded to himself in grim satisfaction. That was honorable if not excellent.

Chapter 10

Longarm approached Canvas Town on foot. It was like approaching the seashore at night. The roar, like the thunder of the surf, grew louder as he drew closer. If Sarah's high white church steeple and her schools embodied the spiritual and moral fortitude of Sarah Starbuck, the section beyond Main Street, the section called Canvas Town, embodied her fiery red hair, bedroom eyes, and hot, sensual femaleness. The proper side of Sarah immortalized a fine woman, but Canvas Town was that woman by night, sparked by her man's embrace.

In Canvas Town there were no street lamps—no streets, for that matter. Longarm went from the glare of the brightly lit tent entrances to the pitch-black, grassy fields in between. Ambling about, he listened to the squeak and groan as the tents swayed against their ropes in the night breeze. There rose everywhere the sound of tinny piano music and the hearty laughter of men who were tired, but not so tired that they might give up their fun. Voices would swell out of the darkness only to fade as shadowy forms blundered past, drunk, night-blind, or a little of both.

The hissing kerosene lanterns by each tent entrance were surrounded by fluttering moths, and farther out, by the rail-road tracks, other tents with faintly glimmering red lanterns attracted a different sort of moth to flutter and beat its wings before burning up in a flame far, far too hot. How could this honkytonk, carnival atmosphere, this wild abandon just a street away from the gas lamps and whitewashed picket fences, not remind Longarm of the two sides of every woman's personality?

The sharp tang of cheap whiskey, and the smoky grease-smell of even cheaper food both attracted their share of cowboys. In one relatively well-lit area, gunsmiths, saddlemakers, clothiers, and cobblers peddled their wares from small booths or the tailgates of wagons. Competing for the cowboys' hard-earned dollars were the stalls that offered games of chance. These lured their marks with a pretty girl standing by the entranceway. Only the greenest lad could think that he had any more chance of winning the woman outside than he did of winning the game inside, but still the hands streamed in, not caring whether they won or lost, only looking for a good time.

By morning's light, Canvas Town would look sordid and dreary, Longarm knew. But that was tomorrow. Tonight the shadows and kerosene glow only softened and beautified, and the whiskey did not punish but instead rewarded the drinker with sharp wit and boundless energy. Come morning, both Canvas Town and cowboy could lick their wounds and swear never again—until nightfall.

It would all last as long as the roundup lasted. Sarah had no need for tent hotels and soft-roofed saloons once the free-lance hands had drifted from the area. The tents owned by the town would be taken down and folded up for another season. The peddlers would hitch their swaybacked teams to their gaudy wagons and slowly head for other parts, other gatherings of men with time and money on their hands.

Longarm entered a saloon tent and bellied up to the bar—which happened to be a couple of planks laid lengthwise on a trio of high sawhorses. There was no floor to the tent, and consequently no floor to the saloon, except for well-trampled grass, but there were tables and chairs, lit by candles stuck into empty whiskey bottles, or by small, hissing lanterns. Behind the bar were beer kegs and a motley assortment of half-filled bottles.

"What's yours?" the bartender asked in a weary, punch-drunk voice. He had a day's worth of beard on his cheeks, purple shadows beneath his eyes, a cigar clamped between his yellowed teeth, and, incongruously, a shiny, brand-new derby, about one size too small, perched like a bird directly on top of his bald head.

Longarm gave the bottles a quick perusal. Sure, he could order Maryland rye, and the label would probably even assert that it *was* Maryland rye, but what would he get? "I'll take a beer," he told the barkeep, who filled a mug with the draft, and then gave Longarm his change from a leather purse strung about his ample middle.

As the bartender performed his services, Longarm noticed him scanning the tent with ever-watchful eyes. The place was crowded and rowdy. The bartender carried no gun, but when he turned around, Longarm saw the braided leather handle and wrist loop of a blackjack sticking out of the back pocket of his pants. Behind the bar, in a corner, a fellow with a double-barreled scattergun sat and watched the crowd from a high-chair contraption.

Longarm took his mug to a nearby vacant table. Toward the rear of the tent, two liquored-up hands began to fight over which way a deck was stacked. The bartender pointed to the two men and hollered, "Quiet down, there!"

The hands ignored him, of course. Longarm lit up a cheroot, sipped at his beer, and leaned back in his chair to watch the show.

The fellow in the high chair climbed down, scattergun in hand. He wasn't very tall, but he was well built, with thick forearms and large, capable-looking hands. He was wearing a sleeveless undershirt, and a derby that seemed the identical match for the bartender's. Maybe they were brothers.

The scattergun was more than likely a means of intimidating the patrons rather than blowing their fool heads off. Usually such fearsome-looking weapons were loaded with birdshot. A rowdy cowboy might end up enduring the taunts of his friends as he searched out a doc to pick the pellets out of his backside, but he'd heal up pretty soon. It would not do for any saloon, permanent or canvas-roofed, to earn itself a reputation as the sort of place where a patron could be killed by the help. As the man passed Longarm's table, he saw that in addition to the scattergun, the fellow wore a .44 derringer in a tiny stitch of a holster, high up just behind his right hip. In the unlikely event that killing should be required, the tiny handgun's range was adequate in the close confines of the tent.

Both cowboys quieted down as the bouncer approached their table. Longarm could not hear what passed between the bouncer and the rowdy pair, but he did see one of the cowboys make a grab for the scattergun, a stupid move in any case, but especially stupid against such a handy opponent. The fellow with the derby stepped nimbly back, swinging the barrel of his shotgun as he did so, to crack the steel against the other's outstretched fingers. The cowboy howled and let his injured paw hang limply at his side. His buddy scrabbled for the revolver crammed into the waist-band of his jeans—the fellow was plainly no gunslick—and was rewarded for his clumsy efforts by having the twin barrels of the scattergun shoved hard into his belly. The cowboy doubled over, his revolver falling out of his pants to thud against the grass as he did so, and the fellow with the derby spun him around and booted him right through the doorway of the tent.

Throughout the short-pitched battle, the bouncer had kept on his face the relaxed but alert look of a seasoned veteran. That expression signaled to Longarm that the fellow knew that nine out of ten bar brawls ended in low comedy, like this one had, but every once in a while there was one that could suddenly burst out of control, like a forest fire in woods gone too long without rain.

The cowboy with the swollen hand scurried after his drinking partner. The derby-wearing winner of the fight tossed the fallen revolver after the two, then sauntered back to his lookout post behind the bar. The din of conversation and clinking of bottle against glass went on as it had before and during the confrontation. As far as Longarm could tell, he was the only man who had even bothered to look in the direction of the commotion.

Longarm sent blue wreaths of smoke toward the pitched cloth ceiling. Canvas Town was an interesting place to while away the hours, but its pace and commotion were such that no information or gossip could be gleaned. For his purposes, Longarm needed a quiet saloon where the barkeep had time on his hands and was grateful for company, paying or otherwise. The bartenders in Canvas Town were just passing through, like the cowboys themselves. The place was too fleeting a phenomenon for anybody to learn much about anybody else.

Longarm would have spent his time at the Union Saloon, the largest of the permanent watering holes in Sarah, except that Ki had warned him off, saying that the place was stodgy and stiff, that nothing ever happened there because it was on the regular patrol of Town Marshal Farley and his deputies. Longarm decided to head over that way anyhow, since he'd tied his horse up in front of the Union. Besides, there he could get himself a drink of bona fide Maryland rye.

Longarm was finishing off his beer when he felt a heavy hand clamp down on his shoulder. He twisted around in his chair to see that he was bracketed by two men.

"Howdy there, gunslick. 'Member us?" one of them said.

It took Longarm a second to place them. The one who had spoken had a wispy, billy-goat beard. "Sure. You're the fellow named Ray. Both of you were Higgins's boys. You still with him, now that he's out as the Starbucks' foreman?"

"Now we're with *you*, gunslick." Ray grinned, showing broken teeth. "Or should I call you by your name? Longarm. Musty, get us some chairs. Us and Mr. Longarm is gonna have a drink."

While Musty did as he was told, Longarm checked the two cowboys out. They were still each just a pair of gleaming Justin boots, an expensive Stetson, and a long, dusty road in between. They smelled of horseshit, and their guns jutted out from their right hips like the hammers in a work-man's belt.

They sat down, one on either side of Longarm, so that they were positioned more like three men abreast than facing each other. Longarm thought about the danger of the situation, but he figured he was safe from being shot here in the saloon with the bouncer watching over everything from his high vantage point. The one named Musty, a youngish, curly-haired man with pale gray, squinty eyes and sun-reddened cheeks, pulled out a plug of tobacco and bit off a chaw. He set the plug down on the table.

"How'd you boys find out my name?" Longarm asked, not

that he really expected them to answer, but you could never tell with horse turds like these two. "Pretty slick of you, anyway, I'll give you that." He poked Ray in the ribs, pleased at the angry glare the poke provoked.

"Never you mind, lawman," Musty mumbled around his mouthful of chewing tobacco.

"Who said I'm a lawman?" Longarm asked, casting his bait.

"Not just a lawman, but a federal marshal," Musty replied.

"Fetch us both a drink, Musty," Ray growled disgustedly. "Longarm here don't need one. He's still got an inch of warm beer left in his glass."

"You two are real sports," Longarm grimaced.

"We can't be buying you drinks." Musty indignantly spat a long, brown stream of tobacco juice on the trampled grass. "We lost our jobs on account of you snooping around—"

"The drinks," Ray barked.

So they not only know my name, Longarm thought, they know why I'm here. That eliminated the possibility that his being recognized was just a bit of bad luck brought on by his being spied by some jailbird he'd arrested in the past. That sort of thing happened all the time to undercover men. You took the time to build a painstakingly exact cover, and then, from out of the blue, some joker who saw you strolling down the street pointed his finger and sang out, 'He's a lawman!' to anyone who had reason to be interested in such news.

But an ex-convict, or any outlaw, would have no way of knowing *why* Longarm was in Sarah. Town Marshal Farley might have spilled the beans, but it also could have been either Jessica or Ki. Right now, Longarm had his money on Farley. But why would any of the three who knew his business talk about it to men like these?

Musty returned with two shots of whiskey and two mugs of beer. The men tossed off their drinks and then chased the rough liquor with cooling swallows of brew.

Longarm watched, pleased. They were trying to drink their courage, of course, but more alcohol would also loosen their lips. "Buy you gents another round?" Longarm began to rise, but he stopped as Ray, on his left, snaked his right hand beneath the armrests of their side-by-side spindle chairs. Longarm looked down at the six-inch blade Ray was holding against his vest, just about where his heart would be.

"You just sit back down, Longarm, 'less you want me to pop your pump," Ray said jovially. "It wouldn't be no trouble at all on my part."

Longarm realized that Ray's knife was out of sight of anyone else in the saloon. Amid all the noise and confusion, Longarm could be stabbed dead and left for a drunk sleeping it off in his chair, and no one would be the wiser.

"You gonna sit, or you gonna bleed?" Ray softly insisted.

"Bar's a little crowded anyway," Longarm said, and sat back down.

Musty reached over and plucked Longarm's Colt out of its holster. He was about to slip it into his own waistband when Ray ordered, "Give it here, boy."

Musty did as he was told, scowling all the while. Ray held the double-action weapon up to the lantern light. "Fine gun, Longarm. I promise to think of you every time I plink away at a coyote with this here Colt."

"Hey, you!" came a shout from behind the bar. It was the bouncer, the man with the scattergun, high up on his tower-chair, addressing himself to Ray. "You want to stay in here, put that piece away."

Ray tucked Longarm's Colt into his gunbelt. "Musty, take his wallet, see if he has any papers that could help—No! Wait a minute, that bastard with the shotgun is still watching us," he grumbled. "Longarm, real pleasant-like, you take out your billfold and lay it down on the table."

"I'd be careful with the likes of him, Ray," Musty warned. "He could have another gun stashed in his coat."

"Hmm, do you, Longarm?" Ray coaxed. "Iffen you do, think on this. I'm no gunslick like you, but I've spent a lot of time around campfires with nothing better to do than practice with my knife. There's no gun on earth that can be drawed and fired before I'm able to push these here six inches of steel between your ribs."

"Except one gun, maybe," Longarm suggested as he slowly removed his wallet and placed it on the table. "The kind of gun that shoots .25s?"

"But you ain't likely to have one beneath your coat," Musty guffawed.

"Shut up about them guns," Ray snapped at his partner. "Give me the money in the wallet."

"There's no papers in here but travel tickets and the like," Musty said. "Hot damn, here's his shiny badge."

"Hold on to it, and the wallet," Ray said. "That way they'll find a corpse with no identification. We'll all be long gone by the time they figure out that a lawman's been killed, and not just some drunk got himself involved in a knife fight."

"Let's get it over with, Ray," Musty whined.

"I guess I'm a dead man, eh, boys?" Longarm made his voice rise high and trembling, the way Henry, the clerk in Marshal Vail's office, sounded when Billy began roaring and fuming over some misplaced report.

"Keep your voice down," Ray hissed, anxiously eyeing the bouncer surveying the scene.

"Lord, I hate the idea of it being a knife." Longarm reached into his pants pocket, the action bringing Ray's glinting blade close by, just like a cat will pounce at the first sign of movement around a mouse hole. "Easy now," Longarm soothed. "Here, see?" He held up a double eagle. "I just thought Musty could fetch us all another round. I know I sure could use a shot. What do you say, boys?"

Musty snatched up the money, as Longarm had known he would. The nineteen dollars and change would carry an out-of-work cowboy quite a ways. Poor Musty! He wasn't even smart enough to figure out that Ray would never let him keep a cent. Not that Ray was going to profit for very long from this little exchange. "I suppose you boys know more than you're telling concerning the murder of Alex Starbuck?"

"Plenty more," Ray boasted. His knife hand rested on the seat of Longarm's chair, although the blade was still tickling Longarm's ribs.

"What you know doesn't seem to be paying you very well," Longarm observed.

"The ransom hasn't been collected yet," Ray shrugged. "When it is, we'll get our share. Higgins said so."

"You boys believe *that?*" Longarm mocked.

"Shut up! We'll do all right. We already got your money,

lawman. And after tonight's Cattlemen's meeting, the whole town will pay off. Too bad you won't be around by then," he laughed, as Musty returned with three shots of whiskey.

"Reckon that meeting will be starting in just an hour or so," Longarm mused. "Well, let's drink up, boys."

"And then get the other part done with," Musty added meaningfully as he tilted his head toward Longarm and shifted his mouthful of tobacco to one cheek to give the rotgut an unobstructed chute down his gullet.

Longarm felt Ray's knife blade momentarily lessen its pressure against his ribs as the man lifted his glass and knocked back his drink. Slamming his own left hand down upon Ray's right, so as to pin the knife in place, Longarm shouted at the top of his lungs, "Don't stab me, boys! Please!"

"Christ, Ray!" Musty gasped. "Get it done!"

"I'm trying, dammit!" Ray's face contorted with effort.

"Help!" Longarm shouted, doing his best not to break out laughing. He pressed down with all his strength as Ray's sweat-slippery fist slipped another fraction of an inch closer. Now the man redoubled his efforts to stab Longarm, but he just couldn't make that last crucial inch.

"Here now! What's going on?" It was Mr. Derby, with his scattergun. He'd climbed down from his chair and was coming over to see what was the matter. Just as Longarm knew he would.

"Ah, shit," Ray moaned. "Can't stab him with this bird watching."

"He's going to throw you two out," Longarm chortled. "Just as well, I've gotten to like you two jokers. It'd be a shame for me to have to kill you both."

"All right, you two," the bouncer growled, his scattergun hovering ominously. "This here gent was sitting peaceably enough, and then you two come in and start a ruckus. Out of here, now!"

Ray and Musty exchanged anguished looks. "Please—" Ray began.

"I said now!"

Haltingly, both men rose. "Aren't you coming with us, old pal?" Ray coaxed Longarm. The knife had somehow disappeared from sight.

"No," Longarm drawled. "I think I'm staying right here. This is a fine establishment that knows how to look out for its patrons." He beamed at the bouncer, who smiled back.

"Come on now, Longarm." Musty tried to laugh. "Come with us!"

Longarm looked at the bouncer. "Weren't you throwing these two out?" he asked innocently.

"That I was." He tilted his derby forward and cocked both barrels of his scattergun. "Now git! Both of you."

Like two boys being sent to the woodshed, Ray and Musty began to trudge away. The bouncer turned and began to head back to his chair. Musty took the opportunity to spin around and spit a glob of chewing tobacco squarely against the back of the bouncer's neck.

The fellow almost lost his derby as he clamped his hand against the thick sludge. He turned, his face at first pale with anger, but his expression soon changed to aghast horror as the shit-brown, sticky mass began to run down beneath his undershirt. His fingers came away with gruesome webs of the stuff stringing down. "Who?" he managed to say, his voice shaking with fury. "Who did it?"

Without a word, Musty pointed to the plug of chewing tobacco still on the table where Longarm sat, and then at Longarm himself.

"All right, you son of a bitch! You go with your friends!"

Longarm was about to argue, but when the bouncer shoved the scattergun into his belly, he decided that now was not the time to claim he only smoked cheroots.

As he stood up, Ray put his arm around Longarm's shoulders. "Let's go, old pal!" he said triumphantly.

"I would have missed you fellows, anyhow," Longarm sighed. As they walked toward the tent saloon's flap doorway, Longarm realized that the knife had materialized once more in Ray's right hand, and that its blade was once again against his ribs. As before, no one could see what was happening, not the way Ray had his left arm around Longarm's shoulders, and his knife hand buried beneath the tails of Longarm's frock coat.

"Once we're outside," Ray whispered into Longarm's ear, "once we're in the dark, I'm going to cut your heart out!"

As the bouncer returned to his chair, Musty took up a position on Longarm's left, but when they reached the flap doorway, he had to fall back behind the other two.

Longarm made his move. He brought his left hand around to grab hold of Ray's knife, but not before he felt the icy bite of the blade slice through his vest and shirt to pierce the skin across his ribs. Ignorning the pain, he brought his right fist up in a short, stiff uppercut. The force of the blow drove Ray back, although the cowboy still kept hold of his knife. Longarm's hand snaked out to pluck his double-action Colt from where it was dangling in Ray's belt, but before he could get a shooting grip on the gun, Ray pressed his attack. His knife came around in a deadly windmill motion to slash down toward the point where Longarm's neck joined his shoulder.

Longarm threw himself backward to the ground, managing to send two shots Ray's way before he even hit the grass. Out of the corner of his eye, Longarm saw Musty draw his Peacemaker. There was nothing he could do about it in time. Longarm prepared to take at least one of the young cowboy's bullets—

There was a loud boom, and Musty screamed. His gun fell as he dropped to his knees, his shirt in tatters, his back peppered with birdshot. The bouncer, from his high vantage point, had sent his swarm of pellets over the heads of those in the crowded tent.

Longarm looked back at Ray. The man's knife lay in the grass, forgotten, as Ray concentrated on the two holes the .44 slugs had punched into his chest. He rocked on his legs like a seasick landlubber experiencing his first sea storm, and then fell forward, his head coming to rest between Longarm's boots.

The bouncer was making his way toward the scene, trying to get through the gaping crowd, as Musty—still on his knees—picked up his Peacemaker and pointed it at where Longarm lay sprawled.

"Don't do it, boy," Longarm warned him, but Musty wasn't listening. Longarm brought his own gun around.

"Gonna kill you!" Musty babbled. He clicked back his revolver's hammer.

Longarm fired first. He aimed high and to the left, to put his round into Musty's right shoulder. The bullet's impact knocked Musty backward, off his knees. Longarm rode the .44's recoil up, then brought the gun back down into position as Musty wailed in agony, his pellet-peppered spine scraping against the rough turf. Still he held on to his cocked Peacemaker.

"Please!" Longarm begged. "Drop that damned gun!"

Musty slowly brought up his revolver. He was holding the Peacemaker in both hands now, to steady his wavering aim. "Gonna kill you—"

Longarm fired again, an instant before Musty squeezed off that one damn shot he'd been working on. Longarm's shot went true, thudding into Musty's heart. As the young cowboy died, his own bullet ploughed a furrow through the grass just a foot in front of him.

"Throw it down!" the bouncer demanded. He'd exchanged his scattergun for his derringer. Longarm guessed that was his way of saying he was serious.

Longarm set his Colt down on the grass. His side was slick with blood and stung like the devil, but he didn't think it was a deep wound. Christ, he hated a knife! "I'm a federal marshal." He told the bouncer, thinking that his cover was blown to shreds anyway. His wound hurt, and the Cattlemen's meeting was due to begin and Longarm wanted to be there to see or hear whatever Ray had expected to happen.

"If you're a lawman, where's your badge?" the bouncer asked craftily.

"My badge is in my wallet," Longarm sighed; he'd been through this routine before. He gestured toward Musty. "That one lifted it." He'd underestimated these two cowboys, it seemed, and it had almost cost him his life. Longarm dabbed gingerly at his side with his pocket handkerchief.

"How come you spit at me if you're a lawman?"

Longarm pointed at Musty, his bloodied handkerchief balled in his hand. "*He's* your damned spitter, not me!"

"Then how do I know he isn't the marshal as well?" the bouncer roared triumphantly, to the general approval of the crowd. "Somebody go get Farley!" he shouted. "And you—"

"Long's the name."

"You, Long, you sit right there and wait for the *real* law."

Sighing to himself, Longarm got comfortable on the grass. It looked as though he wasn't going to get to stop off at the Union Saloon before the meeting, after all.

Chapter 11

Ki surveyed the action from his vantage point at the Union Saloon. He was standing shoulder to shoulder with others at one end of the fifty-foot, polished mahogany bar. He had one foot on the brass rail—a booted foot. As Longarm had remarked about the hotel, the Union was not the sort of place where they let you in barefoot.

Poor Longarm, Ki thought. He felt a little guilty about fibbing to the lawman, telling him that the Union Saloon was a dull place, and that the best area to snoop around was Canvas Town. The truth of the matter was, Ki wanted to stake out the Union himself, and didn't want Longarm around to attract attention. Well, at least Longarm would stay out of trouble in Canvas Town . . .

Several bartenders were being kept busy by the crowd in the saloon. They drew mugs of draft from built-in taps decorated with ornate metal spigots, or poured shots from the extensive display of bottles on the backbar beneath a wide, gleaming mirror.

Ki stared into the mirror. He was, of course, known in Sarah, and had been recognized by several people, but there were enough out-of-towners in for the roundup for Ki to blend in. Those who knew him tended not to say more than a few words to him anyway . . .

He was, after all, a 'chink' to those who were American,

just as he was a 'round-eyes' to the Japanese. He belonged to no race, no country—but then, he never really had.

Ki stared into that mirror behind the bar. He was wearing a blue-gray tweed suit, a sky-blue cotton shirt, and a black shoestring tie. His Stetson was steel blue. On his feet he wore black, ankle-high Wellington boots. The low cut of the boots gave his feet the freedom they needed . . .

All around him, reflected in the mirror, people went about enjoying themselves. Ki watched them, or their reflections in the glass, but he felt as much apart from them as he would have staring at aquatic creatures below a pond's flat, gleamingly clear surface. The saloon, the oldest and largest in Sarah, was a cavernous place brightly lit by gas lamps. Gaming tables, including a wheel of fortune, took up half of the room, with tables for drinking taking up the other half. Leading up to the second floor was a wide, red-carpeted staircase. If a man wished, one of the saloon's "hostesses" would escort him to one of the many rooms on the second floor, and there she would entertain him in private.

Ki turned around to lean against the bar. He hooked his fingers in his gunbelt. Wearing a firearm was a nuisance, but it was his experience that to blend in, a man had to look like everybody else. Not wearing a gun invariably attracted attention in these parts, so he wore one.

It was not that Ki was unfamiliar with firearms, or with any weapon. The study of weaponry, of killing, had been his life's work. His life had been decreed worthless on the day he was born. The only path of honor open to him had been the path that led to his becoming a warrior.

Ki sipped at his scotch, neat. Over the years he'd developed a taste for the spirits imported from Scotland in exchange for Texas beef. Once, scotch had been hard to come by, but now imported foods and distilled spirits from Europe were becoming commonplace in the larger cities and towns of America. He sipped at his whiskey, and remembered the past . . .

His mother had been high-born, a member of an aristocratic family in Japan. She was beautiful and full of life—the exquisite product of centuries of culture and high, fierce, Nipponese blood. When the Yankee barbarians forced their way into

Japan, his mother fell in love with one of the American adventurers who came to take his fortune from the island nation originally dubbed *Jibon* by the conquered Chinese. *Jibon*, literally meant "origin of the sun."

Against all warning, and totally realizing the horror she was causing her family, his mother took the Yankee barbarian as her husband. The family disowned her in disgrace, society shunned her in disgust and contempt. To Ki's mother, all this made no difference. So completely and totally did she love her husband that she willingly made plans to leave her homeland and journey with him to America. Ki—but that was not his name then—was born to them a year later. He was to be their only child.

For six years the child's father labored, and then, finally, his business in Nippon was done. The long years of loneliness for the mother and son were soon to turn into a future of great adventures. Both mother and son had learned English, for they had no company other than barbarian company; the Nipponese shunned them totally. The child was only able to attend school because of his father's mighty influence, but even then, Nipponese children would have nothing to do with him. It made no difference that he claimed his heritage, for he looked like a Yankee, a barbarian.

It did not matter, the child told himself countless times, every day. It did not matter. A new world waited, his father's world—surely, in the fantastic land called America, the land his father had lovingly told him about, surely in such a place a soul would not be judged merely by how he or she looked? Surely in America he would belong!

Only a month before they were due to set sail, the child's father took sick. The finest physicians were sent for, but they could do nothing. 'A disease of the blood,' they'd said, shaking their heads. A disease of the blood; the little boy who would grow up to become Ki had always thought that funny . . .

His father died in Nippon. His mother, heartbroken, did not know what to do to protect herself and her son. She was a simple woman, for all of her noble heritage. Her husband's holdings were looted by rival businessmen in Nippon, and in America she was totally dismissed by her husband's relatives as a bizarre anomaly in the man's past. Without his father's patronage and funds, the little boy was soon expelled from his school. Soon after that, his mother died of a broken heart.

Her funeral was attended by the curious only, for no one would consent to mourn her. "This is what comes of the barbarians," the curious laughed at her funeral. "This is what comes of foolish love . . .".

But the hecklers at his mother's funeral would not consent to mourn. The five-year-old hoped that his lone mourning would be enough to soothe his mother's *Kami*, her spirit . . .

Ki grinned to himself as he sipped at his whiskey. Never had he blamed his mother for falling in love. Never had he taken from his origins the moral others had taken: that love could be wrong, a foolish thing. Love could be impossible, love could be doomed never to blossom—Ki knew firsthand about such love—but this did not taint it with foolishness. A man's love was like a wild horse, like a powerful animal that had to be controlled, but could never really be broken or tamed. One could not let love interfere with one's duties, with one's vow of service. Love had to be kept in its place, but never was love foolish.

Of course, such high-flown thoughts belonged to him now, but in the days following his mother's death, the little boy that he was then had no thoughts except for thoughts of fear . . .

His mother's relatives had disowned her, and so they had disowned him. He did not exist for them. He went with the other urchins to sit outside the monastery gates, as was the custom for orphans. Most were, of course, turned away by the priests who taught spiritual matters and who conducted *ryu* in which the *bugei*, the martial arts, were taught.

Ki sat with the other orphans. He sat with them at gate after monastery gate, traveling with—but never befriended by—those who were successively turned away. When it came Ki's time for an interview, the results were always the same.

"It is not that you are lacking in any spiritual, physical, or intellectual capacity," the priests would intone serenely, sitting in their fine silk robes, their shaven heads glistening like ivory carvings in the lambent glow of a thousand candles. "It is because your blood is impure that we must turn you away. Despite your mother, you are not Nipponese, you are the son of a barbarian. You must go."

The little boy would trudge from the light and warmth of the monastery, to try the next one. And then the next.

And then there were no more. What the little boy had once dismissed as childish taunts, he now realized were in fact a prophecy . . .

"Mongrel!" his schoolmates had jeered. "You are a cur, fit only to scavenge in the gutter!"

Months passed. His clothing became rags. He fought the dogs—his fellow mongrels—for the garbage tossed in the back alleys. He dodged merchants' sticks, criminals' knives. At night he solemnly prayed that his ancestors, and especially his mother and father, were not suffering disgrace and humiliation as they looked down from heaven at his poor circumstances.

It was during his wanderings that the boy stumbled across a blind alley buried deep in the heart of the city. Here there was a shack, and in front of it, a large, strong-looking man of fierce expression. His possessions were few, as far as the little boy could tell, and most of them were shabby, except for the man's gleaming, obviously well-tended collection of blades and weapons. This man, the child knew at once, was a *bushi*, a warrior.

The man sat on a thin, threadbare *tatami* mat. His hair was long and lacquered in back, shaved in front, as was the samurai's custom. The man's clothing was of thin, threadbare cotton. The little boy stared in awe at the man's arms and torso, marbled with muscle. Off to one side was a cooking pot over a small fire. Steam rose from beneath the lid of the pot, the fumes rising toward the heavens like incense, and oh! didn't the aroma smell just as wonderful! The little boy's senses had grown quite sharp since he'd lost his home, as sharp as the constant pangs of hunger in his belly. There was chicken cooking in that pot, and pungent vegetables—

The samurai looked the little boy over. "What do you want here, termite?" he growled. "Begone, you with your big eyes staring at my dinner."

The little boy took no step back or forward, but just stared, and wondered how to ask. Dinner meant little to the boy; how many times had he gone without it, or lunch or breakfast, for that matter? What the little boy wanted to ask . . . but how could he ever hope?

"Get out of here!" the samurai shouted. "Go, or else, instead

of looking at my dinner, I'll cut you up and cook you with it!"
The samurai pretended to start to get up, hoping to frighten the
boy away, but the ruse didn't work. He settled back on his mat,
to glower darkly at the little snip.

"It's not your food I want, noble warrior," the little boy
began, but then he lost his nerve.

"Not my dinner, eh?" the samurai grumbled. "What, then?
Money?" He waved away the boy in disgust. "I have no money.
You wish money, go beg the *bushi* who have it, those who call
themselves true warriors, and yet disgrace themselves and the
warrior's code by teaching the martial arts to any student who
has the coin to pay for the lessons. Once, before the cursed
barbarians came to our land, there were plenty of excellent
wars for a samurai to fight! Now it's gotten so a warrior can't
make an honest living, unless he wants to open a stall next door
to the flower-arranging teacher, and the tea-ceremony teacher,
and the music teacher! Never! I for one, Hirata Soko, will never
dishonor the *bugei*, the martial arts, by revealing them to a
bunch of spoiled brats. Nor will I degrade them by turning
them into what is being called these days *budo*—"Martial
Ways," indeed! Just a rationalization so that dishonorable samurai can make money!"

"It is neither food nor money I wish, noble samurai," the
little boy replied.

"Samurai!" the man snorted derisively. "I am no samurai!"

Startled, the boy replied, "Then what—?"

He was silenced by a wave of the man's hand. "I *was* a samurai, once. But a samurai is a warrior who serves a great lord. I
serve no one! And what is a servant without a master? A *ronin*,
a 'wave man,' blown here and there like the waves of the ocean,
owning nothing, owned *by* no one."

Abruptly his fierce manner changed, and he beckoned to
the boy.

"Come closer," the *ronin* said. "Come on! Hirata will not hurt
you. I was only joking about cutting you up and putting you in
the pot."

"I know," the little boy said bashfully.

"You know, do you?" Hirata laughed. "Tell me, how do you
know?"

"I'm too skinny to eat."

At this the man threw back his head and roared his laughter. "Come closer, boy. Your voice is like the squeak of a mouse, I can hardly hear you." Hirata peered and squinted. "My eyes aren't what they once were, but you do seem strange to me, boy. Come closer, I'll not say it again . . ."

"Samurai!" the man snorted derisively. "I am no samurai!"

Startled, the boy replied, "Then what—?"

He was silenced by a wave of the man's hand. "I *was* a samurai, once. But a samurai is a warrior who serves a great lord. I serve no one! And what is a servant without a master? A *ronin*, a 'waveman,' blown here and there like the waves of the ocean, owning nothing, owned *by* no one."

Abruptly his fierce manner changed, and he beckoned to the boy.

The little boy slowly came forward, within an arm's length of the huge *ronin*. The child had to stare up to look at the man's face, even though the warrior was seated cross-legged. The boy felt like he was standing next to a boulder of a man, a mountain of a man. Inhaling, he could smell, mingling with the food's aroma, the *ronin's* man scent, the smell of brute animal.

"How can it be?" Hirata exclaimed. "You are a barbarian child!"

"My father was . . . barbarian," the little boy said, lowering his eyes. "My mother was high-born . . ."

"And what is it you wish of me, boy?" the man growled, his ill humor revived by this living reminder of the rape of his homeland.

The little boy took a deep breath. He sent a prayer to his parents in heaven to prepare the way for him should the warrior chop off his head in a fit of anger brought about by his arrogant request. Fully expecting to be slain for his impetuousness, the boy said, "I beg that I be allowed to pledge myself to you as your servant and apprentice, that you teach me—"

That was all he got out. With a flick of his wrist, the man swept the boy's feet out from under him. He placed his hand across the boy's neck to pin him fast. Such was the breadth of Hirata's hand that he was able to place thumb and little finger on the ground, with his palm across the boy's windpipe.

The boy stared up at the fearsome face of the *ronin*. He was pinned fast, but so thin and scrawny had he grown that he felt

no discomfort beneath the *ronin's* hand. The boy was about to
beg for forgiveness, and to be allowed to wander on his way,
but before he could, the man began to berate him.

"How dare you ask to be taught the *bugei?*" the warrior spat
scornfully, his words causing the boy more pain than could
any of his assortment of razor-sharp weapons. "You are not
even fit to learn the *budo*. You are tainted with barbarian blood!
You are impure! A—"

The boy closed his eyes, and allowed his soul to wander
through the depths of his own anguished heart deep as a cave,
so that the taunts and jeers of the *ronin* grew muffled and
distant. Shame and guilt for his predicament fell from him.
Lying on the ground, pinned by his tormentor, the boy felt anger
and defiance wash over his frail, tiny body. The boy opened
his mouth, and made a sound . . .

Just as the eerie howl of the wind is the aural manifestation
of the terrific potential force of moving air, so is the *kiai*—
the shout of spirit—the aural manifestation of *ki*, the all-
encompassing, indefinable spirit of the universe, focused
through the body and will of the master of *bugei* . . .

At that moment the little boy felt just that power grow in
him. Another boy might have cried out in surrender, in a plea
for mercy; in *this* boy it was a shout of utterly fearless determination.

It was the *kiai*, the shout of spirit. The boy sounded it as
his tiny fist the size of a butterfly struck the *ronin's* massive
forearm.

Hirata unpinned the boy at once. Awed, he stared at the
place on his arm the boy had struck. The blow did not harm
him, of course, but it did astound him, and touch his heart. This
child's body—to be sure, a tainted body—housed a soul
stripped pure and clean by adversity. This soul had been pitted
against the world from birth. It *had* to tread the warrior's path.

"What is your name?" Hirata asked, and after the boy had
told him, the *ronin* said, "Yes, I have heard the story of your
mother's marriage. It is a well-known bit of gossip." He pon-
dered the pale, frightened, but stoic lad lying sprawled before
him; as he did so, love, pity, and sympathy flooded his heart,
for the *bugei's* code decreed that such emotions must live in

every true warrior. Corrupted *budo* be damned, Hirata thought. Here, at last, was a worthy protege to whom Hirata could teach the strict, stern *kakuto bugei*—the true samurai's way. The boy *had* to tread the warrior's path, there was no other path for him to follow . . .

All of this the little boy did not then know, of course, but Hirata told it to him toward the end of their ten years together. As the little boy grew in both stature and strength, he learned the *kyujutsu, kenjutsu, bojutsu,* and *shuriken-jutsu*—the arts of bow and arrow, sword, staff, and throwing-knife—and all the other fighting arts. The two of them, mentor and protege, had many talks about duty and destiny and how those two guiding principals had merged on the day of their fateful meeting, during the ten years that the boy spent becoming a warrior . . .

Ki's keen ears picked up a strange-sounding voice. Instantly it seized his wary attention, hauling him back from the reverie into which he had drifted, floating on whiskey. The voice, with its European accent, catapulted him into the present, and his duty toward the woman he had sworn himself to protect, Jessica Starbuck.

A stranger had entered the Union Saloon, to take a table near the bar. The man looked to be in his thirties. He was tall and fit-looking, with close-cropped blond hair the color of goldenrod, and eyes as heartlessly pale blue as the sky during a Texas drought. The man's handsome looks were marred by a thin red scar running the length of one cheek. He was dressed in a suit of black, but wore no hat. Beneath the man's long coat, Ki could see the bulges made by a brace of pistols.

Ki stared at the man from his own place at the bar. It was not the stranger's thick Germanic accent as he harangued the bartender for service that had tipped Ki off. It was the way the man carried himself. There were, after all, many Europeans who visted Sarah on legitimate business. The Scottish cattle barons were buying up ranches, as were the English and others, from the Continent, but this blond, scarred, pistol-packing stranger was no cattleman. Ki knew that it was quite possible that the stranger would sense him in the room and turn in his chair to stare at him. Instantly a silent sort of mutual recognition and acknowledgment would flow between them, even though they had never before laid eyes on each other. They would recognize each other not as men, but as warriors.

It was the *ki*, the focused energy, or perhaps just the faint heat of it, that warriors could sense in one another. Ki had felt it radiating from Longarm that first time they'd met, up on the rise overlooking the place where Alex Starbuck had died. In Longarm, the fierceness was tempered by mercy and honor. Ki knew that Longarm suffered a tiny bit of each death he brought to his adversaries. Longarm was a warrior who still fought the most important battle, the battle to maintain a hold on his humanity while he lived by the sword—or gun. This was a battle Ki still fought as well. The first thing Hirata had taught him was that all of a warrior's prowess could turn into a thing of shame rather than pride if his soul was weak and he surrendered to the thrill of spilling blood.

Yes, Ki nodded to himself. He had instantly recognized this European stranger for what he was: a warrior, but not one like Longarm or Hirata, a warrior who had given himself over to dishonor, who plied his trade not out of duty and destiny, but for the dark and addictive joy of killing.

The bartender brought the stranger a bottle and two glasses. Ki watched and waited. When the stranger's drinking partner arrived, he would be distracted. Then Ki could perhaps move closer without tipping the man off. He would like to hear what this European killer had to say. Ki only hoped the conversation would be conducted in English. Unlike Jessie, he did not have a command of German, Spanish, French, and Italian. He could speak only English and, of course, his own Nipponese.

As the stranger looked about the room, Ki pulled his hat down over his eyes, so that the other could not see them. It was the eyes, mostly, that gave away a man's secrets. Even the most experienced warrior could not keep his eyes from telegraphing a warning to his adversary a moment before he struck his killing blow. Hirata had always taught that this did not matter, that the aim of a *bushi* was to strike a blow so perfectly executed that his adversary could not block it, no matter how much advance warning he had received.

Ki had never fully accepted this teaching, and that had been the only source of disharmony between himself and his teacher

over the ten years of his apprenticeship. Hirata was proud and
pure-blooded, after all. There was no question as to his place
and stature in Nipponese society. He had been samurai, like his
father before him, and his father's father. The only question was,
how excellent a samurai. The ancient *bugei* tradition decreed
that a warrior walk loud and proud, and in that way give lesser
beings an opportunity to scurry from his path. Should a man
even accidentally touch the scabbard of a samurai's *katana*, his
long sword, that man could be instantly slain; the samurai's
code demanded that the guilty party be cut down then and
there. Hirata's way of handling this particular situation that Ki
now found himself in would be to stride up to the blond stranger,
demand to know what his business was in Sarah, and then kill
him, then and there, if the man refused to say, tried to defend
himself, or, in Hirata's estimation, attempted to lie.

This Ki would not do, just as he would not carry or willingly
use the *katana*. Ki had often thought that it was this decision on
his part that had finally broken the bond between himself and
his teacher, effectively ending his ten-year apprenticeship.

"I simply do not understand," Hirata had shouted. The *ronin*
had grown older and grayer over the years, but he was still a
mountain of a man with hard stones for muscles and tree trunks
for limbs. "The *katana*, the long sword, is a divine weapon, a
badge of honor that links a warrior to his noble ancestry." They
were sitting in front of Hirata's shabby house, situated at the end
of the blind alley. As always, every evening, the cookfire was
burning, and the pot of food the two would share was quietly
bubbling away, the puffs of fragrant steam rattling the lid. "For
the life of me, I cannot understand why you are so stubborn
about using it!"

The young man only smiled. "Honored teacher, it is precisely for the reasons you have mentioned that I refuse to use
it, even though I have practiced and mastered its techniques."

Hirata drew his *katana* from its scabbard, as if to seduce
the young man with its exquisite, deadly beauty. The fine steel's
lovingly polished length caught the fire's reflection. *Hirata*
turned the blade this way and that, so that the flame's reflection
glittered, captured in the gleaming sword, reminding the young
man of precious gems, of the jewellike Siamese fighting fish

in their crystal bowls, of the light in a woman's eyes when she is joined in blissful sexual union with a man . . .

"Honored teacher," the young man began, "you have described the *katana* as the link between a warrior and his noble ancestry. For this reason I turn my back on it."

"Explain yourself," Hirata growled like a tiger, and lifted his hand as if to cuff his pupil. He restrained himself only because it had been his experience that some unlikely seeds of wisdom had a way of sprouting from this half-breed's mind.

The young man, meanwhile, had not flinched from the threat of the blow. An apprentice can learn nothing until he trusts his teacher, and the ultimate sign of such trust in the world of the warrior is for the pupil to calmly await any sort of strike from his master, knowing that an expert *bushi* can perfectly control the force and intensity of the attack. "How can I carry a symbol of noble ancestry?" the young man explained, not even looking at Hirata's unpraised ham of a fist. "Society has shunned me, and even my mother's own family has denied me my birthright."

"Ah . . ." Hirata sighed, and looked away from his pupil. What the young man had said was, of course, quite true. The *ronin* felt his heart grow heavy with pity. The young man had an indomitable spirit, a spirit that had not been broken by the stigma of his barbaric sire, but oh, how that spirit—once so tender and vulnerable—had been scarred! "I did not mean literal ancestry," Hirata said gruffly, "but *spiritual*, my boy. This spiritual link you have with all the great warriors of the past, despite your unfortunate parentage."

"That I understand," the young man said. "That I believe, just as I believe you are my spiritual father."

"Ah . . . go on, now," Hirata sputtered, turning eyes grown liquid away from his pupil. "None of that, else I *will* cuff you . . ."

"But despite the spiritual link, honored teacher, I will not carry the *katana*," the young man continued. "I would have to kill far too many men who I suspected were scoffing at my pretensions. No, I will make it a point to use the *sai*, the *bo* staff, the *nunchaku*, and the small, deadly *shuriken* throwing blades and stars. I will use the weapons perfected by our homeland's vanquished foes, the weapons of China and Okinawa, the weapons of the downtrodden, the underdogs. If I am to be a samurai, honored teacher, I will not be samurai to the noble class, as you were. I will be samurai to those who suffer through no fault of their own, in the land where my father was born."

"To this vow of yours I have no answer," Hirata replied softly. He sheathed his sword, then reached out and took his pupil's hand. "Tradition compels me to reprimand you, and yet the barbarians have taken over our country. I, once a noble samurai, have been reduced to living in a hovel. I have my pride, my strength, my *katana*, and my honor. But each day I grow a little older. Soon my strength will be gone. How then will I sustain my pride? What then will become of my honor?"

"You are the last true samurai," the young man answered. And then he smiled. "You are the last because you would not degrade the code by teaching *budo*. You would not take on a student for money."

"And I never did," Hirata smiled back. "I took on the last true pupil. In you I have been able to turn the wheel of my life one complete cycle. Now that I have taught you all I know, you must go off to wherever your vow shall take you."

"When?" the young man asked.

"Now," the old *ronin* answered. "Come back in a little while."

"I understand," the young man said, very, very softly, taking care to keep his tone totally neutral.

"Of course you do," Hirata chuckled. "You were my student."

The young man rose, bowed to his teacher, and then walked off to a quiet park in the city, where he meditated for an hour. When he returned to the old shack that had been his home for a decade, he saw the still, lifeless body of Hirata. The master was slumped over, his two hands still holding the hilt of the short sword lodged in his abdomen. The young man did not have to examine the body to know that his teacher was dead, just as he did not have to examine the long, self-inflicted horizontal and vertical slashes in his teacher's belly to know that the cuts were crisp, clean, and totally excellent. Even in dying, the old man had remained true to the ancient spirit of *bugei*. In recent times it had become the custom among samurai committed to *seppuku*—suicide by ritual disembowelment—to appoint a second who would stand by, prepared to lop off the suicide's head as soon as he had made the first thrust with the short sword, thus sparing him the agony of the two long, deep cuts. Typically, the noble Hirata had shunned this cheapening of the samurai's ultimate act of courage.

The young man turned to where his belongings had been neatly stacked. On top, in its scabbard, was Hirata's *katana*. Smiling, the young man drew the sword, and with it saluted his teacher. Smiling he slid the blade back into its scabbard. He did not thrust it through his sash, as was customary, but holding true to his vow, he wrapped it in his clothing and carried it on his back as he left Hirata for the final time. He brought the blade with him to America. He kept it clean and sharp, and when he was sure he was alone, he practiced with it, hearing Hirata's whispered instruction in the singing of the sword as it sliced through the air.

But he never used the *katana* in battle. In battle he used the common weapons of his culture and background, for he had declared himself samurai of the common man. Accordingly, when he journeyed to America, he told no one of the aristocratic background from which he sprang. Had not both "noble" families—his mother's and his Yankee father's—disowned him? America was to be the starting place for his new life, and so he chose for himself a new name. In America he would be known by a name that symbolized the unifying spirit of all men, all creatures. Some he met, men like Alex Starbuck, understood, while others did not, but Ki was sure his ancestors, and Hirata were pleased.

From his place at the bar, Ki watched a short, fat man approach the blond stranger's table. The newcomer's blue crushed velvet suit, his red and gold paisley silk vest, only emphasized his girth.

"I've been looking all over for you," the fat man said in a clear, American-accented voice. "It's going to be wonderful! The town is packed with people!"

"I've been waiting here for fifteen minutes," the blond man said. Ki could see the arteries in his neck pulse with anger. That almost made him feel a more positive kinship with the blond European. How difficult it was to suffer all the fools in the world! Truly, avoiding a fight was often the most difficult test a warrior could face . . .

"I *told* you I would meet you here," the blond man growled

through clenched teeth. Then, calming himself, he stood up to shake hands.

"Lord, I suppose I forgot," the fat man laughed.

"Well, sit down now, and have a drink. You technicals are in the clouds, yes? Absentminded . . ."

"Scientist, not 'technical,' my friend," the fat man corrected him, careful to keep his voice good-humored and his manner polite. "And I will have a drink."

Ki looked the new man over, grateful that their exchange, so far at least, was in English. The man looked to be about fifty-five. He was bald, with gray tufts of dry hair sprouting on both sides of his head, just above the ears. He wore steel-rimmed spectacles with thick lenses. If he was carrying a firearm, it was small enough not to make a bulge in his snug-fitting clothes. The blond man had already identified his friend as a scientist. If he hadn't, Ki would have guessed that he was a barber, merchant, or town mayor. Only two things about the man belied his soft-looking image. Ki noticed that his fingers were blunt and callused-looking, the nails either missing or blackened. Whatever work this man did, it took its toll on his hands.

The other odd thing about the soft-looking, fat man was his *smell*. It was smoky and crowded in the saloon, but Ki's sharp olfactory sense picked up the odor immediately. Emanating from that suit of crushed velvet and that silly vest of red and gold silk, was the unmistakable scent of cordite, the eye-stinging pungency of spent gunpowder.

The two men were talking more softly now. Ki began to wander toward them, but was foiled in his attempt to eavesdrop when several drunk and rowdy cowboys beat him to the only nearby vacant table.

Ki stood rooted to the floor, totally frustrated. Not only did he risk discovery if he attempted to get any closer to the quietly conversing pair, but now the rowdy cowboys were making so much noise that Ki could only pick up an occasional word coming from the two men.

" . . . twelve men, all with coffee grinders . . ." the fat man beamed, but the rest of what he said was drowned out by the shouts of the cowboys for more beer. " . . . both sides of town. It'll happen at . . ."

Three of the cowboys broke into a chorus of a filthy ditty

currently popular with the hands, and Ki gave up in disgust. He returned to the bar and ordered another drink. He sipped it slowly, and about the time he was finished, the two men stood up to shake hands. The one in the velvet suit hurried out, while the blond man signaled a hostess—a pretty little brunette— whispered something in her ear that made her giggle, and put his arm around her as they headed toward the staircase, and up to the second-floor rooms.

Ki gave them a few seconds' lead, and then followed, to slip unnoticed up the stairs. At the head of the staircase the second floor branched out into two wings, but Ki had seen the girl lead the blond man to the left. He carefully and silently hurried that way. The downstairs noise decreased dramatically once he entered the corridor. All he could hear was an occasional thump, and a steady but very muted drone rising up through the carpet.

Ki cat-crept down the long, narrow hallway. He hoped he wasn't too late to catch a glimpse of the blond man and the woman as they chose a room. It would make things more difficult if he had to begin peeking through every keyhole.

He turned a corner and quickly jumped back. The blond man was standing in profile just a few feet ahead. Fortunately his attention was fixed on the girl's backside as she bent to fiddle with the lock on the room's door. Finally she got it open, and the two went inside. The door shut, and then clicked locked. Ki was alone in the still, quiet hallway.

It would be exquisitely difficult, Ki thought as he approached their door. He began to wait patiently. Soon they would be engaged in lovemaking. Then he would silently pick the lock, enter the room, and render them both unconscious before they could have a chance to see him or even sense that he was there. Once that was done, he could go through the blond man's belongings. He'd be gone by the time they came to. The blond man and the girl would think they had dozed off. What else could they imagine? A Nipponese would, of course, comprehend immediately what it was that had happened. One of Ki's fellow countrymen would know that he had been overcome by a *ninja*.

Ki smiled as he leaned against the far wall of the hallway, watching the door in question. He doubted that there was anyone else in this part of the world who could accomplish what he was going to do. Not even Hirata had known much of *ninjutsu*, the art of the "invisible assassin." The samurai's way was to bluster upon the enemy, dealing death to whoever got in the way.

While serving as Hirata's apprentice, Ki had, without telling his teacher, practiced *ninjutsu* until he was as proficient in it as he had become in the other, "nobler" arts he had learned from Hirata. It had not been difficult for a student like Ki; in fact, Hirata could easily have mastered the necessary skills, but he, like all other samurai, considered them beneath his position as a member of that exalted class. This had served as a warning to Ki that even the greatest of warriors have blind spots born of foolish prejudice.

For example, there was *atemi*, the use of pressure-points on an opponent's body. Through the use of *atemi*, Ki would be able to render this couple unconscious quickly, silently, painlessly. Hirata could have learned *atemi* in a day, but he considered the art beneath contempt. Why deign to touch the enemy with one's bare hands, when one could touch the enemy with one's bare hands, when one could touch him so much more effectively with one's blade? Even such limited *te* techniques as Hirata knew were to be reserved for those times of last resort when, for some unthinkable reason, a samurai found himself without his noble *katana*, or without any weapons at all.

Ki watched the thin ribbon of light gleaming from beneath the door. Suddenly it blinked out. Excellent! If the lamp or candle had remained lit, Ki would have had to extinguish it, but he'd known the chances were good that the room would already be dark when he attacked. For some bizarre reason, Americans and Europeans preferred to make love to their partners in the shadows. Well, there was no accounting for taste.

Ki smiled and listened to the murmurs coming through the door. He approached, tossing his hat to the carpeted floor, then pressing his ear against the wood. At the same time, he began to regulate his breathing. His inhalations and exhalations were now very shallow. Someone watching would say that Ki was not breathing at all, for where was the rise and fall of his chest?

There was no chest movement, no physical movement at all, as far as the eye could tell, but if Ki had been shirtless, a palm pressed against his stomach would have felt the rhythms of his diaphragm beneath the thick bands of his belly muscles. For a few seconds the roar of his own blood rushing through his veins filled his ears, but then the internal noise of his own body receded, and his sense of hearing seemed to reach out to encompass the room, the hallway, and even the corridor around the corner. Now Ki did not need his eyes. He could focus them on the lock, let them puzzle out the intricate task of picking the mechanism silently. His ears could hear everything, and what they heard told him that he was alone, safe from discovery, and could proceed with the attack.

From one of the many pockets sewn into the lining of his coat he removed a thin, needlelike *shuriken*, or throwing blade. He inserted it into the lock, and begin the series of tiny movements, mere vibrations, that would coax the tumblers open. On the other side of the door, the key—forced from the lock by his pick—fell to the carpet. Ki heard it thud down like a sack of potatoes. The blond man and the girl in his arms had not heard it at all. Another movement of the pick, another twist and careful shake, and the lock was open.

Slipping the *shuriken* back into its pocket, Ki reached out for the doorknob. He prepared himself. Once the door was opened, there could be no retreat. Light from the hallway would shine in. Both the blond man and the girl would have a moment to turn toward the light before the door was closed again, plunging them back into the darkness. They would not have even seen Ki's silhouette. He'd be no more than a foot off of the ground, slithering toward them on his belly like a snake. The crawling technique was even named after the serpent—Ki could move forward that way faster than many men could run. He'd slide to their bed and then up the side. He would reach out . . . and it would be done.

He could hear the creaking of the bedsprings, as steady as the beat of a song. It was time—

Ki froze, his hand still on the doorknob. Someone was coming down the corridor. He bent to scoop up his Stetson just as a woman turned the corner to confront him.

"Oh! What are you doing here?" she demanded, obviously startled. She was a pretty little honey blonde, with a pert hourglass figure beneath the thin white cotton dress she was wearing. "You're not supposed to be up here alone!"

Ki straightened up, his hat in his hand. He hurried toward

her to keep the conversation from being conducted where the blond man and the woman he was with could hear it. There was a coal-oil lamp affixed to the wall several feet behind her. The wick was turned up fairly high, and by its bright light Ki could see right through the gauze of her dress, see her figure in shadowy but clearly delineated silhouette, see the lovely shapes of her legs as they rose up, the space between them ever narrowing, until his eyes finally came to rest upon the slimmest sliver of light so softly diffused by the soft hair covering her womanhood.

The blonde followed Ki's eyes down her own front, and once she saw where he was gazing, she smiled and said, "I guess it doesn't matter how you got up here all by your lonesome. Something hot in your eyes—and something hot filling out the front of your pants—tells me you're not planning on being lonesome much longer." Then her own eyes, a delicate shade of lavender, narrowed as she looked at Ki's face. "You're a handsome one, aren't you, darling, but your eyes—" She brushed back the black, shiny hair from Ki's forehead, and tilted his head down with the touch of a light, cool finger. "Lord above! You're—"

"I am partly Japanese, as you see," Ki smiled.

"Well, you're a beautiful man, whatever you are." She smiled back at him and licked her lips. "I've never had an Oriental fellow before. I'm on my own time right now. What do you say?" Her fingers tickled down the length of Ki's fly, to brush against his hardness. "Well! You don't have to say anything, you *lovely* man."

Before Ki could protest, she'd gripped his hand and led him to the nearest room. While she fiddled with the door, Ki glanced back over his shoulder at the room he'd been about to invade before he'd been so sweetly interrupted. For a moment he considered placing his forefinger at the side of the girl's neck, pressing ever so gently, and then catching her before she had a chance to collapse on the carpet.

He *could* do that to her. But, truth to tell, Ki couldn't get the memory of her figure—so delectable, glimpsed through the wispy cotton of her dress—out of his mind. Granted, he felt like squeezing various portions of this female's anatomy, but *atemi* pressure-points were not on that list.

As she pulled him into the room, Ki looked back at the other door for one last time. The stranger in there was not likely to go anywhere soon. And considering the grip this little honey blonde with the eyes like violets had on him, he wasn't going anywhere, either.

If he wanted to stay up here without causing a fuss, it fell to him to satisfy this girl's curiosity about Oriental ways of lovemaking. So be it.

As Hirata had always taught, a true warrior ran from no confrontation, but always marched resolutely toward battle, his mighty sword unsheathed. Clicking the door shut behind him, Ki tried hard not to laugh.

Chapter 12

The room she had brought him to was small and scrupulously clean. In one corner stood a pitcher and washbasin upon a stand. The open window in the far wall let in a cool, steady breeze. Pale blue wallpaper and a tan carpet made the room seem larger than it was. The brass bed was large, fitted out with crisp-looking, clean white sheets. If this room was indicative of the others on the second floor of the Union Saloon, the place would have made a very comfortable hotel. Of course, the proprietors were making much more money on the place by using the second floor as a cathouse.

Ki kept an ear cocked toward the door. There was little extraneous noise up here, except for that dull throb rising up through the floor from the saloon. He was sure he would hear the blond man leave his room. If that happened, Ki would have a few extra moments to intercept him. If he was at all like others, he would pause at the bar for a drink to refresh himself after his activities up here.

The girl had undone the bow that kept her dress pulled together at the front. She'd loosened the ties and was about to slip the garment off. She turned and caught Ki looking at the door. "I told you I'm on my own time, so you won't have to pay," she said, misunderstanding the cause of his unease. The white cotton dress had slipped down off her shoulders, but she kept it bunched up in front of her, protecting her breasts with her crossed arms.

"Yes, I know." Ki smiled. "Thank you," he added, meanwhile thinking that this obsession Americans and Europeans had over whether or not they "paid" for sex was a curious thing indeed. Sexual pleasure was always paid for; the unlucky paid with guilt, the majority with money or protection, and the few who understood paid for pleasure by returning that pleasure to the giver. The only woman he had ever met who understood this was Jessie . . .

"Being with a man on my own time always makes me nervous," the honey blonde whispered. "Now don't you smile like that, because it's true!" she scolded indignantly. "My name's Celine, by the way."

"Celine, my name is Ki." This woman was beginning to interest him. Her spirit was strong, and in some way kindred to his own. He slipped off his coat and hung it over the back of a chair. "Tell me why you are nervous," he said softly, genuinely intrigued. He unstrapped his gunbelt and set it down.

"It's kind of like when I wanted to be an actress," Celine said. "When I was on stage playing a part, I wasn't me, so I didn't have to worry about what people thought of me. Now, when I'm with men, um . . . when it's my job"—she blushed, not quite able to look Ki in the eye—"well, then I'm just like an actress. Usually I'm acting for the man . . ."

"Let me see you, Celine," Ki commanded gently.

She let her dress fall to the carpet and stood before him in a slightly pigeoned-toed, bashful stance. If there came to her face a slight blush, it was as nothing compared to the peach-pink flush of shyness and arousal that suffused the large round globes of her breasts, the seductive curve of her belly, and the moist juncture of her thighs beneath the honey-colored fur.

"You are lovely," Ki said, beckoning her to come into his arms. "You are indeed fit for the stage, where all can admire your beauty."

Ki's words brought a happy sigh from Celine. "Thank you, but those dreams are long gone," she said. "The new one is to own a place like this, someday." She turned to blow out the candles, but he stopped her.

"The light sets fire to your golden skin," he told her as he shed the last of his clothes.

Her violet eyes danced the length of his body, feasting upon the sight of his thick shoulders and long, sinewy arms, his hard, rippling belly, and the cords of his calves and thighs. "Anyway, this job does have its benefits," she said merrily. "I'm glad I'm the one who found you wandering around up here. I've never seen a man like you before . . . not like you . . ." She reached out tentatively to touch the hard curve of him jutting out from his center like the spar of a sailing ship. Her tongue slid absently from between her lips as she giggled in nervous expectation. "You sure don't talk much, do you?"

Ki enfolded her in his arms and kissed her, before she could fill the room with her nervous chatter. He captured her tongue beneath his own, as he felt her trembling, satiny body pressed against him like a fluttering bird upon his palm. Now she could not speak at all, but only sing high notes as his fingers stroked the length of her spine, playing along it like a keyboard.

"Lord above," she finally breathed. "This is some sort of magic." She sucked and nibbled her way along his chest, taking satisfaction in the way the lightest touch of her tongue and lips upon his body could make him dance and jerk in place.

Ki arched his back in pleasure. His hands cupped her posterior and lifted her up. She locked her legs about his waist to squirm and buck against him, whimpering all the while. She was so hot and wet that he slid easily into her.

"You're so strong," she marveled between groans. "I'm like a feather in your hands." She painted steamy kisses across his neck and face as Ki stood rock steady, meeting her wildly gyrating hips with perfectly synchronized thrusts. "Oh, I'm coming already," she moaned. "I've never started so quickly before!"

Ki began to run his tongue around and around the dark aureoles of her breasts. Perspiration, wrung out of her by her passion, beaded in her cleavage. His tongue lapped up the salty taste. Her nipples became hard nuggets of flesh. He chewed them ever so gently, while his hands supported and massaged her twitching bottom.

She began to wail, softly and faintly. Her legs, scissored around his waist, clamped together like a vise.

Ki only laughed. "Woman, I have hardly begun with you. Go ahead and take your pleasure. It is only the first of so much more to savor."

Celine delighted in the challenge. "I bet I can make you come too," she cooed into his ear. "Like this, and this!" Her silky furnace gripped and stroked the length of him, embedded inside of her. "You'd just better come, or else!" She tilted her pelvis so that her backside stuck up and out, in that way pulling herself back so that now only the tip of him was still in her. "Are you going to come, or are you going to be left out in the cold!" she crowed in triumph, her tongue teasingly licking his face.

Ki grinned, his dark eyes locking with her lavender gaze. "Before my worthy adversary declares her total victory and issues her ultimatum, she had best look to her rear . . ."

In order for Celine to pull her hips away from him, she'd had to jut out the twin globes of her bottom. Her buttocks were now splayed wide apart, her anus totally defenseless and vulnerable, as Ki's fingers tickled the length of her backside's cleft.

"Ooh!" she squeaked, involuntarily pressing closer to him, taking in fully half of his member. "Oh! Ooooh!" Her ass danced and bobbed as he lightly pressed against her opening. "You wouldn't dare," she whimpered, coaxed by Ki's prodding finger into the preliminary throes of her orgasm. "You wouldn't dare!" But the tone of her voice, and the sparkle in her violet eyes, told him that he certainly should dare!

Ki brought his finger up to wet and lubricate it in the pool of sweat that had collected in the small of her back. Then, as she began the long slide toward her climax, he slid his finger deep into her anus.

Celine threw back her head and sang like a bird. She came like a summer's cloudburst, her bottom sizzling against Ki's hands as tremors ran through her limp body.

Ki, still as hard as a stick of marble, carried her over to the bed and laid her down upon it. He began again, running his fingers through her silky, honey-colored tresses as he kissed the flush of sexual abandon that had spread across her nose and cheeks. His mouth tirelessly worked its way down her neck, breasts, and belly until he was by her side, on his hands and knees, and then he lowered his head between her spread legs, to nip and lick the tender flesh of her inner thighs.

Celine was so paralyzed with pleasure, with delicious sensation, that she could do nothing but stroke and palm his erection, delighting at the way his hardness cavorted beneath her touch.

"My pet . . ." she giggled, giving his tip a squeeze. Her nails tickled and scratched at his groin, forcing a long, low moan from Ki as he darted his tongue between her parted, glistening inner folds.

"Ohhh!" Her cry became an unintelligible garble of noise as Ki's tongue flicked and flicked and flicked like some tiny whip of love against her very core. Her hands became claws pulling him away, and then around to enter her. As he buried himself in her steaming body, she bent her legs to press her calves against the backs of his knees, pinning him down.

Ki worked his hips like a steam locomotive's pistons. He felt his climax rising up from the soles of his feet, coursing through his loins to spin like a deep whirlpool in his groin. He began to shudder as the silvery hot ball inside of him sent drips along his spine.

Celine felt him grow and swell until she thought he might burst. She was tottering on the edge of yet another cascading climax, but before she lost the power of speech, she languidly slid her hand down Ki's broad, muscular back, to press a finger meaningfully against the swell that marked the start of the cleft of *his* rear end.

"Ahhh," she said between kisses. "I've got *you* right where I want!"

Fully delighted to play out this most wonderful game, Ki pretended to plead, "Oh, don't!" He angled up his groin in order to rub his tip against the most sensitive area of her sex. He sawed back and forth, delaying his orgasm for just one more moment, as Celine writhed below him.

Suddenly she slid the sweat-slick tip of her index finger into his anus, and gave a little push, the movement propelling his hips, now turned to hot jelly, forward so that as he came he was locked within her to the hilt. Their voices blended into a chorus of love-sounds as their bodies bucked together mindlessly, their climaxes slowly fading, to leave them breathless and faint.

As they cuddled together, Celine drawled, "Well, I never . . ."

Ki waited a moment, and then said, "You never what?" But

still there was no answer. He glanced at her face. Her eyes were closed, and her breathing had become regular. A moment later her lips parted, and she began to snore.

Laughing, Ki untangled himself from her grip, and quietly went to the washstand to bathe. He dressed silently, but he must have made some noise, for Celine suddenly awoke.

"Where you goin'?" she mumbled sleepily. "Stay . . ."

"I have duty I must attend to, sweet woman," he whispered.

"Maybe I could help you," she pouted. "I want to help you a lot," she added dreamily.

"You may help me by remaining very quiet," Ki instructed.

"Wel-l-l," she drawled. "I don't know . . . you may have to bribe me . . ." She held out her arms and spread her legs.

She leaves me no choice, Ki thought calmly. Saying nothing, moving toward her, he focused the energy within him, sending all of it flooding into the fingers of his right hand. This was the force behind the unarmed combat system of *te*. It was what allowed a man to split a board, shatter a brick, or finger-slice through a man's chest to burst his heart. Ki had done the first two of these things many times—and that last thing once. Now, as he approached Celine's unsuspecting supine figure, he prepared himself to apply that same force to a far different task.

"Ki? Why are you smiling like that?" Celine asked. She shuddered, and tried to rise.

Ki pinned her down with his left hand firmly planted on her belly. He pressed the nail of his steel-stiff index finger against the core of Celine's sex, and then vibrated his digit to send waves of pleasure through her pelvis. In seconds she was caterwauling in the grip of yet another orgasm, her legs flailing in the air as she bucked like a wild horse. She floated in the ever-widening rings of warmth for another blissful minute before her eyes closed, and her snoring began again.

Ki kissed her feather-softly upon her brow before letting himself out of the room. He hoped she was in good with her boss. After that last trick—in Nippon it was called the 'vibrating beak' technique—women usually slept through the night.

Back in the corridor, with his gunbelt slung over his shoulder, Ki once again approached the door behind which the blond man had been taking *his* pleasure. Once again Ki made himself ready for his *ninja* attack. He set his gunbelt down, regulated his breathing, composed his mind, and reached out for the doorknob—

But once again his plans went awry. Before his own fingers could touch it, the doorknob began to turn. Somebody was leaving the room!

Ki flattened himself against the hinge side of the door-jamb. Out of the room came the brunette. He silently wished the American geisha an apology for what he was about to do. After all, the world was a strange place, and the spinning wheel of *karma* that controlled all people's lives could just as easily have ordained that this woman be his sweet Celine. Ki took one soundless step to synchronize his rhythms with those of his victim, and then rushed up behind her, one hand gently covering her eyes while the other found the *atemi* point at the side of her neck.

The frightened woman stiffened, but before she could find her voice, her knees sagged and she collapsed like a rag doll that had lost its stuffing. Ki swept her up into his arms before she could hit the floor, and carried her into a nearby vacant room. He set her down on the bed and then hurried out to retrieve his gunbelt, strap it around his waist, and enter the blond man's room.

The stranger was stretched out nude upon the bed, his double gunbelt draped over the head of the brass bedstead, the grips of his revolvers within easy reach. All looked natural: a man, sexually exhausted, sleeping in a dark room. All *looked* natural—

But a *ninja* knew the difference between what was real and what only seemed real. Ki could tell the difference between real and faked sleep. A person truly dreaming is absolutely still. His bones and joints do not creak, and his snores are uneven. This man, Ki realized, was pretending to be asleep in order to get the drop on him. Nevertheless, Ki pretended to be fooled by the ruse. It would be entertaining to experience the outcome of this little contest, for each man was an expert in some aspect of warrior hood, and each had an advantage over the other. The blond man had eyes grown accustomed to the darkness, and his nearby pistols. Ki had the quickness of wit to pretend to be fooled, and his *atemi* skills.

Of course, the blond stranger lying so quietly might only be pretending to be fooled by Ki's pretending. Ki was within three feet of the bed now. Another step and his adversary would be within reach.

With lizardlike speed, the blond man snapped out his right hand to pull a revolver from his gunbelt. Ki moved in to slam the edge of his palm against the stranger's wrist. It was the *shuto-uchi*, the "knife-hand strike," and its force sent the pistol skidding across the carpet before a shot could be fired.

"*Scheiss!*" breathed the man as he sat up. He brought his arm up and around to catch Ki in a headlock. The man was strong and knew how to use leverage. He twisted to pull Ki off balance and over the man's lap. His fist caught Ki twice against the side of the head, and made him see stars.

Ki jackknifed his legs up and over, to lock about the blond man's neck. Then it was *his* turn to twist, and the blond man was forced to break his hold on Ki as he went somersaulting toward the foot of the bed. The man's hands reached out to break his fall, in lieu of breaking his neck, and Ki's stiff fingers punched at a point just above the man's collar bone and to the right of his Adam's apple.

The blond man managed a last feeble jab at Ki's ribs as he faded into unconsciousness. The whole fight had taken less than ten seconds, and had been totally silent except for the light thud of the gun upon the soft carpet, the man's one whispered curse word, and the creaking of the bedsprings.

Gingerly rubbing at the bruise on his temple, Ki lit a candle and began to go through the blond man's belongings. The first thing he did was extract the other pistol from the gunbelt. If the blond man came to, Ki did not want him to have a gun within reach.

Ki carried the weapon over to the candle's flame in order to examine it. He'd never before seen such a weapon. The nickel-plated handgun looked to be a .38, but was smaller than a Colt of comparable caliber. Instead of wood or hard rubber handgrips, the pistol had a long, slender, rounded butt of fili-greed metal. Ki searched for the catch and then broke open the pistol to extract its six shells. Then he closed it and experimen-tally worked the action. There were diagonal groovings on the outside of the revolver's cylinder. As the pistol was cocked and dry-fired, a pin in the frame moved back and forth, riding in these zigzag grooves, rotating the cylinder.

Ki tucked the emptied weapon into his gunbelt, at the small of his back, and continued his search through the man's clothes. There was nothing in his pockets or wallet to identify him, but Ki did find a yellowed, tattered newspaper clipping, folded into quarters and tucked into the watch pocket of the man's vest.

There was a photo pinned to the clipping. It was of the short, fat man whom Ki had earlier seen drinking downstairs in the saloon. Ki couldn't make out what the article was about, for it was written in German.

What he'd found were slim pickings, but intriguing ones. Perhaps Longarm could garner some clue from the unusual revolver; Jessica could certainly translate the German newspaper article.

Ki slipped out of the room and down along the corridor. He ambled down the stairs, keeping his hat pulled low and his eyes on the floor, meeting no one's gaze—assuming anyone was bothering to look at him—as he cut across the saloon and out the batwing double doors.

He began to walk down the wooden sidewalk, toward the Cattlemen's Association. He sensed a presence behind him and had begun to turn when he felt the cold, hard barrel of a gun thrust behind his ear, and froze in his tracks.

"That's right, chink," rumbled a familiar voice. "Thought it was you. We were having a drink when we saw you leave."

"Hello, Higgins," Ki said. His eyes flicked right and left as two of the ex-foreman's men bracketed him on both sides. "It's no use pleading, you know. You will not get your job back."

"Just start walking, and turn into that alley coming up," Higgins snarled, careful to keep his cocked .45 pressed against Ki's head. "Once we're off the street, we'll see who does the pleading, boy."

Ki did as he was told. The street was deserted. At this hour, those not already in the Cattlemen's building for the meeting were whiling away the time in the Union or over in Canvas Town. Ki could not hope that a passerby, seeing what was going on, might help, or alert the town marshal. He was on his own against three men who had the drop on him.

The alley was narrow and dark; it snaked around behind

the Union Saloon to end where a high wooden fence separated
the saloon's property from the building next door. There was
no first-floor back door into the saloon, but a wooden staircase
led up to the second floor. Ki supposed this was built so the
more illustrious members of the community could partake of
the pleasures offered up there, then slip away unnoticed.

Higgins marched Ki up to the fence, then retreated a few
paces, his two men on either side of him. He lowered his Peacemaker and said, "Turn around, chink!"

Ki turned slowly to face the three men. His back was against
the fence. A beam of light spilling out of a window upstairs
illuminated him as if he were in a spotlight. There was no place
to run, and certainly no place to hide.

"I noticed you're wearing a gun, boy." Higgins grinned like
a man who has dealt himself a winning hand at poker. "I ain't
never seen you wear one before, but seeing that you are, I figure
it's plenty legal for me to call you out on account of that beating
you gave me the other day." The big man glowered darkly. "You
did that to me in front of Miss Starbuck, too." He gestured at
his two men. "These fellows here will testify to old Farley that
it was a fair enough shootout."

"But your gun is already in your hand," Ki observed quietly.

"Well now," Higgins chuckled. "Seeing as how I'm wearing
a shoulder rig, and you've got your gun in a waist holster, I
figure my holding my gun down at my side like this makes it
fair enough." His two cronies smiled and shifted their weight
from leg to leg like a pair of watchdogs straining at their leads.

"I cannot draw on you, Higgins," Ki said.

"Why not? You scared, boy?"

"You're so quick and all, you know, Chinaman?" one of the
other men guffawed.

"If you're scared, you better start pleading." All traces of
humor were gone from Higgins's face and voice. "I'll give you
a few minutes to plead with me, on your knees . . ."

"I am not frightened," Ki said, folding his arms across his
chest. "It is that my gun is not loaded. I only wore it so as not
to attract attention to myself."

The men on either side of Higgins broke out into nervous
laughter. "That's just too bad," the one who had spoken before
said scornfully.

"Loaded or not, how was I to know you were telling the truth? Especially since you drew on me first. Right, boys?"

The two men nodded meaningfully, their eyes on Ki, their hands hovering near their own holstered Peacemakers.

Ki was amused by their agitation. "Tell me, where are your other two hounds, Ray and Musty? Just three of you against me seems like you are taking an awful chance . . ."

"They're taking care of that nosy federal marshal, Longarm," Higgins said. "Getting him out of the way, just like we're going to get you out of the way. Miss Jessie will be all alone. That'll make Danzig's job that much easier."

"Who is Danzig?" Ki asked, but he thought he knew. "That name sounds German," he mused out loud, noting with satisfaction Higgins's surprised look of unease.

"Never you mind who he is," the ex-foreman grumbled, clearly off balance.

"Very well," Ki said agreeably. "How did you find out Longarm was a federal marshal?"

"That was easy," Higgins boasted. "I checked out his horse the day he rode in with you and Miss Jessie. That gelding was carrying a U.S. brand. The Rangers got their own horses. That made Longarm either army or a federal man. I bet on the last, since he didn't carry himself like he was army." Higgins's eyes narrowed. "The time for talking's over, chink."

"Listen to me carefully," Ki addressed the one man who had remained silent throughout the entire exchange. "It is too late for Higgins, as I have already spared his life once."

"You'd do better to use your last time on earth praying to them ancestors of yours," Higgins interrupted angrily.

"And it is too late for this other," Ki continued unperturbed, "for he had insulted me, but you have said nothing. You may go, but you must leave now."

All three men only shook their heads in amazed disbelief. Ki still had his arms folded across his chest. His hands were nowhere near his gun.

"I'll say this for you," the man Ki had spoken to snorted in disbelief. "You're a brazen son of a bitch."

"He's a dead one!" Higgins spat, his voice thick with hate and tension as he brought up his .45.

Ki slid his arms apart so that the inner sides of his forearms

Thompson Nicola Regional District Library System

and palms of his hands rubbed together. The smooth motion forced the two *shuriken* throwing blades out of the hidden sheaths sewn to the insides of his sleeves. His hands rose up, the blades—four-inch knives without hilt or handle—glinting in the light as they left his fingers.

The men on either side of Higgins spat blood instead of screams as Ki's *shuriken* flew to their throats. They were falling to the ground as Higgins fired.

The .45 thundered as the big slug chewed a splintery hole through a fence plank. Ki had somersaulted forward, to rise up in front of Higgins before he could recock his single-action revolver.

At first Higgins didn't even attempt to fight, but turned on his heel and ran back down the alley, toward the street. As he ran, he spun around to backpedal a few steps and snap a shot at Ki.

That was Higgins's final mistake. His shot went wild as Ki reached into his coat to extract another *shuriken*, this one a disc in the shape of a six-pointed star. The disc looked like a spur-wheel, except that the *shuriken* was four inches across and forged of high-grade steel. Ki snapped his wrist to send the lethal star on its journey toward its target.

Higgins saw the metallic thing glitter as it left the circle of light in which Ki stood, to come whizzing and swooping his way like some razor-edged bat. He screamed, dropping his .45 to the dirt as he turned to run furiously for the street. He heard the deadly whir of the throwing star, and uselessly fluttered his hands behind him in an attempt to protect the back of his neck.

The *shuriken* sliced through three of Higgins's spread fingers before burying half of its diameter in the base of his skull, instantly severing his spinal cord. He fell forward, his own momentum carrying him, so that his face plowed a furrow in the dirt before he came to rest. His body twitched and jerked in muscle spasms even as his staring eyes began to glaze.

Ki retrieved his two throwing blades from the throats of the other men, wiping the steel off on their clothes. He walked over to where Higgins lay, and with some difficulty pried the throwing star out of its niche of skull bone. He cleaned it on the lining of Higgins's coat, put it back in its pocket in his own coat, and stared down at the corpse.

"I never make a man a present of his life twice," he said out loud, so that Higgins's Kami, should it be hovering near the body, could take the message along as it began the journey into the destiny long ago decreed for it by the ex-foreman's *karma*.

Ki stepped over the body and made his way to the street. If anybody had heard Higgins's shot, or his scream, they were certainly lying low.

Ki would report the deaths to Town Marshal Farley as soon as possible. The marshal was most likely at the Cattlemen's Association.

Ki strode in that direction. The meeting was where he'd been going before those three had temporarily delayed him.

And Jessie would be waiting for him, Ki knew. He quickened his stride. He'd begun to feel lonesome and just a tiny bit sad. It was the way he always seemed to feel whenever he was away from Jessica Starbuck for very long.

The Cattlemen's Association building was lit up like a Christmas tree. Inside the large meeting hall, the leather armchairs and fine antique side tables had been haphazardly stacked against one of the wainscoted walls, to make room for the rows of backless benches brought in to seat the crowd. The benches filled the room except for a narrow aisle down the center, and the speaker's platform at the front.

The crowd filled the benches. The womenfolk had been left at home, but the cattlemen had brought their foremen and top hands for moral support and physical protection. After all, if a man like Alex Starbuck had been shot down like a dog, who was safe? The agitated voices of the cowboys and their bosses created a general din that echoed in the room and spilled through the open windows that faced Main Street.

Ki stood in the rear of the hall, watching the governor try to call for order. The governor was a tall and stately man, as befit his position, and was dressed in a blue pinstripe suit. He stood ramrod straight, and had a lion's mane of gray hair brushed straight back from his high forehead.

Ki, watching him pound his gavel in a futile attempt to command the room's attention, thought that the fellow looked just like a governor ought to; it was a shame that nobody was paying any attention to him.

The brace of Texas Rangers who stood slouched against the

wall behind the governor looked embarrassed. The governor's mouth was opening and closing, but Ki could not make out the words being intoned. Too many people were shouting and carrying on.

"Where's Jessica Starbuck!" a man yelled.

The governor flushed red and pounded his gavel.

Another of the ranchers jumped up on his bench to address himself to the entire room, totally ignoring the podium as he yelled, "We've got to face facts! Everybody here owes the Starbucks!"

"Please!" the governor shouted, attempting to drown him out. "Let's have order!"

"If Jessie's the new head of the Circle Star spread, she's the only one who can call the roundup on or off!" the man continued. Now he turned to point his finger at the podium. "If things are all right, Governor, where's Jessie?"

There was a chorus of supportive yells, and a smattering of applause. The speaker, pleased, looked as if he were about to continue, but a number of hands reached up to tug him down from the bench that had been his impromptu platform.

Ki, for his part, thought that the man had asked a good question. Just where was Jessie?

While the governor endlessly, impotently pounded his gavel, Ki, spying Farley's rotund form, began to shoulder through the crowd at the rear of the hall in order to make his way to the town marshal's side.

Farley saw him coming. His eyes were red from fatigue, with dark circles beneath them. Before Ki could say a word, Farley sighed, "She's over at Dr. Brown's office."

"What has happened to her?" Ki demanded, gripping Farley's arm.

"Easy!" Farley winced.

Ki let go, and fought to compose his emotions. "Tell me," he said quietly.

"She's all right!" Farley groaned, rubbing at his bicep. "Damn that grip of yours! Anyway, she's just there to hold Longarm's hand while he gets himself stitched up. He got into a ruckus with two hands you fired recently. Anyhow, one of them sliced Longarm's ribs up some—nothing serious—before he shot them both.

I had to go over to Canvas Town myself to straighten it all out. Hell, it's been a long day." Farley shook his head. "I'm satisfied it was self-defense," he added as an afterthought.

"Marshal Farley, I am sorry, but I must make your day even longer," Ki began. "Those two that Longarm shot worked for the foreman we fired, a man named Higgins."

"Yeah, so?" Farley looked suspiciously at Ki. "I've seen Higgins around. What of it?"

"Higgins and two others of his men are lying dead in the alley behind the Union Saloon."

"Oh, no . . ."

"I had to kill them," Ki said apologetically. "It was self-defense."

"That's what Longarm said. I swear, you two are starting to remind me of each other."

Ki only shrugged. He had no intention of telling Farley the obvious connection between the two attacks this night. Higgins had been working for Danzig, the blond man whom Ki had encountered upstairs at the Union, but this was information for Jessica and perhaps for Longarm, but definitely not for this town constable who had refused even to investigate the Alex Starbuck murder.

"Well, let's go clean up your mess," Farley muttered, walking. He looked back at Ki, who had not moved. "I said come on!"

"I think not, Marshal," Ki said absently. "I will remain here, to wait for Jessie."

"Now you listen here, son," Farley said, his temper rising and a note of warning creeping into his gruff voice. "I've got no patience for your high and mighty ways. I said you're coming, and that means—"

Ki cut him off, his black eyes flashing with amusement. "Marshal, I have been living in these parts for fifteen years. Do you really think I am going to hightail it out of town, or Texas, because I was forced to defend myself against three armed men in an alley?"

"I suppose if I insisted that you come along, or tried to pull my gun on you, you'd kill me," Farley demanded furiously. "Is that what you'd do, Ki?"

Wondering if the marshal meant to be funny, Ki merely

said, "Of course not, Farley." He paused. "I would probably only sprain your wrist."

"I believe you. Thanks for nothing!" Farley groused. "Well, you wait here, then."

"Yes, Marshal."

Farley whirled at what he had initially taken to be a sarcastic retort, but Ki's tone and expression seemed totally innocent and respectful. The marshal glanced dubiously at Ki's gunbelt. "How'd you kill those three? Surely not with that?" He pointed at Ki's holstered revolver. "Well?"

Ki gazed at Farley and blinked like a cat. "With blades," he said pleasantly. "Throwing knives."

"A funny fellow, just like Longarm," Farley mourned. Maybe that's why Jessie has taken such in interest in that deputy marshal.

Ki flinched.

"But at least Longarm has blood in his veins," Farley added in farewell. "He isn't a cold fish like you."

Farley wandered away, muttering imprecations beneath his breath. Ki did not notice. He was too busy thinking that the marshal's last hurled accusation had been ironic indeed! If he was such a cold fish, why was his blood just now boiling, his heart threatening to break in two at the thought of Jessie's being with Longarm?

And what right do I have to feel this way? he raged silently at himself. *I am pledged to defend her honor and her person . . .*

Just then, Jessie entered the hall, with Longarm at her side. The tall, broad-shouldered federal marshal was walking stiffly, but he seemed fit enough. Ki composed himself, gathering up the reins of his stampeding emotions. His duty had to come before his feelings. There was some sadness, and a little pain in that, but Ki could live his life no other way.

Chapter 13

The doc had not had to stitch the shallow wound on Longarm's side, but merely plaster down the raised flap of skin with a taped square of gauze. It was more of a scrape than a cut. Longarm had already tested his draw and found it to be unaffected. He'd be healed up in a week or so, and until then he'd just have to put up with an occasional twinge of soreness.

A week or so. Longarm pulled a cheroot from his coat pocket and stuck it into the corner of his mouth. He did not light it, but absently chewed on the end. In a week the army would be patrolling Texas, and he and Billy Vail would be looking for new jobs. Longarm was no closer to finding Alex Starbuck's murderers than he had been when he'd first arrived in Sarah. If the agitated mood of this crowd of cattlemen was any indication, martial law and a flood of bluecoats were just around the corner for Texas.

"There's Ki!" Jessica Starbuck said, and hurried off that way.

She was wearing a green tweed riding jacket, and a skirt made of the same material. Longarm felt himself stirring as, following along behind her, he watched the swaying of her hips. Damn, but the effect of this woman on him was purely magical! Her long, reddish-blond tresses had been pinned up on top of her head. Wisps of hair hung down from beneath her brown Stetson hat. Longarm found himself growing warm as he gazed at the nape of her neck, remembering how it had felt to press his lips against her soft skin during the height of their sexual abandon.

"We ran into Farley on our way in," Jessie blurted to Ki, taking his hands in her own. "Are you all right?"

Ki smiled. He found himself staring into the green pools of her eyes, and then glanced down to see her delicate hands sheltered in his own strong fingers. "I am unhurt," he said quietly, savoring the touch of her, and then letting go. He turned his glistening black eyes on Longarm. "You were wounded, I understand?"

Longarm shrugged. "Hell, my vest and shirt took more of a licking than I did," he remarked absently, still pondering the expression that had been on Ki's face when Jessie had touched him. "Doc Brown is about my size, and was able to lend me a fresh shirt." His vest had been ruined, so he'd transferred his watch, with its gold-washed chain, to a pocket of his frock coat, tucking his unclipped derringer behind the large square buckle of his gunbelt. It wasn't the best place in the world to stash an ace in the hole, but it would have to do until Longarm could replace his vest.

"I am very pleased that you survived tonight's trouble," Ki said evenly. He turned to Jessie. "I must speak with you."

"Reckon the fact that Higgins's gang split up to come at us *both* this evening was no coincidence," Longarm mused.

Ki ignored him. "Jessie?" He reached out to pull her away.

"You just don't let anything happen the easy way, do you old son?" Longarm swore softly. "So here it comes the hard way. Anything you found out tonight comes under the heading of official business."

Ki, said stubbornly, "Jessie, come with me."

"Son," Longarm warned, his eyes narrowing. "I don't have a lot of time to fool with you."

"Careful, Longarm," Ki seethed.

"And I don't have a lot of time to get to the bottom of this damned case. I don't intend to allow you and this young lady to withhold evidence."

"You have no choice in the matter, Longarm," Ki declared, his dark eyes flashing with fury barely controlled.

"I could arrest you, and get what I need to know out of you by making you cool your heels in Farley's jail."

"Incorrect, Longarm." Ki smiled thinly. "You could merely *try* to arrest me."

"Blustery talk, old son, but unless those fast hands of yours can stop lead—"

"Stop it! Both of you!" Jessie commanded, her hands on her hips. "Men! You're both acting like bulls pounding their skulls together to get command of the herd. And you're both as stupid!"

Longarm blushed, recognizing the truth in her words. But he also wondered how she could be so wise and so blind at the same time. *It's you Ki is wanting to impress, girl . . .*

"I haven't forgotten the wild-goose chase you sent me on in Canvas Town, Ki," Longarm said sullenly. He wasn't really all that angry; he would have done the same thing in Ki's position, but he wanted a concession from the man, and he was starting to understand how Ki's value system operated.

"Yes, I apologize." Ki looked down at his boots.

"Farley filled me in." Longarm pressed his momentary advantage. "I trusted you, and got ambushed because of it."

Ki felt very guilty indeed. His ploy had sent Longarm deep into Canvas Town, far from help. He hadn't meant for Longarm to be wounded, of course, but the fact remained that Ray and Musty might not have found him if Ki had not directed him into that wild part of town.

Longarm watched and waited as Ki worked his way through the ramifications of his actions. *Sometimes the only way to crack the toughest nuts is to let them ripen awhile in their own hard shells*, he thought. He struck a match and puffed alight his cheroot. He blew a shimmeringly perfect smoke ring, and winked at Jessica.

Ki was about to acquiesce to Longarm's wishes in partial payment of the debt of honor he had brought upon himself by deceiving the lawman. But when he looked up to see that big, swaggering, mustached Longarm flirting with Jessie, he felt blossoming in his chest an envy whose thorns were as sharp as the meanest Texas cactus. He stamped off, calling over his shoulder, "Jessie, I will wait to speak with you in the foyer."

Longarm watched him go. He shook his head and sighed.

"I just don't understand what's gotten into him," Jessie murmured.

"How can you *not*, woman," Longarm chuckled. "That man is plainly head-over-heels in love with you."

"No!" Jessie said, startled. "No, Longarm," she now said it slowly and seriously. "That can't be. You see, Ki and I, we grew up together. He came to my father when he was little more than a boy. His skills as a warrior were already honed. My father, worried about my personal safety, sort of hired Ki to be my companion and bodyguard. I was just a few years younger. Ki taught me some martial skills, and watched over me." She paused, to stare searchingly into Longarm's eyes. "To say that Ki was *hired* by my father grossly devalues the transaction. Ki pledged his services to my family, to me. There's no question that he would give his life for me if necessary."

"All the more reason for him to love you," Longarm insisted.

"That's *our* concept of love, but not the samurai's concept." Jessica blushed. "Ki and I could never have a real love affair. He could not allow that to happen. His sense of honor and duty would not allow it. Ki's love for me must be totally selfless. His life must be dedicated to protecting me. His vow of service to my father allows for no less than that."

"I'm beginning to understand," Longarm said slowly. "If he and you were, uh, *together* as man and woman, it'd confuse things. He'd be your lover, and not your . . . samurai."

"I love him very much," Jessie smiled. "But our love must always remain chaste. I would never tempt him, for I know that if Ki should lapse from the selfless love he holds for me, thereby allowing his vow of total protection of me to lapse, he'd be forced to commit *harakiri*."

"Excuse me?" Longarm blinked.

"*Harakiri* is another name for *seppuku*," Jessica said.

"Ki told me about *seppuku*," Longarm said. "That's suicide, right?"

Jessie nodded.

"But what's this other thing, this . . . 'hairy carey?' I disremember Ki saying anything about that."

"In Japan, it's a rather vulgar term," she said. "It means 'belly-slitting.'" Longarm frowned, puzzled, and she went on. "I don't really like to talk about it, but . . . well, in *seppuku* the suicide rips open his belly with his own sword and pulls out his entrails. Two long cuts, like this . . ." She drew her hand first across her own abdomen from one side to the other, then upward from pubis to breast bone.

Longarm grimaced and gave a low whistle. He said, "Lordy, these Japans don't do anything halfway, do they?"

"Only samurai are allowed this sort of death," Jessie replied. "It's considered a great honor to die this way. The physical pain means nothing. The greater pain would be in Ki's soul at the knowledge that he'd failed me, and failed my father. That would dishonor him and all his ancestors. The only way he could restore that honor would be through *seppuku*, but he would still have failed, and Ki would never allow himself knowingly to fail. For him to make love to me would be betrayal, the deepest of failure. No, it could never be. He is a true samurai, completely and utterly."

Jessie stood on tiptoe to peck a feather-light kiss upon his cheek. "I think it's not Ki's love for me you're concerned about," she teased sweetly. "I think you're just jealous."

"I won't deny it, Jessie," Longarm said softly, feeling his heart pounding. They stood like that for a moment, as close as a man and woman could be, fully dressed, and in public. Longarm grew dizzy from the perfume scent rising from her cleavage just visible where the undone buttons of her silk blouse allowed the sheer material to gape open. "Go find out what Ki has to tell you," he said, his voice sounding too thick in his ears.

Jessie laughed, and Longarm hurried her on her way with a light and loving pat across the round swell of her ass, so nicely but demurely emphasized by the snug green tweed of her skirt.

"Wait for me here," she winked.

Longarm watched the eyes of every man in the crowded room follow her walk, and he fought down the irrational jealousy he felt. *Relax, old 'son*, he chided himself. *There ain't enough bullets in the world to shoot all the men who find themselves mesmerized by Jessica Starbuck.* A lot of the cowboys lining the hard wooden benches were passing around pints and flasks of hard stuff. The governor was babbling on about something, up there at the podium, but everybody was clearly waiting for Jessie to reassure them concerning their financial and personal security. How the hell was this young woman ever going to handle it all? Longarm thought about her vow to continue the war begun so long ago between her father and his

European enemies. *What some man ought to do, old son, is rope in that female and make an honest wife out of her.* Longarm flicked the ash off of his cheroot. *That's what some damn fellow ought to do,* he thought. *Except that he'd then have to spend the rest of his life taming her—and Jessie would most likely give as good as she got. But hell, that don't sound like a bad life, at all.*

Of course, a man couldn't go traipsing around the West risking his life to enforce the law if he had a wife and maybe a family waiting for him at home. Billy Vail had often said that a man of Longarm's experience ought to be overseeing the work of others and not riding out himself to match his gun against riffraff.

"Whoa, old son!" Longarm laughed, so loudly that several nearby fellows turned to look at him. *Let's eat this apple one bite at a time,* he thought. If he didn't wrap up this case mighty quick, he and Billy would be looking for work, never mind promotions. With a sigh of relief, Longarm turned his thoughts back to the present. The depths of his feeling for Jessie surely did frighten him some.

She was talking with Ki now. As he waited for her to return, he thought over what she'd said.

Well, the girl was only partly right. She'd told Longarm a little something about Ki's past while they were waiting for Doc Brown to finish patching him up. Ki was only half Japanese, of course. His daddy was a true-blue, hot-blooded Yankee. Come to think of it, his Japanese mama couldn't have been an unemotional cold fish, not the way she'd chucked everything to marry the man she loved. Ki's sense of honor, his pride, his sternness—all of that had been forged into him by the harsh, stoic samurai code. But Ki's heart was as warm-blooded, passionate, and loving as any man's; Longarm could tell that just by looking at the fellow, and the way he looked at Jessie. What a war there was going on inside the man! And it was a war Ki could only lose. How long before his heart beat itself to tatters against the warriors steel-clad code, or before that code shattered into gleaming shards against Ki's heart?

Jessie came back into the hall, but there was a determined intensity in the way she brushed by Longarm on her way up the narrow aisle to the front of the room. She sashayed up that aisle like she owned the place. Thinking about it, Longarm was amused. Most likely she *did* own the place.

He began to elbow his way toward the front of the hall. He made good time. As usual, folks who had a mind to complain usually swallowed their gripes when they saw who it was that wanted to get by.

Ki seemed to materialize out of the mob just as Longarm reached the front of the hall. The expression on his face was earnest and troubled.

"Longarm, what I told her upset her greatly. I myself don't understand the significance—" He was about to say more, but both he and Longarm were distracted by a momentary disturbance.

One of the cowboys sitting in the front row reached out for a handful of Jessie's backside as she began to climb the steps leading up to the speakers' platform. The drover was clearly drunk, the situation far from serious, but both Longarm and Ki took an instinctive step forward to come to her aid. They were too slow.

Jessie, smiling, intercepted the cowboy's lurching grasp. She took his wrist in her two hands and twisted. The cowboy yelped in surprise as he found his entire body following the direction Jessie had set for him with just that one twist of his wrist. He landed flat on his back on the floor, looking up— totally flummoxed—into the laughing faces of his chums.

"It is called *jujutsu*," Ki said, anticipating Longarm's query. "A good defense form for a woman. Leverage means more than strength." He winked, "Perhaps *you* would like to learn *jujutsu*, eh, Longarm?"

"Old son," Longarm replied honestly, "I'd learn anything you've got to teach."

The governor was still trying for some semblance of order, but now the crowd was so far gone on whiskey that not even the appearance of Jessie on the platform could quiet it down.

"I'm sorry," flustered the governor to her, pounding his gavel.

"You've been away from the heartland too long," Jessie laughed. "That itty-bitty hammer of yours is going to get us no attention."

Before the nearby Texas Ranger could react, she'd plucked a revolver from one of the holsters crisscrossing his waist.

"This is a Texas gavel." She pointed the pistol toward the ceiling and fired a single shot. The blast echoed loudly.

The noise in the room ceased abruptly as all heads turned toward the platform. Jessie handed the smoking revolver back to the chagrined Ranger. There was an ugly black hole in the ceiling, and flakes of plaster were still wafting down like an early snowfall.

"Now that I've got your attention," Jessie began, shouting out her words loud and clear, "let me straighten a few things out, because right now I don't have a lot of time. It's no secret that my daddy staked about every one of you, and it's no secret that these days, now that my daddy's gone, you're all wondering just when those notes are going to be called due."

She paused then, to let every man in the hall ponder his own financial situation, and how he could keep his outfit going and still meet his commitments at the loan desk of the Starbuck bank.

"Miss Jessie! Your daddy understood that we'd need time to be able to pay it all back," one of the ranchers shouted out. "Give us a straight answer. When will those loans come due? I—"

A chorus of agreeing shouts drowned out the rest of what the man had to say. Jessie held up her hands to silence them.

"The answer is never." She watched the stunned men trying to absorb what they *thought* she'd said. "The Starbuck holdings belong to me now. Your notes belong to me. Just as my daddy built this town to honor my mama's memory, I'm going to do something to honor my daddy's memory. All of you will be receiving your notes back, and they'll be marked 'paid in full.'"

As the hall erupted into cheers, the governor, looking a sickly shade of green, hissed, "Young lady, this is not what I advised you to do this afternoon." He glanced uneasily at the crowd, but they were all shouting and stomping their boot heels to beat the band. There was no danger of their overhearing his stern lecture. "You have no right—" he started to say, but cut himself off as Jessica glanced sharply at him. "What I mean is, not even the Starbuck empire can function without the cooperation of local and federal government agencies."

"Is that a threat, Governor?" Jessie drawled.

"It's a warning," the man said grimly. "I already explained

all this to you. If you don't properly divest yourself of your Starbuck holdings, you're going to leave yourself wide open to the kind of senseless violence that struck down your father—"

"I've just found something out, Governor," Jessie cut him off. "I've just found out that my suspicions were correct, and that my father's death was far from 'senseless violence,' as you put it. My father was murdered in a premeditated act of revenge. I now know what manner of weapon was used against him, but that's not really my concern. I know who killed him, and I know exactly why. The violence is not going to stop, Governor, not after tonight, when I kill the man who was directly responsible for my father's death, and not for a long, long time. My father's enemies were—*are*—many. Their goal is to wipe all traces of the Starbuck name from the face of the earth. I will not let that happen."

The Governor, gone suddenly pale, opened his mouth to say something, but Jessie had turned back to the podium to face the crowd.

Longarm, standing just below them, had not been able to hear their exchange through the noise coming from behind him. But as he watched the governor stand sweating, looking for all the world like a hooked fish just pulled from the water, flopping about, totally out of its element, Longarm thought, *Gov, you may be wearing an expensive suit, and you may be the highest office holder within a thousand miles, but you've got the look I've seen on countless men, from cow thieves to murderers.*

"The governor seems to be troubled by something," Ki murmured beside him.

"He looks guilty as hell, don't he?" Longarm said through pursed lips. "Old son, that apple we've been nibbling has gotten pretty well gnawed down to the core. Just what the hell did you tell her?"

Before Ki could answer, Jessie began once again to address the crowd. "I ask only one thing in exchange: that we pull together to make the roundup the biggest and best ever, even by Texas standards!" After a roar of applause, she continued, "The cattle we sent East have been promised to Europe. We're going to help feed the world. Now there are some good old folks in Europe, folks like us, but there are also some who'd like to see our roundup fail, so that they could buy up our land. They're quite willing to let their own people go hungry if it'll mean our land values get depressed and we have to sell cheap, just to stay alive ourselves. It's damned villains like these folks I'm talking about that had my father killed, because they saw his death as the first step in establishing their own cattle spreads right here in Texas!"

"One of them fellas came 'round to talk to me, Jessie!" A rancher shouted. "A blond man, talked real funny. Hell, I thought I'd have to sell just to meet my debts—" He climbed unsteadily to his feet, obviously drunk. "Until tonight, that is. Ya-hoo!" He pulled his pistol, intending to blast a companion hole to the one Jessie had put in the ceiling, but as his gun bobbed and waved in drunken circles, less boisterous neighbors disarmed him.

"After the roundup, we'll all have our profits!" Jessie declared. "You'll all be able to put that money back into your outfits. Our herds will grow. We'll be able to keep what is ours, what we've worked for. Texas for Texans. Texas for America!"

This time the cheers that went up were deafening. Longarm, standing next to Ki, fought to make himself heard. "Son, you've got to fill me in on what's going on." Longarm watched the governor suddenly scurry from the stage. "Strange, you'd think a politico would want to stand up there absorbing some of that cheering and clapping."

Ki pointed. "Even his Texas Ranger guards have been taken by surprise."

Indeed, the two Rangers were still on the platform as the governor quickly descended the steps to disappear through a side door.

"He left like a man wanting to get away from something nasty that might be happening," Longarm mused. Right then he got one of those *feelings* down along his spine. A man couldn't learn to have those feelings; all he could do was survive enough sticky situations to develop the facility. "Ki! Get up there and get Jessie off the platform—" he began, but stopped. Ki couldn't hear him. The samurai had already launched himself toward the podium. Longarm saw Jessie's eyes lock on to the approaching form of her bodyguard. Her smile faded . . .

She scanned the faces of the crowd until she saw Longarm.

Then she pointed over Longarm's head, to the bank of opened windows. "There!" she screamed.

Longarm whirled, his Colt in his hand. Outside, in the dim glow of the street lamps, there sat mounted on a horse a figure garbed in a canvas duster. The long coat effectively hid his form. His hat was pulled down low over his brow, and he wore a bandanna mask over the bottom half of his face. Some sort of rifle was resting across his saddle, its barrel pointed toward the windows.

The mystery rider raised his weapon to his shoulder. Longarm did not have a clear shot; too many people were between him and those damned windows!

Then the rider fired his weapon. *And fired, and fired, and fired it—*

There was a high, chattering snarl as the weapon's muzzle spouted blue fire. The upper windowpanes rattled in their frames for a split second before the hail of bullets shattered them, spewing splinters and knifelike chunks of glass into the hall.

Longarm threw himself to the floor shouting, "Get down! Get down!" to whoever was still calm enough to listen. The men in the hall were tough, but none had ever experienced such firepower before. The gun kept on firing, chewing a line of bullet holes along the wainscoted walls, bursting wall-mounted oil lamps, so that flaming oil fell into the stacked furniture. Smoke and tongues of flame began to rise.

"Fire!" somebody screamed, only adding to the panic. The men, most of them drunk, were stumbling and falling to the floor, none of them hit, but all panic-striken as they waved their hands in front of them like picnickers trying to ward off a swarm of angry bees.

From out of the corner of his eye, Longarm saw Ki leap from the floor to the platform, easily clearing the six feet necessary to sail over it, scooping up Jessie as he began his descent to the other side. A split second later the firestorm of lead splintered the podium that Jessie had been standing behind into kindling. One of the Texas Rangers had thrown himself from the platform, but the other had both his guns drawn. He was a brave man, furiously returning the mystery rider's gunfire above the heads of the huddled crowd.

The line of bullet holes chewing up the paneling behind the platform abruptly dipped. The black holes being punched into the wall changed to red as they skipped across the chest of the Ranger. The man was jolted backward like a boxer absorbing a fast series of jabs. His revolvers clattered to the floor as he slumped against the wall to slide slowly down into a sitting position, his eyes wide and disbelieving as he stared first at the blood seeping from the holes scattered across his shirtfront, and then at nothing, as he died.

Ki, meanwhile, had Jessie safely cradled in his arms as he plunged downward toward the floor. At the last second Ki twisted around, so that Jessie was above him as they slammed onto the hard planking. He'd straight-armed her so that he'd absorbed every bit of the shock of their landing. A lesser man would have been knocked senseless from the impact. But Ki had her safely huddled in a far corner of the room before Jessie had even figured out just how she'd been spirited out of harms' way.

During the time the rider's weapon was trained on the hapless Texas Ranger, Longarm had begun to make a move for the door. The rider had spied Longarm's movement, and now the seemingly endless stream of bullets was chewing up the floorboards just behind the lawman's heels.

The rider had been aiming high on purpose, Longarm realized. He only tried to kill those who attempted to return his fire, or in some other way attack. Except for when he'd shot at Jessie. If Ki hadn't managed to snatch her up out of the way, the rounds that had turned the podium into sawdust and splinters would have cut her to pieces as well.

The fire, now burst into full flame. The meeting hall was fast filling up with choking smoke. If something wasn't done, and in a hurry, Longarm realized, a whole lot of smoke-blinded, half-drunk men would find themselves running like a herd of stampeding cattle, straight into that rider's incredible gun.

Longarm swung around the doorjamb, crouched low, feeling the hot wind of those rounds as they buzzed by, far, far too close. He took a bellyful of splinters—and was grateful that was all he took—as he slid along the wood-plank sidewalk, just trying to get to a place where he could at least fire back effectively.

Another came loping around the corner. He was dressed the same as the other man, and his weapon was the same as well.

The gun's wooden stock was shaped to hook over the user's shoulder, as it took both hands to fire the weapon. The riders, like Indians, used their knees to guide their horses. Two hand cranks, one on either side of the gun's breech, worked the action, reminding Longarm of the foot pedals on a bicycle he'd seen in Denver.

The two riders rode in a long circle, raking their guns back and forth along Main Street, shattering windows and tearing up walls and doors. A third rider joined them, just as the roof of the Cattlemen's building burst into high, orange flames.

The three riders—drunk with power—began whooping and shrieking like Comanches. Their guns chattered on, stripping the box-planted trees of their leaves and bark and boughs as their weapons filled the air with a high whine. The burning building cast an eerie, flickering crimson light on the scene as the flames crackled loudly. Sarah had been ravished. The town named after Starbuck's wife had been raped. Sarah, along with its fine schools, picket fences and proud, church steeple, had been turned into Hell.

Shiloh, was all Longarm could think as the sky became stained with flame. *Shiloh*, and how futile all attacks were against a Gatling gun . . .

Longarm, still pressed belly-down against the sidewalk, saw Farley and two of his deputies come running toward the riders. They were firing their revolvers as they ran, which meant that they didn't have a hope of hitting anything. One of the riders turned his weapon on the trio. The rounds kicked up dust, and then the two deputies began to flail the air, jerking and twitching like men suddenly struck with the palsey. The rider, laughing, flicked the barrel of his gun like a hose, and like a hose's nozzle, the gun sent a stream of lead splashing Farley's way. The town marshal's pistol went flying as he twirled in the air to come slamming down into the street.

All three riders had watched the local lawmen go down. Longarm used the distraction to launch himself off the elevated sidewalk and into the street, toward the men.

"There!" screamed one of the riders. "Get him!"

Longarm managed to snap off one shot before the hailstorm of bullets came his way. He backpedaled desperately, trying to outrun the rounds kicking up dust spouts inches in front of his toes. He lost his balance in his haste, and sprawled backward to land flat on his back, the wind knocked out of him, his Colt a yard out of reach.

The trio of riders cantered toward him. They turned their guns on a water trough just beside Longarm, laughing as their rounds send gouts of water into the air, turning the trough itself into a leaking sieve.

"That's what we're going to do to you, lawman," one of the men laughed. "Join the others," he told his two companions. "This part of town will burn good. Those poor bastards in the Cattlemen's building are fried crisp by now. They were afraid to come out, I guess."

The two riders turned their horses and rode away toward Canvas Town. The remaining man angled his weapon down toward Longarm.

The tall deputy fumbled for the derringer behind his gunbelt buckle, knowing, even as he did so, that his last-ditch attempt to save himself was useless. He shimmied back, desperate to put even another inch between himself and that deadly gun.

Laughing, the rider began to fire. He stitched the rounds into the dirt between Longarm's widespread legs, inching the barrel of the gun up so that it would eventually be centered on Longarm's crotch.

Longarm waited for the hot bite of lead to smash into his groin and then dance its way up his gut, chest, and head, to split him cleanly up the middle, just like a melon.

Chapter 14

"There!" Jessie cried, pointing over the heads of the crowd, toward the window.

Longarm had been shouting something, but Ki didn't bother to listen. He'd known that the only chance he had to get Jessie out of the hail of bullets was to perform the leaping part of a *mae-tobi-geri*, a flying, front foot-strike. Normally he would have kicked out twice at an opponent at the apex of his six-foot leap, but this time he stretched and arched his back like a pole vaulter, gaining precious inches of elevation. As he locked his arms around Jessie, he jackknifed his legs toward the far side of the platform. It was that power-snap wrung out of his thighs, knees, and calves that gave him the momentum to clear the platform's breadth, while his stomach and back muscles strained to lift her off her feet.

He'd landed hard on the wooden floor, taking the jarring impact of their combined weight along his spine. Jessie did not touch the floor until he set her down lightly. Tomorrow his flesh would be a mass of bruises, but bruises always healed. The throbbing pain in his shoulders and lower back he ignored. Pain was all in the mind . . .

The fire was licking up the walls and blackening the ceiling. The smoke was so thick that he could not see the far side of the hall. He saw Longarm dash through the door, drawing the awesome firepower of the rider along with him.

Jessie was coughing and rubbing at her eyes. "We've got to get these people out," she managed to say.

"You go out the back way," Ki ordered. "I will see to it that they follow. If they go out the front, they will be exposed to that gun."

"I'll help you," Jessie said.

"No!" Ki shouted. He leaped to his feet. Gathering a handful of the back of her tweed jacket, he lifted her up as if she were a kitten being hauled into the air by the scruff of its neck.

"Bully!" she pouted.

"Will you please go!"

"Longarm is out there by himself, Ki. You've got to—"

He nodded distractedly and propelled her on her way with a hard shove against the small of her back. When he saw that she was safely through the door that led to the back hallway of the building, and the rear door, he turned to ponder the situation in the crowded meeting room.

Several of the men, huddled beneath their benches, made a break for the front door. They ignored Ki's shouts, but he was able to cut them off. The first man, fear-crazed, tried to swing at Ki, who deflected the fellow's clumsy uppercut with a circular block and, as lightly as possible, drove his fist into the man's solar plexus.

The rancher collapsed back into the path of the other two men. As they hauled their friend to his feet, Ki said, "You will be shot if you go this way. Go out the back. It is safe!"

They nodded vaguely, and headed back the way Jessie had gone. Others, seeing what Ki had done, and hearing his explanation, turned toward the back door as well. A few stubborn souls still tried for the front door, but Ki stopped them by quickly whip-snapping burning pieces of furniture into the doorway, effectively sealing it off so that now there *was* no front door. Spreading the fire was of no concern to Ki. The flames had penetrated the walls, and had grown to claim the roof timbers. The building could not be saved.

Now that there was someone telling them what to do, the ranchers and cowboys filed out of the building, with few of them panicking.

Ki waited until the last of them were out of the room, then dived through one of the wide-open windows, the glass of which had been shattered away by the gunfire. He saw one of the riders mow down the deputies and Farley, and saw Longarm take advantage of the riders' distraction by rushing toward them.

It was a valiant attempt on Longarm's part, but a man can often be both brave and foolish at the same time. Longarm managed to squeeze off only one ineffective shot before he was swept off his feet by the return barrage of gunfire.

The three riders toyed with the marshal by shooting up a watering trough just beside him, and then two rode away, leaving one to finish the job. Ki saw Longarm kick his heels into the dust, trying for purchase to push himself away from the bullets rushing toward him between his legs.

For one moment Ki thought, *If I let him die, there will be no danger of his stealing away Jessie*—

The thought flickered through his mind even as his right hand automatically plucked the *shuriken* throwing blade from its sheath and hurled it at the rider's back.

His throw had been hurried, without proper time to aim. The blade missed the man's heart, burying itself high in the rider's left shoulder. Still, the shock and pain of feeling himself stabbed, forced the rider to take his hands from his weapon, so that it stopped firing. The gun did not fall to the ground. It looked to Ki as if it was hooked over the man's shoulders . . .

Ki reached for another *shuriken*, but before he could send it flying, the rider wheeled his horse hard around, and rode off in a flat-out run, squealing all the while like a scalded pig.

"You all right?" Ki asked when he reached Longarm.

"You saved my life," Longarm said as he got to his feet. "Another second, and—"

"I have merely repaid my debt of honor to you," Ki admonished, looking away. "Earlier this evening I got you into danger by sending you to Canvas Town. Now I have gotten you out of danger."

"Damn, old son," Longarm said dryly. "For a minute there, I thought it was because you liked me. I didn't know you were playing bank teller with that honor of yours."

Ki merely shrugged. "Let us see to Marshal Farley," he said. Longarm retrieved his Colt and followed Ki, muttering oaths beneath his breath.

Farley's two deputies were stone dead, but the town marshal had gotten off lucky. Only one of the .25-caliber rounds had hit him. He had a broken rib or two, but the round had been deflected outward so that the wound was clean. Doc Brown would have an easy time of it patching him up.

Ki helped Farley hobble along with them while Longarm gave him a clean handkerchief to press against his wound. They wanted to take the marshal directly to the doctor, but Farley would have none of that, not until he knew that everyone who had been in the Cattlemen's building was safe.

Now that the gunmen were gone, citizens were coming up for air. Bucket brigades were hastily organized—not to save the Cattlemen's building, for, as Ki had surmised, it was a lost cause. The bucket brigade worked hard just to keep the flames from spreading to the other nearby structures.

The men who had been at the meeting were sitting huddled behind the now-smoldering ruins of what had been their town's pride and joy. Their eyes were red from smoke, and they were tired, but unharmed. Farley's quick check showed that three men had lost their lives: his two deputies and one of the governor's Texas Rangers.

One other of Farley's deputies came running up, braking to a startled halt as he surveyed the destruction. "Jesus," he gasped. "Marshal Farley, you've been wounded!"

"I'm all right, Harry," Farley grumbled. "What's your report?"

"The rest of the town is all right," Harry muttered. "They kept their attack confined to Main Street and Canvas Town. Canvas Town has been torn up just about as bad as this. A few boys were hurt, but nobody's dead. Just about everybody, drunk or sober, had the presence of mind to hug the ground."

"Makes sense," Longarm observed.

"What does?" Farley asked sharply.

"The way they handled it," Longarm replied. "Some of them terrorize the cattlemen who do the hiring, and some scare the bejesus out of the boys who need the jobs. Reckon you'll find that a goodly number of those cowboys-for-hire are going to seek out healthier regions to make their living."

"The tactic of intimidation," Ki said quietly.

"It'll be harder for you ranchers to run your roundup without your free-lance drovers, right?" Longarm called out.

The men nodded, grumbling dejectedly. "It might just be damned near impossible," one of them offered harshly.

"Come on, now!" Longarm argued. "That's not Texas talk!" He looked around. They needed Jessie to inspire them. But where was she?

"Maybe we do need the army, or at least the Texas Rangers," another man said.

"Well now, the Rangers are an ungodly distance from Sarah," Longarm shouted. "Except for the two left who belong to the governor, and they've got to stick with him." He pulled out his wallet to show them all his badge. "But I'm federal, boys. Working out of Denver. We'll catch those bastards, that I promise!"

The men all looked up, clearly heartened by the fact that there was somebody to stand between them and the horror they'd just experienced.

"Longarm, I thought you wanted to remain undercover," Farley whispered.

Longarm shrugged. "Those two who braced me in Canvas Town knew I was a federal marshal. So did those riders just now. It seems the only folks who didn't know have been the good ones." He gave Farley a hard look. "I sort of thought it was you who spilled the beans."

"No way," said Farley indignantly.

Ki stepped between them. "I found out it was Higgins," he said. "He figured it out the day you rode with us to the Circle Star. He saw the U.S. brand on your horse."

"I see," Longarm smiled at Farley. "I owe you an apology."

"Forget it," Farley laughed, with no real humor. "I've got bigger things to worry about, like putting my town back together."

"It was brave of you to rush those riders," Longarm added.

"Bullshit, sonny," Farley spat back disgustedly. "It was plain stupid. The lives of those two men who got killed following my orders will be my sorrow to bear for a long, long time." He looked expectantly at Longarm. "Well, you're the ranking law. I don't know how to handle this. Should we form up a posse, or what?"

Just then the governor approached, followed by his two remaining Ranger bodyguards, who still had their guns drawn. "Terrible thing, terrible!" the politician muttered. "I hope no one besides my man was hurt."

"Two of mine, as well," Farley replied. "You can put your shooters away, boys," he told the Rangers. "Party's over."

"Where is Jessie?" Ki asked.

"She came our way," one of the Rangers said. "We had her horse with ours, and the governor's buggy. She took it and rode like the devil. Where, I can't say."

"I bet I know," Longarm said.

"She's trailing those riders, of course," Ki agreed. "We must get after her!"

"A posse it is, then," Farley said.

"No!" Longarm cut him off. "You boys all have horses?" he asked the ranchers.

"Ours were all in the stable," one of them shrugged. "If they're all right—"

"They are," Farley interjected. "We were by the hotel, and the stables are near there. Your animals weren't touched."

"Then you men guard your herds," Longarm said. "I can travel faster on my own." He paused. "Except that my horse was tied outside the saloon," he added.

"If it was that chestnut gelding with the McClellan saddle, you're out of luck," Farley said. "He was shot dead by those bastards, along with all the other mounts tied up along that stretch."

Ki swore softly. "My horse as well, then."

"Hell, boys, take two of ours," one of the ranchers said. Two drovers hurried off to retrieve Longarm's and Ki's gear in order to saddle up two other horses.

"How are you two going to face down all those men?" Farley demanded. "My deputy here just told me half a dozen men shot up Canvas Town. That makes at least nine of them, and all armed with those"—he looked helplessly about him—"whatever they are . . ." he trailed off.

"Coffee grinders," Ki said softly.

"Huh?" Farley looked confused.

"It does not matter at the moment," Ki continued. "We must either stop Jessie or rescue her if she has been captured. If they have her, a show of force would be useless. One or two men, who are clever, would be much more effective in safely freeing her." Ki looked at Longarm. "And saving Jessie is our first concern. Agreed?"

"Me and you," Longarm nodded. "Agreed."

As they started off, Longarm told the governor, "You'd better telegraph the army, after all. They can get here sooner than the Rangers."

The governor looked doubtful. "That would mean martial law, after all. I've made campaign promises . . ."

"You've got no choice," Longarm said impatiently. "Farley here doesn't have the manpower. The ranchers have to keep their cowboys watching over the herds in case those riders try to butcher the cattle with those"—he looked at Ki—"coffee grinders."

"Why would they want to do that?" the governor asked.

"To prevent the cattle from going to market, and in that way bankrupt the cattlemen," Ki said. "If tonight's attempt at terrorizing the ranchers fails, the next step may be simply to destroy the cattle."

"With those weapons, nine men could do it easy," Longarm muttered. "And I've got a nasty feeling there are more than nine."

"This is foolishness!" the governor exclaimed. "I suppose you believe that poppycock about Europeans trying to take over the cattle industry. That Jessie has some fool notion, and you boys believe her!"

"It is the truth," Ki said. "Earlier this evening I encountered one of the foreign men Jessie spoke of."

"Probably a businessman," the governor grumbled.

"This man and I struggled," Ki pressed on. "He was no businessman, but a professional killer. From him I obtained proof, which I turned over to Jessie."

"What kind of proof?" the governor asked cunningly.

"This I do not know," Ki admitted. "But the items had great significance to Jessie."

"There you are, men," the governor called out. "I wanted to look out for her because of my friendship with her daddy. But she's going too far—"

"Longarm, we are wasting time," Ki said disgustedly.

"Don't you use that tone of voice with *me*, boy," the governor warned.

"All of you!" Ki shouted, addressing the ranchers. "You know what you owe the Starbuck family." He turned to point at the governor. "You owe this man nothing!" Turning back, he shouted, "Will you stand by your debts of honor to Alex Starbuck, for what he has done for you in the past, and Jessie Starbuck, for what she has given you this night?"

As the ranchers nodded and called out their agreement, the governor told his two Rangers, "Arrest that slant-eyed bastard."

What happened next was too fast for even Longarm to see. One moment the two Rangers were bracketing Ki, and the next they were on the ground, one clutching at his throat and coughing, the other on his knees, his forehead pressed against the dirt, his arms wrapped around his rib cage. Ki had only seemed to flex his muscles; the hand movements had been just a blur . . .

The governor stood quietly as Ki plucked the Ranger's pistols from their holsters and tossed them away. The politician opened his mouth to say something, but then thought better of it.

"If you do not send for the army, as Longarm asks, I will come back and kill you," Ki said calmly. "You might surround yourself with guards. It will not help. At night, just before you drop off to sleep, you will hear a sound. You will open your eyes to see me standing over you." Ki smiled. "Do you understand, Governor?"

The Governor looked at Farley, who seemed suddenly occupied with his gunshot wound. He glanced at his two Ranger bodyguards. One seemed to have slipped into unconsciousness. The other tried to get to his feet, but then collapsed with a long, low moan of pain.

Licking his dry lips, the governor mumbled, "Why, yes, I understand."

"Longarm?" Ki walked away.

"Right. Farley, if he doesn't call in the army, you do it. We'll leave a trail a blind man could follow."

He followed Ki around to the front of the burned-out building, where their two horses were standing ready. Longarm checked his rifle to make sure it was in working order, and was about to mount up when Ki stopped him.

"I must return to the Circle Star to get what I need to battle these men effectively. For me to come with you now would be a waste. I have only a few throwing blades."

"What about that?" Longarm asked, pointing at Ki's gunbelt.

The samurai only shook his head. "I will be several hours behind you. Save her if you can, but if you get into trouble, know that I will save you both." He offered a sardonic grin. "This time, *I* will be your ace in the hole."

"Mine or Jessie's?" Longarm asked sarcastically.

Ki turned away in pain and consternation.

"You love her. Admit it!" Longarm demanded. He grabbed Ki's arm and spun him around. "You love her," he repeated softly. "And you know that I do as well. Admit it."

"My friend," Ki began plaintively, "that my jealousy is so apparent is my shame, but know that I blame you for nothing. It is not a matter of my admitting what is true, but of living the life I have been given. Your love for her steals nothing from me. I cannot be robbed of what I can never have. Longarm, save her if possible. In exchange I will rescue you both, even if it costs me my life."

Longarm watched him swing himself into his saddle. As Ki wheeled his horse around, he called down, "I swear to save you both." He rode off.

Longarm mounted up and loped off in the direction of the mystery riders. His one slim hope was that he could catch Jessie before the riders caught her. Men like those wouldn't kill a pretty girl like her right off. No, they would take their time . . .

If those riders have harmed a hair on Jessie's head, he vowed, *there won't be anything left of them for Ki by the time he catches up . . .*

Chapter 15

It had been easy for Jessica to slip away during the confusion. When the two riders rode out of town, she was mounted up and ready to follow them. She'd pulled her Colt.38 rig from her saddlebags, and strapped the gunbelt around her waist. In her riding jacket's pocket was the strange pistol Ki had earlier turned over to her, and that newspaper clipping that explained so much.

The clipping told of the origins of the awesome weaponry that had been turned upon her town; Longarm would be interested in that, no doubt, since it was now clear that those same guns had been used to cut down her father. But what was important to Jessie was that she now knew who had ordered those guns turned on her father.

Ki had missed it during his cursory examination of the foreign-made handgun, but that was understandable. A family crest, the symbol of European nobility, would mean nothing to a man raised in an Oriental culture. As for the initials WD, the monogram of ownership carved below the family crest, the design had been cleverly worked into the filigree, and besides, no one could know what those initals stood for. Her daddy had told no one but her, and she had told no one at all, not even Ki. That way, when the opportunity to avenge her father's death presented itself—as she'd always known it would—she would have time to kill the man before anyone interfered.

Time to kill the man, Jessie thought as her horse followed the trail through the dark night. But not much time. Both Ki and Longarm would be on her heels by now.

Ki and Longarm—she loved them both, in totally different ways. But neither of them could understand the depths of her passion concerning this feud that had destroyed the Starbuck family. She had to be the one to kill the blond man, the owner of the pistol. It was fitting. It was the wheel of *karma*, making one more complete cycle as it spun around and around, endlessly.

And after it's done? What then, Jessie? she asked herself. *You are a woman, made for love, not for killing . . .*

She slowed her mount, to ascertain that she was still on the trail of the riders. It wasn't hard. There was a sliver of moon to see by, and the riders, confident, had made no effort to camouflage their direction. Jessie knew the area surrounding the Circle Star spread. She had already surmised that the riders were heading toward an old grouping of buildings situated at the base of a marble quarry. The ramshackle compound of buildings, long abandoned, had once been occupied by stone cutters digging out the marble used in the construction of several buildings in Sarah. The marble had run out very quickly. Once sufficient stone had been dug out for Sarah's needs, the operation had been closed down. But there was wood for fires nearby, and a pure water well. It would be the ideal spot to hide a gang of men.

Jessie rode on. She had been careful earlier, letting the third rider pass her while she kept herself and her horse concealed. This third rider, once he'd joined the others up ahead, would make at least a half-dozen men she was following, and maybe more than that. She couldn't be sure how many horses were making the jumble of tracks, but she could certainly tell that the number was considerably greater than three . . .

When the third rider had passed, Jessie had heard him moaning as he tried to clutch at something sticking into the back of his shoulder. There was a dark, shiny patch running down the back of his canvas duster. It had looked like Ki's work.

That Ki would help Longarm, Jessie had no doubt. What she had told Longarm about her relationship with Ki was true. She looked up to and worshiped the man as if he were her older brother. But sisterly love was one thing, and passionate love was

quite another. Longarm was the only man she had ever truly
loved, as a woman . . .

Mrs. Custis Long . . . The thought made her giggle out loud.
She scolded herself for acting so silly while engaged in such a
dangerous activity as trailing a band of armed outlaws. That
alone was proof enough to her that Longarm had wrought
miraculous changes!

Mrs. Custis Long . . . Longarm wouldn't be an easy stallion
to rope, but if there was any woman on earth who could do it,
it would be Jessica Starbuck. She'd never known anyone
remotely like him, except for her father, perhaps, and of course
Ki. She'd let this vendetta rest in exchange for Custis Long's
love and companionship for the rest of her life—let it rest after
this last violent night, for she fully intended to avenge her
daddy's murder by the coming dawn. Then she would docilely
accept Longarm's rebuke and use her womanly wiles to turn
his anger around into passion. They could begin a new phase
in both their lives, leaving their days of hatred and violence
behind as they made love and began to make plans for their
future together.

Mrs. Custis Long . . . Lord, wouldn't that be something. Not
that there wouldn't be problems. A man like Longarm would
most likely stomp the first man who referred to him as Mr. Jessie
Starbuck, but after Longarm had taught all such men their manners, and told them that a fellow didn't need wealth to be a real
man, things would smooth down. But she'd still have to recon-
cile her role as this proud but poor man's wife with her duties
as the head of the Starbuck business empire.

One thing she could do would be to assign control of the
day-to-day decisions to her daddy's trusted advisors. Why not?
They were making most of the decisions now, she only reserving
the final say on the most important ones. She and Longarm could
concentrate on the cattle business. He knew cattle. He could take
the Circle Star over and run things, the way a man ought to . . .

Jessie giggled once again as she let her horse pick its way
along the narrow trail through a dense grove of pecan trees.
The biggest problem she and Longarm would have would be
managing to leave their bed long enough to see that business
was taken care of—

"You hold it right there, lady!" came a shout from Jessie's right.

She peered into the darkness, but whoever was calling to her had himself well hidden among the tree trunks and shadows of the night-dark grove. She set off at a gallop, her Colt .38 in her hand. Damn! She'd ridden right into a trap! Ridden into it mooning and daydreaming over her lover like some silly adolescent—

"I said hold it!" the man yelled at her. He was one of the riders dressed in a canvas duster, his hat pulled low, his face masked by a bandanna. That strange weapon that the newspaper article had dubbed a "coffee grinder" was resting across his saddle. The rider was not trying to kill her, but head her off.

"Back off, or I'll shoot!" Jessie warned.

The man just laughed. "Cool down, little lady," he said, smirking, as her horse instinctively slowed to avoid colliding with his.

"Laugh at me, and you're a dead man," Jessie swore. This was one of the men who had tried their best to destroy the town her father had built in her mother's memory. Who knew how many citizens of Sarah had been killed by this man alone? Who knew whether it wasn't this man who had willingly obeyed the order to ambush her father?

"Don't you threaten me, you bitch," the masked rider spat. "I know what you need." He reached out to grab the reins from her.

Jessie shot him once, in the chest. The man gasped in surprise, then fell off of his horse. One boot stayed caught in his stirrups, so that when his panicked horse trotted off, it dragged the rider's body behind it like a sack.

Another mystery rider broke cover to intercept her. His "coffee grinder" was also secured across his saddle, but he'd drawn his revolver from beneath his duster.

"Don't kill her!" somebody else shouted. "The boss wants her alive!"

Jessie leaned forward over her saddle and rode hard. Her one chance was to get through the grove and into open country where she could goad her horse into a flat-out run. She was lighter than the men pursuing her, and her horse was fresher. There was a good chance she could outrun them.

As the second rider closed in, Jessie fired at him. He

groaned, dropping his pistol as he slumped. His mount slowed in confusion as its reins went slack.

The end of the grove was in sight. Jessie began to think that she just might make it. No other riders were trying to stop her. She holstered her Colt and concentrated on riding.

Blue flame suddenly licked out. The harsh, nasty, chittering sound of a "coffee grinder" enveloped her, and her horse screamed in pain and terror as the bullets stitched along its belly and hindquarters, literally disemboweling it. Jessie kicked free of the stirrups as the horse, eyes rolling upward, began to stumble. She jumped clear as the horse somersaulted forward to crash to the ground. It quivered, its stiff legs kicking in the air, and then lay still.

Jessie broke her fall the way Ki had taught her, slapping the ground with her arm and keeping her body curved, to roll with the impact. The strong tweed cloth of her jacket and skirt, and her high leather boots, protected her from cuts and scrapes, but her momentum had been such that she lay stunned. She was conscious, but the wind had been knocked out of her. She protested feebly, and tried to struggle as men bent over her, stealing away her Colt and taking the foreign-made handgun from her jacket pocket.

"What are our losses?" muttered the man who seemed to be in charge of the party. Through dazed eyes, Jessie had a glimpse of him standing above her, wrapped in his duster, his weapon's long barrel jutting up into the sky.

"She killed the first and lung-shot the second," came an answering grumble from somewhere beyond her field of vision. "Damn, that girl can shoot."

Jessie smiled. "You bet I can," she began, but her voice faded; talking was just too much effort. She tried to hoist herself up on one elbow to get a better look at her captors, but even that slight movement set her head to spinning. She flopped back down and closed her eyes. The spinning increased, tightening into a fast downward spiral. The blackness behind her eyelids deepened—

Mrs. Custis Long, she mused giddily. Well, it looked as if thoughts of marriage had been a bit premature. *If you want me, you'd better save me, Longarm*, she thought, but then even thinking became too difficult, and she lapsed into a dream that faded into darkness . . .

"She's passed out," one of the men looking down at her said.

"Get her across one of the horses," the leader instructed. "One of you double up for the rest of the ride."

Two men hoisted Jessie's limp form up, and set her belly-down across a saddle. One of the men furtively tried to slide his hand beneath her skirt, but before he could, he felt a rough hand gripping his coat collar and pulling him backward.

"None of that now," the leader gruffly reprimanded. "You know he's waiting for her."

"Just wanted a little feel," the other rider shrugged.

"Is that what you want me to tell *him?*" the leader asked.

Shaking his head, the man hurried off. "Let's go, then," he said hastily.

"We'll have plenty of time for taking our pleasure after he talks to her." The leader pulled down his bandanna mask, to reveal a scarred, unshaven face and a mouthful of broken teeth just now split into a dog's grin. "He'll give her to us, till he's ready to slit her throat." He turned toward his own horse, calling out, "Let's ride!"

Chapter 16

Longarm rode hard until he came to the pecanwood grove. Even before he'd reached Jessie's shot horse, he'd smelled the harsh, throat-drying tang of cordite handing in the air.

He dismounted, pulling his Winchester from its saddle boot and levering a round into the chamber. Everything looked quiet, but he reckoned it had looked quiet to Alex Starbuck the day he was ambushed, and to Jessie, who, from the looks of things, had been ambushed just a short while ago. Alex Starbuck had been killed. Was Jessie dead?

Longarm felt a sick feeling building in the pit of his stomach.

Don't think about it that way! he told himself. He squared his shoulders. *Don't think about her that way.* Right now he had to be a professional manhunter, a lawman, just like always.

Over his years as a deputy U.S. marshal, Longarm had built up a tough shell to protect his own heart. Maybe Jessie was hurt—maybe she was even dead, he mused grimly as his eyes traced the line of bloody bullet holes puckering the horse's carcass. Maybe he himself felt like grieving.

But he wasn't going to. He was going to get on with doing his job. That was the difference between foolish amateurs like Jessie and Ki, and professionals like himself. A professional lawman knew enough not to take *anything* personally. A lawman couldn't afford to love anybody. Hell, he couldn't afford even to *like* anybody. People close to a lawman had a way of getting hurt, and the problem was compounded when those people were damned amateurs playing this professional's game of manhunting.

Jessie—an image of her as she'd been that one blissful night, in front of the fireplace, came into his mind. Longarm felt his loins stir. It made him want to laugh, or maybe cry, he wasn't sure which. He was surrounded by danger. He was forced to contemplate the awful possibility that she was dead or dying. He was a man who knew the many faces of death and violence better than he knew any man or woman. He lived by the gun, and he would most likely die by it, and yet—

And yet, as callous as he was trying to be, as cold and as cynical, just the thought of her, as she'd been that night in his arms, forced him to swell and fill the front of his pants. Just the thought of her proved to him that he was a flesh-and-blood man, alive, and that there was goodness in this hard-as-nails world . . .

She was not dead! Longarm suddenly knew it, the knowledge as certain as his ache to touch Jessie, to hold her in his arms. She was not dead, and so he would find her and have her again. And God help any man who had touched her . . .

Longarm froze as his horse whinnied softly, snorting and tossing its head. Now he suddenly knew something else, as well. He was not alone in this grove.

Horses had a way of calling to each other, especially at night, when the darkness combined with a steed's instinctive tendency to run with a herd, and in that way gain safety from the world of predators that craved horseflesh. His borrowed mount was an experienced cow pony, but it had already been panicked by the carrion smell of Jessie's dead horse.

Chances were, the horses of the ambushers surrounding him were not too thrilled about being in such close proximity to one of their own kind, dead. Longarm figured that there were at least two ambushers. In situations like this, two men had a way of comforting one another. One man alone, waiting in the darkness to ambush, had a way of becoming jumpy.

Longarm wanted to get it over with and done with. If he started things off, maybe he could get his bushwhackers to reveal their locations by returning his fire.

Longarm fired into the woods at random, at the same time crabbing sideways into the trees. He saw a flash of blue fire as one of those "coffee grinders" opened up, sending rounds tearing into the corpse of Jessie's horse. The gun was positioned across the trail directly opposite Longarm. The damn fool was counting on his awesome firepower to keep Longarm pinned down and unable to fire back. That tactic could work, but only if the gunner was positive as to the location of his target.

Longarm brought his rifle up to his shoulder and fired once, aiming just above the blue flicker coming from the weapon's barrel. He caught a glimpse of that flashing muzzle rising toward the night sky as the gunner fell back. Then the blue flame winked out and the chattering gunfire ceased.

Longarm caught only a glimpse of this because he'd already begun rolling fast away from his position. He was just in time, for three shots from a more conventional weapon, a rifle, plowed into the fallen tree trunk he'd been hiding behind. He saw the muzzle flash this time as well, but held off firing back. Chances were, the man had already moved from his position. If Longarm fired now, he'd hit nothing, and give away *his* new hiding spot.

There was another reason he did not fire back. He wanted one of these men alive, and he'd already shot the first. He needed to know what had happened to Jessie, where she'd been taken. Blindly following the trail left by the other riders' horses could easily lead him on a wild-goose chase, or right into another ambush.

He heard his man moving through the undergrowth. The fellow was trying to circle around him and come up from behind. Longarm began to move silently to cut across the other's path. He ran parallel to the trail, to avoid the chance of making any unnecessary noise.

The rounds thudded into a tree behind him, even as he heard that firecracker chatter. That damned gunner with the "coffee grinder" wasn't out of commission after all!

"Pin him down for me!" screamed the other ambusher. The man operating the "coffee grinder" answered by turning the cranks on his weapon. This time he restricted his fire to short bursts as he moved and bobbed, weaving in and out among the trees, so that Longarm did not have a steady target.

"There he is!" shouted the man across the road as he sent a burst of rounds Longarm's way. "Hurry up! Finish him off! I'm hurt bad! The bastard hit me before!"

Longarm rolled and twisted on his belly like a snake run over by a wagon. He tried to ignore the bullets kicking dirt into his face. *A miss is as good as a mile*, he reminded himself.

He twisted around as the man on his side of the grove came rushing at Longarm from behind. If Longarm fired at him, he'd exactly pinpoint his own position for the other gunner. Longarm was between the two men, cut off front and rear—

Longarm smiled. It just might work . . .

Leaving his rifle behind, Longarm hurled himself up to run toward the man who was rushing at him. Confused by Longarm's tactic, the man brought up his own rifle and levered off several rounds, but he'd aimed too high. Before he really knew what had happened, Longarm had managed to thrust himself beneath the other's field of fire.

Meanwhile, the man operating the "coffee grinder" was trying his best to cut Longarm down by sending a steady stream of fire after him. The bullets nipped at the lawman's heels like a pack of hungry wolves. The weapon fired fast, all right; what Longarm was hoping was that the hellish thing fired *too* fast.

The rifleman realized what was happening, and dropped his gun to wave in panic at his crony across the road, but it was too dark for the other man to see clearly. As Longarm veered sideways to dive into the brush, the hail of bullets continued along the trajectory he'd set.

"No! Stop!" wailed the rifleman as he zigged and zagged, trying to get out of the other's arc of fire, but he was too late, as was the gunner, who immediately stopped cranking his gun but not before several rounds had peppered his partner's torso. The man fell backwards to lay spread-eagled on the ground.

Longarm listened to the rattle coming from the shot man's chest, and had no doubt that the fellow was just moments away from dying. That left the gunner across the road.

Longarm prepared to move for his life as he called out, "Give it up!" He waited tensely, fully expecting to have to dodge another barrage, but none came. "I'm a federal marshal. You're alone now, and you're wounded! Let me help you!"

Longarm slid sideways to wait for an answer, but none came.

Damn, he thought, *hope the poor bastard hasn't gone and died on me.*

Off to his left, he heard his horse. The animal had trotted back the way they'd come at the first sound of gunfire. Now it was about fifty feet away. Longarm, his eyes grown accustomed to the darkness, could make out the horse's silhouette against the trail so fitfully lit by that miserly portion of moon. The horse seemed to have calmed a bit. It was beginning to browse the tender shoots beneath the trees that bordered the road.

The horse seemed no longer to feel the tension it had shown just before the gun battle had started. Sometimes an animal knew better than a man when the fight was all over and done with.

Longarm found splatters of blood where the gunner had been. He'd managed to drag himself and his "coffee grinder" off into the woods on his side of the road, but from the quantity of blood the man was losing, he wasn't going to get far. Longarm traced the man's path by following the trail of bent and crushed grass and undergrowth. The fellow was crawling, but Longarm kept his Colt ready and his concentration focused. A man didn't need much life left in him to let the hammer down on a revolver. More than one lawman had gotten himself killed by blundering into a dying outlaw's gunsights.

On the other hand, Longarm couldn't afford to close in on the man too slowly. The fellow might get to his horse and make a break for it, or he might curl up and die before Longarm had a chance to question him.

When he finally caught up to him, the fellow was sitting propped against a tree. He was wrapped in that same sort of canvas duster worn by the riders who'd attacked the town. The long coat didn't make the man look nearly as menacing as it had those others. This poor bastard looked like a collapsed rag doll. His knees were drawn up and his head was lowered, his hat tipped forward over his eyes, just like one of those Mexican fellows who liked to take a noontime siesta. Except that this man's siesta was going to last a long, long time.

The ambusher had lost his "coffee grinder," but he held a revolver loosely clasped in his right hand. At the sound of Longarm's approach, he raised the handgun to wave it in the marshal's general direction.

"Throw it away, old son," Longarm told him gently. He kept his Colt centered on the huddled form.

The man did throw it away, quickly and briskly, as if getting rid of his gun had been a great idea he'd been waiting for somebody to suggest. "Good riddance—" he began to grumble, but whatever else he wanted to say was lost in a fit of coughing and groaning.

Longarm crouched down beside the man, and quickly checked him over for hidden weapons. To do that, he had to open the man's duster, and that revealed the full extent of his gunshot wound. The .44 slug had caught the man full in the belly. He was as good as buried.

"How am I, lawman?" the ambusher asked craftily. "Am I going to make it?"

"I'd say so," Longarm nodded. "You'll be fine."

"Then I'd say you're a fool or a liar." The man turned his head to spit out a mouthful of blood. "And from the way you foxed me and Terry, you sure ain't a fool . . ."

"Neither are you, old son."

"My name's Lucas Conrad," the man said. "Make sure they get it right on my stone." He peered up at Longarm's face. "Just who the hell are you that killed both me and Terry?"

"My name's Custis Long. I'm a deputy U.S. marshal. Lucas, we both know you ain't got a lot of time left. Tell me what's happened to Jessie Starbuck. Where has she been taken?"

"U.S. marshal . . . Shit! They must of known . . . and they only left us two to stop you. They said it was going to be that Chinese fellow—"

"Japanese, half Japanese," Longarm corrected. "He's a man who deserves to be called what he is, just like you deserve your rightful name on your stone."

"Reckon so, Long, reckon so . . ." Lucas laughed weakly. "Or maybe a man just naturally feels generous when he knows he's dying. Say, you did kill Terry?"

"You killed him," Longarm replied.

"Maybe so," Lucas agreed resignedly. "But you tricked me into it. Them 'coffee grinders' work real good, but I reckon they ain't meant for close-in, eye-to-eye fighting."

"Where's the gun?" Longarm asked. "I wouldn't mind taking a look at it."

"Don't know," Lucas muttered. "Heavy bastard. I left it in the woods somewhere after Terry got killed. Don't matter, though. Danzig's got twenty-five of them tucked away, every one of them hand-forged by that fellow Brader . . ." After another coughing spasm, Lucas continued, "There's twenty-five men . . . well, maybe just twenty now . . . but all of them are gunslicks brought in from other parts of the country. Me, and Terry over yonder, we was just cowboys who got in over our heads. Maybe that's why they picked us to stay behind and cover the trail . . ."

"They made a bad mistake, then," Longarm said. "You leave your best, not your worst. I'll make them pay for what they did to you, Lucas." He then added politely, "And I'm rightful sorry that I've killed you like I have."

"Don't hold no grudge agin you, Long," Lucas shrugged. "A man decides to play poker, he can't go blaming the other boys for wanting to win. Say, Marshal, you got a smoke on you?"

Longarm gave him a cheroot, and struck a match to light it. As Lucas inhaled, he was again struck by a fit of coughing. This time, Longarm thought it was the end. The man's eyes fluttered, and his breathing became irregular.

"The girl," Longarm demanded. "Is she all right? Where'd they take her?"

Lucas snorted. "All right! She's a damn sight better than all right. Pretty thing, but powerful ornery. She killed two of us before we cut her horse out from under her. Danzig—he's that foreign fellow, hard to understand him—anyway, Danzig wanted her taken alive . . ." Lucas paused.

"Say what you've got on your mind, Lucas," Longarm coaxed. "I don't hold you responsible for none of it. Maybe if you tell me, the Lord will look favorable on you. It's His law you're going to be judged by."

"You believe in the Lord?" Lucas asked softly.

"Don't rightly know if I do, old son," Longarm answered truthfully. "But then again, I've never had a .44 slug nested in my belly."

Lucas laughed. "Lead does have a way of bringing a man around to the religious way of thinking . . ." The cheroot fell from his lips as he wrapped his arms about himself and squeezed tight. "Oh, Jesus, Long. It hurts something awful!"

"Say what you've got to say," Longarm urged. "Before it's too late!"

"It's that this foreign-born fellow, Danzig, hates that girl something *fierce*. He wanted her taken alive so that he could kill her himself. I almost don't mind dying now, 'cause I ain't sure I would've had the stomach for what's going to happen to that little lady. Danzig's got some old boys working for him who've been promised a go-round with her before Danzig kills her. Those boys don't mind cutting up an unwilling gal to make her lay still, you know, Long? Hell, those kind of men *like* it when they can mix some serious hurting in with their loving."

"Where did they take her?" Longarm asked through clenched teeth.

"An old quarry set in among a bunch of hills. You'll hit it right enough, if you just follow along this here trail."

"Don't sound like Danzig is too worried about being tracked down," Longarm mused out loud. "Now, twenty-odd men armed with those 'coffee grinders' could most likely hold off any local opposition, but not the army . . ."

Longarm glanced at Lucas for his opinion, but the man was all finished talking. His breath came slowly, and then faded altogether in one long, hoarse exhalation. Longarm gently closed the dead man's eyes and stood up.

"Well, Lucas, what I think is this. Your ex-boss ain't worried about the army because he knows it ain't coming. I'm starting to smell a rat in this here situation, and I'm starting to think I know who it is. I'm going to need your duster, old son. I mean to get near enough to that quarry where they've got Jessie without starting an all-out shooting war . . ."

He stripped the man of his long canvas coat, and wiped off as much of the blood as he could with handfuls of leaves. "Lucas Conrad, I do pledge that if I live through this, I'll see to it that you get your headstone, with your name carved on it all right and proper. Rest easy, old son. You helped me right fine."

Longarm turned and walked back through the woods to gather up his Winchester. He never even paused to examine the body of the man named Terry, but simply walked on toward his horse. The duster that would be his ticket to reaching Jessica was folded over his arm.

His plan was to dress himself up in the coat and identify himself as Lucas Conrad to whatever sentries were on duty. Chances were good that he could pull the ruse off long enough—in the darkness—either to get past the guards or else take them out quietly, so as not to alert the whole camp.

As he approached his horse, the animal turned its head in the direction opposite him, the way out of the grove. Longarm, eyes narrowed, stood quietly. *There couldn't be more ambushers around*, he decided. *They would've gotten mixed in with the fighting by now, for chrissakes.*

"You're just talking to Lucas and Terry's horses. I hope," Longarm muttered. He wished he still had the army gelding. He's spent some time with that horse, and had been learning how to read the signals it gave. This animal was still a puzzle to him.

He hauled himself up into his saddle and goaded his horse hard toward the encampment Lucas had talked about. He had to hurry. There was no telling when this Danzig character would decide to throw Jessie to his dogs. He hated her, Lucas had said. Hated her so much that he wanted to be the one to actually kill her. And Jessie was looking to kill the man who'd done in her father. What was the link between these two? Were they both just caught up in this generation-spanning feud? Was Danzig just a soldier fighting for the other side? Or did he have a personal reason for wanting her dead?

Just as Longarm reached the end of the grove, he saw the flickers of movement on either side of him in the shadows. He pulled hard on his mount's reins, twisting the horse sideways and forcing it to rear up, but it was far too late to try and make a break for it back the way he'd come.

Longarm heard the reedy whistling sound as the lariats came drifting down, their loops cinching tight around him, pinning his arms to his sides. The two cowboys dressed in canvas dusters kneed their horses out of the woods to trot backward, jerking upon their ropes as they rode. Longarm was jolted out of his saddle. He hit the ground hard, and was dragged, jouncing and jolting along behind the two, for perhaps one hundred feet before there came a shouted command for the two riders to stop.

Longarm, only half conscious, heard the sound of horses' hooves approaching. He tried to move his arms to reach his Colt, but the lariat loops were being kept tight. He was helpless.

"We will not skin him now, but save that pleasure for later," said a thickly accented voice.

Longarm stared up into a face topped with a close-cropped fringe of golden blond hair. The man's eyes were pale blue, and a thin red scar ran the length of one cheek. This man did not wear one of the canvas dusters, but instead a suit of black.

"Herr Long," the blond man began, "do you play chess?"

Longarm let his eyes close. "You're Danzig, right?"

"At your service." Danzig straightened up to click his heels. "Do you play?"

"I have," Longarm muttered. "It ain't my favorite game. How long you been waiting for me?"

"Since you arrived. I placed my two men back there to occupy you for a while, and then lull you into thinking you were in control. I knew you'd easily defeat them."

"So you sacrificed them," Longarm said slowly. "I get it. You sacrificed a couple of pawns."

"Precisely, Herr Long!" Danzig beamed. "I have sacrificed two pawns to capture the first of Jessica Starbuck's two knights!"

"And the other?" Longarm asked.

"The Oriental," Danzig said grimly. "I have a special score to settle with him. I will take him alive, just as I have taken you."

"Why go to all that trouble?" Longarm began.

"To hurt her!" Danzig cut him off. "To make her suffer. I want her to know that everyone she cares for has been destroyed by Wulf Danzig. I want her to know that I have won, that I have wiped the scourge that is the Starbuck family from the face of the earth. Then, and only then, shall I give her to my men, before I personally slit her throat."

"Herr Danzig?"

"*Ja*, Herr Long?"

"I'm starting to understand why everybody thinks you're such an asshole—"

Danzig kicked out savagely, the tip of his boot thudding against Longarm's head. He brought his foot back to kick again at the still form, but hesitated and then got control of himself.

"I must not kill him too soon," Danzig growled. "You two! Take his gunbelt and his coat. Search him carefully for hidden weapons. Hurry!" He smiled. "Jessica is waiting for her knight to arrive. We must not disappoint her!"

Chapter 17

Longarm opened his eyes to see Jessica's face just above his. She was staring down at him with concern. He was lying stretched out on the floor. Jessie was cradling his head in her lap and pressing a cool, damp cloth to his forehead.

He tried to sit up, but the pain that began throbbing in his temples forced him right back down. He tensed his neck and shoulders against the worst of it, and once it had passed, he allowed his head to nestle upon Jessie's soft, warm lap.

"Rest easy," she soothed. She dipped the cloth into a pan of water, then wrung it out before replacing it across his forehead. "You've got a bad bruise. "She traced it lightly where the discoloration ran along the front of his ear, but even that made him wince. "Sorry. There's no bleeding, but you've been unconscious since they brought you here."

"How long . . ." Longarm paused to clear his throat. "How—"

"The whole night. It's about ten in the morning. You kept going in and out . . ."

"Damn." Longarm sat up again, but this time very slowly. He took the cloth from Jessie and gingerly dabbed at his head. "Owww! And my side hurts too . . ." He looked around. They were in the one windowless corner of what seemed to be an old supply shack. Around them, locking them in, were two floor-to-ceiling partitions of steel grating. The door to this cage was held shut by a short length of chain and a padlock. The other walls had windows, and pegs from which hung saws and rope, picks and shovels, buckets and mallets, and other tools and hardware. All of it looked rusty, as if it had been out of service for a long time.

"Any water to drink?" he asked.

Jessie pointed him toward a bucket in which a ladle floated. Longarm drank deeply, then poured a cup of the cool, fresh water over his head, to refresh himself and wash away the last of the cobwebs.

"Where are we?"

"At an abandoned stonecutting quarry," Jessie explained. "This particular building was their tool shed, and in this cage they kept the payroll and stonecutters' valuables."

"When they brought you here, were you able to get an idea of the layout?" Longarm demanded. He'd gone to the door of the wire cage to examine the padlock.

"Well, I was knocked out when they—"

"Are you all right?" Longarm asked anxiously.

"Shhh," Jessie scolded. "I know the layout of the compound. I've been here countless times. Used to play here as a little girl, before my father got wind of it. He considered all these old buildings too dangerous. Near this building is a cookhouse with a well in back, another shack like this where they used to store blasting powder, a long, bar-racks-style bunkhouse, an office, and a stable. At one time this place housed fifty men, but I doubt if there are that many here now."

"Between twenty and twenty-five," Longarm said. "But most of them are professionals. Gunmen hired and brought here by Wulf Danzig." Longarm glared at her. "Just who the hell is this jasper? Why'd you chase after him in the first place?"

"Why don't I start at the beginning," Jessie said mildly. "Did Ki tell you about the things he gave me just before the meeting began?"

"No, only that they meant something to you, but he didn't know what." Longarm reached for a cheroot, and realized his coat was gone, as well as his gunbelt and derringer. His pocket knife was in his coat, as well. Its second blade, filed down into a pick, would have made short work of that padlock.

"He brought me a pistol and a newspaper clipping. The

clipping was in German, and the pistol would have meant nothing to anyone but me. I've seen this model of pistol before. Have you ever heard of the Mauser brothers?"

Longarm was about to shake his head, but decided against it. "What do they have to do with Danzig?"

"Well, they're considered among the finest gunsmiths of Europe. The pistol Ki had brought me was a Mauser. It's a model of revolver called the Zig-Zag, because of a groove etched into the cylinder. A pin on the gun's frame travels along this zigzag groove, rotating the cylinder as the pistol is fired. The zig zag is a popular gun. The Mauser brothers' designs are as common in Europe as Colt's are in America. But this particular Mauser was a special edition, commissioned by one family. When I saw the gun, there was no mistaking the special finish, the custom filigree work on the grips not to mention the family crest or the individual monogram of the owner."

"The Danzig family," Longarm mused. "And I assume you knew this weapon belonged to Wulf Danzig?"

"Yes." Jessie's eyes darkened to a hue resembling the Texas sky when it is suddenly overwhelmed by gray storm clouds. "Wulf Danzig, the man responsible for my father's death."

"I still don't understand," Longarm complained. "What meaning did this special-edition Mauser have for you? Why do you and Danzig hate each other so?"

"There's a pistol just like Wulf Danzig's in my father's gun collection," Jessie said. "Remember that I told you my father had killed a young fop in Europe? A young man who was the son of the baron who had ordered the runaway-carriage attack?"

"That was the incident that took your mother's life," Longarm said quietly. "Your father killed the man's son for revenge, just before his own ship set sail. He had the boy's monogrammed handkerchief sent to the grieving father, along with a Starbuck business card."

"My father took something from that young fop besides his handkerchief. He took the man's pistol. It was a Mauser Zig-Zag, a pistol identical to the one Ki brought me, except for the monogram. The initials on my father's Mauser are KD, for Kurt Danzig."

"And Wulff Danzig—" Longarm began.

"Is Kurt Danzig's son. He was just a child when my father took his father's life."

"To avenge your mother's death," Longarm concluded. "And now Wulf Danzig has killed *your* father to avenge his *own* father's death, and now he wants to kill you, as well."

"The feud continues," Jessica mourned. "The wheel spins around and around." She reached out to press her fingers against his bearded cheek. "I thought loving you could make it end, but it never will, not until the last Starbuck is dead."

"Or the last Danzig," Longarm said cynically. "The Starbucks ain't exactly been innocent victims. Up till now, your family has given as good as it got."

Jessie frowned. "It will get worse. Danzig wants me dead for personal reasons, but the people for whom he is working are very pragmatic."

"Because of that book your father left you," Longarm said sadly. "Because of that book they figure you're dangerous."

"They know I intend to use it to foil and frustrate every one of their schemes to expand their influence in this country. They know I will fight them the way my daddy fought them."

"Well, right now Danzig's got us," Longarm reminded her. "What was the newspaper clipping?"

"I've still got that," Jessie said, digging into her skirt pocket to extract the folded square of newsprint. "It tells of one John Brader, an expatriate American gunsmith who sold his Gatling-style gun to the—"

Jessie broke off as the door to the shack swung open. In stepped Danzig, accompanied by a short, fat, balding man dressed in a blue velvet suit and a garish satin vest.

"That's John Brader," Jessie announced.

"Now how did she know that?" the fat man wondered out loud to Danzig.

Jessie held up the clipping, then balled it up and dropped it to the floor.

"Well, you're a rude girl," Brader frowned. "Never mind that clipping. I have extras."

Longarm took in the gray wisps of Brader's hair, his glinting spectacles, his blunt, callused fingers, and the sharp tang of cordite that seemed to emanate from his skin and clothes. "You're the man responsible for these 'coffee grinders,' I take it?"

"Indeed I am, young man," Brader beamed.

"But you're American," Longarm said. "Why are you working for a foreign power?

Danzig laughed. "Go on, Herr Brader. Tell your story," he coaxed, his blue eyes lit with malice.

"I'll have you know, Deputy Long, that I gave my country every opportunity to appreciate me," Brader began. "I was an officer of the Union Army during the War. Because of my experience and expertise in weaponry, the Army saw fit to call upon me to evaluate Richard Gatling's designs. The Gatling gun was clever, that I will concede," he sniffed, hooking his broad thumbs into his vest. "But nothing I couldn't beat on my worst day."

"So why *didn't* you beat it?" Longarm demanded.

"I did! I did beat it! I worked on my designs until I had a gun comparable to Gatling's in every way. I used every cent I had to build my prototypes. They were the same weight as Gatling's, used the same ammunition, but they could outshoot anything he had to offer. They were more reliable as well, Deputy. My guns didn't jam nearly as often as *his*."

"This was right after the War, I take it," Longarm interjected. "Bad time to try and peddle armaments." He shrugged.

"I demonstrated my prototypes to the army and the navy." Brader stopped. He was shaking with fury. "The United States government, Deputy—your employer—was not interested in what I had to offer them. They came up with some cock-and-bull story about having already spent their budget on building up an armory of Gatling guns. But I didn't believe that. I knew that someone, somewhere, had been paid off. It was bribery and corruption working against me! There could be no other explanation as to why my far superior designs were turned down!"

Longarm said wearily, "Your designs were most likely turned down for exactly the reasons the government gave you."

"Bribery, corruption," Brader staunchly insisted.

"Bad timing, you mean," Longarm said. "Stubborn stupidity on your part." Longarm laughed. "If you were in the service, you should have known better than to try to interest a peacetime government in expensive weaponry. What did you think they would do, throw away all those Gatlings they'd already bought?" Longarm's expression turned to one of disgust. "And for all of your bragging and crowing, you let that one disappointment defeat you."

"No I didn't!" Brader snarled. "I took my plans and prototypes to Europe. They appreciated me! The British Royal Navy bought my guns, and other armed forces are even now getting ready to commit themselves to large purchases."

"Let me guess," Longarm said. "Danzig's organization has generously decided to fund your factories, am I right?"

"That is correct," Danzig said stiffly.

"And what about the 'coffee grinders'?" Longarm asked. "Aren't you going to give your own government first crack at the plans for those, Brader?"

"Actually, no plans exist," Brader said slyly. He tapped one finger against his bald dome. "Except up here, that is. Oh, there might be some specifications and parts lists lying around somewhere, but they'd be meaningless without my overview. No government has yet seen my guns. No one even knows about them, except those who may have seen them in action, and Danzig here. He furnished me the funds to hand-build my prototypes. I personally built every 'coffee grinder' we have, and they are all here."

Danzig rested his hand on Brader's shoulder. "It is the innovation of the century," he said in genuine admiration. "Essentially, it is a one-man Gatling—"

Brader shrugged off Danzig's hand and began to pout like a small boy.

"Pardon, Herr Brader," Danzig smiled. "What I meant to say is that it is essentially a one-man Brader gun."

"Damn right!" Brader declared. "I reduced the weapon's weight by chambering it for a small, .25-caliber round—after all, making lots of little holes in a man is the same as making one big one—and by holding the number of barrels down to just two. The cranks are opposed, so that when one barrel is firing, the other is ejecting its spent casing. A magazine fits into the weapon's breech. The gun weighs no more than two Winchesters—certainly a reasonable enough weight—but the fact the gun hooks over the user's shoulders helps to make it even easier to carry and fire. With my gun, one man has the firepower of ten men, and ten men have the firepower of one hundred!"

Danzig laughed. "We have twenty-five of these weapons, Herr Long, and enough ammunition and magazines for each."

"Enough to do what?" Longarm replied. "What do you think you're going to do with your nasty toys? Take over Texas?"

"In a manner of speaking," Danzig said.

"Never happen," Longarm said flatly. "Twenty or twenty-five men, even armed with those gadgets could never hold the entire state."

"They don't have to," Jessie broke in. "They don't have to *steal Texas, Longarm*," she explained. "They can buy it, lock, stock, and barrel."

"An apt phrase." Danzig ducked his head in appreciation. "You are indeed your father's daughter."

"As you are your father's son," Jessie said evenly. She turned to Longarm. "They can keep the cattle from reaching market, which would mean the ranchers would not get paid."

"That would mean they could not meet their obligations on the notes held by the Starbuck bank in Sarah," Danzig added. "Their land, their herds, their businesses—all of which they have put up as collateral—will be seized."

"Except that Jessie freed the ranchers of their obligations," Longarm pointed out.

"Verbally, perhaps," Danzig shrugged. "But she did not put anything to that effect down on paper, am I correct?" The Prussian looked at Jessie, who sighed and looked away.

"And now she never shall. You must realize that neither of you will leave this place alive," Danzig said.

"I think we will, Danzig," Longarm shot back. "I'm a federal deputy marshal. I turn up missing, and folks start to look for me."

"Not this time, Herr Long."

"I left instructions that the army be sent for."

"The instructions will not be followed, Herr Long."

Brader giggled. "They still don't understand," he said.

"Understand what?" Jessie asked slowly.

"That the governor himself is in cahoots with these two," Longarm said grimly. "It fits, Jessie. Why he pulled the strings way back in the beginning to keep the army out of the area, why he's shown such an interest in your business affairs."

"Oh, Custis," Jessie said faintly. "I've given him power of attorney—"

"The governor was in on it from the beginning, all right," Brader confirmed. "It seems your daddy had decided—rightly—that the governor would make a lousy senator. So the governor helped us get rid of Alex Starbuck, in exchange for financial backing for his campaign."

"He has the connections to see to it that he becomes the executor of your estate, Jessica," Danzig said. He will see to it that the ranchers' holding are foreclosed, and that they are sold to my people at a fraction of their true worth. We will have control of Texas's cattle industry, a foothold in American commerce, and a senator who will do our bidding from that point on." Danzig smiled. "He is a handsome, articulate man, the governor is. Perhaps one day he will be your country's President."

"And what do you and Brader get out of this?" Longarm asked.

"Brader gets wealth, and revenge on a country that spurned his genius," Danzig replied. "I will also receive wealth, but more importantly, I will have the satisfaction of knowing that I was instrumental in grinding the Starbucks into extinction. Not only will Jessie die by my hand, but the empire her father built will, for all intents and purposes, fall into the hands of her father's enemies. I will live in your father's home, Jessie," he continued, staring at her with a mocking grin. "I will control the governor as if he were a puppet, and I will rule over your father's people and his town."

"Brader, don't spend your money yet," Longarm snarled. "And you, you Prussian fruitcake," he spat, addressing Danzig. "You haven't won yet."

Danzig paled with fury. His eyes frosted over like ice, and the long scar down his cheek pulsed visibly. "I could kill you both right now," he said. "But I will wait until the Oriental is caught. I want to see the sorrow in *her* eyes when you and he beg for mercy. I want to see her cry when I kill both of you." Danzig moved closer to the wire mesh. "Then, Long, do you know what I shall do with her? I shall give her to my men to be used like a whore!"

"That's because he can't do the job himself," Jessie laughed scornfully. "And he'd better not try, or I'll—"

But Danzig, sputtering incoherently, had turned on his heel to stride out of the shack. Brader looked reproachfully at Jessica.

"You mustn't make him angry," the inventor warned. "He can be very cruel indeed if he's angered."

"He might kill us twice," Longarm said laconically. "You're as nutty as he is, Brader. Run along."

"He can make it *seem* like he's killed you twice," Brader squeaked in rage. "He can make it feel like you've died a thousand deaths. And I hope he does!" With that, the short, fat man hurried out of the shack, shutting the door behind him.

Longarm turned to Jessie and enfolded her in his arms. "You were great."

"All show," she murmured. "I'm petrified." She kissed him and then asked softly, "What are the chances that someone else might telegraph for the army, or make contact with your superiors in Denver?"

"Not too good, I'm afraid," Longarm answered, hugging her. "Farley's a good man, but not the type to go over the goddamned governor's head. The way we left it before I set off after you, the governor was to telegraph for the army, while Farley and the ranchers organized their men to protect their herds. But twenty-odd professional killers armed with those infernal Brader guns will be able to cut through those cowboys like a hot knife through butter. Hell, most of those drovers never drew their Peacemakers against anything but coyotes."

"Ki will help us," Jessie said. "You need a shave, your beard is scratchy," she giggled as Longarm planted kisses along her neck and cheek. "But your mustache is nice and soft," she murmured as she nibbled at his lower lip. Suddenly she pulled away slightly, still staying close enough, however, for him to rest his hands on her hips. "Darling," she breathed, "there's a time and place for everything . . ."

"And we'd sure as hell be in a different place if you'd listened to me," Longarm scolded. "What got into you to set off after Danzig by yourself? You were sure to be captured."

"Well, you got captured too," Jessie said.

"That's different!"

"Oh, really?" she laughed. "Explain that to me!"

Longarm thought fast. "I wanted to get captured. It was the only way to get to you."

Jessie stared skeptically, but slowly her eyes widened with adoration. She pressed her head against his chest. "I see. How brave of you." She bit her lip to keep from laughing.

"Now we have to find a way out," Longarm said absently, most of his concentration captured by the softness of Jessie in his arms, the fragrance of her hair.

"Yes, dear." Jessie tucked her fingers into his back pockets.

"But I'm still riled at you for breaking your promise," Longarm said firmly, trying his best to ignore her teasing touch. "I thought you said that it was very clear that I was in charge of doing the apprehending."

"I said it was clear," Jessie nodded, a mischievous smile forming on her lips. "I never said I was going to *listen*."

Longarm made a sound that was somewhere between a growl and a groan. "And I also said you needed a spanking!"

Jessie stroked the hard bulge filling the front of his trousers. "Sounds like fun," she said sweetly. "But shouldn't we get out of here first?"

"We've got a little problem there," Longarm mused, letting go of her. "We've got nothing to pick that lock with, and no weapons. We're also surrounded by a band of armed, professional killers."

"Ki will help us," Jessie repeated. "He'll come tonight, close to dawn, when the enemy is most relaxed."

"That still don't get us out of here," Longarm frowned. "Good as he is, he can't take them all by himself."

"Did you say you knew how to pick a lock?" Jessie asked.

"Sure," Longarm shrugged. "Especially one as easy as that padlock, but I need something to stick into it. My pocket knife has a filed-down blade that'd do the job nicely, but they've taken it—"

"Will this do?" Jessica interrupted, removing a pin from her hair.

"Son of a bitch," Longarm chuckled, taking it from her.

"As for a gun," Jessie murmured, looking out through the mesh to make sure they weren't being scrutinized, "I think this will help." She hoisted up her skirt to reveal, high up on her

shapely thigh, a black elastic garter. Sewn onto it was a tiny
holster in which was a derringer. She drew it and handed the
little gun to Longarm.

"Didn't they search you?" Longarm muttered, astounded.

Jessie shrugged. "To a point."

"*I* wouldn't have passed up a chance like *that*," he smiled.
The derringer was a twin-barrel .38. Its grips were of ivory,
and engraved upon them was the Circle Star brand.

Longarm handed it back to her. "Put it back in that interesting
holster of yours," he remarked. "Or, if you'd rather, *I* will—"

"Let's keep our minds on our work," Jessie suggested wryly,
slipping the derringer back into its hiding place.

Longarm tucked the hairpin into the band of his hat.
"Tonight, toward dawn, we'll pick that lock and head for that
shack you told me about, the one where they once stored explosives. I'd wager that's the building Danzig is using for his
armory. We've got to destroy those weapons, Jessie."

"But what if tonight is too late?" she asked. "What if Danzig
decides to raid the herds today?"

"I don't think he will," Longarm began. "First of all, *he*
doesn't know when Ki is going to attack. When I was taken,
Danzig was there, in person. Capturing Ki will mean that Danzig's fun can begin. He hates you more than he cares about this
business scheme. He knows the army isn't coming . . ." Longarm nodded. "My guess is he feels he can afford to wait until
he's captured Ki and has us all locked up. Then he can ride out
with his men to do his dirty work, knowing that he's got his
revenge to look forward to, all nice and neat."

"I guess you're right," Jessie sighed. "Anyway, we need the
cover of darkness, and the confusion Ki will cause, if we're to
succeed in destroying those weapons." She left the last part of
her thought unspoken: *And if I'm going to kill Danzig* . . .

Chapter 18

Ki waited for night to fall before he began his final approach. He'd left his horse two miles back, in order to close in on foot. He'd changed his clothes, donning his old, worn jeans, his collarless cotton shirt, and his soft leather vest with its multitude of pockets.

He'd selected his weapons with care. With him he had his bow and two leather quivers. In one quiver was packed an assortment of twenty-five arrows. The other quiver held twenty-five arrows all of one kind. Ki could only hope that Longarm would remember what Ki had told him days ago.

That Longarm was with Jessie, Ki had no doubt. The story written with blood in the pecan grove had been easy to read. Both Jessie and Longarm had struggled valiantly, costing the enemy dearly for their capture, but prisoners they now were—

Unless they were already dead.

If one was, they both were; of that also, Ki was certain. Still, he refused to allow that particular possibility to take root in his mind. For one thing, forlorn heartache had no place in a samurai preparing to do battle. For another thing, be the two alive or dead, his plan of action would remain exactly the same. He would disrupt the enemy's camp, disabling as many of them as he could. If Jessie and Longarm were alive, they would reveal themselves to him in some way. Ki would then aid them in making good their escape, and the trio would retreat to some sanctuary. Jessica would then express what she wished to accomplish next, and Ki would do his best to carry out her desires.

On the other hand, if the two were dead, Ki would sooner or later come across some evidence proving this. At that time he would stop his random attack to concentrate on finding the one he had earlier struggled with, the blond foreigner. He would kill this man, for he was sure Jessie would desire as much, and then he would go back to battling the rest of those who had sided with this foreigner, until they managed to bring him down. If Jessie was dead, he would fight with the ferocity of a man who does not care what happens to him. It crossed his mind that he probably ought to stay alive long enough to carry out his threat against the governor, should that man disobey his order to send for the army; but if Jessie was dead, what was the point? If Jessie was dead, would it not be better to die where she died, and hope that her spirit, her *Kami*, lingering near the scene, could watch proudly as he wrought havoc upon her enemies?

The how and when of dying were always tricky matters, Ki knew. Better to wait for more facts about the situation before attempting to ascertain the proper etiquette in this case . . .

Rock outcroppings encircled the quarry compound. Ki knew them well. In happier times, he and Jessie had explored and climbed these "baby mountains." As soon as he had surmised which way the tracks were heading, he'd known instinctively that the deserted stonecutting site was the hideout of the mystery riders. There was water there, and timber for fires, in addition to the obvious shelter for men and horses that the deserted buildings could provide. Those high rock walls, broken only by the single trail that led into the shallow canyon, created a natural fortress around the collection of buildings.

Fortress or prison, Ki thought, smiling to himself. It depended on who controlled the walls . . .

He could not afford the luxury of a preliminary reconnaissance. True, it was a dark, nearly moonless night, and he would have the advantage of stealth surprise, but he was only one man against what he was sure would be many sentries. Some might be amateurs, but most would be professionals, men quite experienced in the art of killing and staying alive despite the efforts of other professionals.

In all, it would be a pleasure, Ki thought, for a samurai's greatest pleasure is fighting. But it would not be easy. The only thing he could think to do was to make his way as best he could toward the center of the compound. If and when he found Jessie and Longarm, he would begin to divert the enemy's attention from them by drawing it upon himself. Until then, he would just infiltrate, striking at the enemy as he went.

He checked the glittering array of *shuriken* blades and stars lining the inside pockets of his vest. In addition to these, he had the pair he carried in the two sheaths strapped to his forearms. Both his bow and his *shuriken* would be useful for distance killing, but he carried one final weapon for close work: a *nunchaku*.

Normally, Ki would have depended on his *te* techniques, but his enemies were many and his time was short; the *nunchaku* would help to even up the odds.

Next to the *bo*, or staff, the *nunchaku* was Ki's favorite weapon. This was because its original effectiveness was derived from the fact that it appeared to be only a harmless farm implement, a tool of the common people. The Okinawans had originally used the forerunner of the *nunchaku* as a grain flail. It was only after Ki's own people, the Nipponese, had confiscated all of the Okinawans' real weapons that these proud people developed *te*, and *kobudo*, the art of using tools as weapons. A *nunchaku* consisted of two sticks of varying lengths attached together at one end by a few inches of braided horsehair. Ki owned many different sorts of *nunchaku*. The one he now carried was a *han-kei*, or half-size version. Instead of the two halves reaching approximately from his palm to his elbow, which was the traditional length, the two sticks were each only seven inches long, and flat on one side, so that they fit smoothly together. The *han-kei* form of *nunchaku* was easy to carry; Ki kept it tucked into his jeans like a dagger. With it, Ki could effectively perform virtually every *te* block and strike, but with the extra power brought to the techniques by the hard wood of the *nunchaku's* handles and the centrifugal force generated when he whipped that handle around on the end of its horsehair braid. Flail-like blows from the weapon could shatter a man's bones. Thrusts could smash his face or throat. A finger, wrist, or other joint caught between the two sticks would crack like a pecan shell in a nutcracker. The only *kobudo* weapon that Ki considered superior to the *nunchaku* was the *bo* or staff. But its five-foot-plus length made the *bo* too cumbersome a weapon for the sort of fighting Ki had to do this night.

Ki began to climb the rocks. He would cut a path through the first line of sentries. He would then situate himself to have a clear view of the compound, and then wait for the hour or so before dawn.

It was just human nature, he mused philosophically. That first gray glimmer rising up in the east had a way of comforting men, what with its full promise of another day of light and life on this earth. Men on guard during wartime—even professionals—tended to relax a bit with the first hint of dawn. Some clock inside them seemed to command it. Long ago, Ki had taught Jessica this curious thing. If she was still alive, she would know that the hour just before dawn would be the time to make her attempt at escape, that that would be the time when he would come to help her.

His bow strung across his shoulders, his twin quivers of arrows riding on his hips, Ki climbed the rock face as quickly and quietly as an ape. His climbing techniques were, after all, based on those of the monkey. A samurai soon learned that his bare toes could flex and bend to grip like fingers. A samurai who became a *te* adept also learned the art of sticking, of shifting one's center of gravity this way and that countless times in a moment, so that falling became unlikely. Down and up are, after all, relative terms, and Ki merely reminded himself that to the climbing samurai, down did not exist. Besides, the tall rock was part of the world, and who could fall off the world?

Ki's fingers slid up to hook themselves over the top of the outcropping. He flexed his elbows, biceps straining, to support himself as he peeked about to see if a sentry was anywhere nearby. There was no one. Ki quickly hauled himself up and darted into the shadows cast by the tumbled boulders.

The interior slopes of the ring of outcroppings surrounding the compound descended much more gradually. A man did not have to climb, but could walk down these rock-strewn hills.

From his vantage point, Ki could see sentries, alone and in pairs, scattered about. Evidently he was expected! None of them that he could see were armed with those "coffee grinders," but such a weapon was not really appropriate for this sort of sentry duty, where there was no clear, agreed-upon field of fire for which a man was required to be responsible. Ki also noted that the large clumps and piles of rocks and boulders strewn about the landscape kept the various sentries from being able to see one another.

Ki smiled. All in all, things were working out well. The path down toward the fires that glimmered in and around the compound's buildings was a maze. Guards stood here and there at various turns and twists of that maze. Ki would traverse it, removing the guards as he came—

The gun barrel pressed behind his ear was as cold and hard as the slab of granite upon which Ki was leaning. He groaned inwardly. He was off balance, in no position to attempt a *te* counter-move.

"You even *breathe* fast, little brother, and I'll blow your head off," a deep, calm voice said. "You're carrying a bow, little brother. I'll show you a trick my father taught me."

Ki felt a strong hand tug him up into a standing position. The bow strung diagonally across his back and shoulder was removed as the twin quivers were plucked from his waist.

"Now cross your arms across your chest, little brother," that deep voice instructed. "Do it like you were a shy maid who'd suddenly lost her blouse."

Mystified, Ki did as he was told. That gun was still drilling itself against his head. Then the bow was wiggled back down over his torso. This time the tough, tempered wooden part was in front, across his chest. The curve of wood pinned his arms and hands tightly in the position where he'd been ordered to place them. The string was now across his back. The man behind him gathered up the spare inch of slack and twisted it away by slipping a handful of arrows beneath the string and turning the shafts like handles. Ki felt the circulation in his arms being cut off. The man tucked the arrows through the string a final time, so that the pressure cinched them into place. Ki's upper limbs were now immobilized. The bow stretching horizontally across his chest, and extending for two feet on either side of him like wing bones, was nothing from which he couldn't break free, but doing so would take a little time—

More than enough time for his capable adversary to shoot him dead.

"You can turn around now, little brother."

Ki turned to confront a giant of a man, at least six and a half feet tall. He was built like a grizzly, with long, massive, muscle-slabbed arms. His torso was barrellike, and seemed to make up most of his length. His legs were as squat and thick as two tree stumps. Even in this faint light, Ki could see that the man's skin was of dark hue. He had a large, strong, hawk-like nose that protruded from a craggy face long ago pitted by smallpox. Two black, glossy braids framed that face. The braids reached down to the man's thick shoulders.

Ki, curious, peered up at his assailant. His was not a cruel face, not a particularly nervous one. It was a warrior's face.

"This is a quite interesting use for a bow," Ki remarked quietly. "How did you come by this technique?"

"Like I said, my daddy taught me. I'm a full-blooded Apache, little brother. That's how we used to take other tribes prisoner. 'Course, all that was before my time."

"Very effective," Ki remarked sadly. "What is your name?"

"Hell, little brother, telling an Apache name takes a lot of time. And we—or maybe just you, little brother—ain't got that much time." The big Apache raised his revolver in salute and grinned. "Just call me Joe."

"Joe, my name is Ki."

"Short for something, I'd wager," Joe said shrewdly.

"But we don't have the time," Ki smiled.

Joe was scantily dressed in a sleeveless leather vest and a loin cloth that left his stubby legs bare. Around his belly hung a wide leather gunbelt from which dangled a holster. A sheathed bowie knife hung like a pendant from around his neck. He wore no hat and no boots. Studded metal bracelets extended up Joe's arms from wrist to elbow. Ki knew that those bracelets would act like armor, reinforcing Joe's forearm smashes during hand-to-hand combat.

"I compliment you on the way you crept up behind me," Ki

said politely. He purposely kept his voice meek. It was important that Joe feel confident enough to holster his pistol. Ki could not afford to let his adversary fire even a stray shot, for that would alert all the other sentries.

"Hell, little brother," Joe smiled. "I go barefoot, just like you." He pointed to his feet with his revolver, and then, absently, slipped it back into its holster. "Apaches have feet tough enough to crush rocks, to flex cactus spines till they're as soft as an old man's prick. Apaches are born man-trackers. Little brother, I began my training as a little boy."

"So did I, Joe," Ki murmured, fascinated despite his predicament. He knew that he would have to do his best to kill this man who would try to kill him. But for now, before the killing started, he was content to share a moment with his peer.

"When I was just ten, I had to creep up and pull the tail feathers off a partridge. When I was twelve, I had to snatch a rattler and bring him home alive. When I was thirteen, I had to count coup on a grizzly bear, and live to tell about it." A look of amusement flashed across Joe's face. "No offense, little brother, but sneaking up on you was a mite tougher than the rattler, but a lot easier than the bear."

Ki bowed his head in acknowledgement. "Why did you leave your people? Why do you serve villains?"

Joe's face grew hard. "My people are no more. I was trained to be a warrior, but the Apache nation has left fighting behind. The men have become squaws, as the squaws have become whores. But I must fight. It is all I know. With no people to fight for, I fight for money. I don't care for what cause. There is no longer any cause that can interest me."

Ki stood silent for a moment, contemplating what he had been told. "It is a pity we are on opposite sides. We are much alike."

"Maybe you're right, and maybe you're not," the Apache grunted. "But you're on the button about that last fact. We're on opposite sides. Which brings this conversation to a close, I'm afraid, little brother." He drew his pistol. "Sorry about binding you up like that with your bow. I mean you no disrespect. I only did it 'cause I heard you were a real feisty fellow, real fast, and real clever with your hands. Now, Mr. Danzig said to bring you in alive if possible, or dead if we had to." The giant smiled. "I'd just as soon it was alive. It'd cause me some trou-

bled sleep to have to kill you, little brother . . ." He shrugged.
"Well, let's start on down." He gestured with his pistol in the
direction he wanted Ki to go.

Ki watched the gun turn from him, down toward the compound for one instant. He brought up his right knee to strike
out with a snapping forward foot-strike. His rigid toes slammed
into Joe's wrist, catapulting the revolver up over the Apache's
shoulder.

Both men stood quietly. They regarded one another as the
handgun clattered against the rocks.

"So be it, little brother," Joe whispered. He moved in fast,
his arms held wide, attacking like the grizzly he so resembled.
He was fast, but Ki was able to sidestep the attack. As Joe lunged
past, Ki performed a *yoko-geri-keage*, a sideways snap-kick.
He kept his back and head straight throughout the kick, raising
his striking leg until his knee was in line with his waist. He
brought his foot back, cocking his leg until it was next to his
other knee. When his foot slashed out, its outside edge was
angled like a knife blade toward the front of Joe's knee.

The Apache was able to twist his body around at the last
moment, so that he took the powerful kick on the back of his
knee, instead of upon his kneecap, which would certainly have
been shattered like a fragile china plate by the force of Ki's
blow. In this way, Joe was able to escape real injury, although
Ki's foot, driving into the back of his knee joint, forced him
down into a kneeling position.

Ki danced forward, sending a third foot-strike slamming
into the side of the Apache's face. Joe shook it off and rose to
his feet, forcing Ki to retreat.

The big Indian spat a mouthful of blood. "Ain't that a kick
in the head," he grinned. "You're right fast with your feet as
well as your hands," he observed wryly. He scrutinized the bow
across Ki's chest, trying to evaluate how securely his opponent's hands remained pinioned.

He must not notice the bow's tips, Ki willed. He began to
weave and dip in order to distract the man.

"I could call out for help," Joe said with a ghastly red smile.
The blood still flowing inside of his mouth had stained his
teeth. "I could do that, you know, little brother."

"But you will not," Ki said matter-of-factly. "This night was destined. Have we not both been trained as warriors from childhood?"

"We have, little brother," Joe said, moving in. "Ki, I salute you." He brought up his bracelet-armored arms and attacked.

"I salute you, Apache samurai," Ki whispered. He ducked beneath Joe's first clawlike swipe, but the bow extending on both sides spoiled his timing and balance.

The Apache's second forearm swipe caught Ki across his back. He felt Joe's bracelet studs gouge deep furrows into the leather of his vest as the sledgehammer blow knocked him forward, clear off his feet. With his hands pinned across his chest, he was unable to break his fall. He landed hard, and slid several feet across the jagged stones.

Ki felt his own blood—hot and wet—seeping down his lower spine. He'd purposely landed on his back, letting those arrowheads bite through his clothes and into his flesh, so as to avoid damaging the bow. He would need it later on. Assuming there was going to be a later on . . .

The Apache came lumbering toward Ki. "I'm going to stomp you, little brother," he huffed.

Ki scissored his legs wide, then locked them closed around Joe's massive legs. He swung his hips, letting his higher leg apply most of the pressure. The scissoring, levering action toppled the giant to the ground.

Ki scrambled to his feet, but Joe was right behind him. Ki twirled, trying to get a spare instant to prepare another kick, but the Apache was so close behind him that the two men resembled one dog chasing its own tail.

If only he could get far enough away to turn one of the protruding tips of the bow extending across his chest toward the Apache, Ki thought desperately. Then he could use what Joe had noticed about his strange bow. The bow's secret. The bow's tips were bound in leather to disguise—

Joe locked Ki in a bear hug. With his arms tucked against his chest, there was no way Ki could alleviate the terrible pressure squeezing his rib cage, locking in his lungs, forcing him to exhale endlessly. Time was running out. He could not inhale enough to breathe!

Ki rammed his knees into the other's groin. Joe groaned with pain, but only tightened his grip.

Ki felt his vision funneling down to a small circle of sight. He kicked at Joe's bare legs, but those two massive limbs resisted the kicks the way columns of stone resist a chisel. Ki had no time left to continue hacking away at his enemy by inches . . .

Joe straightened up, lifting Ki off of the ground. Now, ironically, the only thing keeping Ki's rib cage from being crushed and splintered was the barrier of the bow between the two men.

"As I saluted you in life, I now salute your death," the Apache grunted. "I will carry your bow to remember you."

Ki's face was pressed against the sheath of the bowie knife hanging from the man's neck. *If only his hands were free!* His face was slick with his own sweat and the sweat that ran down Joe's bare chest and belly.

"The bow will be yours," Ki whispered. "Alive or dead, you shall have my bow!"

Joe heaved Ki up to get a better grip on his twisting, kicking, sweat-slippery body. Ki used the momentum imparted to him by the Apache to add to his own strength as he butted hard with his forehead against Joe's nose. The Indian gagged in agony as his nose was flattened by the force of the impact. Blood squirted down out of both of his nostrils. Ki butted him again, this time smashing Joe's front teeth. The Indian's bear hug loosened. Ki wiggled free, and then back-pedaled away.

Joe soundlessly wiped away the blood and spittle from his ruined face and attacked once again.

Ki, wobbling on his feet, waited until the last possible instant and then turned sideways, to present the tip of the bow toward his onrushing foe, as if it were a spear.

Which it was!

Ki braced himself, then sprang sideways toward the big Indian. The bow's tip caught the Indian's belly, puncturing through his flesh with an initial crunch, followed by a long, wet, sliding sound. Before Joe could stop himself, he'd run himself through. The bowstring stretched on the curved wooden bow only deepened and extended the wound, sawing it wide.

Joe's chest actually touched Ki's shoulder. His bleeding belly was flush against Ki's side. The bow had come out his back, tent-poling the Apache's vest.

Joe's mouth opened to speak, but he no longer had the strength to form words. His eyes, only inches from Ki's, asked his silent question.

"The bow's tips are of sharpened steel, camouflaged by a thin leather covering," Ki said.

The Apache's legs buckled beneath him. Ki braced himself and twisted to withdraw the bow as Joe's lifeless body fell away.

"Alive or dead," Ki repeated, "you shall have my bow, and now you have." He stared down at the corpse. Steam rose from the gaping crimson slit in the Apache's belly.

Ki, having regained his breath, stood a moment in concentration, and then began to flex the muscles of his back. Moments later the string broke. He caught the flexing bow before it could fall to the ground.

His muscular contractions and expansions had set his own wounds bleeding again. His bow was also bloody. It would have to be cleaned.

He wandered toward where Joe had tossed his quivers of arrows. The few that had kept him bound seemed all right. He would restring the bow—he always carried an extra string—and then find a place where he could rest and regain his physical strength and spiritual equanimity.

"Joe, I am sorry you had to die," Ki addressed the Apache's body. "Tonight, many of my kills will be made in your name. I beseech your *Kami* to wait and watch, and see what your little brother can accomplish!"

He dragged the corpse between two large boulders and piled smaller stones upon it, hiding it as best he could. Ki doubted that any passing sentry would find it before morning, and by then it would not matter.

Gathering up his possessions, he hurried away to find a place where he could safely rest for a few hours. Soon it would be time to begin the final attack.

Chapter 19

"What time do you reckon it is?" Longarm asked.

"About fifteen minutes later than the last time you asked," Jessie remarked, amused. "Calm down. You've been pacing back and forth like a tiger in a zoo." She was sitting on her folded jacket, leaning against a wall, doing her best to relax and rest.

"I know we're supposed to wait until just before dawn," Longarm growled, "But I've had enough of being cooped up. Besides, I want to take a look around to make sure those Brader guns really are in that old powder shack. I've got to put those guns out of action if we're going to stop Danzig."

Sighing, Jessie climbed to her feet. She put on her jacket and raised her skirt to draw her derringer. "Let's do it," she said, smiling.

"Let's do it," Longarm repeated. He took her in his arms to kiss her once. Then he went to the door of the cell. From his hatband he removed the hairpin Jessie had given him. "I think I'll keep this in my hat from now on," he said as he went to work on the padlock. "It's a handy little thing to have around."

It only took him a few moments to pick the lock. He set it aside and removed and then rewrapped the short length of chain so that it would fall smoothly from its position with just a shove on the door. Next he reset the padlock, but only through one link.

"That will fool the guard for the moment we'll need," he said, evaluating his work.

"There are two of them out there," Jessie pointed out.

"Well, all we can do is hope only one will come in," Longarm said. He stretched out on the floor. "If both come in, do your best to keep them both covered. I'll only need a second."

He and Jessie exchanged looks.

"Ready?" he asked.

She nodded. "Guard!" she called. "Help!"

Presently the door to the shack opened, and a man stuck his head in. "What's going on?" he demanded.

"He just fainted dead away," Jessie whimpered, pointing down at Longarm's still form. "I think his head is hurt bad."

Laughing, the guard sauntered into the shack. Jessie, her heart in her mouth, watched the building's door, hung crookedly on its hinges, swing slowly, slowly closed.

"What do you want me to do about it?" the guard asked. He stepped up close to the wire mesh in order to peer down at Longarm.

"He needs a doctor!" Jessie demanded, approaching the guard from her side of the mesh.

"No doctor here, lady," the guard said, and began to turn away.

Jessie jammed the derringer up against the mesh so that it was aimed point-blank at the shocked guard's head. "That's too bad," she hissed. "Because if you make one sound, you're going to need a doctor right quick!"

Longarm was already pushing against the cell door. The chain snaked to the floor. Coming around behind the guard, Longarm drew the man's Colt out of his holster and tapped him behind the ear with the weapon's barrel. He caught the man beneath the armpits before he could slump all the way to the floor. He half carried and half dragged the unconscious guard into the cell, then hurried out.

"What's next?" Jessie asked, at his heels.

"Wait here for a minute. I want to take care of that other guard."

Longarm crept to the door and slowly inched it open. The remaining guard was sitting on a crate, with his back to the shack. He was huddled over a small campfire, and was wrapped in a blanket against the night chill.

Longarm left the shack and walked directly up to the guard.

He made no attempt to quiet his footsteps. His hope was that he would assume it was his partner, returning to the comfort of their fire.

"What was the trouble back there?" the man muttered over his shoulder. "Everything all right?"

"Just fine," Longarm said, and hit him over the head with the butt of his revolver.

As the guard fell back, Longarm caught him and dragged him back to the shack. Inside, he handed Jessie the guard's gun, and chose the corner of the cage area farthest from the door of the shack to prop the man up. Next he put the first guard beneath the other's arm, and wrapped the blanket around both. He tipped their hats down over their faces and stood back to survey the scene.

"Are they supposed to be us?" Jessie giggled as she reholstered her derringer and checked the load in the revolver.

"They might fool somebody who only bothered to glance in through the shack's door, or a window," Longarm shrugged. "Come on!"

They locked the guards in the cell and then left the shack. They kept to the sides of the buildings and hid in the shadows, but were fortunate in the fact that most of the men not on sentry duty on the surrounding slopes were, it seemed, sleeping in the bunkhouse.

"Lead the way to that powder shack," Longarm told Jessie. He had his gun at the ready, but was depending on staying out of sight of any stray guards. If they had to fire a shot, the whole camp would come down on them.

"This way," Jessie whispered. She tugged him toward the center of the compound, close to the other campfires.

Longarm dug in his boot heels. "Are you sure?" he demanded suspiciously. "Damn! Why don't we just drop in on Danzig for a shot of schnapps, or whatever? I'd think the stone-cutters would have kept their explosives on the outskirts of the compound, in case—"

"Oh don't be a mule!" Jessie scolded, exasperated. "They kept their powder where they could keep an eye on it, against thieves!"

Longarm stared at her. "Oh." He nodded. "Well, then, let's get going!" he demanded.

"Men!" Jessie seethed. "I had to fall in love with the most bullheaded—"

"You get what you deserve," Longarm cut her off. He peered around the corner of the cookshack. "The coast is clear. Let's move!"

They scurried across the dark open space, and were halfway to the shack's door when, from around the building's corner, there came strolling a shadowy figure. The man struck a match to light his cigar. Its flare made Longarm and Jessie's eyes ache.

"Stay here!" Longarm hissed, and strode toward the man. He repositioned his stolen gun in the hip pocket of his trousers, angling the butt to make it seem as if he were wearing his gun in a high-cinched holster. Longarm's hope was that the fellow would glimpse his silhouette—a man in a hat, with a gun on his hip—and assume he was just another recruited gunslick.

"Who is it?" the man growled as Longarm approached. The match winked out as it fell to the ground.

"Hold that light!" Longarm called. "Oh, shit. Got another match, old son?"

"Sure," the man replied. His hand was still splayed over his own revolver's butt, but he had not drawn. Now he relaxed as he saw that Longarm's gun was still "holstered." He pulled an another match from his shirt pocket, and struck it against the sole of his boot.

Longarm waited for that blinding flare, and for the gun-slick's eyes to be fixed on the flame as he brought it up, cupped in both hands, to light Longarm's cigar.

"Where's your smoke—" the man began.

Longarm drove his left fist into the man's belly, just above his belt buckle. As the man grunted and doubled over, the wind knocked out of him, Longarm connected with a right cross, catching the man on the tip of his jaw, just below his ear. The gunslick fell to his knees, then slumped.

"We ought get him out of sight," Jessica whispered, coming up behind Longarm.

"I know that," he said. "It's a question of where. I guess we'll just dump him behind the shack." He pulled the man behind the building, relieved him of his sidearm, and left him there.

When they reached the door of the shack, they found it locked.

"Well, that's no big surprise," Longarm said. He reached into his hatband and withdrew Jessica's hairpin. He inserted it into the lock and turned it. He felt some resistance in the lock's mechanism and applied more pressure. The pin broke off in his hand.

"That's no big surprise, either," he said. "What now? I could likely kick the door in, but I don't reckon that would be a very good idea, and I don't want to be out here much longer."

"Come on," she said. Grasping his hand, she pulled him around to the back of the shack, explaining as she went, "I told you Ki and I used to explore around here. Well . . ."

She knelt down and pulled at one of the vertical planks that made up the walls of the building. It moved to one side, not much, but enough for a person to crawl through and get into the shack.

"Woman," Longarm said, "you've come through again. Let's go. Ladies first."

He held the board aside and let her crawl in first, then he followed. It was a tight fit, and he had to go in feet first so he could hold the board aside. He might not have made it, but Jessica grabbed the seat of his pants and pulled, and he squeezed through with a startled curse.

"Where'd you get muscles like that?" he asked her.

She shrugged. "Just leverage," she replied.

Longarm struck a match.

"Where'd you get those?" Jessie asked. "Oh, from that man you knocked out, of course."

"Of course," Longarm said absently, looking around as the match's tiny fire inched toward his fingers. "There! A candle stub. On that shelf. See it?"

"Got it!" Jessie tilted the candle's wick into the sputtering match's flame. It caught.

"That fellow only had the one match," Longarm sighed. He looked around the interior of the shack. Several piles of stacked wooden crates, half-covered with canvas tarps and old, moth-eaten woolen blankets took up the center of the floor. Leaning against the windowless walls were the "coffee grinders." Longarm counted twenty. That meant four of the weapons were being carried by guards outside. Longarm's count assumed that the one carried by Lucas Conrad was even now beginning to rust somewhere back in that pecon grove, the site of the decoy ambush.

Piled in one corner of the shack were several wooden crates of .25-caliber rounds. Other boxes held fully charged magazines for the Brader guns.

"They're all here, except five," Jessie said excitedly.

"Except four." Longarm explained what had taken place earlier in the evening. "Now all we have to do is figure out a way to destroy them." There was a prybar standing against the wall, and he used it to lever up the lid of the crate containing the bullets. "It's going to take a while, but I guess we can build up a charge by emptying the rounds and gathering up the gunpowder."

"Longarm," Jessie called softly. "Here's a box filled with powder!"

Longarm hurried over. It was true. Brader had stockpiled loose powder, ingots of metal, and bullet molds to make his own ammunition.

"Why would he bother to go to all this trouble?" Jessie mused out loud, staring down at all the reloading paraphernalia.

Longarm thought about it. "I seem to remember that one problem concerning Gatling guns is that a soft lead-nosed bullet can get bent out of whack, jamming up the gun's firing mechanism. If Brader's guns work on the same notion—and from what he's told us, I suspicion they do—he can't depend on finding store-bought ammo to suit his needs. He's got to hand-load his own rounds for the 'coffee grinders.'"

Jessie set to work tearing a strip from one of the old wool blankets. "Do you think this cloth will burn?"

"Well enough," Longarm remarked. "I'll tuck one end of the strip into the powder by poking a hole through one of the waxed-paper sacks it's in. And I'll leave just enough sticking out to give us time to get away from here." He sprinkled some gunpowder onto the wool fibers to insure a good burn. "It's not the most dependable fuse in the world," he shrugged. "But it's the only fuse we've got."

"And now we wait," Jessie said. "We've got another hour until Ki attacks."

"*If* Ki is even here," Longarm added.

"He's here . . ."

"Assuming that he is, how will we know when he's started?"

Jessie smiled. "We'll know," she chuckled. She set down her gun and shrugged out of her jacket.

"Well, all we can do now is wait," Longarm said, his voice growing thick. He watched Jessie take off her hat and toss it to the floor. She kept her big green eyes on him as she removed the pins remaining in her hair. Then she gave her head a toss, to let down her shimmering mass of copper-gold tresses. Next she unbuttoned her blouse and took it off. Her breasts jiggled with newly found freedom. Her nipples swelled erect in the cool air. She unbuttoned her skirt and stepped out of it, to stand before Longarm entirely nude, except for her boots and that holster high up on her thigh.

"It's a shame to waste this time we have together," she murmured seductively. She patted the top of the crates piled up in the center of the floor. "All these tarps and blankets make a nice, soft little bed for us."

The flickering candlelight emphasized and delineated the lush curves and swells of her magnificent body. Longarm rushed forward to gather her up in his arms. Their tongues entwined as his hands felt the heat her flesh was generating.

"Oh, Custis, you're the only man I've ever loved," she whimpered, twisting in his embrace to rub her hips against the taut tweed of his fly.

Longarm picked her up and plopped her down on the cushioned tops of the crates.

"I think you better keep your boots and that holster on," he said. "Keep that gun handy, just in case." He gestured toward the door, then began to undress himself. He took off his shirt and hat, but only lowered his trousers and cotton longjohns until they were bunched around his boot tops. He set his revolver down beside Jessie's head, where it would be within his easy reach in case of a sudden intrusion.

"I'm sorry about being only partway undressed," Longarm began, "and about leaving that gun there, but I've got no holster, and—"

Jessie reached out to tickle his jutting member with her fingernails. "Yes, you have, darling," she said, spreading her legs.

Longarm wasted no time. He was hard as stone and dying

to slide into her. He hopped up onto the crates, stretched himself out over Jessie, and penetrated her deeply, to his full length. He withdrew teasingly, until he and she were linked only by the merest kiss of their flesh, and then slammed fiercely into her again.

Jessie bit into his shoulder to keep from crying out in delirious ecstasy. Longarm wanted to prolong the sensations, but he could not keep from hurrying. The constant danger of discovery spurred him on, and truth to tell, he found making love surrounded by all those long, gleaming gun barrels downright inspiring.

Beneath him, Jessie shuddered and let out a tiny birdlike cry. She wrapped her legs around his waist and thrust herself up to meet him. When he came, it was like all those Brader guns going off at the same time.

They rested in each other's arms. Longarm was still nestled inside Jessie.

Twice they thought they heard somebody fiddling with the door, and twice they held their breath, half naked, locked together like Siamese twins, both of them pointing their guns toward the noise. No one intruded, and after both false alarms they giggled like naughty adolescents hiding from their parents.

It was not that they considered their predicament unserious. On the contrary, they both fully realized that they could be discovered and killed at any moment. Accordingly, they were hell-bent on enjoying every moment of whatever amount of living was left for them. Right now, that meant enjoying each other.

"Dynamite," Longarm said.

"Mmm, yes indeed," Jessie said, then realized that he was not looking at her face, but over her shoulder, and he seemed surprised.

She turned her head to see what he was looking at. During their lovemaking, one of the blankets had shifted, revealing black lettering stenciled on the crate beneath: DANGER! DYNAMITE! STORE IN A COOL PLACE.

"I'll be damned," he said. "We've been making love on a bed of high explosives!" He withdrew from her and they dressed, and he used the prybar to take the lid off one of the crates on which they'd been lying. It was filled with neatly packed cylinders covered in thick waxed paper.

"Look around," he told her. "There's got to be blasting caps around. Probably on the far side of the shack . . . There! Under those sandbags!"

In the opposite corner of the small building was a pile of sandbags. Longarm knew that blasting caps were always stored away from the charges they were intended to ignite, and that seemed the most logical place. He removed a few of the sandbags, and sure enough, underneath was a single crate of caps, packed in sawdust. Each had a short length of fuse attached to it. Longarm took several of the caps and inserted them into the ends of some of the sticks of dynamite at the other end of the shack. Then he put the lid back on the box of explosives.

"Why did you do that?" Jessie asked.

"Because I'm about to light this cheroot, and I don't want any stray sparks or ashes setting this stuff off before we're ready."

"Where'd you get that?" she grinned.

"Same place I got the matches. That old boy lying behind this shack ain't going to feel like smoking for a while. He lit the cigar, and puffed its tip into a ruddy glow.

Jessie shuddered. "I think you broke that man's jaw."

"Hope so. That'll mean I won't have to try and kill him. A broken jaw ought to be painful enough to keep him out of the action."

Jessie watched Longarm's face. "You don't like to kill, do you?"

"Few men who've killed like it," Longarm frowned. "Mostly the only folks who do are those that never have, but have strong imaginations." Longarm puffed on his cigar and watched her, hoping that what he'd said had gotten through the layers of hate and anger she'd built up since the murder of her father.

"Like me—that's what you're thinking," Jessie accused. "But you're forgetting something. Earlier this evening I did kill, for the first time. I shot two men in that pecan grove. One I shot dead, the other I wounded badly. He may be dead now, for all I know. I didn't like doing it, Longarm, but I knew why

I had to." She shrugged, and her eyes grew wet with tears. "I'm not saying it was right or wrong, I'm just saying that—"

From outside there came a hoarse shout: "They got away! Search the camp for the prisoners!"

"Uh-oh," Longarm muttered. "Here we go. You've got that gun I gave you?"

"Right here," Jessie answered. Her voice was harsh, her throat dry. "Remember, if anything happens . . . well, I love you . . ."

"Nothing's going to happen to us," Longarm assured her. "And I'll save saying how I feel about you until I can prove it," he winked.

He grabbed his gun, and gathered up the sticks of dynamite to thrust them into his back pocket. Just then the door to the shack was kicked in by one of Danzig's men. He stood, his gun in his hand, blinking stupidly at them in the candlelight. Jessie yelped in shock and fear.

Longarm whirled to whip off a shot the man's way. The round chewed a piece of the doorjamb, chasing the outlaw away. As he backed out hurriedly, his boot heels caught on the threshold. His gun fell to the floor as he stumbled out of sight.

Longarm snatched up the fallen gun and held it in reserve as he pegged a shot out through the door. There were targets aplenty. Men—many of them just awakened and still dazed with sleep—were scurrying past. Longarm took his time and fired again. One of his targets clutched at his side and pinwheeled to the ground.

Jessie took cover on the other side of the doorway. She fired her revolver twice, missing the man she was aiming at both times.

Longarm couldn't help smirking at her. "Need spectacles?" he asked as he sighted at a man crawling across the roof of a nearby building, and fired. The man howled in pain, and slid down the steeply angled shingles to fall somewhere out of sight.

"I'm used to my .38!" Jessie muttered. "This gun you gave me is a .44!"

"Typical of a woman to complain," Longarm laughed.

Jessie swore an oath from between clenched teeth. She gripped her gun in both hands, drew a steady bead, and squeezed off another shot. This time the target she'd been plinking at let his pistol drop as he slumped across the barrel he'd been hiding behind.

"If I use both hands I can steady my aim," she said. "I can handle it."

"Never thought you couldn't," Longarm replied.

Just then one of the gunslicks fired at them. His round slammed into the doorjamb just inches from Longarm's head.

"Do not return their fire!" Longarm and Jessie heard Danzig scream, his accent made thick by anger and frustration.

"Oh, no! My guns!" Brader chimed in. Longarm and Jessie could not see him, but they could hear the helpless flutter in his voice. The pudgy inventor sounded like a mother wailing over her babies trapped in a burning building.

"So that's why they're not shooting back at us," Jessie observed.

"They know what's in this shack," Longarm chuckled. "As much as they'd like to shoot us, they can't risk a bullet hitting that dynamite behind us. Their 'coffee grinders' would be blown to smithereens."

"Yep, for now it's a Mexican standoff," he remarked, puffing on his filched cheroot. "They can't shoot us, but we can't escape, either. We'd never get out through that hole fast enough to make a run for it. We'd be spotted for sure."

"Ki will divert them," Jessie said quietly.

"Well where the hell is he?" Longarm began.

As if in answer, the night air was suddenly filled with a shrill wailing screech. The sound ended abruptly with a dull thud, followed by a shout of pain.

From out of the darkness a man yelled, "I've been hit by a fucking arrow! Indians!"

"I could never forget that sound!" Longarm laughed with relief.

Ki slid down the rocky slope, firing a barrage of "death's song" arrows as he went. He had twenty-five of them packed into one of his quivers. He aimed at a visible target when he could, but for now, just getting the special arrows singing through the darkness took precedence. From his vantage point he had clearly heard and seen the gunfire coming from that windowless shack. The enemy had surrounded it, taking heavy losses as they did so, but they were not returning fire. Clearly there was something valuable—other than Jessie and Longarm—in that shack, something that could be damaged by shots. Longarm and Jessie were safe for the moment, but they were also trapped. Ki wanted to give them a chance to escape, so he kept his dreadful rain of screeching arrows arcing through the night. The technique was called *inagashi*, or "flight shooting." There were many Nippoese bowmen who could fire thousands of arrows—all of them accurately—during a twenty-four hour period.

He raced about beneath the covering cloak of darkness, firing "death's song" as he went. The enemy had been thrown into confusion by the volley of wailing arrows. It was the same tactic of intimidation that had worked so well, so long ago, in Ki's own country. He hoped desperately that Longarm had remembered the story Ki had told him, so that he could put Ki's diversionary tactics to good use.

Ki kept careful watch around himself as he attacked. Up above on the slope, he had left one other man dead to keep Joe's *kami* company. Ki had come upon the man quietly, and snapped his neck before he could make a sound of alarm. Now his head twisted around like a rabbit's as he kept careful scrutiny of his surroundings. His bow made little noise, and there was no muzzle flash for the enemy to zero in on, but all it would take would be one moment's carelessness to put himself in the sights of another's gun. Now that he knew Jessie was alive, he could not afford to become injured—or killed—until he knew she was safe.

Ki fired another "death's song." This one wailed its way close to one of the men keeping his gun trained on the shack. Ki hurried away, but not before he was spotted.

"*Get him!*" he heard the blond foreigner scream. "*Alive or dead—get him!*"

Ki spun around the corner of the cookshack, smack into two of the outlaws, one of whom was armed with a Brader gun. Here a large campfire had been built and kept burning to warm food and drink for the men who had been on watch. Ki had lost the advantage of darkness.

He backed out of sight around the cookshack's corner, just as a pistol round send wood chips flying from the place his head had just been. The man armed with the "coffee grinder" began to fire. His chattering weapon sent blue flame and a rain of lead Ki's way.

Ki shielded his eyes from splinters and crabbed sideways, out from the shelter of the shack, to let an arrow fly. It caught the man firing the "coffee grinder" in the belly. He screamed, and jackknifed in two, the "coffee grinder's" long barrel somersaulting the man forward, over onto his back, where he lay convulsing.

Meanwhile, Ki had let go of his bow in order to throw himself upon the ground. The remaining man fired again, in panic, trying to slow Ki down, but the samurai had a *shuriken* star slicing through the air halfway to its target before the gunslick could get off a third round. The star caught the man in the forehead. He looked cross-eyed at it and began to reach up automatically to pull it out, but then he dropped his gun and pitched forward on his face, burying the star yet deeper.

Ki retrieved his bow just as three more of Danzig's men came careening around the corner to see what all the shooting had been about. Ki went down on one knee to fire off four arrows as many seconds. The last man of the three managed to throw himself back the way they'd all come. The other two went down, two arrows in each of them.

From behind Ki there came two others. Now there was no time to fire an arrow, and they were too close for *shuriken*. Ki charged in between the two, to confound their attempt to use their pistols. He knocked one of the men to the ground by slamming his bow against the side of the outlaw's head. He turned to jab at the other man with the bow's sharp tip, but the string became entangled with the man's pistol barrel as the outlaw used his gun to block the jab, and the bow was torn from Ki's hands.

Ki stepped in quickly and dropped his adversary with a "sweep lotus" kick to the fellow's chin. He next pulled his *nunchaku* to meet the renewed attack of the first man, the one he had felled with a swipe of his bow. This one's pistol was far out of reach, but he had managed to grab Ki's bow while the samurai was busy with the other outlaw. Now the man moved in toward Ki, warily swinging the bow before him like an ax handle.

Ki kept the *nunchaku* whipping in front of him in a

figure-eight pattern. His opponent had bashed in more than his fair share of skulls with ax handles and clubs, this Ki could tell, but no matter how the outlaw bobbed and weaved, trying to land a blow with Ki's bow, the swinging *nunchaku* kept him off balance and at a distance.

Still, the advantage of time was with the outlaw. More men would arrive to aid him at any moment. Ki knew he had to end this stalemate, and fast!

The outlaw feinted with a quick stab of the bow's point toward Ki's chest, but Ki easily blocked it, falling back into a single-footed stance as he parried the jab with the right handle of his *nunchaku*.

The man jumped back, thinking he was out of Ki's reach. He brought the bow up and swung it back over his shoulder and then around, trying with all of his might to knock Ki's head off his shoulders. Ki did not even have to take one step forward, but merely brought his right arm around as if he were trying to chop at the man's neck with the edge of his hand. His arm was too short to make the distance, but the *nunchaku's* length gave him the reach he needed. He held the weapon at one end and whipped the other half into the fellow's neck. The bow fell from his stunned opponent's hands, but before he could utter a cry of pain, Ki had closed the distance between them to deliver an elbow strike to the man's chin. Ki kept the *nunchaku* braced along his forearm to strengthen the blow.

The brawler was now out on his feet, and just in time too. Ki heard footsteps stomping his way. He locked the *nunchaku* beneath the man's chin, and held his sagging form up as a shield against the onslaught of bullets sent his way. Ki felt the rounds thud into the man's body, which was now dead weight.

"Damn it!" one of the gunmen swore. "Don't get near the bastard. Surround him!"

Ki staggered backward, but he couldn't move at more than an awkward shuffle with the dead man's weight upon him, and letting his shield drop would expose him to the others' guns. But there was really no choice in the matter. In another instant he'd be surrounded anyway, and then the man's body would be useless. He let go his grip, and as the corpse fell away he reached for a throwing star, even as he realized it was a futile gesture. He might get one more of the enemy, but then—

The sky seemed to light up, and the awesome clap of noise came close to bursting Ki's eardrums. From somewhere on the other side of the cookshack, clods of earth and rocks flew up. From that same direction there also came angry shouts, and the terrified whinnying of horses. The men who were about to fire at Ki flinched at the explosion, and all heads swiveled toward the direction of the blast. By the time they looked back, Ki was gone.

"Ki's keeping them busy from one side," Longarm told Jessie inside the armory and explosives shack. "We've got to attack from this side. For that, we need mobility!"

They could hear the banshee wails of Ki's arrows. Next came Danzig's furious commands to his men to hunt the archer down.

Longarm nodded in satisfaction. "Good, he's dividing his forces. This is the best chance we'll have!" He tossed Jessie the extra revolver and told her to keep watch to make sure they were not suddenly overwhelmed in a rushing attack, then hurried over to the collection of "coffee grinders." He fetched two of the weapons, along with extra magazines.

"Think you can handle one of these?" he asked anxiously. "I'm going to need covering fire."

"Looks a little heavy for me," Jessie said dubiously. "Help me shove a couple of those dynamite crates over to the doorway. I can rest the thing on them—"

"And also guarantee that they don't shoot back!" Longarm grinned. "Great idea!" He shoved a stack of two crates into position, and set the Bruder guns upon them. Only the bottom crate held dynamite. The top crate was filled with bullet molds, but Longarm figured one was plenty to keep Danzig from risking an explosion.

Fortunately, Longarm had seen enough Gatling guns to quickly puzzle out the odd weapon's mechanism. He showed Jessie how to turn the cranks, and how to reload a clip into the breech, although with two guns primed and ready, he didn't think she'd have to reload.

"What are you going to be doing?" Jessie asked.

"I'm going to go blow something up," he said mildly. "The bunkhouse over yonder looks like a good target. I'll try for that, while you keep me covered with these. I'll run out and throw a stick in that direction. Then I'll come back to work the guns so you can get out—"

"What's the point of that?" Jessie interrupted.

"So I can light the fuse on the dynamite."

"I can do that!" Jessie groaned. She reached up to pluck the cigar out of Longarm's mouth, and then took a few puffs to keep it going. "Not as good as your cheroots," she said, making a face. "Now you take one of these 'coffee grinders' along with you, find cover once you've tossed your stick of dynamite, and give me cover fire to get out of here. I'll leave one stick with a longer fuse burning in here, and throw the other at Danzig and his men just before I make my break for it." She grinned at Longarm. "It's a better plan than *yours*!"

"Can you throw?" he asked skeptically.

She looked at him disgustedly. "Just go," Jessie ordered, "before I decide to forget to give you cover fire!" She gave him a quick kiss. "Be careful," she whispered, as he handed her the three dynamite sticks.

"You too," Longarm warned as she handed him back a stick with a lighted fuse.

They both listened to the sound of shots coming from the other side of the bunkhouse, near the cookshack. Their eyes locked—Ki had been cornered.

Longarm shoved his pistol into his waistband, grabbed a Brader gun, and made his break for it as Jessie began to twist the handles on the remaining gun. The weapon shuddered and shook on its precarious carriage of wooden crates, but the steady stream of bullets—coming *at* Danzig and his men for a change—was more than enough to make them huddle behind their cover.

Longarm ran about twenty yards to a nearby clump of tumbled boulders, and let his stick of dynamite fly. It fell short of the bunkhouse but made a satisfying explosion, nevertheless.

He propped his "coffee grinder" across the rocks, and began to fire. He had a better angle to work from than Jessie did, and he managed to make his burst count, hitting two of the outlaws as the rest scurried around to put something between themselves and Longarm. Jessie, meanwhile, kept firing. Her logic was sound—between them they had Danzig's men trapped in a murderous crossfire—but Longarm cursed her nevertheless. What she'd forgotten was that there was nothing to keep the band from returning *his* fire. Rounds from rifles, pistols, and the Brader guns controlled by the enemy were ricocheting into the rocks. The whine of the bullets whizzing off reminded him of the sound Ki's arrows had been making. Despite the fusillade, Longarm kept firing. His chances, as well as Jessie's, rested on his keeping Danzig's men from being able to take the time to aim.

"Do it, Jessie!" Longarm mumbled to himself. The sky was turning gray with dawn's light. Every moment she waited increased their chances of being shot.

A stick of dynamite flew tumbling out of the shack, to land squarely amidst the half-circle of Danzig's men. It exploded with an orange flash and a roar, and men were sent sprawling in all directions.

Longarm cranked off what remained of the rounds in his "coffee grinder" as Jessie scrambled to the shelter of the rocks he was hiding behind.

"Told you I had a better plan!" Jessie teased.

"You wouldn't have thought of it if you hadn't been learning stuff off of me," Longarm countered. "Give me back my cigar!" He stole the smoke out of her mouth, and went back to raking Danzig's forces until the Brader gun clicked emptily. "Shit!" he fumed.

"Brought you a present," Jessie said sweetly, offering him two more magazines for the weapon. "You don't have to thank me."

"The guns!" Longarm heard Brader shout. He watched the short, fat man waddle as swiftly as he could toward the shack.

"He's out of ammunition!" Danzig crowed. "Attack them now!" His men began to break cover.

Longarm ignored Jessie's proffered ammo magazines, and instead put his hand on the top of her hat, pushing her flat to the ground. He threw himself on top of her, angling both of their bodies as close to the sheltering boulders as possible.

He'd been prepared for a huge explosion, but what occurred

literally took Longarm's breath away. The noise was the least of it. The ground beneath them seemed to heave up and then back into place. The shock wave tore his own hat off of his head, and then the air itself seemed to disappear.

Seconds later, after the worst of the debris raised by the blast had fallen—most of it far beyond Longarm and Jessie—he raised his head to gaze dazedly around.

His ears were still ringing from the thunderous noise, but still he could hear the cries and moans of men lucky enough to have been merely wounded by the blast. They had followed Danzig's command to attack, just moments before the explosion took place. Danzig's band of professional gunslicks, caught in the open, had been chopped to pieces and now lay scattered among the wreckage.

On the shack itself there was nothing left but bits of flaming or charred wood. Brader had unquestionably perished in the blast, Longarm knew.

He rose to his feet, brushing himself off, and then helped Jessie up. Both he and Jessie drew their pistols, but held them uncertainly. There seemed to be nobody left to point their guns *at*. Those men not killed were lying crumpled and broken, crying for help.

Off to their right they saw Ki pop up from behind another rock. He grinned and waved at them, and then hurried to their side.

"It is finished," he said.

"Reckon so." Longarm nodded. "Any men still up in these surrounding hills will be taking off for greener pastures. This fight is over. Jessie, we—" He broke off abruptly. "Where *is* she?"

"Find the foreigner, and we shall find her," Ki sighed.

Jessie didn't bother to search through the rubble for Danzig's body. If he was there, all well and good. If he wasn't—and her instincts told her he wasn't—she thought she knew where she could intercept him.

She made a beeline for the corrals, a fully loaded double-action .44 in her hand. She got there in time to see Danzig leading a saddled horse out of the stable. His black suit was tattered and torn, and his face was smudged from the blast, but otherwise he seemed untouched by it. Obviously he had not followed his own orders, but had been careful to keep himself behind protective cover during the explosion.

An early-morning breeze fluttered Danzig's coat, revealing his holstered brace of Mauser pistols. In his left hand he held one of the Brader guns.

Jessie understood it all perfectly. The murdering Prussian intended to escape with his prize. Other gunsmiths could calibrate the parts of the weapon and duplicate Brader's invention. Danzig could rebuild his arsenal and start this nightmare all over again.

"You're not going anywhere," Jessie called out, leveling her revolver at him. "Except to hell!"

Danzig moved with serpentine quickness. He let the "coffee grinder" fall as he crabbed sideways to put his startled horse between himself and Jessie. The animal bolted away, but by then he had his own pistols drawn and cocked.

Jessie crouched down, and held her gun with both hands. *I could have shot him twice by now*, Jessie thought. *Why haven't I?* Was it Longarm's restraining influence? Longarm understood honor and justice, but that was precisely why the lawman would want her to do her best to take this man alive . . .

"You cannot do it, can you, *mädchen?*" Danzig sneered. His blue eyes were bright with hate, his thin, bloodless lips were pulled back in a canine snarl. "I shall win!"

"I'm telling you to drop those guns," Jessie warned, doing her best to keep her voice calm and steady, doing her best not to show her own feelings of anger and disgust, flaring within her. How she itched to pull the trigger and blast Danzig into oblivion! But Longarm expected better of her, and she would not let him down. She would *not* lower herself to the level of this animal she had in her gunsights.

"I'm not going to kill you, Danzig," she said. "I'm going to turn you over to Longarm. Now drop your guns!"

"Do as she says, Danzig," Longarm ordered, coming up behind Jessie. His own gun was out and pointed at the Prussian. "There's no way you can get us both."

"Certainly not all three of us," Ki added, standing on Jessie's other side. A *shuriken* star lay balanced on his fingertips, ready to be thrown.

Danzig shrugged and smiled. "I am indeed outnumbered," he said. Slowly he lowered his own pistols and let them drop to the ground.

"I'll take it from here," Longarm told Jessie as Danzig walked toward them.

Jessie nodded, lowering her own gun. She kept her eyes on Danzig, knowing him and instinctively distrusting him. It was this instinct that allowed her to cry out her warning in time.

"Longarm! Look out!"

Danzig had dropped to his knees. A third pistol had almost magically appeared in his hand, snatched from his waistband. "Whore!" he screamed, aiming at Jessie.

Both Longarm and Jessie fired at the same time as Danzig. The reports of their three guns sounded as one. The two slugs hit Danzig in the chest, knocking him backward so that his own shot went astray. Nevertheless, Jessie was certain she'd heard Danzig's round sizzle past her ear.

She, Longarm, and Ki approached the still body. Danzig's dead eyes glared up at them. Jessie bent to pick up the weapon Danzig had fired at her. It was her own, .38-caliber, double-action Colt, the one her father had given her.

"I should have known," Jessie murmured. "Of course he would take my gun with him to add to his collection. It was to be his trophy."

Unbidden, Ki had gone to fetch Danzig's brace of Mauser pistols. He showed them to Jessie, then pocketed them.

"And I'll add those to the gun collection in my father's study." She turned to Longarm. "We've got to destroy that last Brader gun. "Men already do an efficient enough job of murdering one another."

Longarm just nodded. He stood beside Jessie, and together the two of them emptied their pistols at the infernal gun until the last of Brader's weapons had been turned into a useless mass of broken steel and splintered wood.

"Now it really is all over," Longarm told her. "Your war is finished. You've won."

Jessie did not answer. She walked silently to the ruined gun, removing a lace handkerchief from her pocket as she did so. Longarm, close behind her, could see that the Circle Star brand had been embroidered in one corner of the fabric. She dropped the hankie above the weapon. It landed on the wooden stock of the "coffee grinder," and before a breeze could flutter it to the ground, Ki pinned it in place with a swiftly hurled *shuriken* throwing star.

"Danzig's confederates will come here to investigate what has happened," she said by way of explanation. "This will tell them that the war will continue." When she turned to look at Longarm, there were tears in her green eyes. "I'm sorry for what it is going to mean to us. But I'm going to carry on my father's fight, wherever and whenever I can."

Chapter 20

Longarm sat sprawled across the threadbare green plush of the railroad car seat. It was late morning, several days after that night of carnage at the quarry. He was on the first leg of his journey back to Denver.

Without Jessie.

As the car rocked and swayed across the New Mexico border, Longarm adjusted his cross-draw rig. He'd found his own guns—his Colt, his double-barreled, .44 derringer, and his Winchester—along with his holster, in the quarry office.

Jessie had begged Longarm not to mention the governor's role in the plot against her father and the state of Texas. It would damage the state's spirit and the cattlemen's morale to know that one of their own had turned against them. In any case, nothing could be proved against them. In any case, nothing can be proved against him with Danzig dead and Longarm had already wired a brief message to Vail, informing him that everything was well in hand, the case was closed, and he'd report in person as soon as he arrived in Denver.

"I still don't understand you, Jessie," Longarm had sighed. They were back at the Starbuck ranch, in Jessie's bed, where they intended to remain until it was time for Longarm to catch his train out of Sarah the next day.

"It's not like you to decide to let a man like the governor

get off scot-free," he continued as the blushing Myobu served them a delectable meal she'd carried up to the bedroom on a laquered tray.

"He's not going to get off scot-free," Jessie said. She sent Myobu away and sat up, letting the sheets fall from her. She poured them both cups of hot tea laced with Maryland rye, and picking up a fork, she began to feed Longarm.

"I can feed myself," he laughed.

"I know, but it's the duty of a geisha to do everything for her man," she insisted. She reached down between Longarm's legs to give him a loving squeeze. "And I mean *everything.* Open your mouth."

"Yes, ma'am!" Longarm said obediently. He knew a good thing when he had it.

"Anyway, the governor will be punished. I sent Ki—"

"Oh, no!" Longarm moaned. "I'm warning you, if you sent him to kill the governor—"

"Of course not!" Jessie said. "You've taught me a lot," she continued docilely. "Killing is a last-resort measure. I understand that now."

"Then what's Ki going to do?"

"Well, he'll go to the capital, and visit the Governor late one night. He won't hurt him, but merely give him a good scare, inform him that we've got enough evidence to get him sent to prison in disgrace, and suggest that he resign his office and retire from political life." She smiled. "Once Ki lets him know that he'll be keeping tabs on the governor from time to time, I think the man will get the message and do as he's told."

"I'm sure he will." Longarm shivered. "I hope Ki doesn't get caught—"

His remark was interrupted by Jessie's silvery laugh. He had to smile along with her. Ki ever getting caught at anything was sort of a silly thing to worry about.

"And you still insist on continuing this vendetta?" Longarm demanded. "On following those leads in that notebook left to you by your father?"

Jessie's face went suddenly grave. "It's something I have to do." She reached out to caress his cheek. "Because of you, I no longer hate, and I thank you—and love you—for that. And for *other* things. But I've got to fight my father's—and this country's—enemies."

"Just you and Ki, against all the forces those bastards can marshal?" Longarm shook his head. "It's too much."

"I won't be alone," Jessie reassured him softly. "Don't forget, all across the nation there are Starbuck offices I can call upon for assistance. Ki is already hard at work designing a special wagon to carry everything I need, and his arsenal of special weapons. He's been referring to it as our 'vengeance wagon.' We'll be able to ship it along with us on trains, and then rent horses whenever we need them. I don't know if we'll use the wagon all the time, but we'll have it when we need it."

"And you'll have me when you need me," Longarm promised, embracing her. "I hope you know that."

"I do," she swore, kissing him. "I love you, Custis. I wasn't a virgin before you met me, but I love you, and when you're ready, and I'm ready, I expect you to come and make me your wife for good and ever!"

"Here now," Longarm pretended to scold her. "I'll do the proposing." He grinned. "When I'm ready, and you're ready, I expect you to let me marry you for good and ever." He looked into her eyes, wanting to say more, but before he could speak, she pressed her finger to his lips.

"But you're not ready yet, Longarm."

"No," he had to admit. "No I'm not."

"And neither am I," she replied.

The lacquered tray clattered to the floor, but neither of them really heard it. They were too wrapped up in each other to let anything disturb them.

Longarm was startled from his reverie by a breeze blowing through the railroad car's opened windows. A marvelous scent had suddenly reminded him of Jessie, but what he had smelled was only a meadow of wildflowers growing alongside the tracks.

Smiling to himself, he pulled a cheroot from his pocket and lit up. Soon enough he'd be back in Denver, reporting to Billy Vail, and most likely getting saddled with another case.

Jessie had been right. He wasn't anywhere near ready to

settle down. But when he was, he'd plant his roots alongside hers. Until then, Longarm knew that his tracks would cross Jessica Starbuck's whenever possible.

She was good, both in bed and in battle. But there were still a few things Custis Long could teach her . . . both places.

Lone Star
on the
Treachery Trail

WESLEY ELLIS

Chapter 1

The sudden spring storm broke with a thunderclap across south-eastern Wyoming. Descending out of Canada and through Montana like a last savage howl of winter, the gale swept in on ugly, bloated clouds and torrential rains, darkening the sky until only a flashing lacework of lightning revealed the looming peaks of the Laramie Range and its wind-whipped foothills, thick with saltbush, cottonwood, and mountain mahogany.

The North Laramie River was a twisting, whorling tide, swelling from the abrupt and unexpected runoff. Paralleling and occasionally crossing the river was a rutted, muddy trail that connected Uva and Garrett and the few smaller cow towns in between, and slowly churning westward along it was a Special Pontiac closed wagon, pulled by two Jenny Lind—bridled Morgans. Obliquely slashing rain beat against the wagon's seasoned wood sides and heavy duck roof, and savagely gusting wind tore at its rubberized curtains that were rolled down and fastened front and rear. And despite its wide stance—seven feet long by three feet wide, with a five-foot track—and its easy-rolling, forty-two-inch high Sarven's Patent wheels, its team constantly had to shift and thrust to keep the wagon on course through the gumbo.

The body of the wagon was painted a ruby-wine color with vermillion striping, making it resemble the sort of rig a snake-oil drummer might use to ply his elixirs. The two who were riding on the buffed leather-upholstered front seat, however, were anything but traveling medicine men.

Concentrating with the reins in both hands was a lean man in his early thirties, his blue-gray suit swathed in an oilskin slicker, his Stetson tugged low against the weather. Shadowed by the hatbrim, his features bore that handsome quality which appeals to women who like their men tempered by experience and bronzed by sun. There was a seriousness about him, too, the glint of chilled steel in his almond eyes and a terseness to his thin lips—all of which would have indicated to a close and knowledgeable observer that one of this man's parents had been Oriental; and that the mating of East and West had produced a proud, rugged, quiet yet determined individual who blended the best of both worlds. He fit well the name he'd adopted when he'd arrived in America: *Ki*, the Japanese word for the vital energy that suffuses all living things, and the mastery of which is the true warrior's life-work.

His passenger was a tall, lissome woman in her twenties; her father had hired Ki to be her companion and guardian some years before. Like Ki, Jessica Starbuck was wearing a rain slicker, its yellowish color almost matching her long copper-blond hair, which she'd tucked up under the crown of her brown Stetson. And although the slicker was buttoned at the neck and completely covered her green tweed jacket and skirt, it did little to conceal her firm, jutting breasts and sensuously rounded thighs and buttocks. Her mother, Sarah, had been a redheaded beauty who'd passed to her daughter a long-limbed, lushly molded figure covered in flesh as creamy and flawless as ivory, and a cameo face with a pert nose and more than a hint of feline audacity to her wide-set green eyes. Yet Jessie's father, Alex Starbuck, had given a steadfastness to her dimpled chin and a shrewd if sometimes humorous twist to her lips. Even though both parents were dead—murdered and subsequently avenged—in a very real sense they lived on, embodied in the spirit and actions of their only offspring.

And whatever might be claimed about Jessie Starbuck's spirit and actions, hawking patent snake oil out of a wagon couldn't be included. She'd had the wagon custom-built and fancied up to her specifications; she had to take the blame or credit if its purpose was mistaken. But other than a few personal belongings, which barely filled the small leather trunk wedged behind the seat, there was nothing in the wagon that she felt was hers—except that generally, everything bought in the name of Starbuck was hers.

Nonetheless, Jessie had wanted the wagon along, and had freighted it with them when she and Ki had taken the Union Pacific to Cheyenne four days ago. After spending the first night in the bustling territorial capital, they had hired the harness team and begun a grueling upcountry trek, stopping the second night at Underwood and the third night at Wheatland, before reaching Uva and turning west. They'd traveled well over a hundred miles, and estimated they still had another ten or so to go before arriving at their destination, the small valley cow town of Eucher Butte.

It would be there, at Eucher Butte, that the wagon would come in handy, if it didn't prove to be downright lifesaving. Because, for all practical purposes, the wagon belonged to Ki, and it was where, in racks and cabinets, he stored some of his considerable collection of lethal weapons.

Sired in Japan by an American "barbarian" who'd taken for his wife a Japanese woman of nobility, Ki had been orphaned at an early age. A half-breed outcast, shamed yet stubborn, he had apprenticed himself to one of the last samurai, Hirata, who for a decade drilled Ki in unarmed combat, and trained him in the use of *kyujutsu, kenjutsu, bojutsu, jojutsu,* and *shuriken-jutsu*—the martial arts of bow and arrow, sword, staff, stick, and throwing knife—as well as in even more exotic techniques and devices.

Such were the weapons, in their numerous variations, that Ki stowed in the otherwise innocuous-appearing wagon. Others he kept on his person, like the *shuriken*, steel disks in the shape of razor-sharp stars, attached in spring-loaded releases to his wrists. Still others, such as his *katana*, the sword left to him by Hirata, Ki preferred to leave behind in the safety of the huge Starbuck ranch in Texas.

Packed with death as the wagon was, its purpose was not to start wars, but to end them as swiftly and victoriously as possible. Neither Ki nor Jessica relished violence. Yet, as Hirata had taught Ki, and Ki in turn had taught Jessica: "To fight with another is wrong, but to lose a fight with another over principles you deem honorable is worse." They had no intention of losing any fight forced upon them.

Ki snapped the traces smartly, goading the Morgans into lunging against their hames and collars. The wagon swayed, lurching on its elliptical springs, its oil lamps shining blurred and dim through the sheets of driven rain. Forked shards of lightning did more to illuminate the trail ahead, and Ki was able to glimpse in their intermittent flashes where the ribbon of mud crested a ridge overlooking the river, and avoided a bouldered cliff by crossing over to the other side on a narrow plank bridge. The North Laramie, deep in its cutbanks, roared in an angry torrent, chunks of trees and uprooted bushes sweeping past, bucking and weaving, careening and jamming against the bridge supports before plummeting on down through the white-water channel.

Jessie, seeing the bridge shuddering from the impact of the water and debris, called over the fury of the storm: "You think it's safe enough to cross?"

Ki shrugged. "No way to tell, unless we stop and inspect it," he answered, as the team headed into the curve. "Do you want to?"

"Let's chance it. The bridge isn't very long, maybe fifty feet or so, and we're relatively light." She started to smile and then laughed out loud. "Remember this morning, when I wondered if it might rain before we reached Eucher Butte?"

"I remember. You hoped it would."

"Well, don't hold it against me. I was in the mood for a little breezy sprinkle, not a downpour. Now I hope it'll just go away."

"It should. It's moving south pretty fast and—"

"Look out!"

But Ki was already aware of the danger, having spotted it a split second before Jessica's shouted warning. The wagon was slewing and skidding around the sharp turn leading to the bridge; the roadbed was poorly banked and wickedly slippery from rain. Ki rode the footbrake and snugged the reins, the treacherous, storm-masked angle requiring all his attention and dexterity.

And the two men emerging onto the trail in front of them undoubtedly knew it. Garbed in nondescript slickers and sodden hats, they raised repeating carbines to their shoulders and began firing a head-on fusillade at the onrushing wagon. In the same instant, two other men rose from the boulders flanking the curve, and started shooting from each side as fast as they could trigger and lever.

"Duck!" Ki yelled, kicking off the brake and lashing the reins, hunching as low as he could while salvoes of lead punctured the curtain behind them and riddled the wooden body with splintering holes. The ambushers had chosen well, he realized fleetingly; they'd planned on the rocks here to give them shelter while hemming in the trail, and had counted on his having his hands literally full just keeping the wagon from toppling over—too full to be able to fight back.

But the bridge ahead was clear. If a tree or some boulders had been thrown across the roadbed, the trap would have been perfect, forcing the wagon to halt or crash. Perhaps there hadn't been time, or there weren't any trees nearby and the rocks were too large to shift, or the gunmen hadn't wanted to risk a forewarning, and figured their ambush was good enough as it was—whatever their reason, they'd neglected to barricade the trail beyond their gantlet.

All this Ki deduced in the blink of an eye.

"We're going to try driving through them," he shouted, urging the team on faster. "Be ready to jump and run if we start to roll over. At the rate we're going, we're liable to, but it's our only hope." *And a pretty dismal one at that*, he thought, grimacing as he battled the wheel-twisting, hubsquealing, erratically tipping wagon. He glanced at Jessica, who was sitting upright on the seat. "For God's sake, Jessie, get down!"

"I *was* down," she replied with a mirthless smile, cocking her two-shot .38 derringer. She had been down crouching behind the curved metal dashboard even as Ki had been first yelling for her to duck—but only long enough to reach up underneath her slicker and skirt to where she wore the derringer gartered to her thigh. Her other pistol, a custom .38 double-action Colt on a .44 frame, was packed in her trunk, it being too bulky and uncomfortable to wear on a long trip. It had been a logical decision at the time she'd packed it, but now it made her curse with frustration.

The wagon continued bearing down on the gunmen in front, leaning to the point of falling, swaying and lurching, throwing off their aim. Bracing herself against the seat, trying to keep her precarious balance, Jessica held her fire, not about to waste her bullets on bobbing targets out of the meager range of her hideout gun.

The man flanking her side of the trail came sprinting diagonally toward them, apparently figuring to intercept the wagon before it could go any farther. He rushed forward, clawing for a handhold, so close that Jessica could see his stubbled, thick-lipped face, and his lidded eyes gleaming with certain victory over a defenseless woman.

She brought the derringer up, caught her right wrist with her left hand, and took a bead on his chest. Her finger squeezed the trigger. The sound of her shot was hardly more than the snap of a finger, lost in the raging storm around them. The man screamed hoarsely and fell back to lie in the mud, inert and unfeeling as the rear wheel of the wagon jounced over him.

The bullet-spooked Morgans surged into their collars, dragging the wildly tottering wagon in frantic jerks. The two men in front and the man on Ki's side were still lined up and firing away. At such close range, both Ki and Jessica should have been riddled like sieves, but the swaying and lurching of the wagon made accurate firing impossible. The wagon was an inferno of flying lead, wood spraying in tiny slivers, the metal dashboard denting from ricocheting bullets. A slug burned along Ki's left arm, raising an ugly welt. But he kept on leashing the frightened team toward the bridge, and the two men in front suddenly realized he wasn't about to stop and let them shoot him, and if they stayed where they were, they'd likely get run over.

The men sprang aside, still firing up at the wagon. The one nearest to Ki dove for the on-side Morgan as it galloped past, in what was evidently a crazy maneuver to stop the team. He caught hold of the side strap and began running clumsily alongside in an effort to get a better grip and swing the horse off stride. The horse shied, sending the wagon into a sideways skid, and for a moment it seemed that the man would succeed. But he had misjudged the speed of the team and the nearness of the bridge. The Morgans lunged onto the planks, the horse with its clinging man grazing the bridge railing. His body was flattened, his single cry of shock and pain cut off as his chest was crushed. The horse dragged him another few feet, his fingers trapped in the strap, then smeared him once again against the railing. His body catapulted into the air, tumbling up over the railing and down into the river.

The wagon careened against the same railing, almost tearing off a wheel, then straightened and lurched, clattering, onto the bridge.

"We made it," Jessie said, smiling broadly.

Ki shook his head. "There's a man in back."

How Ki could sense such a thing over all the commotion and howling storm completely baffled Jessica, but she didn't question it. From long experience she'd learned to trust Ki's uncommon abilities, and she took it on faith that one of the two remaining gunmen had managed to grab the tailgate and climb aboard, and was now lurking in the closed bed of the wagon. She turned on the seat, derringer ready.

And the man launched his attack through the tattered curtain, firing his six-gun directly at her. But already Jessica was pivoting farther to one side so she could see behind her; her action was so swift he had not reacted to it, so he fired at where she had been.

Simultaneously, Ki killed him. His eyes were focused straight ahead at the trembling plank bridgeway, but suddenly, before either Jessica or the man could trigger again, the reins were in his left hand, and his right was slashing back. It was a hand hardened by years of training, and now it sliced unerringly like the edge of an executioner's axe, chopping against the man's throat, crushing his larnyx and cracking his spine.

The man crouched there with his pistol in his hand, staring at Jessica in sheer disbelief, paralyzed in death. Without a sound he rolled sideways as his left leg buckled under him, and toppled back out of sight behind the curtain.

Shaken, Jessie asked, "Any more?"

"Yes," Ki answered, eyes still on the bridge. "But not with us."

"Only one, though."

"Here, perhaps. But these four were hired, Jessie, they weren't the brains. Likely the last man is already going for the horses they hid, and'll be riding to report their failure."

"Eucher Butte. He'll be heading there."

"Assuming he does, he'll be on this trail behind us, faster

than us. Or if he's stupid, he might simply try to pursue us and
cut us down before we reach Eucher Butte."

"Which do you think?"

"Stupid," Ki said flatly, recalling the lack of a barricade.

"Either way, if we do get to Eucher Butte alive, we'll be
prime targets for plenty more treachery."

Ki gave Jessie a flinty grin. "Did we expect anything else?"

"No, but I didn't expect it this soon. How did they know—"

Her troubled question was interrupted by a harsh, shuddering rumble in the bridge beneath them. Almost tumbling out
of the side of the wagon, Jessie clutched desperately for the
dashboard handhold as the bridge trembled violently again,
creaking and groaning.

Alarmed, Ki stood up and peered out over the railing. They
were virtually midway across the span, and the North Laramie
was a dark, boiling cauldren flowing far below. A phosphores-
cent stroke of lightning lit the black sky for an instant, and by
its white glare, he could see that an old thick spruce had been
swept downriver, and had lodged lengthwise against the bridge
pilings. Its gnarled branches and roots were gathering other
debris—pine and yucca and scrub brush—adding to the weight
pressing against the weak, spindly supports.

Ki slapped the reins, sending the team into a protesting
gallop. The bridge began twisting, undulating from the mounting force pushing at its pilings, its creaking now growing
almost intolerably loud.

There was a wrenching shake as the creaking was drowned
out by a sundering roar. The bridge swayed, then dipped, the
railings splintering and the deck buckling, dropping apart. The
planks fractured in bunches, falling, leaving a gaping hole.

The team plunged through the hole, taking the wagon with it.

Chapter 2

The wagon tilted, upending beneath them. Ki scarcely had time to grip Jessica by one arm before they were hurled, tumbling, out into space and plummeted toward the raging river below. The wagon fell like a stone, shattering in the wreckage of bridge supports and driftwood. But thrown free, Jessica and Ki struck open water on the downriver side, dropping deep underwater and striking submerged rocks.

Dazed and gasping, they surfaced, only to be caught by the surging current. They swam with hard strokes, hampered by their slickers, hardly able to keep from being swept toward a series of sawtoothed boulders through which the river was cascading in deadly, foaming rapids. Half drowned, one hand still clinging to her arm, Ki helped Jessica fight out of the tugging current toward the bank, frantically trying to miss the flotsam of bridge beams, wagon parts, and running gear that were churning around them.

They were less than ten yards from the north bank when a side panel of the wagon reared out of the surface and rammed into Jessica. Ki's grasp was torn loose, and Jessica was thrust, rolling, back into the irresistible hold of the swirling flow. Ki made a lunge for her, but Jessica was already gone, plunging with the side panel toward the bone-smashing, whirling rapids.

Ki dove after her, swimming now with the current in an

effort to intercept Jessica. He reached out, missed, stroked, and reached again, fingers tightening on the collar of her slicker. Then he battled one-handedly for the bank again. Taxing his muscles to the utmost, almost losing her again in his frenzied struggle, Ki managed to maneuver them out of the torrent. His boots scraped against stone, and he dug in for a better footing, half climbing, half crawling into a shallow break.

The backwash in this break in the bank created a whirling eddy, and two or three swimming strokes took them to the river's edge. The rain had turned the earth there into a grease-slick ooze, and it was only by clutching at an overhanging limb of a cottonwood that Ki was able at last to drag them both out of the cold rushing water.

Jessica lay on her back, arms flung out, eyes closed, soundless.

Ki knelt and placed his ear to her chest. "You're breathing."

"Of course I'm breathing," Jessie whispered hoarsely, still not moving. "Wait a minute, it's all I can do right now."

A few moments later, Jessie slowly sat up. She coughed, threw up a small quantity of water, then gingerly felt her left shoulder, where the edge of the wagon panel had struck her.

"Are you all right?" Ki asked.

"I think so," she replied, wincing. "It's bruised or maybe wrenched a little, but nothing feels broken."

They rested there for a time, sucking air into their aching lungs, while the storm battered down and the angry river lapped at their feet. Upriver to their right, the rubbled bridge thrust skeletally toward the dismal sky. Downriver, the rapids were collecting the remains of the wagon and the plump carcasses of the team, along with bridge supports and planks, and much of the same mountains pile of uprooted brush and trees that had collapsed the span. But the rocks were tougher, withstanding the ravaging pressure.

Jessie was the first to speak. "Gone, Ki, all gone."

"Nothing that can't be replaced."

"I know, Ki, but your weapons . . ."

"It's not good to become too dependent on weapons. They're merely tools to help in one's task. There are other tools, other ways. Don't worry, the task will be done."

She nodded, biting her lip.

"And our first task," Ki continued affably, standing and offering a hand to Jessica, "must be to find shelter."

Again Jessica nodded, rising and starting with him up the bank to the trail. When he paused on the way to smile encouragingly at her, she managed to respond with a weak smile of her own, sensing that Ki was trying to appear more optimistic than he actually felt. She herself mainly felt anger. As she stumbled over rocks and slipped on the muddy earth, her anger mounted with every step she took, an anger that grew into a grim, purposeful determination to settle the score, barehanded if need be, just as soon as they could reach Eucher Butte.

Angling back upriver toward the bridge, they came to the trail and began following it west again. They trudged slowly, partly from fatigue, partly through caution. The fourth gunman wasn't a threat; he was stuck on the other side of the river and probably thought they were dead. But the unexpected ambush had made them wary, alerting them to the fact that they were known to be traveling this way, at this time. And considering that their only weapons were Ki's *shuriken* and one remaining cartridge in Jessica's derringer, which miraculously had come through entangled in a pocket of her slicker, they both figured that, for now, discretion was a better part of valor.

The trail went along the spine of a low ridge for a while, then came to a plateau overlooking a long stretch of valley ahead. Off to their left, across a weedy field, jutted the angular silhouette of a deserted cabin. From a distance it appeared that some of the roof was missing and the door was sagging on its hinges, but the walls were still standing, and would provide needed protection from the wind and rain. Already Ki could feel a chill seeping through his veins, and though Jessica was uncomplaining, she couldn't keep herself from shivering.

They hastened across the field to the cabin, and went inside; then, propping the door closed, they looked about the dim, musty interior. A crumbling fireplace was built against the far wall, the storm echoing mournfully down its tall chimney. The remnants of a wooden stool and bedframe were cluttering one corner, luckily under a portion of the remaining roof, and when

Ki checked the broken pieces, he found them to be rotten and relatively dry.

Swiftly they scraped up the trash and old leaves that littered the floor, piling it all with the broken furniture in the fireplace hearth. Opening his slicker, Ki took from his suit jacket his waterproof box of block matches, and after a few tries, he managed to light a fire.

Satisfied, he stood for a moment with Jessica in front of the warming flames. Then he said, "I'll be back in a short while."

"You're leaving? No, Ki, not without me—"

"Stay here, Jessie, and get dry. After that dunking you took, you'd risk catching pneumonia if you went out again."

"And you couldn't, too? Ki, where are you going?"

Ki, already at the door, merely answered with a soft, knowing smile. Then, closing the door behind him, he stepped out into the cold, rain-lashing storm. The first task was done; now for the second.

He set off in a steady run back toward the river. It distressed him to leave Jessica filled with questions and doubts; but to have explained, he felt, would have resulted either in her refusing to let him go, or her insisting on coming along. It would have taken too long to persuade her otherwise, and time was of the essence. Alone, he could make better time. Indeed, if he'd been alone before, he wouldn't have left the river; only the priority of finding shelter for Jessica had compelled him to act as he had.

Arriving at the ruined bridge, he angled downriver, veering down the bank and sprinting along the water's edge to the rapids. The turbulent river was swirling against the rocks, spuming over the haphazard dam of debris that was trapped, higher and thicker than ever, like bits of food between the teeth of a giant. Without hesitating, Ki ripped off his slicker, suit jacket, and Wellington boots, and dove in.

The rampaging current carried him toward the nearer of the two channels that formed a fork on either side of the jutting boulders. Swimming furiously, he propelled himself toward the middle of the river, and a moment later he was flung violently against the choking mound of debris. The shock of his impact dislodged one of the dead Morgans, which squeezed between the rocks and was carried away.

Frigid hands clawing for a hold, Ki lifted himself out of the water and onto the rough, scrubby branches of a yellow pine. Balancing gingerly, testing for weight and shifting before each step, he carefully eased among the debris and rocks, poking deep and clearing away, searching to recover what might remain of theirs.

Time, precious time. If he'd been able to begin his hunt earlier, when the shattered wagon had first washed up against the rocks, he'd have had a better chance of finding things. If he'd waited much longer than he had, it would have been hopeless. Every minute, the raging tide was adding new debris, pushing forward what was there already, covering over the old and grinding it up, then prying it loose and sending it swirling away, lost forever.

He spent almost an hour in his search, digging with his hands and clinging precariously with his feet. His weapons were gone. Those made of wood, like his bows and arrows and *nunchaku* sticks, had undoubtedly floated away immediately. Those of metal, like his *sai* swords and studded mail gloves, simply had sunk to the bottom. And his explosive devices would be beyond use, even if he discovered any—which he didn't.

But with a sigh of relief, Ki managed to locate Jessica's bulky trunk. Its top was crushed and one side was stove in, and its Excelsior lock was snapped open and twisted awry. Its two hefty leather straps still held it closed, however, though tree roots were wedged between them and the lid, making it difficult to haul from the debris.

At the other end of the rapids, where the carcass of the second Morgan remained hooked to the harness, Ki discovered his own Bellows case. This took even greater effort to extract, caught as it was in the venturi of two boulders, and firmly held underwater by the leaden foreleg of the dead horse. Launching himself into the water, Ki prodded and shoved and wrenched, struggling to keep from being sucked through the geysering vortex between the boulders. For a seemingly endless time, the case refused to budge, only the fact that it was made of impervious "alligator keratol" saving it from breaking apart in Ki's levering tug-of-war with the rocks. Stubbornly Ki kept working, determined to reclaim the case, which not only contained a change of clothing, but his prized multipocket vest and an emergency assortment of smaller weapons—throwing daggers, spare *shuriken*, and the like.

At last he maneuvered his case free. Thrusting it and himself out of the water, he carried it across to where he'd upended Jessica's trunk to drain, at the edge of the debris closest to the bank. Then, taking a deep breath and an iron grip on the case, he slid back into the river and began an agonizing one-handed crawl toward the shore. He fought the current, counting each off-balance stroke in his mind, savoring each yard he gained. Grabbing at slick tufts of grass growing along the bank, he tossed the sodden case up onto the ground.

Again, hesitating only long enough to fill his lungs, Ki dove back to the rapids to retrieve the trunk. It was larger and heavier than his case, weighing him down like a waterlogged anchor as he hugged it with his left hand and braced himself against the river's brutal rush.

The current pummeled him, tossing him into a dangerous tangent. Despite himself, despite his years of training and experience, a sensation of dread seeped through Ki as he forged again toward the bank. He'd made a mistake, a fatal error, tackling too great and awkward a load this time, and he was going to be swept away and drowned. He forced down his panic, calling on the last of his inner resources to strain forward, wrestling with the pitching, sinking trunk. He could not die this way, it would not happen, it was not a true thing.

God, but it was, it was. His chest was throbbing, aching, and there was a ringing in his ears, and for an instant he thought the feel of stone and sediment under his feet was a hallucination. Ki clawed onwards, knowing that if it was a mirage, it really didn't make any difference. It was all over but the swallowing.

Kicking, frantic to relieve the pressure in his lungs, he reached the shallows, head reeling and stomach knotting with convulsions. Water boiled against his thighs as he straightened, choking and gagging, and shoved the trunk the last few feet to the bank. Wading, he dragged it to the safety of a sloping ledge and slumped beside it. His strength was sapped. He lay there, momentarily helpless, while with wracking coughs he dispelled muddy river water from his lungs.

When he felt somewhat recovered, Ki carted the trunk up

to where he'd dumped the case, and tilted both on end to drain them. Slowly he collected his jacket, slicker, and boots, and after dressing he waited a bit longer, recouping more of his flagging energy. Then, balancing the cumbersome trunk on his back, holding it steady with one hand, he picked up the case in his other hand and set off up the bank toward the trail.

Chapter 3

Ki's return to the cabin was steady but sluggish, the storm flailing about him. Gradually the wind lowered, and in time the rain lessened into a chilling drizzle. The overcast parted, drifting southward, but now the sky was dark with late evening. Stars began to glimmer here and there, and a pale quarter moon was a blurry crescent in the blue-black dome surrounding it.

Ki savored the washed freshness of the crisp evening breeze. He made little effort to avoid detection, walking openly along the center strip of the trail, bending low with the weight of his load, moving by sheer reflex. If he was attacked now, he doubted he had enough strength left to fight, and he was becoming so numbed with exhaustion that he was almost past the point of caring.

Eventually he reached the field, and saw smoke spiraling from the chimney of the cabin. Heartened, he quickened his pace. When he arrived, he put down his case long enough to open the door, then stepped inside.

The interior was bathed in a ruddy glow from the fireplace blaze. Jessica stood with her back to the fire, steam wisping from her tweed riding jacket and skirt, her blonde hair plastered wetly to her head. When she saw Ki enter, she rushed forward to help him, her green eyes widening with relief and surprise.

"Ki! How on earth did you—"

"Never mind how," Ki gasped, dropping her trunk and the case next to the hearth. "It needed to be done, and it was."

"No, it didn't. You said yourself everything was replaceable."

"So I first thought. Then I remembered your father's book."

Jessica paused, nodding thoughtfully. "You're right, Ki, I'd brought it along. But it was still a horrid chance for you to take, and I'm not sure it was worth the risk of losing you as well."

"Ah, but you didn't, Jessie. I'm here, the book is here, and a lot of other things are here that we'd better get to drying."

"And one of those things is you," Jessica said pointedly.

"I'll unpack, it's the least I can do, while you shuck some of those sopping wet clothes and rest by the fire. And, Ki?"

"Yes?"

"Thank you."

Ki smiled wearily in acknowledgement, and gladly accepted her suggestion. He stripped off his slicker, suit jacket, and black ankle-high boots again, adding to them now his socks, sky-blue shirt, and string tie, leaving himself clad only in his drenched trousers.

He settled comfortably, cross-legged, before the crackling fire, and started breathing in through his nose and out through his mouth. When he'd slowed his inhalation/exhalation cycle to ten breaths a minute, he cupped his right ear with the palm of his left hand, and concentrated on one thought: relaxation. After five minutes, he switched to the other hand and ear. After another five, he crossed his arms and covered both ears, still breathing inaudibly, his tongue adhering to the roof of his mouth. And in that position he remained.

Meanwhile, Jessie was busily emptying his case. She laid out his denim jeans, collarless shirt, rope-soled cloth slippers, and brown leather vest near the hearth and wiped and cleaned his weapons with the hem of her skirt. Then she arranged the case so that it too would dry. Nothing, she was relieved to find, appeared ruined.

Then she turned to her trunk. Opening it, she realized bleakly that it was beyond salvation and would have to be replaced. Blessedly, it had stayed together enough to protect the contents. Most of her extra clothes were ruined, but her wide brown belt was fine, and there wasn't much damage that could be done to her well-worn jeans and matching denim jacket—except maybe to shrink some more, and they already fit her as snugly as a second skin.

Resting on the trunk's linen-lined set-up tray was her custom .38 Colt revolver, still in its waxed holster, along with a gun-cleaning kit, a cut-crystal perfume atomizer, and a few other feminine trinkets. These she set aside, lifting the tray's bottom, which acted as the lid of a second compartment underneath. She removed a letter and a black calfskin-bound pocket notebook, silently thanking Ki again for having endangered his life to recover them.

Taking the letter and book to the hearth, she propped them up to dry. Then, on second thought, she picked up the letter again to see if the soaking had made it illegible. The notebook worried her less; she knew its entries were in india ink, having frequently studied the pages of names, dates, and places since her father, the author of the notebook's contents, had died, leaving it in a hidden compartment of his old rolltop desk.

The letter was on a single sheet of tablet paper, and though some of its writing was smeared a little, it had been protected by the envelope. Postmarked six weeks ago at Eucher Butte, it had been penned with exquisite script in stilted, formal language:

To Whom It May Concern:

This is to inform you that my husband, Uriah, recently passed away. I must mention this grievous tragedy in detail for two reasons, one being the peculiar nature of his death, and the other being the resultant inability to continue business relations as contracted between the Flying W and the Circle Star.

My husband, a star rider all of his life, nevertheless was found by our foreman after apparently having fallen from his horse and been dragged a considerable distance. When I questioned this and insisted on a fuller investigation, I was subsequently informed by Sheriff Quincy Oakes that inspection revealed a massive blow inflicted to the forehead, and other indications that this

*injury had not been inflicted by a horse, but had caused
death before dragging took place. Unfortunately, as
suspicious as this might sound, I have been unable to
gain further help or to alter the verdict of accidental
death.*

*I suspect my husband met his untimely demise
through foul play. Shortly before his supposed accident,
he turned down an offer to sell the Flying W to Captain
Guthried Ryker, owner of the nearby Block-Two-Dot
ranch. Shortly afterwards, I was approached by this
same man To be perfectly candid, I am afraid I hold a
low opinion of Captain Ryker's basic nature, in spite of
his outwardly civilized manner, and cannot but wonder
if he felt that his purchase would be easier to negotiate
with a widow.*

*I am adamantly opposed to selling, particularly to
Captain Ryker. I believe I should warn you, however,
that soon I may be forced to put the ranch up for auction.
My husband brought me here from Boston just a few
years ago, and I know little about ranching. Rustlers
have been raiding our stock. I have been required to
withdraw heavily from our savings, and face having to
borrow funds to operate. If matters continue as they
have, we will surely be unable to meet the quota of cattle
we agreed to supply the Circle Star by this coming
autumn.*

*I have no proof, and you could very well regard me
as a silly and incompetent hysteric. Yet I am convinced
that my late husband and I have been the victims of an
unscrupulous plot to wrest ownership of our ranch. I
beg your indulgence and understanding, and remain*

Y'r m'st ob'd'nt s'rv'nt,
(Mrs.) Amabelle Pons Waldemar

"I certainly don't think you're silly or crazy, Mrs. Waldemar,"
Jessica sighed aloud, spreading the letter back out on the hearth.
She crossed to her slicker and took out her derringer, then
went to her trunk and unwrapped the gun-cleaning kit. All the

while she mulled over the letter, pondering how it fit with other facts she knew. Closing the lid of the trunk, she sat down on it and began drying and lubricating the derringer, then hesitated, frowning as she glanced over to where Ki was still squatting motionless.

"Ki, how did Ryker know we were coming?"

"Your supper with Governor Hoyt," Ki murmered, unmoving.

"Of course," Jessie said, mostly to herself. Finishing with the derringer, she picked up her revolver and started to clean it, her mind shaping small links into a pattern, as a child might fashion a delicate pine-needle chain. Her eyes flashed a peculiar greenish shade, the hue of an iceberg's edge when salt water washed it. Her father would have said she was in one of her "damned moods."

Amabelle Waldemar's letter, which had started it all, had been addressed to the general offices of the huge Starbuck cattle operation in Texas, headquartered at the sprawling Circle Star ranch. Initially it was treated the same as the many other missives received every day, and was transferred to the section that handled sales and purchases for routine response. On the surface, it *was* routine. Starbuck contracted with hundreds of small, underfinanced ranches to supply beef for the burgeoning markets in America and Europe, and a certain percentage of failures and bankruptcies were expected.

In the case of Waldemars' Flying W, it was one of a half-dozen borderline ranches in the area, which the Circle Star had helped to arrange into a loose sort of cooperative. Banding together allowed the ranches to operate as effectively as larger spreads, but the Circle Star's motives were not entirely altruistic, for it also guaranteed a reasonably steady source of meat.

The previous October, the Circle Star had been notified that the Block-Two-Dot ranch had been sold and was dropping out of the co-op. Starbuck field men, going there to try renegotiating the deal, reported back that they'd been tossed off the property at gunpoint. At the time, neither this nor the name of the new owner sparked any alarm. Then Amabelle Waldemar's letter arrived. A sharp-witted clerk, perceiving that an anguished plea for help was implied in the message, and remembering the strange incident at the Block-Two-Dot, sent the letter and a memo explaining the connection on to his superiors for review.

It didn't take long for Jessica to get the letter—after all, the Starbuck buck stopped with her. Reading it and the memo, the name of the Block-Two-Dot's owner struck her as sounding familiar, and she then began leafing through the pages of the little black book.

Guthried Ryker was listed in it.

Another connection was now forged, one far more sinister than the lowly clerk could have imagined. Contained within the notebook's leather covers was a ledger detailing the names and activities of a vicious international ring intent upon gaining control of America's business and political establishment. Jessica's father had started compiling the information while in the Orient, during his first meager years of building what would ultimately become the Starbuck business empire, and had scrupulously kept the book up to date ever since. In his subsequent battles with this criminal conspiracy, his wife was killed while Jessica was still a baby. Eventually he too was murdered; though, by then, Jessica was a young woman, old enough to know and understand his persistent fight.

Vowing revenge, and aided by Ki and her wealthy inheritance, Jessica continued her father's war against the insidious network of graft and corruption—against the traitorous businessmen, lawmen, politicians, and outright crooks who'd sold out America to this merciless cabal that had slaughtered her parents. Guthried Ryker was one of them.

The entry stated that Ryker, Guthried Hannibal, aged forty-seven, had been born to a socially prominent family in Philadelphia. He was well educated, with no military service—putting the lie to his aggrandizing title of "Captain." He was unmarried, and a frequenter of prostitutes who specialized in whips and ropes. Currently he was the figurehead president of Acme Packers & Purveyors, a front company for the ring, which operated out of the Chicago stockyards.

Evidently, Ryker was quite the city-slick bastard . . .

And at the moment, as Jessica sat on her broken trunk, rubbing whale oil on her revolver, she couldn't help wondering why the devil Ryker had chosen to move to Eucher Butte. She could envision the kind of man he was: ambitious, greedy, devious, with a streak of cruelty just beneath his sophisticated facade. He would likely enjoy the role of cattle baron, but she couldn't figure how he hoped to attain that by owning such piddling ranches as the Block-Two-Dot and the Waldemars' Flying W. Nor could Jessica see him running them. If the report was accurate, and she'd no reason to doubt it, Guthried Ryker had never roped, branded, or castrated a calf; had probably never, in fact, stepped in cow dung. He was the type who'd stay comfortably away and hire lesser men to do his dirty work for him.

Dirty work like the ambush that had been laid for Ki and herself.

The surprise attack at the bridge still puzzled her. Ki had answered the *how* behind it: Ryker had undoubtedly heard they were coming, thanks to John W. Hoyt, territorial governor of Wyoming. Hoyt had greeted Jessica and Ki in Cheyenne, admitting that he'd learned of their arrival from the Wichita stationmaster, who'd recognized Jessica when they'd boarded the Union Pacific there, and had wired ahead for red-carpet service, thinking he was doing her a service.

Hoyt had insisted that *the* Starbuck of *the* Starbuck empire dine with him at the capital. On trips like this, Jessica preferred to keep a low profile, but there hadn't been any way to decline his offer graciously. She'd been politely vague about their destination, even though she knew the governor to be an honorable man beyond reproach. Nor did she believe he'd purposely tipped off Ryker—except perhaps in the same respect as the stationmaster had, by innocently requesting other important personages to host her royally wherever she went. And certainly, as president of a Chicago packing company, Ryker was the most—probably the only—person of any note around Eucher Butte. On the other hand, the news could just as easily have been sent by an eager reporter or political flunky keeping tabs on the governor's doings. Whatever, the dinner's high visibility had resulted in warning Ryker, giving him plenty of time to arrange an appropriate welcome . . .

But that still failed to solve the *why* of it. Obviously, Ryker had deduced that he was the reason for their trip, and had figured to kill them before they could threaten his schemes.

Jessica didn't know what those schemes might be, yet for Ryker to have tried such a drastic act as that ambush convinced her he was after more than merely grabbing the Flying W. No matter what his motives, one fact was clear: their journey to Eucher Butte was already proving to be complicated and dangerous, far more than their original purpose of helping Amabelle Waldemar would have led them to believe.

"I hate to admit it, Ki," Jessica said, setting her revolver aside and smoothing her skirt, "but Ryker has got me baffled."

Ki said nothing.

"I mean, what's he up to?" she continued. "The region's pretty remote, lacking mining potential and only fair for grazing, and the only rumors of a possible new rail line are about the Chicago & Northwestern laying track way to the north. What do you think?"

Ki still did not respond.

Jessica looked carefully at Ki, wondering if something was wrong with him. He remained quiet and motionless in his cross-legged, cross-armed position—a position she knew he used for more than simple relaxation. As Ki had often told her, it was a position he practiced for fifteen or twenty minutes almost daily, as an exercise to strengthen what he termed his "intrinsic energy," that inner concentrating force which permeated most Asian martial arts systems, and which was the underlying basis of his own power and agility.

No, nothing seemed to be wrong. In fact, as Jessica started toward him to check, Ki appeared to look superbly healthy. With his lithe-muscled naked back, his bronzed bare arms, and his mane of blue-black hair cascading around his corded shoulders, he resembled something like a pagan earth god, virile and primally desirable.

Reaching Ki, Jessica felt her breasts begin to tingle perversely, and she told herself to be a good girl. Ki was out of bounds, just as she was for him. It wasn't because he worked for her; Ki may have been on a different social level, but so had been many of her lovers. And it wasn't because he would have rebuffed her seduction; though unspoken, she was aware of how greatly he cared for her. Rather, it was because they were as brother and sister, two halves of a partnership equal and compatible. To have surrendered to a moment of physical bliss would have ruptured forever that deeper, more fundamental bond of admiration, trust, and affection that they held for each other.

She touched him lightly. "Ki?" she whispered.

Ki did not answer. He was sound asleep.

Chapter 4

The night passed without incident.

Jessica and Ki awakened just before daybreak, to find that the residue of the storm had blown itself away, wheeling south into Colorado. But the fire had long since burned out, and the gray false dawn was cold, adding impetus to their movements as they hurriedly changed their clothes and left the cabin for Eucher Butte.

In the flush of a serene, fiery dawn, they began their long hike down the trail. Jessica was now in her figure-squeezing denim jeans and jacket, her derringer concealed behind the wide square buckle of her belt, her custom .38 holstered at her thigh, her notebook safely hidden inside her silk blouse, pressing against her flat belly under the swell of her firm, unbound breasts. Ki too was wearing jeans, along with his cotton-twill shirt and moccasin-like slippers, the weapons he'd salvaged from his case now hidden on his body and in the many pockets of his worn leather vest.

They reached Eucher Butte with the noon sun overhead, the Wyoming sky a soft powder-blue enamel, warm and benevolent.

The town swelled like a festering sore near the banks of the North Laramie, sprawling in the same pattern as a thousand other small cow towns, with an outscatter of corrals and sheds at one end, and a rutted main street leading to a cluster of frame houses at the other.

Walking along, Jessica and Ki passed a livery stable and yard, a funeral home, a gunsmith, and an imposing saloon with the name THUNDERMUG painted on its etched-glass windows. Directly across from the saloon was a combination barbershop and bath house, and a tucked-away restaurant with no name at all. Farther on could be seen a bootmaker, a general store and feedlot, and a false-fronted three-story hotel called the GRAND CONTINENTAL, with most of its ground floor taken up by a bank. Flanking the hotel was a telegraph and post office, and a bleak stone building with a weathered sign over its door reading ALBANY CO. SHERIFF. Buckboards and wagons were almost as prevalent as horses, and the boardwalks were crowded for this time of day, sure signs that, come evening, a lot of merry hurrahing would break loose in the gaming rooms and crib parlors of the large, obviously profitable saloon.

They went as far as the restaurant, where they ordered the first decent meal they'd had since yesterday morning. While eating, Jessica thought that probably Eucher Butte wasn't too awful a place—it merely seemed that way. It was wild, typical of the territory and the breed infesting it, no worse than other small cattle towns and maybe a little better. She doubted they'd get much cooperation here; likely the townsfolk wouldn't be partial to strangers poking their noses in local affairs, especially now that Ryker, forewarned, had had a chance to cover himself and spread a bunch of horse manure around. But it would furnish their more immediate needs, and from that point of view, Eucher Butte was quite satisfactory.

Leaving the restaurant, Ki said, "No telling what Ryker has in mind, Jessie, and I'd hate for him to catch you with empty pistols. Let me go buy you some fresh ammunition. Then, if you want, I'll hire a horse and ride back to the cabin to collect our luggage."

"It's liable to be all stolen by now."

Ki shrugged. "No great loss," he replied, adding with a sly grin, "besides, if any thief looked finer in your tweed outfit than you do, I'd say you ought to let him keep it."

Jessica laughed. "I would, gladly. Better yet, Ki, see if you can find some kid who'd fetch it for you, and ask directions to the Flying W. If there's time, we'll ride out there today. If not, we'll stay over at the hotel and leave early tomorrow."

"Good idea. Then where will I meet you?"

"At the sheriff's, I imagine."

"You're going to report the ambush?"

"I might. Won't know till I size up the man," Jessica said, "and get a feel as to which side of the ambush he'd have been fighting on."

They parted, and Jessica strode along the boardwalk to the sheriff's office. Even before opening the door, she could hear an angry voice shouting inside. Entering, she faced a fat, fifty-ish man sitting tilted in a swivel chair, and the back of a younger man standing with his fists clenched on top of the littered desk between them.

"Haul your ass out and put a stop to it, Quince!" the younger man was yelling. "My crew's threatening to quit, and after that raid the night 'fore last, when Rasmussen got shot dead and three others got winged, I can't rightly blame 'em if they ske-daddled. Just like all my goddamned rustled cows you can't find went and skedaddled."

"Easy, Daryl, a lady's present," the fat man growled, seeing Jessica and straightening in his chair. "Yes, ma'am?"

"Are you Sheriff Oakes?"

"Deputy Sheriff, yes," the fat man answered, preening one end of the graying mustache that drooped around his pudgy mouth and jowls. A tobacco dribble stained his vest next to his tarnished star. "Something I can do for you, ma'am?"

"Maybe the same thing you can do for him," Jessica answered, indicating the other man with a glancing nod.

She judged the man, who'd now turned toward her, to be about thirty, six foot one or two, maybe two hundred pounds, with a hardness that didn't come from riding a brass rail. Tousled hair the shade of dressed hardness leather, brushed long under a wide-brimmed, flat-crowned Kansas hat. Big beak of a nose and an anvil for a chin. Magnetic eyes that appraised her squarely. His frayed range clothes were sweaty and dirty, and the Remington .44-40 stuck in his belt was a relic with cracked grips, but this was no saddle tramp; he was a man used to giving orders and having them obeyed. She liked him immediately.

Regarding Deputy Oakes again, she continued, "You can track down and arrest these rustlers and killers hereabouts, that's what you can do. But I gather you haven't been much good at it."

Stung, the deputy frowned, puffing his cheeks. "Can't say I place you, ma'am. Forgive me if I ask just who you are, and if you've got any special interest in our local problems."

"I most certainly have," Jessica retorted archly. "My name's Starbuck, Miss Jessica Starbuck, and I've got a considerable interest in the Flying W." Which, in a manner of speaking, was true enough.

She left it at that, deciding not to mention the ambush. Even if Deputy Oakes acted on it, she figured he wouldn't be able to do or prove much; Ryker was too clever not to have removed his dead gunmen and cleaned up any other evidence that might incriminate him. And the deputy didn't look like the sort who'd bust a gut investigating; he looked like he'd been in that swivel chair a mighty long time, and was tired of hearing about trouble.

Jessica's name seemed to spark recognition in the other man, but if Deputy Oakes realized who she was, he didn't show it.

"Poor widder Waldemar, a shame, a shame," the deputy murmured, then eyed Jessica glumly. "I'm not surprised she's sold to an outsider, it's a terrible lot for her to try running all by her lonesome. But like I was about to tell Mr. Melville here, I've been worn to a frazzle chasing one blind lead after another."

"Well, if you won't do more'n you have," Melville snapped, "then I reckon us ranchers will have to protect ourselves."

Oakes leaned back again, shifting uncomfortably. "It's not that I won't, Daryl, it's that all I've got is me and my night man. Sure's I ride out to your spread, the coyotes are hitting the Double Diamond. I ride there, and they strike Leach's Lazy L."

"As Miss Starbuck said, Quince, track them down."

"Don't think I haven't tried. But once off the flatlands, we lose them up in the rock canyons. Can't even get a line on where the cattle's being sold, either, no sign of any of your herds showing up anywhere in the territory. It's just like the mountains opened up and swallowed them whole, and I tell you, it's got me buffaloed."

"Well, I guess that means me and the others will have to form a vigilante committee," Melville said, glaring as he leaned over the desk again. "I know it's illegal, but we're fed up with losing our men and cattle."

Deputy Oakes brooded, as if considering the ultimatum. "Daryl," he finally said, "I'll ask you not to go off half cocked. Let me wire my boss in Laramie to send some more deputies. I'll scatter them around, and we're sure to get a lead on where the rustlers are rat-holed. You tell that to the others, will you?"

"I'll try," Melville replied. "They might not listen."

"Make them listen. Letting your crews run around with itchy trigger fingers can only lead to worse trouble, not less. I mean this for your own good. I'd really regret having to arrest you or any of your men for taking the law into your own hands."

"All right, Quince, I'll string along with you awhile longer." Straightening, Melville started for the door. He paused, hand on the knob, to add, "But things have to change around here, and fast."

"They will, Daryl," Deputy Oakes replied with an earnest heartiness. "You've got my word. You can count on it."

Melville nodded and opened the door, then hesitated again to look at Jessica. "Coming, Miss Starbuck?"

It was less a question than a command, and normally such a tone would have provoked Jessica. But she had no more to say to Deputy Oakes, and plenty to ask Daryl Melville. Besides, she was interested in knowing why he'd raised his eyebrows when he heard her name. So, with a parting smile to the deputy, she went out the door that Melville was holding open for her.

Before she could utter a word, Melville started angling across the street, his long swift strides hard for her to follow.

"Where are you going so fast?" she asked.

"To get my father," he said, slowing so she could catch up. His onyx eyes were flashing more irately than ever. "He's over in the Thundermug, half swacked by now. The damn dog-bleeding crooks."

"Who?"

"Halford and Kendrick, bartender and gambler, the owners of the dive. If one doesn't rob you, the other one will. Say, by any chance would you be related to the Starbucks in Texas?"

"Yes. Why?"

"I'm one of the ranchers in the Circle Star co-op."

"Oh? Which one?"

"Spraddled M. M for Melville." Reaching the boardwalk on the opposite side of the street, he stopped and smiled at Jessica. "Daryl Melville. And my father, Tobias, of course; he started it after driving cattle up from Texas back in the early seventies."

"You sound proud of it."

"Dirt-proud, mostly, but it's home," he responded wryly, and gestured down the street, where the trail continued west to Garrett. "There's a fork in the road a fair piece from here, that goes to five spreads back in the slopes, including ours and the Flying W. There ain't none of us but hasn't fought everything Mother Nature has to throw, and we were winning until this thieving and murdering came along. Hate to say it, but you rode into a range that's raring to explode."

"I've done that before," Jessica said quietly.

"I admire your spunk," he said, starting up the boardwalk again, "but it's too bad you didn't know this before buying out Mrs. Waldemar."

"I haven't. My only interest is to protect the investment Starbuck has in her herd. In all your herds, if possible. But are you ranchers truly serious about forming a vigilante committee?"

Melville gave a laugh, short and bitter. "I was pure bluffing. The big ranchers don't need to, they've got their own guards. And the smaller ranchers are afraid that to fight back would goad the rustlers into wiping them out, man, woman, and child. So all they're willing to do is stand pat like sheep, doing nothing 'cept bleat and leak in their pants, if you'll pardon the expression, Miss Starbuck."

"Jessie."

"All right, but only if you call me Daryl. And don't get me wrong, but I can't see how you hope to help the lady, Jessie."

"First, by riding out there this afternoon for a talk."

"Won't make it before dark, I'm afraid, and the Flying W isn't much set up for overnight guests. Or are you already expected?"

"Not especially, no. I'd better wait till tomorrow morning."

"Well, you can leave word with her crew that you're coming," he said caustically, thumbing toward a knot of horses tied in front of the saloon. "Crews are like mavericks, they have to be taught who's boss and be ridden on short rein. Otherwise they run wild."

Melville moved through the batwings without holding them open for Jessie; it never dawned on him that a rowdy saloon would be a place she'd visit. She followed anyway, her curiosity piqued by his comment about the Flying W crew, and stood unobtrusively along the wall by the entrance. The Thundermug was aptly named, she thought.

Melville was brushing between the mostly empty tables, thrusting toward the card tables and chuckaluck layout clustered near the rear. It was far too early for much action in the saloon, not even any drink-cadging bar girls around yet, and what patrons there were seemed more interested in boozing than gambling. Only a small group of players and kibitzers were gathered at a single smoke-obscured card table, and from what Jessica could see of it, there didn't appear to be any high-stakes excitement going on.

The drinkers were mainly in two separate clumps at the shiny mahogany bar that stretched along one wall. The nearer men were sullenly quiet, a ferret-eyed watchfulness on their lanky, stubbled faces, a challenging bravado to their display of bristling weapons. The other bunch were nondescript cowpunchers, wearing pistols out of habit, the tools of their trade the rope and ring and branding iron. It was from them that Jessica heard the dull roar of talking and laughing, the clink of glasses and bottles.

Behind the bar, two white-aproned tenders were busily pouring. Brackets and chandeliers reflected in the polished backbar mirrors, and gleamed against the huge portrait of a buxom reclining nude. Seated on a high stool next to the nude, presiding over it all, was a frog of a fellow with slicked-down balding hair and a handlebar mustache, a nugget chain looped across a flowered vest, a torpedo cigar clenched in his gold-capped teeth.

He, Jessie surmised, would be Halford, one of the owners. And the boys happily lapping up his rotgut would be Mrs. Waldemar's crew. Melville was right—they were going to have to learn some loyalty and earn their keep. Before Jessica or anyone else would have a prayer to saving the Flying W, those men would have to be out there riding, and riding with everything they had. And the more Jessica looked at them and considered their failings, the more incensed she became.

Finally, beyond endurance, Jessie strode up to the crew. "Drink hearty," she snapped in a cold, cutting voice. "Because this'll be the last drink you'll have on the Flying W payroll."

Startled heads turned. A hush fell over the bar.

Then one of the men chuckled cynically. "Aw, hell, it's only a female." He was a bowlegged, weatherbeaten man with a nut-shaped head of narrow, sly features; he was older than the others, who were rawboned youths with devil-may-care in their eyes. "Don't pay her no mind, boys, you know how women go on the prod."

Jessica eyed him sharply. "You must be the foreman."

"Uh-huh. Nealon's the name, but you can call me Lloyd."

"I call you a bum."

"What?" He reared back, glowering. "Just who d'you think you are, comin' in here where you don't belong, pesterin' and insultin' us?"

"I'm Starbuck," she said flatly. "By contract, I own the beef you're not herding. Mrs. Waldemar wrote that she had problems, and now I can sure understand why, with a slob like you rodding a pack of lazy, elbow-bending drunks."

The others were staring dumbfounded, but Nealon was growing crimson, champing at the bit. "Okay, sweets, enough of your gag."

"It's no gag. And if you think it is, Nealon, you're dumber than you're acting already." She stepped closer, surveying the crew, her hands in fists on her hips. "Now open your ears, because I'm going to say this only once. I've come a long way to help the Flying W, and I don't have the time or patience to fool around. I'm going to be out there early tomorrow morning, and any of you who aren't up and out working, and working hard, will be fired."

A babbling broke out among the crew—all except for Nealon, who was now the one to stare gawking, silent and stupified.

Before they could collect their wits, Jessie pivoted to stalk away. And two things happened, almost simultaneously. Ki walked through the batwings and, seeing her, started across. And from the card table rose an infuriated bellow: "You skunk, Kendrick, I oughta break every bone in your body with my bare hands!"

"Lay a finger on me and I'll kill you!" a second voice shouted almost as loudly. "I run a friendly, honest game here, and your old man sat in of his own free will. Now get him and get out!"

Jessie and Ki, along with most everybody at the bar, headed toward the back, joining the watchers around the table. Cards and chips were scattered all over. Two players were seated with their eyes wide, mouths shut, hands flat on the green felt—the best position to hold when a game was in dispute. A third player was a bull-bodied, whiskery brute who was obviously enjoying the ruckus and was feeling immune, lounging back in his chair with a contemptuous smirk pasted on his brutal, scarred face.

Slumped in a fourth chair, his head resting on the table, was a white-haired elderly man. Tobias Melville, Jessie assumed. His son Daryl was towering behind him, face gnarled with rage and nearly as red as Nealon's had been. Across from them, standing where his chair had tipped over, was the fifth player, a squat, plumpish man with a cherubic face and pouty lips, garbed in a black cutaway coat, ruffled shirt, string tie, and a rakishly tilted green Keevil hat.

As Jessie and Ki approached, Melville was snarling at him, "Sure, you run it friendly and honest, all right. About as friendly as a rattler, Kendrick, and you give a man just about as much chance."

"I won't take no more of this," the gambler warned.

"You'll take it," Melville raged heedlessly, one hand gripping his father's lax shoulder. "You've been taking everything else from us for months now, when you know we can't pay, only go deeper into debt to you. You and Halford have been addling him with whiskey till he can't tell an ace from a queen. Just look what you've done to him!"

"Yeah, the old fool's passed out cold," the smirking player cut in snidely. The other players stayed quiet and still, unwilling to intrude. "Tell you what, Melville, I'll help you. I'll help you carry him out and dump him in the closest horse trough."

The man snickered at his own joke. He was big enough to

get away with it, taller than Melville and heftier by a good ten pounds. But Melville was beyond caution now, and he focused all his pent-up fury on the sneering giant, his voice like the edge of a scythe.

"Shut your mouth, Volpes, before I shut it for you. I've had it with you too, just like the other ranchers have had it. We're out there working, trying to live decent, but for some reason all you can think to do is sneer and bully like the king of the shitpile."

Volpes rose swinging.

An uppercutting haymaker crunched against Melville's jaw with a meaty impact, sending him reeling off balance. Wincing with pain, Melville shook his head to clear it, falling back a pace to regain his footing, as Volpes confidently charged to polish him off.

Melville ducked the onrushing roundhouse fist, dancing aside and striking back with a jolting right-left to Volpes's stomach and heart. The attack caught Volpes surprised and unguarded, but he moved in undaunted, hammering with abandon. Melville shifted and feinted, evading the blows, stabbing two lefts to Volpes's face so fast that one had scarcely hit before the other had landed.

Then a roundhouse knuckler cracked alongside Melville's cheek, momentarily stunning him. Before he could recover, Volpes got an arm around him and smashed him twice in the face with stiff, short-range punches. Melville butted him hard, breaking free, and launched another one-two combination. His left opened a gash over Volpes's eye, the right flattened the bridge of his nose. Volpes staggered, spurting blood from his nostrils, and the customers yelled.

And the gambler went for a belly-gun. Or at least it appeared that way, Kendrick barking an oath and darting his hand inside his coat, where a stubby-barreled weapon would be hidden in a shoulder holster.

Before Kendrick could produce whatever he was after, Ki took a step forward, his arm blurring up and out. A throwing dagger winked across the table. Kendrick choked on his oath, his hand still dipped inside his coat, and stared down at the jutting hilt of the knife, which had sliced through his coat pocket, skinning his ribs.

"The next will be closer," Ki called, smiling.

Kendrick grinned weakly and removed his hand.

The fighters traded blows, Volpes the stronger and cruelly effective, and Melville the faster and angrily impervious. Ignoring the battering jabs and chops, Melville returned rights and lefts until he'd wiped Volpes's smirk off his face, and sealed up the eye with the cut over it. Volpes dove, grappling, to wrap him in another crushing hug, but this time Melville was prepared, catching Volpes by the beard and jerking his face downward, mashing Volpes's already broken nose against his rising right knee. Pushing Volpes away then, Melville hit him a half-dozen more times in both eyes. Like a blundering, blind bear, Volpes tried to slug back, but Melville went under the swings and pummeled him in the belly and face, driving Volpes against the table, overturning it, punching him the length of the saloon and pinning him against the bar. Dazed and bleeding, Volpes sagged to his knees, bewildered by the unleashed fury of Melville's assault.

Melville hauled Volpes to his feet, while the crowd closed in around them, baying for the finishing blow. They weren't disappointed, Melville brought his right fist up from somewhere down around his boots. It hit Volpes's chin with the sound heard in a slaughterhouse, when a steer was brained with a maul. Volpes arched backward and slid five feet along the sawdust-covered planks, coming to rest when his head struck a brass spittoon. He didn't get up.

Melville stood catching his breath, looking moodily down at Volpes. Then, turning, he thrust through the congratulatory throng to where his father sprawled snoring on the floor, the old man having fallen there when the table overturned. Jessica and Ki followed, and Ki helped Melville pick up his father and dust him off.

Kendrick, who was righting the table, paused to give the two men a murderous glare. "From now on, you're both barred from here."

Melville, misunderstanding, snapped, "That's dandy by me. I've been trying long enough to stop Dad from coming to this snake pit."

"Oh, Toby's welcome anytime. I mean you—and *him*."

Melville regarded Ki and then the gambler again, and then

he frowned quizzically. "Say, isn't that a knife sticking outta your coat?"

Ki answered for the gambler, "He was trying to do what your opponent couldn't. With lead. I thought it wise to discourage him."

Livid, Kendrick blurted, "Why, you slant-eyed—!" And then promptly shut up, seeing Ki smile the same pleasant smile as before.

Now Melville laughed. "Serves you right, you sidewinder," he said to Kendrick, and lifting his father by the shoulders, he began carrying him toward the front. Passing the bar, where the customers were thirstily debating the finer details of his fight, Melville glanced back and grinned at Ki, who had hold of the father's ankles. "I guess I owe you my thanks, Mr . . ."

"Ki."

"Just Ki, no 'mister,' " Jessie added, opening the batwings.

Outside, Melville said, "Our wagon's by the barbershop." Starting across the street, he gave Jessica a sidelong appraisal, seeming to want to say something, but only managing to clear his throat a number of times. Finally it came out: "Maybe I shouldn't ask this, Miss Star—uh, Jessie—but are you . . . *with* Ki?"

"You bet. Ki's my guardian and sometime chaperone," she explained teasingly, intrigued by the way Melville's bruised mouth went from a crestfallen droop when he'd asked, to a smiling curve when she'd answered.

Melville stopped in back of a scruffy one-horse farm wagon, whose swaybacked horse dozed placidly at the hitching rail. Opening the wagon's tailgate to climb up inside, Melville started to speak again with faltering embarrassment.

"This is plumb shameful. Please don't think the worse of me or Dad, Jessie. It's mostly on account of him being so powerful lonely and sad, ever since my mother died four years ago."

"I understand, Daryl. Misery makes it easy for men like Halford and Kendrick to take advantage—and take your money."

"You don't know the half of it. We're in hock up to our ears to Kendrick, and we'd have to sell out or simply give him the whole blamed Spraddled M, if we ever had to pay him off all at once."

"You think he's rigged the games to win it?"

"He doesn't want our ranch," Melville replied, as he and Ki slid his father into the wagon bed. "Besides, Dad plays so badly, Kendrick would have to cheat to lose. What makes you ask, Jessie?"

"Nothing I can pinpoint. But the way the man you beat rose to Kendrick's defense makes me wonder a little bit if they haven't got something going between them."

"Nope, that tussle was personal 'tween me and Volpes. We've locked horns before, but nothing like this, and I suppose I shouldn't have lost my temper. But he's been swaggering and bullying around too long, and needed the stuffing knocked outta him." Melville jumped down and untied the horse, adding sheepishly, "Think he knocked some stuffing outta me, too. Anyway, maybe this'll be a lesson for Cap'n Ryker to keep him on a shorter leash."

"Ryker? Guthried Ryker?"

"Yeah. Know him?"

"Strictly by reputation," Jessie said grimly.

"Well, Volpes is Ryker's foreman. He's mean enough to steal the blanket outta his mother's kennel, but he's kinda at odds with Kendrick and Halford, him working for Cap'n Ryker and all."

"How's that?"

"Well, when Kendrick and Halford arrived here about this time last year, they bought the old saloon and put options on some other properties like the hotel, and generally began acting like bigshots. Then Cap'n Ryker showed up with even more money to spend speculating, and naturally it's stirred up resentments and competition."

Jessie was still perplexed. "That much makes sense. But if Kendrick and Halford are interested in gaining property . . ."

"Sure are," Melville said, nodding, as he climbed up onto the wagon seat. "Them and Cap'n Ryker, squabbling over this and that like two dogs over a bone, to see who'll wind up lording it over the other."

"Then why'd you tell me Kendrick doesn't want your ranch?"

"Because that's what he's told us, Jessie. Says he's only interested in town property, moneymaking property. Says if he took over, he'd have to abandon it and write it off as a total loss, or else try to run it and end up scratching and starving like we are. He says he'd rather have us make payments to him like a loan, than to have us hand over a spread of skin and bones and worthless dust."

Jessica pursed her lips, pondering for a moment, suspicious of saintly gamblers unwilling to rake in the entire pot the instant it was won. And her brief exposure to Kendrick had not left her impressed with his charitable qualities. She gazed skeptically up at Melville, asking, "Have you offered the ranch to him, Daryl?"

"No, and I don't aim to, unless I'm forced. But speaking of our worthless ranch, I'd best be getting Dad home to bed. Are you still planning to ride out to the Flying W tomorrow morning?"

"At the crack of dawn. Though I wish we could go now, and not waste time spending a night at the hotel," Jessie replied, then turned to Ki. "We are staying there, aren't we?"

Ki nodded. "It's all arranged. Luggage too."

"Well, you just remember that fork in the road," Melville said. "When you pass our place tomorrow, Jessie, you stop in."

"Thanks, we might, if it won't be any trouble."

"No trouble, no trouble a-tall, 'cepting you don't come a-calling like you're expected to. *Then* there'll be trouble." Grinning broadly, Melville released the brake and lashed the reins, and the horse started plodding down the street, the wagon creaking behind it.

Jessica stood beside Ki, watching Melville slowly haul his besotted father home. Daryl was a smooth hairpin, she had to admit; and he already had so many problems that she certainly didn't want to cause him the slightest bit more trouble. So of course she'd visit.

Chapter 5

Moving to the boardwalk, Jessica and Ki watched the departing wagon, Ki remarking, "I looked for you at the sheriff's, Jessie. He told me he'd met up with a dratted female of your description, but otherwise he couldn't help any."

"You can say that again, Ki," Jessie replied with disgust. "How'd you know to find me in the saloon?"

"That's where the thick of the uproar was. Where else would you be?" Smiling, Ki took a pocketful of .38 cartridges from his vest and handed them to Jessica, adding: These are from four boxes I bought. The rest I put in your room."

"Thanks." Loading her revolver, she glanced at the bath house next to the barbershop. "Does the hotel have a bath?"

"Two. Fifty cents extra, fresh water daily, reheated noon and evening, and I've already reserved the one on our floor for us."

"That's a relief," she sighed, starting along the boardwalk. She felt grubby and unkempt and in need of a good scrub, from all that had occurred since the ambush. But the bath house, like most cow-town bath houses, would be a male preserve where men would mingle, arguing such weighty issues as women and liquor. She had little interest in bathing with them and airing her differences.

Ki fell in beside Jessie, and they walked in the same direction as the still visible wagon. He hadn't been blind to her interest in the ruggedly handsome rancher, but neither was he so crass as to pry, other than to ask, "Daryl, did you say his name was?"

"Daryl? Why, yes, Daryl Melville, and his father, Tobias."

"He seems to be shouldering a heavy load."

"I believe he is," Jessie replied, and briefly sketched what she'd learned. "And call it a hunch or feminine intuition, Ki, but I also believe there's some kind of link between what's happening to Daryl and what's happening to Mrs. Waldemar."

"What?"

"I don't know," Jessie said grimly. "Not yet."

They entered the combination telegraph and post office that butted against one side of the hotel. Approaching a wizened oldster who sat behind a barred window, Jessica asked, "Are you acquainted with the owners of the Thundermug Saloon?"

"Yes'm. Halford and Kendrick, know 'em well."

"Know their first names? And where they're from?"

That almost stumped the grizzled clerk, but after scratching his chin thoughtfully, he answered, "Woodrow and Barney, I recollect. Can't say positive where they hail from, 'cepting they've gotten and sent mail and wires to an' from back East, Washington way."

"You're a dear," Jessie said, dimpling a big thank-you smile. She then composed a long telegram that caused the clerk, sworn to secrecy by the rules of the telegraph company, to regard her with even livelier interest. Addressed to the Circle Star ranch in Texas, her message directed that a large draft of money be relayed, and a quick investigation be done on Woodrow Halford and Barney Kendrick, both from Washington, D.C.

"Hold all replies for either me or my friend," Jessica instructed, indicating Ki. "Nobody else, no matter what you're told."

After paying the clerk, they stepped back out onto the street, Ki turning automatically toward the hotel. But Jessica, shaking her head, said, "There're a few things I wish to buy first, now that we're spending the night. Or do you want to meet me here later?"

"No, I haven't anything special to do," Ki replied, and began to walk with Jessica back up toward the general store. "I hired a stablehand at the livery to fetch our things from the cabin, but I doubt he'll return much before nightfall. Oh, and I also rented two saddle horses, a pair of matching bays. The hostler assured me they can be hitched to a buckboard, if you prefer."

"I don't. My suspicion is that before we're through, we'll be having to ride where there aren't any trails."

In the store, Jessie took her time perusing the slim stock of ladies' articles. At length she decided on a plaid flannel shirt to replace her ruined blouses; a calico wrapper and a frilly Empire-style nightgown made of fine nainsook; a bar of castile soap; a box of hairpins; and a traveling set consisting of a Russian bristle hairbrush, nail and toothbrushes, and an imitation ebony comb, all packed in a seal-grain leather case.

Ki, bored silly, made the common male error of asking, "Just what are you planning to do with all that, Jessie?"

"Well, I don't plan to wear filthy clothes after I've bathed, and I don't plan to sleep naked in any hotel," she declared with womanly logic, "and I certainly don't plan to go visiting tomorrow looking dirty and smelling and with my hair all in a tangle."

From the store, they went to the hotel. The Grand Continental may not actually have been grand, but it had a distinct air of faded gentility. Its oak front door had an oval window in it, thick and bevelled, with chintz curtains hanging behind it. There was a well-worn but clean carpet of flowing rose pattern on the lobby floor, and through the scarlet portiers toward the rear was a dining room with a crystal chandelier and linen settings. The wiry, thin-lipped, gimlet-eyed clerk at the reception desk had a different air about him, that of *eau de lilac*, and was obviously an insufferable prig.

Collecting her key, Jessica asked, "Is there a laundry service?"

"Of course," the clerk said with a sniff. "Anything accepted by eight in the evening will be washed and ironed and delivered by morning."

Jessica took her purchases to her room, which was on the second floor, at the rear. The room was in keeping with the rest of the hotel, with a plain bureau, a drab armchair, and a large wardrobe sporting a full-length, discolored mirror. The bed, though, looked clean and comfortable. On the side of the room opposite the bed, a dreary blue curtain hung from a rail, covering, she assumed, a communicating door to Ki's room.

She opened the window a crack, to let out the mustiness, glancing out at the roof of the sheriff's office, and then down at the dark, narrow alley that ran between it and the side of the hotel. As a view, it left much to be desired. She pulled the blind, and after lighting the kerosene banquet lamp on the bureau, she locked the door after her, and went back down to Ki in the lobby.

They ate an early dinner in the dining room, the food palatable if not interesting, the waiter surly and prone to swatting flies with his serving tray. The young stableboy arrived with their luggage, and after he'd left with a generous tip, Jessie and Ki ordered brandy and coffee, and sat discussing what little they knew.

When it was time for her bath, Jessie returned to her room, where she reloaded her derringer, stripped naked, and put on her new wrapper. She bundled what she'd been wearing with her clothes from the trunk, then took them next door to Ki, asking him to give them to the clerk downstairs.

Then, gathering her toiletries and locking the door behind her, Jessica placed the room key in her wrapper pocket along with her derringer, and went down the corridor to the bathroom. The hook on the bathroom door worked, but just in case, she folded the wrapper so the derringer could be quickly reached from the galvanized tub of tepid water. Cautiously satisfied, she slipped into the tub and settled down in the water for a long, well-deserved soak.

Ki, meanwhile, was deciding that he might as well add some of his own dirty clothes to the bundle Jessie had given him. Tossing in most everything except his jeans, vest, and rope-soled slippers, he waited until he heard Jessica close and safely latch the bathroom door, then left his room and walked down to the lobby.

The twit of a clerk wasn't there. The only person in the otherwise deserted lobby was the girl who cleaned the rooms and made the beds. Ki recalled passing her in the upstairs corridor earlier that day, when he'd first checked in, while she'd been carrying a stack of linens similar to the bundle of clothing he now had in hand. She was now perched on a rickety stool behind the reception desk, concentrating so hard on the game of solitaire she was playing that she failed to notice Ki's approach.

"Excuse me," Ki said.

Stiffening, the girl hastily began to gather the dog-eared cards together, as if he'd caught her doing something very wrong.

"You don't have to stop," Ki said.

"Oh, I should," she replied guiltily. "If Uncle Humphrey catches me sinning like this, he'll whup me good."

She was a vivid creature, as fiercely pretty as a panther kitten. About twenty, Ki judged, with flaming red hair and great and amethyst-blue eyes set in a freckled, tanned face, and with a wide red mouth that was slowly beginning to soften into a relieved smile.

"Uncle Humphrey?" Ki asked. "The clerk?"

"And manager, and owner," the girl explained. "He's out for dinner right now, and I'm just holding down the fort till he gets back. That can be a spell at times, but if you want to come back . . ."

"No, I only want to leave some laundry."

"Well, you can put what you've got 'round back here."

Ki moved to the end of the counter and dumped the bundle. He could now see that the girl was wearing a cheap muslin dress cut rather high on the knees, laundry-boiled over the years almost to the transparency of lace gauze. Her legs were long and bare, her feet encased in low-cut moccasins. He also noticed that although her body was slender and wasp-waisted, she had the large, succulent breasts and thighs of a mature woman built for breeding.

She twisted on the tall stool and regarded the bundle suspiciously. "You've got some lady's things in there, too."

"Miss Starbuck's."

She paused thoughtfully, then said, "Are you two . . . ?"

Ki chuckled. "Not in the way you're thinking."

She giggled and then neither of them said anything more for a while. She just kept looking at Ki, appraising his tight-fitting jeans and vest and his bronzed, muscular form that they barely covered, until her scrutiny and the silence grew embarrassing.

"I hope Uncle Humphrey doesn't come back and find me sitting here doing nothing," the girl said at last. "He doesn't like me to become familiar with the hotel guests, he says. He's afraid something might happen to me, I guess."

Ki grinned. "What kind of something?"

"Oh . . . you know. Men in here all the time, coming and going. Uncle Humphrey gets powerful mad if I stop and talk to any of them."

"And you never do?"

"I am now, ain't I?"

She lifted her brows when she said that, and looked sideways at Ki. And Ki found himself wondering if there was anything under that dress of hers. Somehow he thought not. There wasn't any reason to believe that it was the only thing she was wearing, but he got the idea, and then he tried imagining what it was like beneath it.

It didn't take much to imagine her breasts. Her lips were full and red; big nipples, then, strawberry in size and color. She had fire-red hair. Between her legs would also be a frothing mass of red, bushy between the cheeks of her big solid rump.

Ki licked his lips. "And is your uncle right about it?"

"What do you think?"

Ki glanced down at the bundle, then across the lobby toward the door, then finally back to the girl. What a vixen, he thought; she exuded sex like her uncle smelled of lilac perfume. He needed her like he needed a bad case of poison ivy, but if a woman's offering, a man will take, even if he has to get off his deathbed for her.

Huskily, he answered, "I think I know what you need."

She sat with a light smirk on her face and then, because she evidently wanted him to make the first move, Ki stepped over the laundry and went to her stool. The girl tilted her face up to him and pressed her lips to his, her tongue darting between his teeth.

Ki held one hand on the stool to keep it from falling over, and slid his other hand over her shoulder, down her dress front. She wriggled some but didn't object, and in a second he was massaging one of her breasts. All things considered, she had damn big breasts for her size, because Ki didn't think she could weigh more than a hundred pounds, but her breasts would have worn well on any woman. She didn't say a word when he started kneading them, but after a long moment she broke her kiss and watched his hand caressing her nipples.

" 'I wonder why she ain't trying to fight me,' " she said. "Is that what you're thinking? Why I'm not putting up any struggle?"

"I'm not thinking at all right now."

"All right. But you wonder just the same, I'll bet. I do, I know. And I don't know the answer. I can't imagine why I'm such a pushover. I'm one of those girls who're easy to get, I guess."

"This stool is liable to collapse," Ki said, wanting to change the subject. "Let's either stop or go somewhere."

"I can't leave the desk. We can do it here."

"Your uncle or somebody might come in."

"Maybe. But let's try it anyway and find out." She slipped from his embrace and went to the front door, snapping the catch on the lock and pulling down the window shade. *This is crazy,* Ki thought as she turned and walked back toward him. But her eyes had that vacant, burnt expression that some women got when they were ready to be seduced, and she was breathing hard, as though there weren't enough air in the lobby. Here was blatant challenge, here was passion deluxe. And what man could turn his back on that?

The girl went around the end of the counter and settled down on Ki's bundle of laundry. Slowly, sensuously, she stretched back across the dirty clothing, her dress hiking up above her knees, and she crossed her arms behind her head and gazed invitingly up at him.

Ki sat beside her, and she said, "Don't undress me."

"I'd like to see you naked."

She rubbed her leg against his, and pulled her dress up a little. "I know. It's better when you're naked, but you were right, Uncle Humphrey or somebody could come along."

"Has your uncle ever caught you doing this?"

"Almost. I had to hide in a closet for two hours."

Ki eased her dress higher and saw that she was wearing a pair of short lacy pantaloons, tied by a drawstring at her waist. "Don't wrinkle my dress in back," she said, arching her bottom so he could get it up from under her and spread it out beneath her back. "I guess I'm stupid, letting you do this at all. How'd you know I would? You didn't seem to be worried about me raising hell or anything."

Ki untied the drawstring and began to take her pantaloons off. They were tight from having been washed and shrunk a lot, and were hard to slip over her hips. "I don't know," he replied.

That seemed to satisfy the girl. She helped him tug her pantaloons down past her knees and off her feet.

That big fluff of crimson hair stuck out on her just as he knew it would. He ran his hands across her belly and thighs and dipped down between her legs, stroking her rounded slit. Her legs spread, and she slid lower against the bundle when he hooked his fingers under her pubic hair and speared inside her moist canal.

Still fingering her, Ki used his other hand to unbuckle his jeans and open his fly. She reached, clutching the shaft of this erection and stroking him delicately, as he struggled to lower his pants down around his ankles.

"You stay dressed too," she whispered hoarsely, and wrapped her left arm around his neck, drawing him up and over her, the hand clasping his hardness, guiding it into her warm moisture.

Ki felt himself sinking inside her a long way before he realized how tight she was. He paused then and looked down at her. She was smiling all over. "Don't stop," she said. "It feels good."

He lanced deeper into her again, and this time he could almost feel the juice springing out of her. He began to thrust very hard then, and she seemed to grow even tighter around him, until every time he would pound into her, she would gasp, shuddering, from the squeezing impact. Yet she kept smiling and undulating her buttocks on the pile of dirty laundry, eager for more. There was nothing timid or gentle about this union, Ki thought.

Her hips writhed and pumped under him, her thighs clasping him as if she would hold him in her forever. She began to moan, and her eyes closed, her fingers stroking down over his buttocks as she tried to match Ki's quickening movements. Her moans grew deeper, more prolonged, and she caught at his thighs where they were pressed against the undersides of hers, pulling them at her while her mouth opened and closed as if she were gasping for air.

Then, as her moanings became continuous and high-pitched,

the girl began babbling, "Fast, fast, fast, fast . . ." in a cascade of incoherent emotion. Her hands clutched him savagely, digging into his thighs as her face contorted and her whole body shivered in a series of convulsions.

"Ahhh . . ." she mewed, as her wet passage compressed around Ki's surging shaft, the force of her orgasm drawing the breath from her lungs in a furious, aching sigh.

As he felt the girl gripping him in her ecstatic release, Ki burrowed deeper, pressing and grinding against her for seconds without pumping his hips. Then he withdrew, thrust slowly in again—and again—and with a final deep thrust, his own climax erupted far up inside her welcoming belly.

Slowly he settled down over her soft warm body, and he lay, crushing her breasts and belly with his weight, until his immediate satiation began to wane. Finally he rolled from her and gently stroked her quivering breasts.

The girl smiled at him with lazy, satisfied eyes. "I guess if Miss Starbuck's and your clothes didn't need washing before," she whispered, "they sure do now . . ."

While Ki was down romancing the girl, Jessica was relaxing sleepily in her bath. Eventually stirring from her lethargy, she sat up and began to soap her breasts and loins, every inch of her trim yet voluptuous body. Kneeling then, she lathered her long blond hair, then bent, with the nipples of her distended breasts brushing the water, to rinse off the lather. Briskly she dried herself with a large, fluffy jacquard towel. Her nude flesh tingled, her skin glowing a burnished pink, as she slipped her wrapper on again, collected her toiletries, and left the bathroom.

Padding barefoot along the corridor again, she unlocked her door and found a man in her room. He was stooping over her trunk, one hand on its open lid, the other pawing through her set-up tray. Hearing her enter, he straightened and turned, his clothes grubby work denims and shirt, his face lean-jawed and the color of old paper.

"Well, well, what have we here?" the man said, ogling.

"A burglar, that's what," Jessica retorted sarcastically, in no mood to tolerate the way the man was studying her nudity under the clinging wrapper. She drew out her derringer and pointed it at him. "It's a bit early in the evening for larceny, isn't it?"

"Whoa there, lady, let's not be hasty," the man said, abruptly losing interest in ogling her. "Little mistake in the room, is all. May haps I'm a little drunk too."

"Get out, and I'll call the matter closed, if not forgotten."

"Yes, ma'am, just what I had in mind," he said nervously, sidling out around her and into the hallway. "Let's leave it at that."

The man rushed pell-mell down the corridor. Jessica waited until he'd vanished down the staircase, then examined the door lock and jamb plate, finding they hadn't been forced. She wasn't surprised.

Closing and relatching the door, Jessica figured the incident wasn't worth disturbing Ki about. What could be gained? The man was gone, and had gotten nothing except an eyeful and a scare.

Discarding the wrapper, she slid the flowing nightgown down over her head, and discovered that it was a size smaller than her figure demanded. She smoothed it out as best she could, the fabric like a lover's clasp, squeezing her breasts and pressing around her thighs and buttocks. She continued trying to stretch the gown looser, as she stood in front of the wardrobe mirror, brushing her damp hair and pinning it up so she could sleep on it.

Eventually satisfied, Jessica blew out the oil lamp on the bureau and climbed into bed. She was asleep the instant her head hit the pillow.

She was awakened by Ki.

She felt his presence at first and, opening her eyes, saw him moving through the connecting doorway into her darkened room, wearing only his jeans, his bare feet noiseless on the floor. When she sat up, still foggy with sleep, he put a finger to his lips as a signal for absolute silence, and pointed at the window with his other hand.

Jessica froze, breathless. For an agonizing moment she heard nothing, and she realized it was probably sometime between three and five in the morning, in that predawn stillness when most everybody is sleeping their soundest, and those awake are at their most relaxed. And when Ki was at his most alert.

Then, from below the window, against the side of the building, came a slight scraping noise and a soft squeak of stressed wood. Ki was beside the window now, poised motionless, staring intently at the drawn blind like a cat watching a mousehole. Gently, Jessica rose, slipping from the covers and easing over to the other side of the window. Ki gestured for her to back away, but before she could, the sash creaked slowly higher and the blind began to quiver.

A hand raised the bottom edge of the blind. Whoever was out there then stuck his other hand underneath, gripping two dynamite sticks tied together, fuses sparking and hissing.

Ki pounced. He grabbed hold of those two hands by their wrists and thrust them back out the window, leaning way out before letting go with a final shove. The dynamite went with them, and so did the blind, ripping off its roller to flap out like a flying tail.

A startled howl, which had begun at the height of the window, was swiftly falling away and down. Jessica, peering out the window with Ki, saw a tall spindly ladder teetering in an arc away from the hotel wall, its legs firmly rooted in the alley below. The hunching silhouette of a man was perched on its top rungs, clinging helplessly as he was catapulted backwards toward the sheriff's stone office.

The ladder struck the edge of the building, toward the rear of the structure where the jail cells would be. The man was flung onto the roof, his howl cut off as the dynamite detonated with a terrific, brilliant flash. The hotel quivered, glass shattering, while down across the alley, the rear quarter of the sheriff's office hurtled out, stone, beams, and masonry cycloning up and about in a blinding white cloud. The roof collapsed in the hole the explosion had punched, fire blossoming through the wreckage.

By the suddenly sprouting incandescence, Jessica saw Deputy Oakes stumble out the front door, wearing long red underwear and nothing else. Other doors and windows were opening, the street swirling in a confusion of shouting men and women both dashing about, cursing and questioning, gaping at the ruined building that was now being consumed by hungry flames.

Ki turned, surveying Jessica. "Are you all right?"

She nodded, though she was still shaky, still dazzled by the glare, her head whirling from the concussion of the blast.

"Somebody doesn't like us," she said, smiling weakly. "I can't imagine who."

"And he knew where to find us. If I hadn't been lucky enough to hear that ladder brushing up against the wall, he would've succeeded," Ki added, slamming the window and starting back to the connecting door. He paused before closing it to say reassuringly, "But I think that's all he'll try for tonight. Sweet dreams."

Jessica went back to bed and pulled the covers up close around her neck. She listened to the continuing noise from the street, and watched the reflection of the fire in the wavy glass pane of her window, and she wondered what tomorrow would bring in the way of death.

She lay there a long time before going to sleep again.

Chapter 6

The rising sun had scarcely cleared the mountains behind them when Jessica and Ki turned at the fork in the road west of Eucher Butte. They rode for the next two hours through a vast upland basin that was hemmed in by the river to the south, and by granite-toothed and canyon-gashed foothills ahead and to the north, the peaks of the Laramie Range towering beyond, seeming to float above the horizon on a sea of morning mist.

The trail kept to a course that meandered toward the foot hills, the broad sweep of the basin slowly falling behind, being replaced by increasingly rugged country of tumbling creeks and high, timbered plateaus. The sun had become hot and bright against their backs by the time the two riders reined in their mounts before a narrow lane that cut away from the trail. A board nailed to a tree beside the lane bore the brand of the Spraddled M.

Heeling their bays into a trot, they followed the rutted lane through a belt of spruce and yellow pine, then down into a verdant swale speckled with the first buds of spring. Along a stream that flowed across one side of the swale were strung the few low buildings of a ranch: a long, thin, cabinlike ranch house; a squarer bunkhouse, against which leaned a grub shack; a clapboard barn and a scattering of sheds; and a pole corral in which a few horses stood.

The Melville spread did not look rich, Jessica thought as

they approached the stretch of bare yard in front of the ranch house. But it was neat, and the buildings appeared to be in good repair, showing a desire to work hard and do the best with what there was.

A gallery ran the length of the ranch house. There was a small amount of clutter and discarded saddlery at each end of it, but in the middle, next to the front door, was a rocking chair. Sitting in the rocker was Tobias Melville, clad in a loose-hanging vest and denims of the range, and a plaid shirt not unlike the one Jessica was wearing. A faded bandanna was knotted around his throat, a thatch of white hair peeking from beneath a floppy-brimmed, sweat-stained hat.

Daryl Melville was standing nearby, one boot on the gallery and the other on the ground, as if he couldn't make up his mind whether to come or to go. He had on a clean set of clothes, and was hatless, his hair slicked and combed. But he was also wearing, Jessica saw, the same dark scowl as he'd worn yesterday, when he'd been angered at Deputy Oakes, and then later in the saloon.

Daryl and his father were looking at whoever was in the buggy parked alongside the gallery by the rocker. The buggy had a piano-box body and a leather quarter-top, and was hitched to a sleek dapple gray. Because the fancy top blocked their view, neither Jessica nor Ki could tell who was in it until they rode all the way up to the gallery. But they could hear a deep, well-modulated voice coming from within, saying to the Melvilles:

"Let's be realistic. You don't have anything to sell but debts and scarecrow cattle, but I'll take them to secure your range—"

"Hello, there," Daryl interrupted, smiling as he spotted Jessica and Ki drawing near. "Sure glad you could make it."

And the words from the buggy came to an abrupt halt.

Two men were sitting in the buggy, their eyes veiled, as Jessica and Ki pulled up to the gallery. The one holding the reins was a bucktoothed, hatchet-faced man with an impassive, secretive expression. The other was middle aged, sporting bristly muttonchops, his once handsome face and deep-socketed eyes webbed with lines of dissipation. And it was obvious from his apparel that he was more accustomed to rich city reveling than hardscrabble ranch life, wearing as he was a pair of flat-heeled patent-leather shoes, a square-crowned Governor hat, and a dark brown town suit of expensive broadcloth, its jacket unbuttoned to relieve his paunch.

The tense silence stretched on, until Tobias Melville rocked back and remarked affably, "Sure got peaceful of a sudden."

"Yes, well, where're my manners?" Daryl said hastily, clearing his throat. "Dad, I'd like you to meet Miss Jessie Starbuck."

"Heard something about you this morning," the father said, grinning. His gaunt face was creased with wrinkles, but his eyes, as black as his son's, were sharp and bright as he looked Jessica over. He seemed to like what he saw.

"Call me Toby, Jessie."

"And her friend, Ki," Daryl continued.

"Heard about you too, feller. But you ain't Mexican."

"Mexican?" Ki echoed, nonplussed.

"Ain't Mexicans the ones who're best with knives?"

"Pa!" Daryl snapped, scowling afresh. But Toby just continued grinning unregenerately, looking incredibly chipper after his long bout of drinking. Jessica, smothering a laugh, thought it was amazing, the vitality these leathery old ranchers seemed to have.

Forging ahead, Daryl said, "Cap'n Ryker? Let me intro—"

"We're aquainted," Ryker cut in, a sharp edge to his mellow voice. "That is, we know each other by reputation. As president of Acme Packers, I am well aware of my competitors, of which Starbuck is definitely one. As I'm sure Starbuck is similarly aware of me."

"Oh, you bet we are," Jessica said.

"The Captain's trying to buy us out," Toby explained, obviously tickled by his chance to stir things up. "Plans to run us together with the Flying W, when he takes that place over, too."

"Now, now, Mr. Melville, I said no such thing to you."

"But that's what you've got in mind, ain't it, Cap'n?"

"Well, I suppose I'm forced to admit it is," Ryker replied gravely, and turned from Toby to Jessica. "To be perfectly honest, Miss Starbuck, my company needs the same thing yours does—a constant, reliable supply of beef without the fluctuating prices and conditions we've all experienced. I'm here on behalf of Acme, trying to persuade the smaller ranchers to sell out to one large combine, rather than join a cooperative of the sort you've been attempting to establish. I'm afraid that if I succeed, the ranches involved would no longer be able to honor their commitments with Starbuck."

Jessica clucked her tongue and looked downcast. "You understand if I hope your plans fail. But will you be staying permanently?"

"Goodness, no. When my negotiations are finished, win or lose, I'll leave whatever I've obtained in capable hands, and move on."

"Then you might as well move on from here, Cap'n Ryker," Daryl said sternly. "Unless you're willing to meet our price."

"Thirty thousand?" Ryker's chuckle was amiable. "My good man, I could buy all of Eucher Butte for that much money."

"Be my guest. Halford and Kendrick mightn't agree, though."

"Ah, yes, Kendrick. Now listen, I'm offering a fair price, more than a fair price, almost double what you owe Kendrick—what, in effect, you'd be getting for your ranch by turning it over to him."

"Don't intend to settle for Kendrick's price, either. We intend to keep it for all it's worth. Thirty thousand worth."

"You may not have that choice much longer," Ryker continued in his shrewd, persuasive voice. "Oh, I understand how you feel, how you believe your ranch is worth a great deal, how you place a high value on the sweat and tears you've spent improving it. But consider this—will your crew shed more blood to help you keep it?"

Daryl stepped forward, fists clenched. "Is that a threat?"

"Simple advice. Even supposing Kendrick held off claiming your ranch as payment, there's a ruinous crime wave going on in this area that Deputy Oakes seems incapable of stopping. If it continues as it has, it could ultimately rob you of all your assets, and leave you crippled, in a worse position to bargain than you're in now."

"Our land'll remain. Like you said, that's all you want."

Ryker threw up his hands in frustration. "You're not being sensible, son. Very well, I won't pursue this further this morning. But I'll be at my Block-Two-Dot in case you want to get off your high horse and talk down on the ground. Good day to you all."

With a tip of his hat and a nudge at his driver, Ryker sat

back in the seat, looking sourly exasperated. Behind the dapple gray, the buggy veered about and jounced, swaying, out of the yard.

Apart from the noise of the departing buggy, and the clucking of some scrawny hens foraging by a pile of manure, nothing stirred for a long moment. Then Jessica, referring to Toby's initial comment, said lightly, "Yes, it certainly is pleasant and peaceful here."

"Like blazes it's peaceful," Toby snorted. "We and the boys are shot at, our cows are run off . . . not that I'd allow Cap'n Snake-Eyes the satisfaction of hearing tell."

"Snake-Eyes?"

"That's what Dad calls Ryker's Block-Two-Dot brand."

"Looks just like dice showing twos," Toby added, grinning.

Jessica laughed. "But aren't you trying to sell to him?"

Daryl shook his head. "We were only funning him, Jessie. We picked the figure of thirty thousand 'cause nobody'd be dumb enough to pay such a price. C'mon, step down and rest a spell."

"Thanks, but we're awfully late as it is."

"I know a shortcut," Daryl offered hopefully, and when Jessica didn't refuse, he grinned, saying, "Wait a minute, I'll saddle up."

As Daryl began sprinting for the corral, Toby yelled, "You ain't leaving me ahind to rot, blast you!" He lurched up out of his rocker and chased bandy-legged after his son. "Hell, you get lost goin' to the outhouse! You better let me do the pointin'!"

A short while later, the four were riding as a group across Spraddled M range, Daryl on a linebacked buckskin gelding, and his father on a tubby roan mare. They headed west-northwest over mountain meadows and among thick stands of spruce, fir, and lodgepole pine, at one point spotting Spraddled M hands chousing a small bunch of young stuff down by some creek brakes. Then Daryl shifted to a slightly more northern track, and climbed higher along a tangent through the forested benches and rocky slopes.

Eventually, their hard-breathing horses struggling with the steepened grade, they topped a ridge and Daryl reined in. Ahead stretched the vista of a wide, shallow valley, through which coursed the wavering thread of a stream. Beyond the stream was the distant outline of a ranch, its cluster of buildings vaguely resembling the Spraddled M's, a windmill in its yard briskly revolving, sunlight glinting faintly off the whirring blades.

"Like the view?" Daryl asked cheerfully.

Jessica nodded. "It's beautiful out here."

"Well, it looks better'n usual. We had a good snowpack this winter, and spring's been pretty wet so far, but generally we suffer from poor runoffs and low rainfall. A couple of years it's gotten as bad as being drought-dry." He jiggered his buckskin closer to Jessica's bay, until they were almost touching stirrups. "That's the Flying W you see down there. Actually, it was doing fine, despite the weather and all, till Waldemar met with his accident."

"And now?"

"It's going to hell in a handbasket. Frankly, I'm glad Dad is coming along. He and Uriah—Mr. Waldemar—loved feuding over cribbage a lot, and I think he misses him almost as much as he does my mother. But, 'cept for the funeral, Dad hasn't been by to pay respects to Mrs. Waldemar, and I know she must be feeling lonesome and miserable about everything, and could do with an old friend cheering her up some."

"You leave me to my own socializin', son," Toby snapped.

Daryl turned to his father, grinning. "You an' Uriah, the orn'riest pair of mules ever born, I swear." He kneed his horse forward, and with Jessica following closely, Ki and Toby trailing a few feet behind, they began their slow, winding descent into the valley.

Jessica said to Daryl, "That accident was pretty convenient. I understand Mr. Waldemar refused to sell out to Ryker."

"I don't know what you mean by his death being convenient, Jessie, but yeah, Uriah wanted nothing to do with Cap'n Ryker. There was bad feeling 'tween them right from the start, when the Cap'n first moved onto the Block-Two-Dot. It's way over in the next valley, and it's probably the largest and richest of the smaller spreads. Anyway, Uriah was a tough, stubborn, but honest cowman, and you know how some of them can feel about Easterners taking over spreads."

"The ol' grunt-and-grab," Toby added from behind.

Daryl twisted in his saddle again. "Dad, you're only saying that 'cause that's what Uriah used to say. But if you consider it from Ryker's angle, he's buying up a wad of mortgages and debts, offering a way out, often the only way out, from bankruptcy."

"Maybe," Jessica said, "but he drives a hard bargain."

"Why shouldn't he? He's a businessman. We're the damn fools who've bitten off more'n we can chew, trying to make a go with a handful of cattle and a wagonload of furniture. He's not accountable if we end up dragging ourselves down into poverty and misery."

"He is if he helps do the dragging."

"He doesn't have to, Jessie. Failure seems to come natural to some folks, just like it's human nature to blame the winner who comes to buy up what's left. A body resents it, resents what's given."

"Maybe Ryker should grow whiskers and drive reindeer," Jessica retorted, angered to hear Ryker described as a benefactor for gobbling up other peoples' property and dreams. On the other hand, Daryl was speaking without having her information, her black book, her background and experience in dealing with such skunks. And at this point she didn't feel ready to educate him, either.

They dropped out of the hills and onto the gently rolling floor of the valley, and for a while rode roughly parallel to the creek. Where the creek was bridged by a wagon road, they turned and followed the road until they reached the home pastures of the Flying W. The windmill appeared first, flickering in the sunlight atop the wrinkled steppes of a hillock. Then, as the road curved around the base of the hillock, the ranch itself came into view, sprawling in the mottled shade of a grove of cottonwoods.

Riding into the yard, Jessica saw a couple of punchers moving around the outbuildings. When they saw who she was, they sped up; and Jessica, smiling inwardly, thought the crew must all be madder than a boil at her. Then, pulling up in front of the ranch house, she eyed its weathered clapboards, dirty and paint-peeling, though its windows were washed and were framed by spotless curtains.

They were dismounting as a graying woman came to the door. She appeared colorless and subdued, with a lurking sadness to her eyes, but she wore a clean house dress, and her hair was neatly plaited and pinned around her head.

"Howdy, Am'belle," Toby greeted, lifting his hat.

"How do, Toby, Daryl." Her voice was throaty and warm. "And you must be Miss Starbuck. Please, all of you, come on in."

At the door, Jessica asked her, "Your crew told you?"

"Did they ever!" Mrs. Waldemar's lips perked with a wry smile. "They larruped in like a posse was after 'em, and got to working bright and early, fit to beat the band. All save Lloyd. He quit."

Jessica frowned, recalling the aggressive Lloyd Nealon. "I'm sorry. That leaves you short a foreman, and that's not what I had in mind. I guess I overstepped my bounds, and I do apologize."

"'Tain't accepted, Miss Starbuck. You did what Uriah would've done, and what I should've done if I'd had the gumption of a ninny." She shut the door and headed for the kitchen, adding, "Now sit. I've got coffee on the stove, and an apple pandowdy in the oven."

Inside, the parlor was meagerly yet tastefully furnished. Jessica and Daryl settle on a horsehair tête-à-tête sofa, while Toby relaxed in an easy chair with his hat balanced on his knees, and Ki stood beside a French marquetry-work side table.

"Don't you want to sit comfortable?" Mrs. Waldemar asked Ki, when she returned from the kitchen bearing a loaded tray.

"No, thank you. I feel quite comfortable standing."

"Ain't used to a saddle, I betcha, and 's just sore from our ride," Toby declared. Which was anything but the truth; Ki simply preferred to stand, finding most American stuffed furniture, including beds, too soft and spongy for his taste. But then, Toby probably didn't believe what he was saying anyway, and promptly forgot about it as he started eating the fresh-baked apple pandowdy. "This is plumb scrumptious, Am'belle. Best I've ever tasted."

"If you didn't make yourself so scarce, Toby, you'd find I can cook more'n that," Mrs. Waldemar replied, as she finished pouring coffee and serving wedges of apple pandowdy. "And you'd also find I'd whup you at cribbage worse'n Uriah ever could." Setting the tray aside, she sat down in an armless reception chair and regarded Jessica appreciatively. "You received my letter. I truly didn't expect anyone to come here about it, but I am most grateful."

"You still suspect your husband was murdered?"

"I've learned nothing to change my mind, Miss Starbuck. I can't say I don't wish to have his killer brought to justice, but I doubt the crime will ever be solved, and nothing can bring Uriah back. No, I must put that behind me, and think of the ranch."

"Well, that's why we're here, Mrs. Waldemar. If you'll allow me, I'd like to take a look at your books and some of your land, and see if we can't come up with a few suggestions to help you."

"Feel perfectly free, and my prayers are with you. The banker and my foreman—that is, my *ex*-foreman—and others who should know have all insisted it's too late, and there's nothing left but to sell."

"Yes, to Ryker. Has he made you a reasonable offer?"

"I can't judge, and I'm not sure it'd matter if I could. It's the only offer; no other buyer is willing to buck the Captain."

"You're bucking him, Am'belle, and good for you."

"You know why I am, Toby. Because Uriah would spin in his grave if I let Captain Ryker buy the Flying W. Besides, the ranch was profitable before, and I can't help believing it can be made so again, if . . ." Mrs. Waldemar paused, getting to her feet and pacing the room, looking troubled and embarrassed as she halted in front of Jessica. "If, Miss Starbuck, you'll bring in some men. Some real men, who won't scat to the tall timber whenever the rustlers cut our herd or torch our graze. Men who won't hesitate to kill."

Jessica studied the coffee in her cup. She finally answered, "Hiring gunhands isn't a solution. It'd only mean we'd have two packs of wolves to get rid of, instead of one."

Mrs. Waldemar sat down heavily. "Of course. Two wrongs never made a right. I'm ashamed of myself for even thinking such a thing."

After a few more minutes of small talk, Mrs. Waldemar ushered Jessica into her late husband's study, and showed her where the books were kept. Spreading the books and related papers out on the study's battered rolltop desk, Jessica began a cursory investigation of the ranch's financial status, and almost immediately found it to be deeply in the red, bordering on collapse.

Beef receipts from the last co-op gather had been spent before Starbuck had paid off, the Flying W's income going to back wages, supply and feed credit chits, and an overdue mortgage payment. Current expenses were not being met, other than a few of the worst bills, which apparently had been paid through withdrawals from Mrs. Waldemar's savings account back in Boston. Rustlers had whittled at the Flying W stock until the latest tally recorded by Nealon revealed less than two hundred three-year-olds, yearlings, and heifers. Even if Starbuck accepted them at top market quotations, Jessica realized that it would barely pay the crew what they were owed.

Squaring her shoulders, Jessica replaced the books and rolled down the top of the old desk. She returned to the parlor, where Ki and Daryl were standing by the sofa, watching Toby and Mrs. Waldemar play cribbage, the scoreboard and cards on the cushion between them.

"I know, it's as bad as I've been told," Mrs. Waldemar sighed dejectedly, glancing up. "The Flying W is finished, beyond recovery, and I should resign myself to losing it to Captain Ryker."

"I'll admit it can't continue as it is," Jessica replied. "But we're here to try to save it, not bury it, and before anything's decided, I want to take a quick tour of the property with Ki."

Daryl grinned. "Well, I'm your guide. Dad?"

Toby shook his head, fuming. "Go ahead, son. Am'belle's just skunked me with pairs royal, but she ain't going to get away with it."

Leaving the ranch house, Jessica, Ki, and Daryl spent the rest of the day in their saddles. The unfenced range of the Flying W took in the valley and some of the broken hills that surrounded it, much of the land having a short, tough grass cover that was not the best, but was adequate for grazing. The hands they encountered appeared to know more or less what they were doing, though the lack of supervision was evident in their choice of tasks. The spread would never be a gold mine, Jessica concluded, but it had once been healthy—and with a lot of luck, leadership, and hard labor, it could be again.

Their inspection took longer than expected, and dusk had fallen by the time they returned to the ranch yard. Dismounting, Daryl asked, "Well, shall we go report to Mrs. Waldemar?"

Jessica, glancing at the lighted windows of the cookshack, said, "Not yet. There's one more thing I want to get straight."

She led the way to the cookshack, noting, as they went, the littered, unkempt appearance of the barn, sheds, and bunkhouse. It shocked and angered her to think how, in just the few short months since Uriah Waldemar's death, the Flying W had declined through indifference and neglect. Amabelle Waldemar was a fine, decent lady who had no experience in running a ranch and, not knowing any better, had placed her trust in the wrong men. If Jessica did no more than turn the ranch around and keep Ryker from grabbing it, it would be adequate reason for having come to Eucher Butte.

Inside the smoky cookshack, the Flying W crew lined both sides of a long plank table, demolishing platters of meat and potatoes, and steaming pots of coffee. At the head of the table was the empty chair of the foreman; Jessica sat down in it and reached for the coffee, while Ki and Daryl stood flanking the door.

The crewmen studiously ignored their presence, other than to dart surely glances in their direction while they ate. Finishing their meal, the men shoved their plates aside and rose to leave.

"Sit tight," Jessica snapped. "You're not through yet."

The crew hesitated, giving her hard, belligerent looks, then slowly settled back on the benches. In the tense hush that followed, Jessica sipped her coffee and thought how they all must be silently wishing she'd go away, preferably straight to hell. Well, she wasn't about to go; she was going to stay and find out how many of *them* were going to go.

Draining her cup, she returned their harsh glares and said, "But in another sense, you're through. Through for good."

One of the feistier hands protested, "Lady, it's not—"

"Miss Starbuck, if you please. And yes, it is."

"Miz Starbuck, okay, but it's not right to fire us now. We came back and worked all day, like you wanted. It's not fair."

"I don't have to fire you. You're firing yourselves, with all your hurrawing on the ranch's time and money. And the rustlers are firing you too, by raiding and looting till the Flying W is stone broke, and Ryker can take it over as a favor." She leaned forward, sternly eyeing the shaken crew. "Ryker says he's planning to form a combine out of the ranches he buys, and you know what that'll mean? It'll mean most of you'll be canned, and those who aren't will have to work twice as hard for half the wages."

Another puncher shrugged. "Nothing we can do to change it."

"That's where you're wrong, dead wrong. You're going to start tomorrow dawn, by weeding out the stock of everything four years and older, and shipping them to Starbuck. We need them like the plague, but it'll help pay your wages, help keep you *hired*. And I want a couple of you to take some Giant powder to the west end of the valley, where the stream flows down out of that long canyon. I found plenty of tracks heading up it, and the cows didn't get there by straying."

The second puncher nodded, brightening. "Not a bad idea. A little blasting up in the rocks oughta close that gap to rustlers."

"It'll also dam the stream," Jessica continued. "It'll form a reservoir to provide extra water for the herd, and for crop irrigation."

That startled a third hand. "Crops? We're not sodbusters."

Jessica favored him with a flinty smile. "It's not hard to learn. And you'd better, because that whole section by the canyon will be fenced off for native hay and maybe some sugar beets. What you don't use for the ranch will be sold as another source of income."

By now the entire Flying W crew was gaping at her. Daryl, as well, was studying her in wonderment. She was moving fast and decisively, this Jessica Starbuck. She was ramrodding hard—which, though unsettling, was also generating fresh enthusiasm.

And then she dropped the bomb. "You're going to need a foreman, what with Nealon gone—and from what I've seen so far, good riddance—so I'm going to ask Toby Melville to stay on awhile, as guest of Mrs. Waldemar. From now on, you'll take your orders from him."

There was an outburst of voices, including Daryl's: "But Jessi—"

She shushed them with a wave of her hand. "Listen, Toby Melville's forgotten more about ranching than most of us will ever learn. And you all get along with the Spraddled M crew, don't you?" When she wasn't contradicted, she forged on: "The two spreads will remain separate. I'm only taking about banding together till we've licked the rustling. A common herd can be defended by fewer men, freeing others for nighthawking—and fighting."

A fifth hand balked at this. "Fighting, like in shooting? Not me. I was hired to nurse cows, not toss lead."

Jessica nailed him with steel-cold eyes. "You're hired to side the Flying W, a fact you've managed to ignore." Surveying the others, she added, "You're bogged down and sinking fast, and if you hope to save your ranch and your jobs, you're going to have to lay your brains and guts and, by God, all your loyalty on the line."

"By damn, I've heard all the manure I plan to," a puncher way in the back sneered, "and the only reason I say 'manure' is on account of a female's present. Leastwise, she *looks* like a female."

Daryl stiffened. "Hold on, watch your tongue there."

The third Flying W hand who'd spoken now chimed in. "Yeah, Wylie, ain't no call to—"

"Shut up, Croft," the man called Wylie snarled. "Maybe your spine is made outta smoke, but as for me, I've had my fill of bein' lectured at by strange wimmen." He got up from the table, a dark, squat man with a barrel chest and black, beady eyes. "I'm doin' nothin' till Miz Waldemar tosses these troublemakin' talkers offen the ranch. If anybody else feels the same, come with me."

The two burly punchers who'd been flanking him on the bench rose and fell in, swaggering behind Wylie as he began shouldering his way toward the door. Apparently his close buddies, they laughed when he glared at Jessica and taunted, "Yeah, if I craved preacherin', lady, I'd go to Sunday school." Then, turning to Daryl and Ki, he added, growling, "Step aside, 'lessen you wish to get busted apart."

Almost to the front of the table now, he drew abreast of Croft. Foolishly, Croft shifted on the bench and reached out to place a cautioning hand lightly on Wylie's arm. "Simmer down, Wylie," he said. "Hear them out. Maybe these folks've got something to—"

"Leggo!" Wylie wrenched away from Croft's hand as though it were a snake biting his arm, then pivoted and shoved his palm flat into Croft's face. "I'll learn you to shut up!" he snarled, and mashed Croft's head down into his dinner plate with a dull, meaty crunch. Dazed and half-blinded, Croft reeled to one side and began falling off the bench, and Wylie drew back his right foot to kick his boot into Croft's unprotected belly. "I'll learn you good!"

Ki reacted before the kick could land. With an odd smile that masked his anger, he launched himself at Wylie, who immediately turned to meet him with clenched fists. Ki ducked Wylie's first and last punch, catching the puncher's outflung arm and angling to drop to one knee, swinging him into *seoi otoshi,* the kneeling shoulder-throw.

Wylie arched through the air, over the heads of the seated men, and came down on the table, atop the meat platter and the bowl of mashed potatoes. He sprawled there, dazed and breathless.

Even before Wylie hit, Ki was swinging around in the cramped space between the bench and the wall, to check whatever Wylie's two friends might be up to. The nearer one was charging him with outstretched arms, as if he were tackling a drunk in a barroom brawl. Ki chopped the edge of his hand down at the fellow's nose. He purposely held back a little so he would not break it, but it struck forcefully enough to hurt like hell, and tears of pain sprang into the man's eyes. Ki followed through by kicking the man in the side of his knee, collapsing him to one side. He caught his right arm, crunched down on it with his elbow, and then brought his own knee into his hip.

The man dropped to the floor, leaving the way clear for Wylie's second pal to lash out at Ki with his wide leather belt. Ki had already seen this second one slide off his belt and fold it double, which was one of the reasons he'd had to dump the first man, for now he was able to step over the first man and catch hold of the second one's right arm and left shoulder with his hands. At the same time, Ki moved his right foot slightly in back of the man so that as the fellow began tumbling sideways, Ki was able to dip to his right knee and yank viciously. His *hizi otoshi,* or elbow-drop, worked perfectly; the second man catapulted upside-down and collapsed jarringly on top of the first man, flattening them both to the floor.

And Wylie, face purpling with rage, launched himself off

the table, a well-honed bowie knife clutched in his right hand. "I'm gonna carve you apart!" he bellowed, slashing at Ki.

Ki calmly stepped aside and then kicked up with his callused foot. His heel caught Wylie smack on his chin, so hard that Wylie flew backwards onto the table again. This time he sprawled cold on his back, staring sightlessly up at the rafters and cobwebbed ceiling of the cookshack.

The rest of the Flying W crew gaped at Wylie, his two moaning pals, and then at Ki with stunned disbelief. They said nothing.

Jessica broke the silence. "If these three want to quit, then they can quit. If any of you others want to quit, you can. Or you can stay. It's up to you, but make up your minds. As I said last night, I don't have the time—and the Flying W doesn't have the time—for you to sit on your butts. Either start kicking or packing."

The feisty hand who'd first spoken, now spoke up again. "Well, boys, I reckon Miz Starbuck might have something. She sure has a powerful persuader, and she's got me convinced. We gotta pitch in and stop the raidin', else we'll all be grub-lining. 'Sides, none of us is safe from a bushwhack bullet 'lessen we do rare up and fight back."

"Okay, count me in."

"We gotta do something, I see that now."

"Sure, we couldn't face Miz Waldemar if we didn't."

A consensus of agreement quickly swelled from the crew, including the one who'd refused to fight. "Might as well," he growled, moodily building a smoke. "Guess it don't make no difference how I bleed, fast or slow. I'll be dead here anyways."

Diplomatically thanking the men for their splendid cooperation, Jessica rose and left the cookshack. Ki followed, amused as ever by how much she was her father's child, equally as competent as Alex Starbuck had been in defusing and mastering tricky negotiations.

Daryl stood momentarily by the shack's open door, staring in bewildered at the sudden and complete change in the crewmen. Then he turned and swiftly caught up with Jessica and Ki, as they were walking toward the ranch house. "Jessie, that was great, but . . ." He faltered, still stunned by her volunteering of his father. "But Dad can't do it, you know how he drinks. He won't want to."

"We've got to make him want to," Jessica replied, and with a twinkle in her eye, she added, "I suspect that between handling those men, and Amabelle Waldemar's cooking and cribbage, Toby's going to find staying here to be a sobering experience."

Toby, when confronted, ranted and blustered. But he didn't argue all that hard, and eventually he caved in with surprising grace. Or maybe it wasn't so surprising.

Chapter 7

After enjoying a dinner with all the trimmings, Jessica, Ki, and Daryl bade goodbye to Mrs. Waldemar, who was now feeling greatly heartened, and to Toby, who was crankily washing the dishes, his penalty for having been thoroughly trounced at cribbage. The trio stepped to the barn and resaddled their fed and rested horses, then rode slowly out of the yard toward the main trail.

Moving alongside Jessica, Daryl said, "I sure do like your notion of combining the two spreads. I think my boys will go for it, once we've pointed out the advantages."

"Problem is, Daryl, it'll only work temporarily. We've stirred up the crew here and stiffened their spines, and maybe we can do the same for yours. But after a while, it's bound to wear off."

"Meanwhile," Ki added, "the rustlers can lie low, waiting for your crews to grow lax and drift apart before striking again."

"I don't think they'll wait," Daryl responded. "They seem to be a nervy bunch of polecats, and I wouldn't put it past them to try anyway, just to prove they're stronger. Even if they did hold off our spreads a while, they'd still be able to hit the other ranchers."

Jessica nodded. "You're right, there's a good chance of that. But if the other ranchers haven't gotten together before this to protect themselves, there isn't much we can do now to help them."

"Well, there is one thing you can do now," Daryl said with

a grin. "You can both come to the Spraddled M and stay overnight. There's lots of room, especially with Dad gone. And Jessica, after watching you twist the Flying W crew around your finger, I'd sure like you around in the morning, when I have my confab with the boys."

"Nice of you to offer, Daryl. Maybe we will, later."

"But I insist. You can't mean to ride half the night, all that long way back to Eucher Butte."

"I don't."

"Then where . . . ?"

"I mean to ride to the Snake-Eyes."

"The Block-Two-Dot?" Startled, Daryl jerked erect in his saddle. "Jessie, by the time you get there, Cap'n Ryker'll probably be in bed, in no mood to welcome a visit."

"I don't want his welcome. I don't want him to know."

"You're talking in riddles, Jessie," he said impatiently.

She reached across and placed her hand fondly on his arm. "I'm sorry. You're simple going to have to take my word for it—for a lot of things, right now."

Daryl gnawed his lower lip, frowning. "All right," he said at last, "I know it's useless to try changing your mind, once it's made up. And I'll take it on faith that you've got good reason. So I'm coming along and making sure you keep outta harm."

"Believe me, Daryl, Ki's very good at that."

Daryl twisted in his saddle to look over at Ki. "I've got every respect for your fighting abilities, Ki, but you and her don't know the country like I know it." He turned back to face Jessica. "Whatever you're planning to do at Ryker's, it plainly involves sneaking in. Well, I'm the one who can get you there unseen, and if trouble pops, I'm the one who can get you two out."

"We accept," Ki said, before Jessica could answer. "But you'll have to promise to do what we say, when we say it."

"I promise to consider it. Now follow me."

Spurring his buckskin, Daryl led Jessica and Ki northeast across the Flying W valley. When they reached the hills that separated the Flying W from the Block-Two-Dot, they climbed in a wide circle to hit Ryker's spread from almost due north. It took them over an hour to work their way through the jagged, forested heights and down around to where they could first glimpse the ranch.

Spied at a distance, the barns and corrals and other buildings appeared dwarfed by the tall, sheer cliffs surrounding
them on three sides. It was as if the Block-Two-Dot were set in
a canyon-locked lagoon, facing a gentle sea of waving grass,
and fronting a thin beach of roadway that cut in from a nearby
pass. And it looked silent and deserted from where they paused,
seeming to sleep in the clouded moonlight. But as they watched,
a tiny figure left the bunkhouse and strolled to the corral. In a
few moments it returned to the bunkhouse, and the yard was
empty again.

"They're still awake," Daryl commented dryly.

"Then we'll wait," Ki responded, his eyes surveying the
stone walls around the ranch. "Up there." He pointed toward
a fault in one cliff face, which formed a steep but not impossible
slope to the top.

Skirting the open valley meadow and keeping to the cover
of rocks and trees, they eased along the base of the hills until
they reached the cliff. Horses and riders struggled up the slope,
hooves slipping and gouging out small avalanches of stone and
dirt. When they struck the rim, they rested their mounts awhile,
then cautiously rode toward a concealed ledge closer above the
ranch.

Finally they dismounted and picketed the horses, moving
ahead on foot to a flat rock projecting out from the face of the
cliff. They slid out and crouched at the edge, pleased to find
they could view the dark, corrugated uplands and the bleak
mountains beyond; the purple valley pastures that were mottled
with the dunkier splotches of cattle; the lofty walls of the box
canyon in whose notch the shadowed ranch was nestled. Their
perch was ideal, and they settled themselves for a long vigil.

Time passed. A few hands left the bunkhouse now and then,
for the outhouse or the barn or corrals. Nothing else happened.

"Let's go," Daryl said restlessly. "It's dead down there."

Jessica shook her head. "As you said, they're still awake."

"Playing poker in the bunkhouse," Daryl retorted. "So
what? Why are you and Ki so determined to keep tabs on Cap'n
Ryker?"

"Because he's been lying through his pearly teeth."

"C'mon, Jessie, I know you're competitors, but—"

"It's because we're competitors that I know he's lying. Listen,

Ryker's been saying he's here to consolidate your ranches into one big operation. Well, if he had enough legitimate money to swing such a big package, he'd send representatives and agents to deal for him."

"So he likes to handle it all himself."

"Daryl, does Ryker look like the kind of man who'd come out here if he could avoid it? No. And the only reason he'd have to do it himself is if his finances are so shady and his reasons so sneaky that he can't afford the risk of hirelings finding out. He wants the land, Daryl, I don't question that, but his fancy story about Acme needing beef is only a cover to hide his real motive."

"Which is?"

"That," Jessie sighed, "is why we're waiting."

Abruptly they stiffened, hearing the faint beat of horses hooves echoing hollowly from the pass. More lights began glittering in the Block-Two-Dot buildings, and crewmen from the bunkhouse came out into the yard. Ki stared into the darkness toward the pass.

"Riders," he said.

Jessica kept her eyes on the ranch house. Only two windows were showing any light at all, one being where a front sitting room would be, and the other at the side, in what appeared to be a relatively new addition tacked on to the existing structure. Ryker's office? It was impossible to tell. The window was draped, allowing only a thin crease of lamplight to filter through.

Six or seven riders streamed out of the pass and along the wagon road, reining in when they reached the yard, the bunkhouse hands closing to meet them. Ryker's big bulk was silhouetted in the ranch house doorway as he stepped outside. The men clustered around him for a short while, and Jessica wished she could somehow be down there to overhear the conversation.

Ryker disappeared back into the house. There was more activity in the yard as some of the bunkhouse crew saddled horses and, together with the riders, galloped out of the yard. Hoofbeats drummed loudly and then receded as the men vanished back along the road and up into the pass. Quiet descended across the ranch again, the remaining hands returning to the bunkhouse and closing its door.

Daryl rubbed his ear. "Wonder what that was about."

"Suppose I told you those were the rustlers?"

"No!" Daryl gasped, stiffening. "Jessie, are you sure?"

"Like I keep trying to tell you, Daryl," she replied irritably, "I *think* I have some of the answer to what's been going on hereabouts, and I *think* more of the answer is down at that ranch. But the only thing I *know* right now is that I can't be sure of anything yet."

"But—but if you're right, then we've got to go warn—"

"Warn who? Which rancher, Daryl? And by the time we could follow that bunch to wherever they're raiding, and then get help, they'd have struck and moved on. Relax, Daryl, we're waiting."

Shortly, the lamp in the sitting room winked out, followed by another one being briefly lit at the far end of the house, presumably in a bedroom; Rykcr was getting ready for bed. Fifteen minutes later, the lamp in the study was snuffed, and the entire ranch house was now dark, silent, undisturbed. Jessica hesitated for a while longer, but nothing suspicious occurred.

"All right, let's give it a whirl," Jessica said, moving away from the edge. "I figure Ryker's had time enough to fall asleep."

"But the men in the bunkhouse," Daryl protested. "I know there ain't many of them there now, but they're all still awake."

She smiled tautly, "Why, they're busy at poker, remember?"

As they hurried to their horses, Jessica was glad to stretch her cramped muscles. Worming back down the steep, narrow crevice was ticklish business, but at last they reached the base of the cliff and cautiously began to approach the ranch.

Coming to a small clump of trees at the extreme edge of the yard, Ki reined in and said in a low voice, "We'll walk from here."

They dismounted and ground-hitched their horses, and Jessica whispered to Daryl, "You stay here and guard them for us."

"Not on your tintype," he declared adamantly.

"Daryl, you wouldn't have gotten this far," Jessica snapped crossly, "except you insisted on jumping into things you don't know anything about."

"And you don't either," he reminded her. Stooping, he tugged off his boots; his socks had holes in them, but he ignored his bare toes sticking out, adding, "My feet are tougher'n rawhide, and when it comes to creeping around, the only one quieter'n me might be Ki, in those slipper-shoes of his."

Jessica turned to Ki for support, but Ki only shrugged, a slightly amused expression on his face. Grudgingly she gave up arguing, realizing Daryl could be just as stubborn as she was, and together the three glided from the trees and crossed into the yard.

Reaching the near corner of the first outbuilding, they paused and listened, checking every shadow for the presence of a guard. They had seen none from the rock, but this was not the time or place to rely on assumptions. Again, they saw no sign of one.

From the outbuilding, they cut swiftly through the yard, making a wide circuit around the bunkhouse. They melted into the night beyond the corral, then eased back toward the ranch house.

They stopped just under the short overhang of the rear porch. Again they strained to hear, to peer into the blackness around them. A coarse laugh sounded from the bunkhouse; a horse in the corral snorted and stamped. Satisfied, Jessica rubbed her palm along the butt of her holstered revolver, and nodded to Ki. Ki took a skeleton key and a thin, pliant strip of metal from his vest and, squatting, went to work on the porch door. A moment later, the latch snicked back, and he warily pushed open the door.

They slipped inside and stood in a dark pantryway, listening, gaining their bearings, before padding into the kitchen beyond. They passed through the kitchen by the glow of the banked fire in the large cast-iron stove, and entered a dining room with an oak table capable of seating a platoon, with elbow space to spare.

At the other end of the dining room were double doors, luckily unlocked. Ki inched one open and they squeezed through into a sitting room. Near the single window was the wide front door, and opposite was a stubby corridor and an inner door, which she surmised led to Ryker's bedroom.

Straight ahead, therefore, would be the new wing containing his study.

Breathlessly they crossed between the front door and hall-way, fearing their footfalls might be audible. Jessica hesitated before continuing, bird-dogged by apprehensions, even though they heard nothing. Nothing at all . . .

That was what concerned her—hearing nothing at all.

They crept onward nonetheless, through a succession of smaller rooms, pausing before entering each one to assure themselves of unobserved passage. Finally they arrived at the study door. This too was closed and locked. Swiftly, Ki picked the lock and pushed, hearing from its other side the rattle of a key in its escutcheon. They waited. All remained silent. Ki gradually eased the door wider, until there was room for them to dart into the study.

The study was black, save for a trickle of pale moonlight around the edges of the poorly drawn drapes. Jessica immediately went over, rearranging the drapes so they completely blanketed the study's small paned window, while Ki lit a small reading lamp and Daryl gently closed and relocked the door.

Most of the study was taken up by a massive six-foot curtain desk, made of quarter-sawn golden oak, with sycamore inlays and pigeonhole cases. It rested with its matching swivel chair on an Oriental carpet, and was surrounded by walls of book-shelves that were crammed with leather-bound books and looseleaf folders.

"What're we looking for?" Daryl murmured.

Jessica shrugged, and started poking into drawers and pigeonholes, while Ki began sifting through the material on the shelves. She unearthed very little useful information, other than a curious letter postmarked from Washington, D.C.:

My dear Guthried:

I trust you're finding life among the savages and cut-throats not overly unbearable. Your endurance will be well rewarded, I assure you, and this is to confirm that I've already taken steps to arrange for five percent of the stock to be issued in your name. Of course, this is

*predicated on your success in purchasing all the land
we require, and the subsequent merger of Acme with our
new corporation. I'm also pleased to report that we've
decided on the name of American Federated Development, which has a nice solid ring to it, I believe, without
meaning anything. As soon as I receive your wire, I shall
introduce my bill and guide it through to passage.*

Yours respectfully,
Dilworth Trumbull

Jessica pocketed the letter, frowning as she tried to remember precisely who Dilworth Trumbell was. A congressman,
obviously, but—

"Jessie," Ki hissed, interrupting her thoughts. "Come here
and take a look at this, see what you make of it."

Jessica and Daryl crossed to where Ki stood by one book-
case, his hands holding wide an unfurled surveyor's section
map of Wyoming Territory. A red ink line had been drawn
along the same hazardous trail Jessica and Ki had traveled from
Uva to Eucher Butte, apparently indicating where an improved
road was to be built. Another line ran in a haphazard wriggle
from Eucher Butte north to the site of Fort Fetterman, then
west and down to just below Casper, then south to intersect the
Little Medicine Bow River, and then back across the Eucher
Butte. Roughly estimated, the box-like shape it formed encom-
passed some 3,700 square miles of territory.

"Unbelievable," Daryl gasped. "He's buying all that?"

"I guess so," Jessica whispered. "Trying to, anyway."

"He's already bought or optioned some of it," Ki added,
indicating where, within the box, blocks of property had been
marked with X's. "And hardly any of it is good as range or
farmland."

Daryl shook his head in amazement. "Whatever Ryker
wants it for, it'll be the largest land-grab since we revolutioned
from the British—"

A moan cut him off, freezing all three of them. It was a low,
muffled sound coming from somewhere nearby, and when,
after a long moment, they didn't hear the groan again, Ki

rcrolled the map and picked up the lamp, whispering, "I'll go out first."

"Wait," Jessica cautioned. "Cast some light around. I swear that moan didn't come from inside the house—or outside, either."

Ki held the lamp higher, so that its feeble glow could better illuminate the dark nooks and crannies. At first nothing appeared out of the ordinary, until the study, concealed in an easily overlooked corner where two bookcases met, was reflected the outline of a small inset door.

On a wild impulse, Jessica went to the door, her saner self rebelling even as she eased down on its handle. The door opened against her gentle pressure. She peered down a short flight of stairs to a basement landing, glimpsing a dim finger of light lancing from somewhere farther back. And wafting up came the familiar odor of a wine cellar—that distinct blend of tannin, cork, and mold, which woke in Jessica's memory the many genial excursions she'd taken with her father's servants, when hunting bottles for dinner in the cellars of the Circle Star ranch.

"Shut the door," Daryl pleaded. "It's only a wine—"

There rose from the basement another moan, longer this time, with a clearly pleading tone to it, as though someone was being tortured.

"Oh, no, it's not," Jessica whispered back to Daryl. "It's another Ryker lie, another trick to cover up something wretched."

Hesitating only long enough for Ki to move ahead with the lamp, Jessica followed him down the steps, Daryl trailing reluctantly, gripping his old Remington revolver. At the bottom stretched two rows of bottles stacked in ceiling-high tiers, and the finger of light she'd seen from upstairs was emanating from a half-open door at the end of this corridor. The bottles, the tiers, the cellar itself were all quite new, Jessica observed, probably dating from the same time as the addition of the study to the main house above.

Moving between the rows toward the door, Jessica rationalized her reckless urge by arguing that the more she learned about her enemies, the more effectively she could defeat them. And for starters, she wanted to find out who was moaning and why, and if it had anything to do for the reason behind the

cellar's existence. That it was a ruse, a blind to disguise some
other purpose, was clear to her; no host in his right mind would
build a wine cellar so far from the dining room.

Reaching the end of the tiers, they saw that the door was in
a plank wall that partitioned the rear of the cellar into a separate
room. Open to view through the widely ajar door, the room
was brightly lit by a library lamp hanging from a ceiling joist.
Its floor was matted with straw, and its walls were thickly padded with canvas quilting; spaced around the room were big
wooden blocks carved out in places to fit the shape of the
human body, with leather thongs and belts, and innumerable
chains dangling from their fronts and sides.

A woman was shackled to one of the blocks. She was on
the good side of forty, Jessica judged, with black hair to her
waist, pendulous breasts, and large quivering thighs. She was
entirely naked, except for leather sandals and metal-studded
leather cuffs at her wrists, to which the chains were padlocked.
Her lips, breasts, and loins were painted to accentuate her sexu-
ality, and her eyes were treated with mascara to look twice their
normal size. And from her neck to her knees, her flesh was a
mass of lacerations, new redder welts laid crisscrossing over
older pink scars.

Guthried Ryker was similarly naked, except for a leather
belt heavily studded with iron, which he wore around his pudgy
waist. He also had on sandals, but instead of leather cuffs,
he wore gauntlets. He was patently aroused, his erection jutting like a ship's boom from his hairy groin. And held in his
right hand, slapping lightly against his leg, was a vicious
cat-o'-nine-tails.

Sensing an intrusion, Ryker wheeled to face the group in
the doorway. His pursy mouth gaped open, and instinctively
his right hand made a slight whipping motion with the tails,
which he instantly checked. Ki remained still, guardedly
poised. Daryl stared dumbfounded, his revolver pointing downward. Jessica glowered rigidly, infuriated and disgusted.

"What are *you* doing here?" Ryker snarled.

"What are you *doing* here?" Daryl blurted in shock.

Ryker blinked, then chuckled throatily. "Why, just a little
recreation, m'boy. A little stirring of the blood to relax me."

"Release her," Ki said, coldly but calmly.

"Come now, let's not be naïve about this. My friend is being well paid for her pain." Ryker moved almost imperceptively into a crouch, adding: "And I do believe Dolores enjoys it, too."

"I'm sure Trumbull will enjoy it, when I write him," Jessica retorted with poisoned sweetness. "I'm sure he'll be delighted to share this with the other stockholders of American Federated."

She had no intention of writing Dilworth Trumbull or anyone else; her threat was merely to throw Ryker off his stride, and see what came of it. Nothing did, at first. Ryker showed no alarm, no fear, only a deep surprise. A tense silence gripped the room.

Then, with the suddenness and speed of a striking snake, Ryker's hand shot back the tails and snapped them forward. Jessica had no time or space in which to avoid the blow, so she caught the full blow of the lashes across her breasts and belly. It felt like a shatter of glass in the skin, in the sensitive lair of flesh beneath—it was not one red-hot sting of fire, but a general cracking agony that caused her to shudder, screaming.

But even before Ryker could complete the arc of his swing, Ki had released one of his *shuriken* throwing blades from the sheath strapped to his arm under his shirt. The spinning, razor-sharp star glinted in the lamplight as it left his fingers. And simultaneously, Daryl raised his revolver and triggered.

The .44-40 bullet hit a split second before the *shuriken*. Daryl's hasty shot blew most of Ryker's left ear off. Ryker howled, clapping his left hand to the stump of his ear, toppling back and to one side. It wasn't until he'd bumped into the block where the woman was chained that he noticed Ki's *shuriken* embedded in his right shoulder, close to his neck. If he hadn't jerked off balance when first struck by Daryl's heavy lead slug, the *shuriken* would have sliced into his throat and killed him instantly.

"Goddamn you!" he bawled, still falling against the block, sending it and the woman over with him as he crashed to the floor. The woman was shrieking now, struggling futilely in her chains, kicking out and managing accidentally to catch him in the groin with one sandal. Which pretty well took care of his withering erection, and any other notion of resistance he might have had. The cat-o'-nine-tails dropped from his nerveless fingers, and with eyes filming and legs turning to jelly, Ryker collapsed, unconscious, on the straw.

"Let's move," Jessie snapped, moving from the door. "Fast!"

Daryl hesitated, bewildered. "But that lady in there—"

"We don't have the time, the keys, or a way to take her if we could get her loose," Ki yelled, propelling Daryl along between the rows of bottles. "What we've got are your poker-playing pals from the bunkhouse, doubtless coming fast after hearing your shot!"

Chapter 8

Up the stairs to the study they raced, then through the ranch house, back to the pantry. They reached the rear door just as the crew from the bunkhouse came rushing in across the yard.

Both Jessica and Daryl had their revolvers leveled, when they and Ki stepped out. The half-dozen men hauled up short, their own pistols drawn, pointing every which way but the right way.

"Far enough," Daryl ordered. "Toss your guns away."

The crew milled indecisively, stymied by the two revolvers aiming straight at them. Then, one by one, they gave in, throwing their weapons off into the darkness. Eyeing them warily, Jessica, Ki, and Daryl moved off the porch and began edging around toward the side of the yard where, beyond, they'd posted their horses.

"Your boss isn't dead," Jessica told the crew, her large-framed .38 never wavering in her fist. "Fact is, he's down in the wine cellar, way in the rear, waiting for you boys."

They continued backing away from the disarmed group, and were almost to the corner of the first outbuilding again when they stiffened, listening. Hoofbeats sounded in increasing tempo, heading along the road from the pass, directly for the yard.

"Hot damn!" one of the gang cried. "They're coming back!"

"Yeah, we've got this bunch trapped!"

It was true. The three could hear the riders sweeping in toward the ranch behind them, and the men they were covering were regaining their nerve, already scrambling for their thrown pistols.

Jessica, Ki and Daryl pivoted as one, and started running for the protection of the outbuilding's shadows. "Get them!" they heard a raspy voice shout, and the bunkhouse crew, finding their weapons, began firing eagerly in their direction.

When they came to the back of the outbuilding, Daryl swiveled and his Remington spat flame. A man dropped and another cursed. Joining Daryl, Jessica fired with deadly precision, scattering the initial charge of Ryker's men, downing two more. Thundering battle broke loose in the yard, pistols bucking, lead searching.

In the dark, bloody confusion, the trio managed to run in a crouch away from the outbuilding. They streaked, ducking and zigzagging, to the edge of the yard, then cut toward the grove where their horses were waiting. They knew they had a bare minute before the approaching riders would descend and spread out hunting for them—and in that minute they'd have to be gone, or be dead.

They were merely flitting silhouettes in the field between the yard and the trees, when the riders galloped in. A quick, shouting uproar and the blood-cry of pursuit rose from the yard, and the riders turned, roweling their mounts toward the fleeing trio.

They dove into the trees, Jessica and Daryl holstering their pistols as they all grabbed reins and leaped for saddles. " 'Bye, boots," Daryl said regretfully as they wheeled their horses away from the Block-Two-Dot. Then, breaking from the grove, he shouted, "It's a race for it! Head for the pass!"

They bent over their horses' withers, and the animals chewed up the ground. Shots snarled after them, but the swaying riders behind them couldn't aim effectively, their bullets off target, high and wild. They didn't bother to return the fire. It would be nip-and-tuck all the way to the pass.

The earth blurred under pounding hoofs. The rolling beat of pursuing horses echoed loud and thundering. The pass was an eternity away. The fusillade of avenging lead buzzed close by their heads.

The murky slopes of the hills loomed closer, and finally they could see the black maw of the pass. Jessica risked a quick glance behind her. She could plainly hear the onrushing riders, but could only make them out as a group bunched together in the hazy darkness. From her brief glimpse of their bulk, however, she estimated they were just the bunkhouse crew, and not the combined force.

At last they plunged into the narrow pass, Daryl slightly in the lead, urging his buckskin to greater speed. Short moments later, the towering walls of the pass echoed as the pursuers swept in after them along the rutted trail. The chase continued, the pass gradually rising and blending into the foothills and opening out into a draw. Beyond, a wide rock-strewn plateau extended to another maze of night-heavy ridges and canyons. Naked of trees, the plateau gleamed under moonlight, which made pearls of the stones littering their path.

The three rode hard across the flat. The only sounds were the deep panting of the horses, and their drumming strides against the rocky soil—and the faint rataplan of hoofbeats coming after them.

"Ryker's boys still have us in sight," Jessica said loudly.

"Not for long," Daryl shouted back. "They're going to wind up chasing their tails all night, when I get done confusing them. Nobody 'cept my dad knows these hills better'n I do."

Reaching the edge of the plateau, Daryl began skirting a twisted ravine, gesturing toward a side trail some distance ahead. Jessica and Ki veered to the left, following him as he swung onto a barely visible track at a dead run. A canyon embraced them, shrinking to a sinuous gorge of solid stone that reverberated with their passage.

Daryl slowed his buckskin and motioned for Jessica and Ki to do the same. Their huffing bays were glad to oblige. They moved on along the granite floor, their easy lope giving off very little noise that could be traced. Behind, the sounds of galloping horses echoed off the rock as the Block-Two-Dot crew entered the canyon.

"Haven't lost them yet," Ki said, glancing back.

"We will," Daryl replied confidently. "Thing is, I don't want them to be able to hear when and where we cut off. It's up a ways—"

"Wait," Jessica interrupted. "Listen."

The two men tensed, straining to catch what she was hearing. Then, from ahead, faint at first, but growing swiftly, rose a deep, earth-trembling roar. Still riding at a loping pace, they became increasingly alarmed the farther they went along the snaky gorge. But they couldn't stop or go back, because of the pursuing riders; they couldn't turn aside, because of the steep slopes and flanking boulders on both edges; they could only continue heading toward the rolling, pounding, fast-approaching tumult.

A few rags of clouds shuttled across high stars, blown by a rush of wind from the north. They caught the moon, released it again; and as the pale light trickled back into the gorge, the trio rounded a sharp bend and faced a looming herd of cattle.

Hastily they reined in, aghast at the sight of this brown wall bearing down on them heads tossing, eyes rolling, horns clacking. It was not a big herd, but it didn't need to be, squeezed as it was within the narrow gully. It was being driven at a rapid clip by punchers on horseback outlined against the starry sky, their prodding shouts lifting above the drubbing beat of hoofs. A little in front trotted one curly-horned, wall-eyed steer that seemed to be the leader.

"I know that brute!" Daryl yelped. "Them're *my* cows!"

"You can have them!" Ki retorted. "Back! Quick!"

His voice was drowned in the deafening roar, but Jessica and Daryl saw him wheel and start heading back the way they'd come. They wrenched their horses around to follow, Daryl's buckskin kicking and plunging, Jessica's bay dancing, ears laid back and eyes wild.

Fear was in the air, fear of this mass of flesh closing inexorably, no more to be halted than a tornado. To yell and wave would be futile; to shoot would be like damming a flood with loose rocks, and could easily result in panic, spooking the steers into stampeding in the only direction they could go—straight ahead.

The dark trail blurred under their horses, their pace too swift for talk, and none was needed. Each could sense the tension and dread in the others, as they galloped around another tight curve, and surged directly toward the oncoming Block-Two-Dot gunhands.

The crew were caught by surprise, but not so much that they didn't react. Predictably, they spurred their horses on, whooping with certain victory, their pistols spurting flame and lead. At such dead-on range, Jessica, Ki and Daryl should have been riddled, but in firing from speeding horses into night shadows, the crew's aim proved inaccurate. Bullets ricocheted off the boulders and whistled past their bodies uncomfortably close, one searing along Daryl's ribs in a long gash. But they continued their suicidal charge, figuring their only chance was to somehow break through the line of gunmen and return to the plateau.

And then the herd came lumbering around the curve.

The gorge abruptly erupted in howling, rattling confusion, the Block Two-Dot crew shouting in shock and fear, trying to check their horses and spin them about. Some went down as their horses slipped and fell on the shale. Others windmilled arms and hats in a vain attempt to stop the front. Still others, the really stupid ones, turned their fire from the three riders to the crowding steers beyond.

The cattle spooked. Lowing and snorting, they began picking up speed, and as one would stumble or drop with a bullet, the other would leap the barrier and stream on even faster. More gunfire peppered the advancing herd as the crew splintered frenziedly, a few retreating, most of them still attempting to stave off the stampede.

A panic-triggered slug caught Ki's horse in its breast-bone. The bay reared with the impact, causing Ki to lurch half out of his saddle, his balance lost. Frantically he grabbed for the saddlehorn, missing it, and started falling headfirst as the horse folded beneath him.

He wriggled clear. Jolting agony jarred through him as he struck the ground, the bay tumbling on its side, its hooves slashing close to his face.

"Ki!" Jessica pivoted her horse toward him, heedless of the oncoming stampede. The curly-horned leader dashed bellowing past her, other steers thronging right behind, and it was almost more than Jessica could do to maneuver her horse out of their path. Daryl, spotting her, swung his buckskin in an arc to intercept her, as the rush of steers surged perilously around him in an increasing tide.

They saw Ki rise, then begin bobbing and weaving in a desperate effort to reach the boulders at the nearest side of the trail. "Leave me!" they heard him cry as he dove among the swelling torrent of hoofs and horns. "Save yourselves—or we'll all die!"

Jessica ignored his plea and made a last convulsive try, struggling against the flow of crazed cattle to save him. But that shoving melee flung her back as easily as a baby. She reeled, tilting far off balance, and the flinty tip of a longhorn snagged her jacket, tearing through it and her shirt, gouging a burning furrow diagonally across her side and back. She would have lost control, had not Daryl swerved alongside and grabbed the cheekstrap of her horse's bridle, pulling the animal around in line with the maddened herd.

"No!" Eyes wide, face chalky white, Jessica fought to stop him. "Let me go, Daryl, we can't leave Ki—"

"Dammit, we have no choice!"

They were swept along shoulder to shoulder with the steers, shoulder to shoulder with sudden death, but at least they were going in the right direction. The Block-Two-Dot crew was not. Men fell, horses tripped, and the stampede crushed them in its relentless pressure, trampling and slashing them under sharp hooves. The agonized cries of the injured and dying were faint in the overwhelming, thunderous maelstrom.

And the avalanche of beef rolled implacably on toward the plateau, moonlight glinting on tossing backs and piercing horns. Carried along in the hemming current, Jessie and Daryl could hear the bellowing of frightened animals and the pounding of hooves drumming the stony trail. This was no place for a poor rider, or for a coward.

The gorge widened into the short stretch of canyon, and from the canyon the herd funneled out, spreading across the plateau. Daryl angled for a narrow crevice at one side of the canyon mouth, Jessica followed, slumped in her saddle. The herd kept plummeting past in a swirl of dust and horns and hooves, not a dozen yards from the spot where they hid.

Eventually the drag drained through, the rustlers behind them yelling and cursing as they tried to stem the runaway, paying no attention to the narrow crevice. Watching them, Daryl commented disgustedly, "They'll never turn them. By morning, my cows will be scattered from hell to breakfast out there in the brakes."

"We've got to go back," Jessica said dully.

"We can't."

"We can't leave Ki!"

"We have to." Daryl turned, leaning across to wrap a comforting arm around her, being careful not to press her bleeding wound. "Listen, Jessie, I know how you feel, but you've got to understand. Maybe half the gang chasing us wasn't skinned or stomped, and they're still back there, sorer than kerosened snakes. We couldn't go looking for Ki, or stop to help him if we found him."

"But he could be hurt, or . . . dead."

"If he's dead, he's dead, and getting ourselves shot won't make him alive. If he's hurt, he's got a better chance of living by lying low, staying put, instead of us drawing attention to him."

"Tomorrow . . ."

"Sure, Jessie, tomorrow. We'll come back for him tomorrow, but right now, tonight, it's more important to take care of you."

Chapter 9

They rode in silence through the murky hills, hearing the bawling of cattle and the shouting of rustlers receding behind them.

Jessica hunched despondently in the saddle. Daryl was beside her and a bit ahead, leading the way back to the Spraddled M. As they dipped down across a fingerling valley, he noticed on the right a craggy outcropping. Bluestem grass appeared to be growing in foot-high tufts there, an indication of a spring or brook. He pulled alongside Jessica, gesturing, and angled toward the boulders. She headed after him, the horses speeding up as they smelled water.

The outcropping proved to encircle a small patch of bottom, with a thin trickle of water oozing from the ground. A few small animals fled as they approached, but otherwise the area seemed deserted. They dismounted, stiff and exhausted, and knelt in the grass, cupping their hands to drink. The horses lapped thirstily.

"Well, we lost them this time," Jessica said with irony.

"We better have. The horses are too tired for any more fancy prancing. We should give them a short breather."

She nodded wearily. "No argument from me."

Leaving the saddles on, they picketed the horses by the water and went to the outcropping, where the grass was dryer. Jessica sucked in her breath, grimacing from pain, as she slowly sat down. Frowning, Daryl hunkered beside her and tentatively touched her back.

"Bend forward a tad," he said. "If you can."

She leaned over, biting her lip to stifle a moan, feeling him gently peel away the ripped fabric that was stuck to her coagulating blood. The long gash opened up again, a line of warm moistness seeping out and riveting down her back.

"Doesn't look too deep," Daryl said, still frowning with concern. "My guess is, with a cleaning and bandaging and a good smear of ointment, your cut should heal up right fine."

She tried to make light of it. "Nary a scar, doctor?"

"Probably not, if we treat it right soon. I ain't any doc, though; I'm just going by how I tend my cows."

Shortly they were up and riding again, across the range of wooded slopes, stony ridges, and brushy draws. Jessica fell to following Daryl again, more than willing to let him find their way through. He did, competently. And as fatigued and aching as she was, Jessica made sure to memorize the route he took.

When they cleared the hills and entered his ranch yard, the buildings dozed dark and still, appearing abandoned, as if the rustlers had not only made off with a small bunch of Spraddled M stock, but with all the hands as well.

Inside the house, Daryl lit a glass stand lamp and ushered Jessica into the kitchen. "Stay here," he said, and then made two trips outside, one for wood with which to stoke the cast-iron Duchess stove, and the other for water to fill the washtub he placed on the stove's burners. While the water was heating, he hauled out a heavy tin bathtub, and placed it near the stove.

"This ain't the height of modesty," he said, beginning to redden around the ears. "But I reckon it'll just have to do."

"I'll manage nicely, thank you," Jessica replied, managing to keep a serious expression. She trailed him into an adjacent bedroom, saying, "Bad as it was, we learned a lot tonight."

"Sure did." His back was to her as he ransacked a tall wardrobe. "Now, I know I've got a clean towel in here somewheres."

"We learned that Ryker wants a big chunk of Wyoming for no good reason, and that in order to get it, he's resorting to rustling."

"The one don't mean the other. Ah, here're a couple."

"Yes, it does. When we ran into those steers—your steers—they were being herded toward the Block-Two-Dot, weren't they?"

"Yeah, along that rocky gorge. No wonder Deputy Oakes could never find no tracks," Daryl said, as they returned to the kitchen. "I'll use this one for freshenin'. Here, you take the bigger one."

The bigger towel was the size of a child's blanket. Jessica refolded it and laid it on the kitchen table, continuing, "And I'll bet you anything that the men who were herding them are the same men we saw earlier—that first bunch who rode into the Block-Two-Dot yard, and then rode off again with some of the bunkhouse crew."

"Okay, so supposing there is a connection. But why? Ryker don't need more stock; he already owns more'n his range can handle."

"Daryl, Ryker isn't a rancher like the rest of you, struggling to make ends meet, hoping to build a future. He's a crook, tied in with a whole ring of bigger crooks who'll stop at nothing to gain control of that block of land we saw on that map. It follows like night follows day that he's using the rustlers to cripple you ranchers, as a wedge to buy you up for nickels and force you off your property."

Daryl brooded for a moment, then stepped closer, searching her eyes. "Jessie, you'd best leave Eucher Butte as soon as you can."

"Leave? I don't want to leave, I want to stay."

"I want you to stay too, of course, but you must leave, for your own sake. I won't have you dying for a fight that isn't yours."

"This *is* my fight, Daryl. More than you know."

"You've already done as much as any man could. More!" He gripped her tenderly by the shoulders. "But if you're right, and in my gut I know you are, then Ryker and these other crooks won't stop at nothing. They sure won't stop at brutalizing or killing a woman."

"And what about . . . about Ki?" she asked, faltering, a lump gathering in her throat. "We made it our fight when we came in answer to Mrs. Waldemar's letter, and now that Ki is missing, I won't rest—I *cannot* rest—until I finish the fight we started together."

Daryl heard her sob, as she pressed her cheek against his chest. It seemed so natural for her to melt in his arms, as natural as lowering his face to kiss her, the pressure of her body like an eager promise. Shaken and chagrined, Daryl released her, taking a step backward. "F-forgive me, Jessica, I didn't mean to be forward."

Jessica looked as though she weren't paying the slightest attention to his apology. She placed the open palm of one hand flat against his cheek. "You need a shave," she said, stroking upward against the stubble. "When I rub down, it's smooth, and when I rub up, you're all whiskers."

Daryl shivered, speechless from her caress, staring at her affectionate smile. There were rents in her clothes, and one sleeve of her plaid shirt was almost torn away. Bloodstains and scratches marred her smooth, tanned face and delicate hands, and her long hair, tangled and hatless, gleamed like the hue of fireweed honey where the glowing fire from the stove reflected against it. She was a lovely thing, and Daryl battled hard to retain his control.

"The, ah, the water is warm," he finally managed, blushing to his hairline. "We . . . I mean, you can have a nice bath now."

Hastily he poured the steaming water into the plunge-tub, leaving a little in the washtub for his own use. He tossed her a cake of soap, grabbed another and his towel, and fled with the washtub into the front room. "Soak as long as you like," he called.

"I will," she replied lightly, shedding her clothes in a pool on the kitchen floor. "But Daryl . . . I expect you to shave."

A throat-clearing sounded from the other room, causing her to broaden her smile as she eased naked into the bath water. She washed carefully, thoroughly, wanting to be squeaky clean in case anything developed—which, considering Daryl's flustered behavior, was not entirely impossible.

She was not in the habit of seducing men, although occasionally she enjoyed a bit of coy flirting; it was a pleasing game, and it gratified her to know she could arouse the stuffiest, most virtuous of males on a basic, primitive level. Nor was she a promiscuous wanton, the victim of some insatiable sex drive. It was simply that Jessica Starbuck was not a prude or a hypocrite; she was pure woman, proud of her femininity, and she relished the sensation of being attractive to those few men she found desirable.

And Lord, Daryl Melville was desirable! She had thought so ever since their first meeting, and thinking of him now caused her taut breasts to tingle, her rosy nipples to harden involuntarily. Daryl possessed a rare allure that seemed to captivate and fascinate her, to bore to the very essence of her sensual nature. The easy grace of his motions, the strong muscles flexing along his thighs and chest, the hard bas-relief of his loins in his pants . . .

Whoops! Jessica straightened in the tub, chastising herself. It was one thing to admire him, or even to desire him; it was quite another to get herself worked into a frazzle.

She stepped out of the tub, dripping water and trying to wrap the large towel around her. "Are you decent. Daryl?"

"Yes."

"Well, don't peek. I'm having trouble with this towel of yours." She sauntered into the front room, the towel perversely slipping and unraveling, no matter how she tried to hold it closed.

Daryl ignored her warning, naturally. He was standing in front of the fireplace, shaving by the reflection of the large mantelpiece mirror. He was barefoot and shirtless, wearing only his trousers, and Jessica could see the muscular power of his naked torso as he stroked his cheek with a straight razor.

She also saw him nearly slice an ear off, when he took a look at her, bare-breasted. Hastily, Jessica struggled to raise the hem of the towel back over her bosom. Which she managed to do, but at the cost of one edge of the towel behind her parting like an errant stage curtain and fully, if briefly, exposing her firm buttocks and lithely tapering thighs.

The razor dropped to the floor.

Jessica retreated, scampering. "I said not to peek!"

"I didn't see a thing, Jessie. Honest!" There was a pause, then Daryl asked, "Was there something you wanted?"

"Well, you told me my cut needs ointment and bandages,

and I can't very well reach all the way around my back and do it, can I?"

"Oh." There was another pause, longer and somehow more profound. Then, nervously: "I, ah, I'll do it. You go get arranged on my bed, and I'll be in as soon's I finish here."

In the bedroom, Jessica stretched out on her stomach on the iron-framed single bed, and very carefully made sure the towel was draped properly over her from the waist down. Mentally she kicked herself, flaming with embarrassment, for that impromptu strip-tease with the towel had been truly accidental, and not like her at all.

Daryl entered, clearing his throat a lot, and put a roll of adhesive tape, some gauze bandages, scissors, and a tin of ointment on the bedside table. He sat down, balancing on the edge of the bed with all the caution of a man expecting the mattress to explode.

"Just consider me one of your cows," Jessica said, hoping to relax him, her face buried in the covers. "I'll moo, if it'll help."

With a tight chuckle, Daryl opened the tin and began to spread the ointment hesitantly along her wound. It burned like a branding iron.

"My God, Daryl, what is that stuff? Acid?"

"Arnicated carbolic salve," he answered, pausing to quote the label: " 'The best in the world for burns, flesh injuries, boils, eczema, childblains, piles, ulcers, and fever sores.' " He started smoothing it on again, assuring her, "Dad swears by it for his salt rheum and ringworm. Don't worry, it'll smart for just a minute, and then it'll just feel nice warm."

Jessica lay still, skeptically waiting for the salve to stop burning and start warming. Amazingly it did, the warmth penetrating while Daryl continued rubbing gingerly with his fingers. He leaned over her back, so close that she could feel his breath against her flesh and smell the fragrance of his masculine body . . . and gradually, against her will, she sensed budding tendrils of pleasure beginning to curl deep down in her belly and loins and gently clenching buttocks.

"Jessie . . . ?"

"Mm?"

"Remember Ryker's cellar? His chains and whips?"

"Mm."

"Does that kind of thing . . . do girls go for that?"

"A few, maybe. Me, I'm strictly a soft touch."

Daryl touched her softly. Massaging, kneading, his hands eased from where the wound started high on one side, down along her spine to the dimple of flesh just above the crevice of her tensing buttocks. His fingers explored very slowly, almost fearfully, and she could hear his breath deepening, his pulse quickening. And she could feel her own lungs sucking in air, her blood racing with a fire that flamed through her flesh and goaded her to reckless abandon.

She turned over. A slight twinge of self-consciousness stole through her as she sat up facing him, seeing his eyes roaming heatedly over her naked, thrusting breasts. "You'll make some lucky girl a real fine husband," she teased in a throbbing voice.

His own voice was husky, choking. "I—I'm sorry, Jessie. That's twice now that I've . . . I don't know what's come over me."

"There's nothing to be sorry about." Intimacy crept into her tone, and she touched his arm. "Only to be happy about," she continued in a sultry purr, her other hand pulling the towel aside. "You want me. After all, I'm a woman and you're a man . . ."

His tongue licked his lips to moisten them, as he stared quivering at her delicately molded thighs and golden-fleeced loins. Desire stirred within him, despite his best intentions. Jessica was not for him to take, he told himself; she was offering her love in a moment of anguish, out of grief and hysteria over the loss of her friend Ki, as a desperate effort to forget and drive out her torment. He would not be the cause of her further suffering—he could not be, and live with himself.

"But Jessica, you . . . you're an angel . . ."

"I'm also a beast," she murmured tauntingly, reaching down to unbuckle his belt. "Let me prove it, prove both of us are."

And then Daryl found himself moving, his body responding of its own volition. His fingers fumbled with the buttons, his hips trembling as he rose to slide his pants down, his flesh aching as Jessica ran her hands around his chest and thighs while helping him rid himself of his clothing. Then he was as naked as she, tanned and muscular and admirably masculine.

Daryl joined her on the bed, his mouth coming down on hers. He kissed her and she kissed back, and fire was in their lips. Awkward with passion, he tried to push her flat and enter her from above, but the press of the covers against her wound was too painful for her to accept. Daryl was a solid man, she realized, without a great deal of imagination or experience, and was probably only familiar with the standard position. Well, that was definitely out of the question tonight.

"Daryl," she whispered, "my back."

He reared as if scalded. "Jesus, I'm sorry, we can't—"

"We can." She drew away slightly, just enough so she could turn and crouch on her knees and elbows with her buttocks thrusting up. It was a submissive position many women dislike, the cow-hitch posture, but what with one thing and another, it seemed exceptionally appropriate for the occasion. She stifled an urge to moo, saying, "This is how beasts do it, isn't it?"

Daryl was eagerly game to try playing the beast. He slid behind her on his knees and took her gently, his hands gliding along her sides and up around to fondle her breasts. He moved deep within her, and Jessica felt him clearly, with a joy that surged through her. It was this elation that made her anchor her feet against the bed, raising her hips to press up and back to match his passionate thrusts. The world spun in a rainbow of colors, but in reality there was no world for Jessica just then—there was only this throbbing, this pulsing rhythm inside her gripping belly. Together they worked in frenzied ecstasy, until at last they reached sweet release, and he spilled his passion deep inside her while she squeezed around him, shuddering.

Daryl sprawled beside her on the cramped bed, his erection fading, his breathing trembling in her ear. But greater indeed was the fulfillment inside Jessica, the effervescent sensation of contentment and satiation. Stirring, she eased from the bed, reaching back with one hand to retrieve the blanket.

"No," Daryl said, smiling up at her. "No blanket."

"But Daryl," she teased, standing naked beside the bed, "what about your modesty that you were so worried about?"

He laughed. "Too late for that, little heifer."

She sashayed to the doorway, standing there in the warmth

from the kitchen stove, feeling no embarrassment at all. She felt pleased and natural, basking in his adoring gaze, admiring in return his openly displayed, handsome body.

He rose on an elbow. "You've got me going in circles, y'know."

"About what?"

"You. Us. This."

Smiling, she parried, "You mean about us having sex?"

"Yeah, in a way. I guess I just won't ever figure women out. A man, now, is pretty straightforward. I like a drink when I'm thirsty, and a steak when I'm hollow inside. I've never been much for the notion that there's just one woman in the world for a man, but all the other women I've met up with before don't seem to agree."

"Then it's simple, Daryl. You've merely met up with a woman who's as straightforward as you, and agrees with you." She crossed to the bed and knelt beside him, and as he put out his hand to caress one of her distended nipples, she whispered: "Have you ever studied sex, the art of making love?"

"In Eucher Butte? I'd be tarred and feathered."

"Well, I've tried to avoid living in the Eucher Buttes of this world. I've lived in a lot of other places, and studied and learned."

"And practiced," Daryl added, his mouth closing around her breast, suckling it as if he were an infant seeking milk.

"Japan, the Far East, Arabia, Europe, ahh . . ." she sighed dreamily. "And I've found that passion and desire never made anyone feel sick or guilty. Only the hate and destructiveness that can be hidden in them will produce sickness and bitter regrets."

Daryl's lips left her breast, and he helped lift her back onto the bed. He was ready again to sample her talents, his erection reviving hard and strong as she stretched out beside him, snuggling affectionately, her legs slightly parted.

"Make it as good as the last time," she whispered.

Daryl ran his hand over the mounds of her breasts and down across her smooth belly to the soft, pulsing warmth below. Jessica moaned, her flesh coming alive to his caresses, and her voice sighed in his ear, urging him to quench the fires kindling in her loins.

He kissed her lips, her cheeks, the tender hollow of her neck. Slipping lower, he darted his tongue across her hardened nipples, then moved it wetly along her abdomen, feeling the satiny skin ripple under his tauntings. Then still lower, his lips probing and exploring as she cried out in ecstatic pleasure. She rolled from side to side while he licked at her inner lips; she whimpered deliriously as her throbbing arousal increased, her fingers entangled in his hair.

The splayed thighs beneath his mouth arched and swiveled. Daryl gave them room. Jessica again stretched out alongside him, but now facing the foot of the bed, her legs still spread wide on either side of his bobbing head. Daryl could feel her hands move from his hair and down along his body, clutching his buttocks, pulling him toward her face. Her tongue began teasing him, dancing like a waterbug on the crown of his erection. Daryl pressed her loins harder against his sucking mouth, and a deep animal sound escaped from his nibbling lips.

From below, between his own wide-stretched legs, Jessica dipped further, licking along his rigid shaft, and then plunging her mouth voraciously on it, swallowing it in a soft clinging pressure. Daryl felt his hips writhing, stirring, swaying, his entire lower body seeming to swim in a vast sea of tense sensation.

Jessica's seemingly disembodied lips, her mouth, her throat were eating him, trying to draw the whole of him into her yearning flesh. Daryl could distinguish no external detail of touch. Doubtless her teeth were there, nipping gently; her tongue was there, licking and twining; her lips were there, pressing and sucking . . . but no detail was clear, only the combining vacuum of suction drawing all of his vital juices down to his groin.

And in response to her own urgent yearnings, Jessica was pressing her naked body full-length against him, undulating back and forth, around and up, so that the potent force of his own tongue was being drawn deep up inside her sensitive flesh. His head was hot, his mouth working, gasping, and a tumultous eruption was growing, growing in his scrotum . . . and from the way Jessica was reacting, he thought she might also be on the verge of climaxing.

Too soon, he thought, *too soon . . .*

On the verge, on the very crest of his orgasm, Daryl felt

Jessica pull away slightly, perfectly timing and tapering off,
no more ready to end their ecstasy than he. For a long moment
longer her mouth lightly suckled his thickened shaft, her tongue
dancing teasingly on its bulbous tip. Then she pivoted up,
squatting over him, astride him, knees on the bed on either side
of his hips.

She gazed down at him with eyes filmed with passion, and
then impaled herself on his spearing erection, contracting her
strong inner thighs, her muscular action clamping her moist
passage tightly around his shaft. "This one, a knowing French-
man would call *monde renverse*. You like?"

"I like," Daryl groaned, clenching his buttocks, thrusting
his hips up off the covers in greedy response "Oh, I like . . ."

Jessica splayed her kneeling legs, settling down until she
contained all of his rigid, lust-hardened shaft within her. Slowly
at first, then with increasing fierceness, she began sliding up
and down. This was a posture more to her liking, allowing her
to be the dominant partner, freeing her to control the pace and
stimulation. Her head sagged, then tautened again in arousal,
a vein standing out at the side of her throat with the fury of her
pumping exertion. Her mouth opened and closed in mute testimony to the exquisite sensations plundering her loins, her
long blonde hair swaying and brushing down over her shoulders
and across his chest.

Daryl grasped her jiggling breasts, toying harshly with them
until hoarse moans were drawn from her slackened lips. She
bent for a brief moment with a whisper of a kiss, then arched
up and back as she plunged deeper, faster, reaching behind to
caress Daryl's scrotum, massaging with delicately stroking
fingernails. The backward angle made her body toss precariously on Daryl's hips, her thighs descending with building
force, only to reverse at the last instant and draw up again on
his penetrating shaft.

Daryl, tensing upward, felt the gripping of her sheath tearing
at his entrails. "God, Jessica, you're like a vice," he panted.

Her passage kept squeezing, squeezing, as she crooned
above him, her mouth open, her eyes wide and sightless. The
squeezing grew unbearable until, bursting, Daryl came again.

Jessica's loins worked and sucked as if his juices were some invigorating tonic, to be ravenously swallowed in her belly, as her own face contorted and twisted with spasming climax.

Then, with the ebb of passion, Jessica crouched limp and satiated over Daryl. Slowly, sighing contentedly, she eased off his flaccid body and lay down on the bed alongside him. Daryl felt drugged, unable to move. He wanted to say something, but was at a loss for words. Instead, he silently cradled her in his arms and dozed off, their bodies remaining loosely entwined . . .

Jessica awoke from a restless sleep.

Tensely, she remained quiet beside Daryl, listening to his easy breathing and watching the rhythmic rise and fall of his sweat-slick chest. Then, gradually, gently, she sat up and eased from his lax embrace, slipping noiselessly from the bed.

Cautiously, so as not to disturb him, she took the gauze, the roll of tape, and the pair of scissors, and padded into the kitchen. By the frail glow of the stove's embers, she awkwardly patched her wound and began gathering her clothes. Her jeans and boots were still in fair shape, but her shirt and jacket were virtual rags. She went into the front room and snitched Daryl's heavy cloth workshirt; it fit her like a tent, but at least it was in one whole piece. She wrapped it around her, tucking it in and rolling up the sleeves, then put her ripped jacket on over it. It would have to suffice.

Soundlessly she moved to the front door, boots in hand, and twisted the handle. The hinges squeaked. She hesitated, licking dry lips, glancing fretfully back toward the bedroom.

There was a sound of Daryl fidgeting, but his breathing continued guttural and even. She thought of the angular lines of his naked body stretched out on the covers, and was filled with the desire to strip again and climb back in bed next to him. She fought her temptation, furtively crossing the threshold and closing the door behind her, leaning against it for balance as she tugged on her boots.

It was just before dawn, and a cold, silvery light touched only the jagged rim of the distant hills. Spying the outline of the otherwise murky slopes just increased Jessica's bitter resolve. Swiftly she crossed to the barn where her horse was stalled, and walking the bay out and safely away from the house, she stepped into the saddle and rode west toward the hills.

The dawn had evolved into an overcast morning of melancholy grayness by the time Jessica had retraced Daryl's route back to the rocky gorge. She passed the spot where the Block-Two-Dot crew had been trampled, and saw that most of the men and horses had survived; there were only a few corpses dotted around. Even fewer steers were sprawled lifeless in a short line from there back up the gorge trail, the results of the crew's panicked shooting.

When she located Ki's dead bay, she dismounted and started her search. Ki was not anywhere in open view, which gave her hope—though he could just as readily have been thrown into the boulders, or been injured and crawled out of sight. To die.

"Ki!"

His name echoed mockingly. Grit and pebbles crunched under her boots as Jessica ran along both sides of the trail, calling for him over and over. When she failed to find him at first, she sought him a second and then a third time, up and down the edges, going farther than where they'd encountered the herd, and back to the mouth of the canyon, where she and Daryl had hid.

"Ki!" she continued crying out, her voice rising with growing alarm. Increasingly frantic, she stumbled over and over across the sharp stones, her breath coming short and hurting under her breast.

"Ki!"

There was no answer. Except for the scattered remains from the stampede, Jessica was utterly alone.

Chapter 10

Ki, thrown by his dying horse, had scrambled in a frantic dash for the bouldered side of the gorge. He'd whirled and leaped to keep from being trampled, and when he glimpsed Jessica and Daryl struggling to reach him, he had to strain his lungs to be heard. "Save yourselves . . . or we'll all die . . ."

Then the stampede rampaged close and enveloped him. A hoof caught him in the shin and almost broke it; he swallowed the pain and plowed on through the churning, trampling herd. The boulders . . . he could see the boulders . . . an arm's length away . . .

And then he saw the maddened longhorn plunging straight for him, head down, horns rolling, nostrils leaving a stream of foam in the moonlight. There wasn't any time to dive out of the way. He could only fling himself flat and let the steer leap over him. As he did so, the stampede and its thunder grew vague and gray, blending into a swirling black fog . . .

Consciousness returned, along with a staggering headache. Ki lay where he was, propped on one elbow, his thoughts slowly clearing. The steer must have kicked him a glancing blow; luckily it had been a straggler, in the drag of the herd, or else he'd surely have been run over by others. Dazed, holding his head in his hands, Ki sat up and peered groggily around.

The gorge was quiet. The herd was gone, the only steers in sight the few dead ones the Block-Two-Dot crew had shot. But facing Ki in a haphazard semicircle were six men in range garb, dirty and sweat-streaked, their expressions hard. He would instantly have perceived them to be some of Ryker's riders—perhaps the only uninjured survivors after their mauling by the herd—even if he hadn't recognized one of them as the ranch ramrod, Volpes. The man was standing back, strangely poised, eyeing Ki as if he were a casual bystander; but the carbine nestled in the crook of Volpes's arm didn't look casual at all.

"Be up in a minute, I said, didn't I?" Volpes grinned and spat. "Always said chinks have cast-iron skulls."

Nobody confirmed or denied it.

"Okay," Volpes said, "grab him and tie him up. The boss'll want this smart turd alive."

The five moved in with more relish than caution.

Ki scrambled upright, his face purposely fearful while he threw up both hands as if in entreaty. But what he expected didn't happen; no *shuriken* sprang from his sleeves to appear in his hands. He flicked his wrists. Still nothing. Jammed! Somehow, with all the grit and banging around, the damned release mechanisms had broken!

Not that the five crewmen were aware of this, of how near to death they had all come, as they sprang for him. Seemingly trapped by their swift convergence, Ki had time for only a *kapalabhati* cleansing breath before embracing their attack—*nukishomen-uchi*—drawing them and himself into the circular harmony of the universe.

Ki stunned the nearest man with a back-knuckled "ram's head" jab between the eyes. Without turning, without apparently seeing his target, he stabbed the second with a left-handed thumb-and-forefinger thrust to the throat, constricting the flow of blood through both jugular veins and dropping the man unconscious. Meanwhile, he stopped the man tackling from the rear with a sideways snap-kick; his solar plexus paralyzed, the man sank to his knees, convinced he was dying. But the fourth man managed to come in butting from the other side, knocking Ki just enough off balance so he could gouge his knee in the small of Ki's back and apply a full nelson.

"I got him now! Beat the shit outta him!"

"You betcha!" The fifth man grinned, plunging forward.

Using the man behind him for support, Ki bunched both

legs in a flying upward thrust, his heels catching the fifth man square in the balls. The man doubled up, uttering short croaks of agony and confusion.

Then, planting his feet firmly on the ground again, Ki simply backed up. The man behind him, who had both arms and one foot engaged in the lock he had put on Ki, was thrown immediately off balance, and had to remove the knee he'd put in the small of Ki's back, to keep himself from falling. So Ki just relaxed and bent his knees and dropped out from under the full nelson, turning as he did so to deliver an elbow-strike just beneath the fellow's breast-bone. The man went down, and Ki was just preparing to finish the job with a heel to the groin, when he felt the press of cold steel against his temple.

"You move," Volpes said coldly, "and I'll blow your fuckin' pigtail brains out."

Slowly, Ki lowered the foot he was planning to stomp with and stood motionless. His face became taut, expressionless, as the rifle continued to bore into his temple.

The five fallen men began stirring, crawling and gasping raggedly, then tottering upright, holding themselves, hacking and wheezing.

"S'mbitch," the one who'd been hit in the balls croaked. He was still in a crouch, one hand cupped over his groin. "The bastard's nailed. C'mon, let's pay him back!"

The men all staggered forward, lunging at Ki. They were big, husky, range-toughened brawlers, used to absorbing a lot of punishment and dishing it back out. Yet it was likely none of them would have been alive, much less standing, if Ki hadn't been caught weakened and groggy, before he'd had a chance to revive his flagging energy. But he had been caught, so the men were standing, crowding in, while Volpes held Ki at bay with his finger tight around the trigger.

The infuriated men surged forward, bent on revenge, arms seizing and fists smashing. Ki stumbled, blinding pain seeming to shatter his skull. He was pulled to the ground, dragged and kicked.

"Hey, don't kill him! He's worth somethin' alive!"

Ki gritted his teeth against the brutal impact of boots. He fought his way to his feet again, using fists, elbows, teeth, knees, his entire body as a weapon. But it was useless. Despite his spirit, his defiant will, Ki was only human—a human being whose mind and body were exhausted from his brush with the murderous stampede, and drained of their inner force. Blackness overcame him again, and he slumped unconscious to the trail.

His senses returned gradually, as numbed impressions:

The bent-over hunch of his body . . .

Jarring pain in his wrists, ankles, and belly . . .

The sight of moonlit ground moving past him at the pace of a horse's walk, and the sound of a complaining voice in back of him . . .

One other thing Ki knew: he was alive.

He finally became aware of the fact he was tied hand and foot, and that he was jackknifed over a saddle. Craning his head about, he caught sight of two Ryker crewmen, one in front and the other behind him; and of Volpes riding point, mounted on a close-coupled grullo that bore the Snake-Eyes brand on its rump.

"Dunno why the boss picked me to go," the rider in back was whining. "My guts're all busted up inside from that kick, I just know they are, and this jouncin' hurts like pissin' hell."

"Shut up bellerin' like a sick calf," Volpes retorted harshly. "You ain't half as bad off as Mike or Lonnie are, and Fletch here, he can't talk much above a squeak after his throat got squozed."

The riders lapsed into silence, emerging out onto a thin strip of a pass between the mountains and the foothills. They were high, Ki realized, and climbing higher, on a wandering, little-used trail no better than an animal track. More than that, he couldn't tell.

Ki closed his eyes and slumped his head, and quietly tested the ropes binding him. They were tight and well-knotted—but not tight or knotted enough. A slight, humorless smile creased his mouth as he twisted and flexed his wrists and ankles, sensing the weak points. The men, having put their faith in the ropes restraining him, would be less watchful and cautious.

He relaxed then, feeling a bit more confident, and began rebuilding his vital psychic strength. Calming his mind, Ki focused his concentration on an internal point just below his navel, the place the Chinese call *tan t' ien*. As he adjusted his breathing, he continued pressuring the ropes lightly with his wrists and ankles, but he made no overt move to break loose; he was more concerned with restoring his essential energy, and was willing to wait, playing the prisoner, to learn why he was alive. It was no accident; Ki did not believe in luck, but in cause and effect. So there was a reason why he hadn't been killed. To be questioned, he supposed, though he sensed there was more to it than that . . .

For all its meandering, the trail kept generally climbing. In single file, the riders crossed a winding bench and passed through a cloaking pine forest, coming out on the sharp-breaking rim of a narrow canyon. The timber and brush closed down so thickly that the canyon could not have been discovered, even in full daylight, until it was actually entered.

The men veered northward, angling once more over sloping ground until, between two towering rocks, a break in the jagged canyon rim disclosed another ribbony path. As they turned onto it, a guard on the connecting rim came out to the edge, where he could be seen outlined against the soft, starry sky. He did not yell a challenge, but waved questioningly with his arms. Volpes signaled the guard to go on with his job of watching, and they continued along the second trail.

The going was slower now, long night shadows cast by the surrounding mountains blanketing the canyon in darkness. Before he saw the shallow creek, Ki heard Volpes's grullo splashing into the water, followed by the others. They progressed up the stream, its bed widening and deepening as it flowed down around a bend in the now narrowing canyon wall.

Turning the bend himself, Ki glimpsed a point ahead where the two canyon walls apparently joined together to form a land bridge. The water was now up to the withers of the horses, pouring out of what appeared to be the end of a box, over a waterfall some twenty feet in height and about ten wide.

First Volpes and then the next rider disappeared under the falls. Having no choice, Ki moved under the cascading sheet after them, his clothes and aching flesh becoming drenched in the frigid mountain water beating down over him and the horse. On the right, pale moonlight filtered through a narrow passage. They rode into the vague opening, and almost immediately emerged into another, much smaller canyon that was hardly more than a natural pocket dug in the hills.

Not far inside the pocket was a bare-earthed clearing, fronting an elongated log cabin with a flat roof. A few steps from its door were the smoldering embers of a campfire, the silhouettes of three or four men spread out around it. If there were more men in the camp, they were sleeping in the small tarpaper-roofed shacks that dotted the scrub flanking the house; but Ki suspected the shacks were empty, the men out chasing a scattered herd of terrified steers.

They rode across the clearing and up before the main cabin. The door opened and a young woman stepped out-side, holding a brass night lamp, and looking puffy-eyed and irritated at the men as they dismounted. The two crew-men moved away, out of range of Ki's limited vision. Volpes went up to the girl and said something too low for Ki to hear; and she said something back that was also inaudible, though, judging by the sharpness of its tone, it was probably a rebuke. Ki guessed she was Volpes's girl.

Volpes turned around and walked toward Ki, the girl trailing grudgingly, evidently having been told that her lamp was required. Volpes stopped beside Ki and unsheathed a Green River knife. The girl eased closer, shining the lamp on Ki, her other hand clutching the neck of a long raglan coat, which was draped open around her shoulders, over her nightgown.

Her nightgown was the sort beloved by maiden aunts, of thick daisy-cloth flannel gathered at a yoke in front and back, making it hang very full. But it didn't matter, not on her. Her breasts were plump and high, their large nipples protruding out from the already straining material; and she was leggy down to the warped, mud-caked cowboots that peeked beneath the hem of her gown. Her hair was wrapped in a loose bun at the nape of her neck, and was as raven-black as her eyes, and her butternut-brown face was heart-shaped and matched her body's promise of sensual passion.

One other thing Ki noticed: the girl was Eurasian.

Ki managed a slight nod. *"Yü nü,"* he said.

"Hello yourself." Her black eyes widened, curious, though her mouth remained drawn in a hard, suspicious line.

Volpes had jerked as if bitten. "You've got a fat lip that's gonna get fatter," he snarled, slicing the rope that held Ki down across the saddle.

Ki dropped like a feed sack to the ground, landing on his side. His skull still throbbed and his brains felt as if they were scrambled, from the twin knockouts suffered from the herd and the crewmen. He lay still, breathing through his mouth, as he felt Volpes cut the ropes around his ankles. Then he was hauled to his feet.

"Fletch, goddamn it, c'mere," Volpes yelled, and the man Ki had jabbed in the throat hastened out from the side of the cabin, running bowlegged while he buttoned his fly.

"Put this sassy-assed sonofabitch in the empty shed 'round back," Volpes told him. "And make sure he stays there, 'y'hear?"

Fletch nodded, and pushed Ki ahead of him, causing Ki to stumble slightly, and Ki used the opportunity to glance back and see if the girl was looking his way.

She was, frowning as if perplexed while she stood with Volpes's arm possessively around her waist. Ki grinned. She stiffened, then was hurriedly propelled toward the cabin door, Volpes gripping her tighter and muttering curses.

Ki was pushed forward again, across the yard and along the cabin to the rear, where off to one side stood a small plank-walled shanty with a dark, gaping door. Fletch shoved him inside, and the door slammed shut, and he heard a padlock snapped in heavy chain.

Ki placed his ear against the door. When he could no longer hear Fletch's receding footsteps, he slid down onto the floor and rested his back against the board wall. For a while he merely sat relaxing, and then he began freeing his wrists from the rope.

Focusing all his concentration on the task, Ki purposely dislocated the bones of his wrists, then his hands, even his nimble fingers. Then, by merely twisting and stretching his ligaments and muscles, he slowly wormed his limp, formless flesh through the encoiling bonds. The rope dropped empty to the floor behind his back.

Snapping his bones back into place, Ki swiftly checked his vest pockets. They were all empty, as were his shirt and pants pockets. His daggers were gone, and even his jammed devices holding the *shuriken* were missing. Obviously he'd been searched while he'd been unconscious that second time; and once the men had found the first of his secreted weapons, they must have turned him virtually inside out to locate the rest. He was fortunate to have been left his clothes. Grinning mirthlessly, Ki wondered what they must have thought when they discovered his devices.

He stood, stretching his cramped muscles, and started to cautiously feel around the dark, gloomy shed. He quickly realized that when Volpes had called it empty, he'd been telling the truth.

He settled on the floor again, and fell asleep.

Chapter 11

Dawn.

A vague dribble of light began seeping through two thin cracks in the boards across the shed. With a patience he had learned over the years, Ki remained sitting on the same spot where he'd slept, watching the dull gray light ease in time across the flooring. There was no use trying to beat himself against the door and walls, hopelessly wasting his energy. Sooner or later someone had to come in, or he would be led outside. Given a split-second's chance, he would take full advantage of it.

A field mouse scuttled out from a hole and raced around the floor in the feeble light, before returning to its burrow.

Ki thought about that for a while.

Steps sounded outside, and Ki flattened his back to the wall, arms behind him as if the ropes still bound his wrists. The chain rattled slightly, and the padlock made a soft, muffled click. Gently someone pulled the chain loose and eased open the door.

The girl stood outlined against the dawn sky.

"*Yü nü*," Ki greeted her with a mocking bow of his head. "What, no Volpes?"

"I'm alone. But don't let my nighty fluster you."

"I don't care if you're naked," Ki said. "What I want is in your hands. That is a bowl of soup you're holding, isn't it?"

"Yes," she replied crossly, moving toward him. "And if you

don't stop calling me 'fair lady' in that horrid Chinese accent of yours, I'll beat you to death with it. My name is Daphne."

"How fitting," Ki murmured sarcastically.

"Daphne Chung," she continued, "daughter of a coolie spiking track on the Central Pacific, and an Irish camp follower on the Union Pacific. Not that I'd have to kill you, Ki—"

"You know me?"

"I know *of* you. You're all he talked about last night." She squatted in front of Ki and regarded him with her proud onyx eyes. "*He'll* kill you," she said, obviously still meaning Volpes. "Soon's Ryker's finished and turns you over to him, he'll kill you as fast as a trench can be dug. You're dead, Ki, dead."

"Is that why you're here, Daphne? To rub it in?"

"I suppose even a condemned man deserves food," she replied grudgingly, and began spooning soup from the bowl.

Ki kept his arms behind him, getting perverse pleasure out of fooling her. Yet, as she silently helped him eat, another part of his mind was in a quandary, his emotions strangely ambivalent toward this cool-eyed, terse-lipped Eurasian. And when he finished and she asked if that was enough, Ki could only nod dismissively, finding himself unable to thank her for her solicitude.

"That's right, spurn me," she snapped, sensing his rejection. "Daphne the doxy, no better than a second-generation *ukareme*."

Ki gave a sardonic laugh, amused by her use of the antiquated Japanese term for a lewd and dissolute woman. "You're not Japanese," he retorted. "Instead, how about *yü chi?*" Which was equally obsolete Chinese for a third-class "flower girl" who serviced the general public.

She slapped his face, hard, anger flaring in her smoldering black eyes. "Of course, I see now. It's not that I'm a tramp, it's that I'm half Chinese! And the Japanese half of you finds that repugnant, doesn't it? Well, the Japanese make me just as sick."

"Just my luck," Ki sighed. "One of the few times I'm not taken for Chinese, I'm hated for being Jap—"

"Invading us for centuries," she rushed on in her fury, "Ever the conquerer, lording it over us, bloated with superiority and smug contempt!" The girl leaned closer, eyes narrowing, lips peeling back over short, sharp teeth. "But you're the lesser, Ki. At least I'm true to whatever I am. But how false you are to the *yang* of kindness and the *yin* of righteousness, to which you pay lip-service as the basis of your *tsui-kao jih-shih*, your supreme instruction."

Stunned and chagrined by her bitter outburst, Ki could not utter the slightest word of rebuttal. "Daphne, where did you learn . . . ?"

"I was raised by my father, my mother didn't want me. He was a dirt-poor coolie to the West, but to the other Chinese he was a teacher of *T' ai-chi Ch' uan*, the 'supreme ultimate', which makes your pugilism possible—"

She stopped with an abrupt sucking in of air, the sound of heavy footsteps growing louder as they neared the open shed door. Paling, she straightened and backed into one corner, where the shadows were deepest, lines of fear suddenly creasing her almond-hued face.

"Hell, looky there," a man's voice growled. "The door ain't locked like it orter be. Guess this's my lucky day."

A weasel-faced man strutted bowlegged into the shed, and stood with legs apart, fists resting cockily on his hips. "Well, now, I heard tell you was here," he said to Ki, walking closer, and then his sneering grin widened when he glimpsed Daphne hunching in the corner. "Didn't know you was here too, gal. Guess none of us did, 'specially Volpes. Maybe we can fix it so he don't find out, eh?"

Snickering, he turned back to Ki. "Know who I is?"

"Not by name," Ki said with a slight quiver to his voice, hoping to draw the man out. "Didn't I see you the other night in the saloon?"

"Right, boy. You saw me there, gettin' my hide blistered by that uppity galfriend of yours. Seems she ain't the only bitch liking yaller meat, is she?" the man added, leering at Daphne again.

"I'll tell him," Daphne hissed. "I swear I will."

"You ain't tellin' Volpes nothin'," the man retorted snidely. "You ain't got the guts to. Ain't got much brains, either. If'n you're gonna fool around on him, you orter leastwise have the sense to do it on the sly. Keep it private, like this." He pulled the door shut, plunging the shed into murky dimness, and returned to Ki, nudging him with the toe of his boot. "Ryker's sendin' a note to your gal, boy, tellin' her he's got you hid, an' if 'n she wants you back, she'd better come collect you. You're bait, boy, live bait. 'Cept I've gotta a few scores to square on my own, an' the way I sees it, I got the chance, and nobody's told me how 'live you've gotta be."

"Leave him alone, Nealon, and get the hell out!"

"I'll tend to you in a minute, slut," Lloyd Nealon snarled, and rearing, he kicked Ki viciously in the stomach.

Ki, anticipating, had already used an exercise to relax his muscles, and the kick hurt hardly at all. Straightening from his sitting position, arms still behind him, he said coldly, "Try that again, and I'll kill you."

The former Flying W foreman laughed derisively. "Why, you nervy asshole, I'm gonna give you a taste of whupping, like I whupped ol' man Waldemar." Drawing his six-gun, Nealon swung a pistol-whipping blow with his right hand while gut-punching with his left, adding, "Only this ain't gonna look like no accident!"

Ki killed him.

Ducking, Ki gripped the revolver and bent it back, breaking Nealon's trigger finger with a spasmodic firing of one shot. Ignoring the bullet slamming upward into the low roof, and the explosion thundering in the tiny shed, Ki firmed the hold of his other hand on the arm of the first aiming for his stomach. In a blur of motion, Ki spun Nealon with *kuwatago*—a short "flying mare" toss that sent Nealon sailing over his shoulder.

Nealon landed on his back, screaming as his pelvis cracked. Then he stopped screaming as Ki kicked in the side of his head, crushing the temple bone like an eggshell.

"I'll dump the garbage," Ki said affably, glancing at Daphne. She was standing rigid in the corner, face flushed, mouth wide, and it seemed to Ki that a faint gleam of hope lit her eyes. He wasn't sure; perhaps he imagined it, he thought as he lifted Nealon, but it seemed that way to him.

He dragged Nealon by the collar and belt, using the man's broken skull to push open the door. With a swing, he heaved the corpse outside, where it landed, mucous and blood spewing from its mouth and nose, just as seven men came rushing up, pistols in hand.

The man in the lead was yelling, "The shot came from—"

Then, seeing the body and Ki standing in the doorway, they pulled up short. "Look what he done to Lloyd! Gun him!"

"Go ahead," Ki called, smiling. "Shoot."

Seven revolvers were leveled, fingers squeezing triggers.

"Shoot me," Ki urged again. "Ryker will love you for it."

The men hesitated, frustrated by uncertainty.

Shrugging, Ki stepped back inside and calmly closed the door.

Daphne came toward him, her voice a whisper. "You are a *lei jen*, a man of thunder . . ." Her words were momentarily lost in the noise of the men running up outside and rechaining the door. She went ashen, hearing the snap of the padlock, and when she spoke again, her voice was no longer hushed. It was hard, loud, and angry. "You're also a fool! Why didn't you just keep going while you were out there?"

"I wasn't finished."

"You're finished!" she said furiously. "Oh, God, you are!"

"A man of thunder? What difference if I'm made of thunder or not?" Ki snapped back. "I'm still a man, and a man can't get far with seven revolvers aiming point-blank at him."

"We're both finished," Daphne moaned, slumping to the floor. "We're both locked in here now. We're trapped!"

Chapter 12

Jessica continued her dogged search, going over the same ground again and again, trying to spot fresh details each time. But Ki was gone, vanished, most likely dead. As long as he had been with her, his optimism and courage had sustained her. Now, without him, Jessica felt at her heart the cold hand of futility and grief.

Yet she refused to admit her fears, to accept the obvious. Some small doubt wormed in her mind, and its persistent squirmings sharpened her eyes. Bloodstains. In a wide patch near the boulders across from Ki's dead horse, she glimpsed splattered blood like freckles, and wondered how she'd missed them all the times before.

She stood back a short distance to survey their pattern, curious about how these stains looked different from the smudges and pools around the dead steers, horses, and rustlers. It almost looked as if it had been caused not by the stampede, but by a fight, a scuffle of some sort.

Moving into the area, Jessica hunkered down and began to study it inch by inch, trying to sort out and piece together what had happened here. She found boot prints, a lot of them, pivoting and squirreling in all directions, as if following the call of some odd, macabre dance. Then her practiced eye caught the faint, scuffed outline of Ki's distinctive rope-soled slippers.

Pulse quickening, she hunted for more. She found a few, a very few, but was able to make out where Ki had evidently been dragged to where six or seven horses had stood. All the hoof prints that left the area were pointing toward the plateau. One of the horses, she saw, had a cracked fore shoe.

Swiftly she returned to her horse and rode out of the gorge. Reaching the mouth of the canyon, where the herd had spread out across the plateau, she dismounted and started another painstaking search for some sign of that broken shoe. Locating it, she swung back into her saddle and followed it across the plateau to the entrance of the pass leading to the Block-Two-Dot.

There the horse had stopped with the others for a long enough while to leave droppings and splashes of urine. Scouting, Jessica determined that the bunch was definitely seven in number, joined by an eighth horse coming up out of the pass. She felt a sneaky hunch that the eighth had been ridden by Ryker, after she'd found the butt of an expensive Havana cigar doused in one of the urine puddles.

The meeting had split up, with four of the horses going into the pass. The other four, including the horse with the broken shoe, had angled westward toward the rising slopes of the mountains beyond.

Jessica trailed the broken shoe. It was easily traced across the plateau, but once it entered the rocky, forested uplands, the going got more difficult.

Jessica took her time, gauging the vast raw stone and wooded scrub for the dim, indistinct clues of passage. Much of her tracking was done by instinct; once she went a half-mile up a culvert free of any sign at all before she found that her trust had been good. A white scratch, the iron of a horseshoe against a rock . . . and then, a little farther on, a stepped-on twig, cracked and showing pulp.

The path kept close to the contours of the foothills, rarely along the ridges, but through clefts and hollows. Most of it seemed little used, and at that, mostly by game.

Once, when she discovered a solid imprint of a hoof, she stopped and examined it closely. The edges hadn't crumbled, but there were indications of dew; the track had been made early last night. She continued on with grim satisfaction. Twice more she had to rein in and study the terrain, unraveling the path as it wove higher among the crags and spurs and overgrown canyons.

The creek brought her to another halt. It was a fast-rippling flow cutting right across the trail—but it quickly became apparent that the tracks didn't come out the other side. They entered at an upstream angle and stayed in the water. Turning, Jessica headed up along the creek, riding slowly while scrutinizing both banks for wet impressions of the horses having left the creekbed.

The canyon slopes rose higher and drew nearer, becoming cliffs hemming her into a narrow culvert. The only tracks she found were those of animals that had come to drink. By now it was well into midmorning, the day proving to be overcast, the air cool and very still. Too still. The lack of noise bothered Jessica, for if the rocks ahead were devoid of humans, she should have been able to hear little scuttlings, tiny chirps and buzzings.

She moved on, increasingly wary of her surroundings.

The creek grew wider and deeper, making an S-curve, a swath of tall grasses and a few saplings sprouting in its bend. Rounding it, Jessica saw that the creek rushed disjointedly from between boulders, down from a collecting pond and a short waterfall. Slowly she continued parallelling the creek on a moss-covered ledge, a cold clammy sensation nestling between her shoulder blades.

A gravelly voice said, "Hold it, sister, and get down."

Jessica reined sharply and dismounted, seeing a thickset man with stubbly cheeks and watery eyes emerge from the rocks just ahead. The Winchester he pointed was all the more dangerous for his shaky trigger finger.

"Been spyin' you since you came into the pass," the man said, coming closer, eyeballing her and licking lips like slices of liver. "What's your name, sister, and whatcha doing way up here?"

"Imogene," Jessica said demurely.

"Yeah? Imogene what?"

"Just . . . Imogene. I find last names kind of get in the way between friends, don't you?"

The man laughed once, derisively. "What're you doing here?"

"Well, I was out riding, and I got ever so lost."

"Balls."

"Truth, mister. If you could direct me back to—"

"Nobody can get so damned lost that they wind up back in this buzzard's roost, and you know it. Now, why're you really here?"

Jessica smiled shyly and folded her hands in front of her, thumbs hooking behind her belt buckle. "I reckon I can't fool a big smart man like you. I'm looking for the rustlers."

"The—? What'n hell you want us—them—for?"

"You got to understand, mister, I'm new to Eucher Butte, having run out of luck down Cheyenne way. But the dance places, like the Thundermug, are all full up and don't need new talent, and I'm kind of broke, and a girl has to make a living, y'know what I mean?"

The man's face remained poker straight. "No, tell me."

"Well, when I heard about a bunch of men hid out up in these hills, it seemed to me that if they couldn't come to me, I'd go to them. So, if by some chance you could help me—if you could escort me to their camp, I'd be grateful. *Very* grateful."

"I ain't that crazy! Once you got in there with all them, I wouldn't get nothing for a month of Sundays." The man backed a pace, raising his rifle and gesturing with it. "Get into the bushes, Imogene, I'm taking you all for myself."

The bullet entered his stomach while he was still gesturing with his rifle. It hit low, straight, shot from Jessica's derringer when she snapped the hidden pistol out from behind her belt buckle. The man seemed paralyzed from the impact of the .38 slug, mouth wide as if to scream, but no sound coming out.

Jessica was in motion even as the bullet struck. She leaped for the man, snatching the rifle from his nerveless fingers and springing for the cover of the nearby rocks. She crouched, waiting.

The man stayed upright, although his knees were gradually bending. He clasped both hands against the wound, trying to hold himself together, his rolling eyes glazed and disbelieving as he stared down at his red-staining shirtfront. His legs buckled; he toppled over, slowly crumpling to sprawl inert.

Jessica stayed put, drawing her revolver, then reloading the derringer and slipping it back behind her buckle. Her horse browsed near the stream, shaking its head once. The man lay absolutely still, his hands pressed to his midriff, his face retaining its startled expression, as if sealed by wax. Jessica ignored them both, her attention centering on the crevices and shadowed nooks above and around them.

She had killed again. To keep from being raped, true, although she'd purposely tricked the man into believing she was a whore. And if he'd agreed to take her to the rustlers' hideout—where, she was convinced, the tracks she was following ultimately led—she wouldn't have shot him. At least not right then, and maybe later it wouldn't have been necessary. But she had only a moment to spare for remorse; there was a job that needed to be done.

By the time flies had begun to gather on the man, Jessica was pretty sure no partner was hiding, anticipating revenge. Nonetheless, she took care. She dashed from the rocks and grabbed the man's legs, then hustled them both behind cover. After another long pause, she darted out again and led her horse into the rocks, where, out of sight of the brook, she tied its reins to a tree.

Alive, the man had virtually admitted being one of the rustlers; dead, he told her two other important facts: he must have been posted as a sentry, and he hadn't gotten wet on the job or while stalking her. Which meant, Jessica figured, that the hideout had to be nearby, on this side of the stream. On the surface, that didn't add up too well, because obviously neither the rustlers nor the horses she'd been tracking were anywhere in the canyon, and the waterfall ahead was pouring over what was essentially the canyon's rear wall. Yet she felt her hunch was right when she glimpsed a pale drift of smoke rising from the hills beyond; it was scarcely more than a thin, indistinguishable smudge against the drab skyline, but it was enough to confirm that somewhere up there to her left, somebody was using green wood to fuel a campfire.

From here, she would go on foot.

Chapter 13

Tempering her impatience, Jessica scouted the area, then cautiously started up the slope of the canyon. She climbed at a crawl as the morning eased toward noon with a light sprinkling of rain. There was a tenseness to the cooling drizzle, a hush as if the hills resented her and the thickening slurry of clouds, and it made Jessica watchful and slightly nervous. Nearing the rim, she groped for handholds in the weathered rock, testing each one before placing her weight on it; the cracked, fissured stone crumbled easily in her fingers. Once she almost lost her balance and toppled back into the chasm of the stream. She clawed frantically, pressing against the cliff face and grabbing onto an outcropping that trembled and fell loose as she hauled herself to another high point.

Easing over the top, she flattened herself, trying to catch her breath from the last desperate pull. For long moments the pounding blood in her ears made her deaf to the gravel and dirt trickling down the way she'd come. Then she started forward, keeping low and in line with the upper course of the stream, as it bubbled and stewed toward the surging waterfall on her right.

She entered a tangle of shrubs and stunted trees, whose windswept limbs were twisted at every conceivable angle. She stood in their shadows a while, silently listening for men and looking for that telltale ribbon of smoke. Then, moving to her left, away from the waterfall, she struggled through a cluttered grove of conifers, eventually emerging where a rotted tree had settled, roots upended, by the very edge of a straight-sided drop.

Crouching on the ledge and concealed by a low hedge of brush, Jessica peered over the side into a small, box-shaped pocket canyon. It was slightly at an angle to the other canyon, a land-bridge connecting the two; and either through erosion or upheaval, the bed of the stream skirted the pocket and formed the waterfall at the narrowest point of the land-bridge. A curious quirk of nature, but not uncommon; mountains were like this, concealing deep pockets till one stood on their very brink.

Most of the pocket was overgrown with tall grass, scrub, and thickets of aspen, fir, and pine. But a quarter of the way in from the land-bridge, at a tangent to the waterfall, she saw a log cabin and some motley shacks clustered around a wide clearing, in the middle of which burned the fire whose smoke she'd spotted. A path led from the clearing to a point below and just to one side of the waterfall—the pocket's only entrance, Jessica assumed, though she couldn't make it out precisely because of her distance and poor angle.

Four men were standing at the fire, cooking something in a cast-iron kettle. Another fourteen or fifteen men could be seen elsewhere in and about the clearing, walking, talking, or doing nothing, ignoring their scattered equipment and the loose cavvy of untended saddle horses. Obviously the men were lazy, badly organized, and poorly disciplined, which didn't surprise Jessica; and whatever else they were, they were not defense-conscious. The chain of tall ridges surrounding the pocket, watched over by the now-dead guard, was evidently trusted to be protection enough; a single shot would warn them, and they were camped in a natural fort, a hole-in-the-wall that had one hidden gap through which they could be attacked.

Since it was impossible from here to detect which, if any, of the horses wore a broken shoe, Jessica ignored the cavvy and concentrated on the men. She searched out each one to see if she could recognize any. They were depressingly similar, dressed in grubby shirts and pants, needing shaves and trims, none with a three-fingered hand, say, or only one ear. No peculiarities at all. No Ryker, no Volpes, and most discouragingly, no Ki.

Jessica sat back, contemplating. If Ki was in the pocket, he was either imprisoned or buried. Of course, she had no way of knowing if he was down there; she'd been following horses, not men. Back when the eight horses had split up at that pass, she'd chosen the broken-shoe trail because the other trail appeared to simply head to the Block-Two-Dot. For her to brave Ryker's stronghold alone would have been foolhardy; to have gone there first, and not found Ki, would have also allowed time and weather to obliterate the meager traces and signs leading to the canyon. But whether Ki was down there or back at Ryker's, there was no doubt in her mind about the men she could see. Trash. Nor did she question *if* she should do something about them, only *what* she should do about them. Afterward, she'd allow herself the luxury of feeling regret. But only afterward.

Jessica thought a bit longer, then slipped back into the brush and began hiking back to the bluff overlooking the canyon. She took her time, not risking detection, yet she wanted to hurry, knowing that sooner or later someone would be detailed to relieve the dead sentry. Reaching the spot where she'd climbed up, she started her treacherous way back down again, sliding and plunging, digging in her heels and clutching with her hands to keep from tripping into a headlong dive.

Once at the bottom of the creek, she hurried to remount her horse and ride back out of the canyon, still keeping a cautious eye on the terrain around her. Without lingering, she entered the maze of crooked ridges and twisting gorges, hoping her sense of direction would not fail her, scouting steadily through the roughs of brush, rock, and forests for familiar marks that would lead her back to the plateau. Twice she followed false sign and had to backtrack, the wasted time frustrating her, making her edgy. If she was a good enough tracker to find the canyon, she chastised herself, then at least she ought to be able to track her own goddamn backtrail out again.

Finally she reined in and smiled, seeing the plateau up ahead. She headed out across it, toward the mouth of the canyon from which the rustled cattle had fled, figuring to pick up the path there that would return her to the Spraddled M. Approaching, she saw that the last leg of her trip was unnecessary. Daryl Melville was standing just inside the canyon mouth, holding the reins of his buckskin. Beside him, Deputy Oakes had one foot on the ground and the other lodged in his stirrup, in the process of either getting on or off a moro with tan leggings. Spotting her, Daryl began gesturing and moving forward to meet her, while the deputy merely put his stirruped foot down and waited.

"God, but I was worried about you," Daryl called, even before she could come to a halt and dismount. "When I woke and you weren't—I mean, I guessed you'd come here to look for your friend, but then when I couldn't find you . . . you should've told me, Jessica!"

"Oh, it wasn't that important," she said vaguely, smiling as if the whole thing had been just a whim of hers. "Certainly not so important that you should've called the law in."

"He didn't, ma'am," the deputy said, answering for Daryl as he politely removed his hat. "No, ma'am, I was over looking for you at the hotel, and they said you might've gone to the Flying W, so I rode there and they said you might've gone visiting the Spraddled M. Then I got tooken here. My, you sure do lead a feller a merry chase."

"He don't believe what happened," Daryl said grimly.

"Now, Daryl, you're givin' Miss Starbuck the wrong impression," Deputy Oakes replied gruffly. "I ain't deputin' that a wad of steers broke crazy down that gorge, or that a few Block-Two-Dot punchers were trompled. I'm only queryin' the drift you've put on it, is all. Seems to me it's as liable that the men were trying to head off them rustlers behind the cows, or coming in to help you."

"They were after us, I tell you, aiming to kill us!"

"Well, if they caught you trespassin', like you admit, I can't rightly blame them if some tempers got a little het up and—"

"Deputy," Jessica cut in sharply, "why're you looking for me?"

"Oh, yes, that," Oakes said with a haggard sigh. "What with this here in the gorge and everythin', the day's been kinda discombobulatin'." He reached into his hat and brought out a rumpled, slightly sweat-stained envelope. "Here, this is addressed to you."

The envelope had no marks or postage on it, only her name

and the words URGENT, DELIVER IMMEDIATELY written on its front, and what appeared to be a knife-slice through its middle. Jessica ripped it open and removed a sheet of onionskin, also cut, and read:

> *Dear Miss Starbuck:*
>
> *I believe you're missing an item of sentimental importance. If you wish to arrange a recovery, you know where to contact me. I urge you to do so promptly, to assure undamaged condition, and I also insist that as proof of your goodwill, you come alone.*
>
> *Guthried Ryker*

"Horseshit," Jessica murmured under her breath, then louder, to Deputy Oakes, she snapped, "Where'd you get this?"

"The workmen found it stuck with a knife to my office door, when they went there this morning to rebuild the cells. Gawd, what a mess." Oakes nervously clutched his hatbrim in both hands. "Can't add more'n that, ma'am. It's all I know."

Jessica refolded the note and stuck it back into the envelope, saying to Daryl, "Ryker's got Ki. He wants me to go to the ranch."

"The bastard! You can't, Jessica, it's a trap."

"Sure it is," Jessica agreed, nodding. "I know it, and Ryker knows I know it, but he's counting on my coming anyway. I don't have any choice, he thinks, because I don't have any idea where he's got Ki hidden. I'm forced to play his game his way. But Ki isn't at Ryker's place. Ryker's too shrewd to risk a charge of kidnapping. He made sure not to write anything incriminating in his note, but he wouldn't have sent it at all, if he had Ki where he could be found at the ranch. Though that's what he'd like me to believe." Jessica paused, eyes narrowing, a tight, flinty smile creasing her lips. "But what Ryker doesn't know is that I *do* know where Ki is."

Swiftly she sketched the events since she'd discovered the blood-spattered scene of the struggle in the gorge, as the two men listened with mouths gaping in surprise. She told of tracking the broken-shoed horse to the canyon, and described the natural pocket in which she'd located the camp, while Daryl breathed harshly with increasing anger, and Deputy Oakes grew redder in his fat jowls.

"So," Jessica concluded, "Ryker's note has backfired on him. He's unwittingly answered which of the two places Ki must've been taken."

"Him and his filthy kidnappers!" Daryl roared furiously. "God knows how long he's had them nesting up there, swooping down like vultures to steal our stock and now people! There you are, Oakes!"

"There I am, what?"

"She's found our rustlers. What're you going to do about 'em?"

"I, uh . . . I suppose a posse, and, uh . . ." The deputy hesitated, scratching his hair, and then he clapped his hat back on, a crafty glint coming to his eyes. "Hold on, won't do to go off half cocked. I gotta investigate this first, legal and proper. Now, Miss Starbuck, did I hear you admit that this here letter you got don't exactly spell out a kidnapping or ransom demand?"

"No, but it's implied, and Ki was taken by Ryker's men."

"Your friend may be missing, ma'am, but did you actually see him being taken, or being held against his will in that camp? And these here kidnappers—can you prove they're Block-Two-Dot men, and if so, that they're following Mr. Ryker's orders? Or that they're the rustlers, who you figure are also working for Mr. Ryker?"

Jessica glared at Oakes.

"No?" he said. "Well, ma'am, I need evidence 'fore I can organize a posse and go rousting innercent folk. I mean, d'you have proof the men in the camp are the rustlers? Did you see any stolen cattle with 'em?"

"Of course not. That pocket's too small for much more than their camp," Jessica replied frostily. "But I've got a strong hunch, Deputy, that maybe you can tell us where those cows are."

"Me? Not me," Oakes retorted indignantly. "I haven't any idea who the rustlers are, or what they've done with the stock."

"You should. It's part of your job, only Ryker's paid you to be blind to it, hasn't he? That's why you could never trace them."

"Lady, you're loco," Oakes growled, but his voice was quivering. Sensing that his denials were getting him nowhere, he again tried to attack: "Fact is, I'm thinkin' you're trying to trick me! You're trying to ruin me and disgrace Mr. Ryker, our most prominent citizen, so you can go ahead with your own dirty work!"

"Stop blustering," Daryl raged. "You're caught."

"Nope *you're* caught, both of you!" Oakes stepped closer to Daryl, his pudgy hand groping in his hip pocket for his handcuffs. "For trespassin', disturbin' the peace, bearin' false witness, and suspicion of havin' a hand in stampedin' them cows—"

Daryl's fist whipped out in a short, pistonlike punch that connected with the deputy's chin. Oakes's head whipped back and he crumpled to the rain-dampened earth, blood oozing from his mouth.

Jessica stooped and snatched his revolver from its holster, while Daryl rolled him over and snapped the cuffs on his wrists.

"There are some spare piggin' strings in my saddlebags," Daryl said, as he wrestled to lift the mud-splotched deputy onto his horse. "See if you can use them to tie his legs to the stirrups."

Fetching the strings, Jessica asked, "He's coming along?"

"Yeah, to make some arrests, even if he's in no mind to."

Oakes, regaining his wits while he slumped in his saddle, glowered and cursed them, swearing to have them both in jail by nightfall. His mount didn't seem to appreciate his language, and started prancing, its tan leggings flashing droplets of the continuing drizzle. Oakes promptly shut up, straining to keep his seat.

"I hope you fall on that fat head of yours," Daryl told him, then turned to Jessica. "Now let's get to gathering all the hands from my ranch and the Flying W, and then we'll go rescue your friend."

Jessica, startled, restrained him with her hand. "Please, Daryl, I appreciate your offer, but I can't have all of you risk—"

"Don't you argue, Jessie," he fumed. "I thought we had this all sorted out last night. You may've come here to make this your fight, and Ki may be the reason you're fighting now. Hell, I like the feller too. But this was *our* fight first, and it goes a lot deeper than just one man—or woman. And by God, I aim to see it finished."

Jessica nodded and smiled. "All right, offer accepted."

"Y'think we should get the other ranchers in on it?"

"Frankly, I don't. If you're determined to do this, then it'll take too much time to reach them, explain, and get their crews together. Besides, wc'll have enough men to surround the rim of the pocket and cover the entrance hole. The rustlers don't realize it, but if we can hold them down in there, they're virtually sitting ducks."

Daryl mulled it over for a moment, then said with a frown, "Listen, I'd better warn you, and if you don't like it, you'd better say no. Way I see it, it's going to be a fight to the death, no quarter given. If we bottle them up like you say, and knock them all to hell an' gone, Ki is liable to get hurt permanent-like."

"Daryl, Ki is either already dead—and as you told me last night, dead's dead—or he's being kept locked in someplace. And if that's the case, what we've got to do is attack so swiftly and surprisingly that the rustlers won't have a chance to bring him out and use him as a hostage. They'll be too busy fighting us."

"Well, I still figure his odds stink."

"Maybe so, Daryl, but they're worse every other way. If we tried to simply ram through the pocket's entrance, we'd suffer awful losses, and never reach Ki in time. If we do nothing, eventually he'll be killed anyway, and if I do what Ryker's note demands, it'll only result in my dying with him. I know Ki; given a sliver of a chance, he can take care of himself better than any man alive. And I also know that this is the way Ki would want it."

But she was equally aware that Daryl was right—this was a frightful risk to take. If Ki wasn't gunned by the rustlers in retaliation or panic, he could just as easily be caught in the murderous crossfire that the two crews would be pouring down into the pocket. That is, if Ki was still alive—if Ryker's cutthroat gang hadn't already slaughtered him out of sheer cussedness.

Chapter 14

Ki was very much alive.

And he was feeling more alive with each passing moment. He was in trouble, but it was trouble he'd been figuring might be turned to his own disadvantage. Daphne Chung was spoiling his chances of that. Just the mere presence of Volpes's willful, mischievous lover was adding a potentially volatile threat he couldn't predict and guard against. Yet he couldn't look on her barely clothed, provocative sultriness and miss the feeling that here was a devastating female whose survival ability was centered between her legs. Her fiery challenge was unspoken, an undercurrent he was determined to defend himself against.

Not that he didn't want her.

That was the problem. He did.

She was staring up at him from where she was slumped beside him on the dirty shed floor. The frightened sheen was dimming from her eyes, and she was watching him with, it seemed to Ki, something like fascination. He expected her to continue tongue-lashing him. He waited, but no more furious outbursts came.

Finally he said, "Stop sulking. If anybody's trapped in here, it's me, not you." He said it harshly—too harshly, as if directing some of it inward—and instantly relented. "Hell, Daphne, you've got nothing to worry about. When the door opens, you can explain."

"No, he'll kill me. He owns me."

"Volpes just wants to scare you into thinking he does."

"He owns me, Ki. And he's warned me that if he ever catches me with another man, he'll kill me. He means it, he will."

"A bowl of soup isn't very compromising."

"In my gown, without getting his permission first, it is. Oh, he'll know the soup was only an excuse, he'll know what I was after."

"Mind letting me know?"

"I was going to make you promise that if I . . . if I released you, helped you escape, you'd take me with you."

Ki raked her face with a quick, questioning look, and saw that her gaze was intent and pleading. "You vixen, you really were."

"I certainly was." Her voice was low and husky with emotion, and made Ki feel warm inside. She caught his arm and tugged him down to sit with her, then leaned over and pressed her lips against his mouth. When he started wrapping his arms around her, she pushed away. "There, you see? Any way I had to, I was."

Ki felt her warm breath against his face and smelled her womanly fragrance, and read in her anguished gaze the strength of a soul living with a truth that is against it. "Oh, yes, Ki, I'm a passionate girl. I take lots of loving. But you know, all I've ever really wanted was to be liked. I've been pushed down, sat down, thrown down, and upside-downed, but never turned down. Never simply liked for myself. Who could, considering what I am?"

"Don't hate yourself, Daphne. I don't."

"You do, you don't have to lie. It's too late now, but the worst part is that I'd been waiting for you a long, long while."

Again, Ki studied her eyes for meaning, and this time she smiled. "That's a silly thing for me to say, isn't it?" she murmured. "When I couldn't have been waiting for you, since I didn't know you existed till late last night."

"It could do with some explaining, yes."

"It's not a pretty story." Her voice was unsteady. "Volpes bought my contract from a house in Salinas. Utah, that is, not Kansas. It cost him a bundle. I was the . . . resident virgin, and virgins can make a house a fortune. Anyway, he's always led a gang, long as I've known him. His men change, but it's always the same—thieving, rustling, robbing trains—and he's kept me with him in a dozen different hideouts, getting his money's worth, you could say."

Daphne was clinging gently to Ki's midriff as she confessed her torment, her fingers circling of their own volition. Ki felt a prurient stirring in his loins, triggered by her longing, and sparked by a perverse physical yearning that was building between them. He tried to resist. Another time, another place, he'd have flattened her to the nearest bed without hesitation, but here?

"Okay, I get the picture," Ki said curtly, feeling himself hardening against his will. He tried to shift where he sat, his beginning erection bulging out the crotch of his pants. "So you don't like it, you're fed up with him. Fine. So leave him."

"I have, quite a few times. He always brings me back and beats me, beats me so hard he's broken my bones before. Now that Ryker's hired him and his gang, and installed them up here, there's no way I can get free without . . ." There was a sob in her voice now. "I could only wait, Ki. Wait for a strong man I could trust."

"For a crazy man willing to die for you, you mean."

"No, no!" she replied in a thick whisper, and on her face was a look of sudden excitement. "To live for me, Ki, not die! Haven't you ever felt that about a girl, Ki?"

Ki didn't answer.

"Not ever?"

"Never mind." He glanced away from her searching eyes, from her lips and breasts and legs, her nightgown hiked up almost to her thighs from the awkward way she was sitting.

"Ki?"

"Yes?"

"I don't know if I love you, but I want you."

"Stop it."

"I've wanted you since the second I laid eyes on you. I want you now, right now, in spite of everything. *Because* of everything."

"You don't want me, Daphne. You're just upset."

"I do . . . and you want me. You're hard, hard as a bar of iron. I can feel you poking my arm, Ki." She giggled lightly, and languidly began to strip off her nightgown. Unbuttoning it at the throat, she crossed her arms and with slow, tantalizing suggestiveness, eased the gown up over her head and tossed it aside. "There. Now you."

For a moment Ki did not move, could not move, his eyes feasting on her nudity. Her breasts, golden and firm, nipples large and jutting like ripe black cherries. Her belly, taut and flat, flaring down into rich black curls of pubic hair, the pink flesh of her vaginal lips peeking warmly from underneath. Her thighs, smooth and tapering into long legs that he instinctively knew would wrap around him in a squeezing grip of passion.

Then, goaded to recklessness, Ki removed vest and shirt, and rose to unbuckle his pants, aroused, throbbingly erect, aching to penetrate her voluptuous body. Her hands reached high, her fingers burning his flesh as she began pulling his pants down, her gaze riveted on his naked loins, her breath coming in short, hissing gasps. Daphne was in heat, animal heat, and Ki knew there was no longer any denying her—or himself.

His left trouser leg off, he balanced on his left foot while they both tore at his right trouser leg. Daphne, gazing hurgrily at his jutting instrument, giggled again. "Position eighty, *Chin Chi Tu Li.*"

"What?" Then Ki got it. "Oh, yes, your father's *T' ai-chi* exercises—'Golden Cock Stands On One Leg'."

He settled alongside her, moving one hand down over the smoothness of her buttocks, marveling in their warm texture and beautiful shape. She tilted her face and kissed him urgently, her hand searching down between them and closing around his burgeoning shaft. He sucked in his breath, his blood pounding as she stroked him with her fingertips and nails, and then he crushed the full length of her body against his, grinding his pelvis into her.

"Yes, now," she moaned. "Now, I beg you . . ."

Ki pulled her beneath him, and she opened her legs to accept his thrust between them. He could feel her crevice moist and tender against the blunt crown of his erection, and thinking to repay her, he taunted, "Position sixty-three, *Yeh Ma Fên Tsung*—'Partition of Wild Horse's Mane,'" as he slid gently through her pubic hair.

"And *Shê Shen Hsia Shih,*" she moaned, " 'The Snake

Creeps Down,' " feeling Ki plunge fully into her loins, her hips slowly undulating against him. Her thighs pressed against his legs as her ankles wrapped over and locked around his calves. He pumped deep into her soft flesh while she strained under him, moaning beneath his rhythmic surges, opening and closing her thighs, her head thrashing from side to side on the cold shed floor with total abandon. *"K' ua Hu! K' ua Hu!"* she chanted. " 'Ride The Tiger'!"

Ki could feel himself growing and expanding inside her till he felt as if he were going to explode from the exquisite pleasure building in his groin, and he could sense that Daphne was also nearing completion as she gripped him tighter and moved more frantically under him, reveling in his trusts, hot and pulsating and deep.

"Now, Ki, now! *Pao Hu Kwei Shan!* 'Carry the Tiger to the Mountain'!" she pleaded, urging him on with the pounding of her heels on his legs. Then she cried out shrilly, loud and piercing, uncaring if it brought the camp running. Ki didn't give a damn either, ejaculating violently into her as she shuddered convulsively beneath him with each of his pulsing spurts.

Then Daphne's body collapsed limply and she was still, except for the uncontrollable quivering of her thighs still firmly pressed around his loins. And Ki remained inside her, feeling himself drained of energy, placidly satiated.

"Forgive me . . . forgive me . . ." Daphne murmured crushing her lips against his mouth before he could respond, then pulling away as abruptly as she'd clung. "You must think terribly of me, Ki, and I don't blame you. But, oh, I wanted you . . , needed you . . . I still do . . ."

A shaft of waning sunlight filtered through a crack in the wall, illuminating her face under him, and revealing a smile that was sad, and yet warm and tender. Ki wanted to tell her now that he didn't think less of her, only of himself for having given in to the risk of being caught like this. And to tell the truth, he didn't even care much about that. Their coupling somehow seemed natural, even though the circumstances were unnatural; their joining had served to release their dangerously pent-up emotions.

But Ki was a fighter, not a poet. He found it impossible to voice what he only dimly perceived in his instinctive reaction to her sensuality. He drew her to him instead, answering her fears in his own way, by hungrily kissing the smoothness of her lips, her neck, the swelling nipples of her breasts.

"Ki . . . Ki . . ." Daphne cried, while her naked flesh began to tingle with renewed excitement. Tears blurred her eyes, and her voice was thick with desire and fright. "Don't leave me, don't . . ."

"I won't," he assured her as he tongued one nipple.

"Take me with you. Please, take me away from here."

"If I can."

"And don't die for me, Ki, live for me . . ."

"I'll keep living . . . living as I am now."

And he was alive, he had to admit wryly. He could feel himself harden within her, swelling into stiff, reinvigorated passion. He tentatively thrust deeper into her.

Daphne gasped with delight. "You can't . . . !"

"I am," Ki chuckled throatily. *Hai Ti Chên.*"

" 'Needle at Sea Bottom,' it is indeed," she sighed, arching and writhing underneath him—then she suddenly screamed, freezing rigid.

Ki twisted his head sideways to see what had shocked her into mortal terror. And he just kept on twisting, withdrawing from Daphne and swiveling around in an upright crouch, readying to strike.

The shed door was open. Not by very much, but enough to admit Volpes. "I thought I heard that squawk of yours," he snarled at Daphne, stepping closer as she scuttled into an almost fetal position. "So I was real quiet about unlocking and sliding the chain loose, and I'm glad I was. But shit! I could've fired a cannon off in here and not disturbed you, the way you were bucking and snorting!"

"I—I'm sorry," she whined. "I'll never do—"

"You're right, you won't." Volpes loomed menacingly over her; and Ki, who'd been cursing himself for being as blindly preoccupied as Daphne, made a motion to stop Volpes from touching the girl. Volpes, pivoting and drawing his pistol, yelled out, "Boys!"

The door swung wider and three more men rushed in, grinning rapaciously and bristling with revolvers. Ki tensed to take them on too, but then thought better of it; Volpes now had his pistol aimed at Daphne, and he looked ready to shoot her at the slightest provocation.

"No, I wasn't ignoring you," Volpes told Ki with a sideways glare. "I was saving you. Killed one of my men, I hear. Just bashed his head in. And now you've been dipping your wick in my woman. You've got brass balls, boy." He glanced at his men then, ordering, "This chink so much as breathes, blow those balls off."

There was a chorus of lewd snickers, while the girl huddled naked and cringing.

Volpes, concentrating on Daphne again, shouted, "Get up, you slut!" And when she didn't, he holstered his revolver and wrapped his hand in her hair, whipping her upright. "You fuckin' li'l whore!" With his other hand, he smashed a brutal fist to her jaw, and she sagged limply, still held standing by her hair.

Volpes dragged her to the nearest two men. "Take her out," he said contemptuously, dropping her into their eager arms. "You know where—same place I'm taking this here squint-eyed bastard."

Volpes palmed his revolver again and, with the third man, marched Ki outside, a few steps behind the two who were carrying Daphne. Down along the side of the cabin they went, and openly across the clearing. Daphne had begun to regain her senses by now, groggily staggering between the two men, whimpering as they fondled her breasts and fingered her loins, still damp from Ki's secretions.

The clearing lay bleak under an overcast sky, cooled by a leaden drizzle and shadowed by the advance of evening. Only ten or so rustlers were out of their shacks, most of them milling about the fire to warm themselves. Whey they glimpsed Daphne and Ki being paraded naked past them, their first reaction was one of astonishment. But when they saw how the two nude prisoners were being mauled and manhandled, they quickly began jeering and hooting obscenities.

"Get an eyeful now, fellas," Volpes yelled back, " 'cause this'll be the last you'll be seeing of 'em!" Then, jabbing Ki in the spine with the muzzle of his revolver, he said in a lower but nastier voice, "Ryker'll fart a blue streak when he finds out.

But I'll just tell him you were too tricky to let run around loose."

They entered the scrub at the other side of the clearing, where thorny vines and briars scraped Ki's bare legs as he was prodded up a rocky defile. He walked without giving resistance, without showing any defiance, while his mind worked swiftly to figure out when and where to make his stand. But mainly he walked feeling sadness for Daphne and bitterness toward himself. The gleam in Volpe's eyes was of pure malicious hatred—the implacably murderous kind that Daphne had warned him Volpes would feel—and that now was directed against them both. Yet Ki understood this kind of hatred, and in a sense he could not blame Volpes for it. In fact, he held a certain rueful respect for it.

Fifty yards from the clearing, Volpes called a halt in a wide spot of the defile. The ground was relatively soft here, a bit sandy and fit only for grass and stubby weeds—and for three oblong mounds of earth, just beginning to sprout fresh growth.

A rusty shovel was stuck like a grave marker at the end of one of the mounds. Volpes crossed over, still covering Ki with his revolver, and with his free hand he wriggled the shovel loose.

"Here," he ordered, handing Ki the shovel. "Now dig."

Chapter 15

Ki took the shovel and rubbed his hands along its rough wooden handle. He considered it in terms of a weapon; and then he wondered about the three victims already buried here, who they'd been and if they'd thought the same thing about the shovel while digging their own graves.

"Go on, start digging," Volpes snapped. "Right where you're standing will do fine, I reckon."

Ki glanced fleetingly at Daphne, who still needed to be held upright, her face a mask of mute terror. Then he began to dig. Under the thin top layer of soil, the shovel struck clay pan, and his digging became more difficult. The evening lengthened; Ki's naked chest and back soon became beaded with sweat, which riveted down his flesh and mixed with the drizzly rain. By the end of an hour, he had gouged a three-by-six pit to the depth of a foot.

"Keep digging," Volpes growled. "But I'll let you off easy. You don't have to dig two holes, just make yours double-wide."

The two men flanking Daphne chuckled snidely; they were smugly relaxed after an hour of waiting, and Daphne was giving them no trouble. She was slumped in despair between them, speechless and glassy-eyed with her mounting horror. The third man was leaning against a boulder directly across the pit from Ki, holding his pistol lazily in his lap and appearing to be bored stiff. Volpes was a couple of yards to the near side of the man, facing Ki as alertly as ever, keeping his revolver leveled and taking no chances that his prisoner might attempt a break.

Ki continued digging. When the dual grave was a foot deeper and wider, he was positive he and Daphne would be shot firing-squad style and dumped into it, to be covered over and never found again. Whatever he was going to do, he'd have to do in the next few seconds.

"Enough digging," Volpes said suddenly, as if reading Ki's thoughts. "Okay, boys, bring the bitch over next to him."

The two men hauled Daphne closer, while the other man, now holding his pistol firmly, rose and moved beside Volpes. Daphne was now mewing and writhing feebly, and when Ki said to her sharply, "*Tao Nien Hou*," he couldn't be sure whether she was nodding with understanding, or merely shuddering with mind-numbing dread. But it was too late to repeat; it had either sunk in or not, and if not, they were both virtually dead. Volpes and the man beside him were foolishly close together, but that still left Ki's back exposed to the two men holding Daphne.

"That's it," Volpes was snarling in response to Ki's words, "Say your yaller prayers." And he thumbed back the hammer . . .

And Ki dove across the pit, gripping the shovel lengthwise by its handle. A thunderous flash exploded before him, the heavy .45 slug whispering past his ear as it sped harmlessly into the woods. Before Volpes could trigger again, before the man beside him could fire his own pistol, Ki had leaped the short space and flattened Volpes with a combination of shovel to the face and flying kick to the chest. The wooden handle smashed between Volpe's upper lip and nostrils with a driving upward thrust, shattering his nose and spearing shards of bone and cartilage into his brain. This, while Ki's driving feet were crushing his chest, snapping ribs into his lungs and rupturing his stomach and kidneys.

Volpes was dead before he hit the ground, and Ki was attacking the other man. He seemed to pivot in midair, using the shovel again to swipe the man's wrist with a lightning sideways chop, and all in the same motion, as the pistol dropped and discharged, he added a thumb-jab to the man's neck. The man began wilting, his brain bursting from the eruptive pressure on his carotid artery. Lurching, spinning, dying, he fell backward into the open pit.

Again Ki swiveled, bracing himself against the expected fusillade of bullets from the men behind him. But Daphne had heard him, had understood, and with courage born of hope and desperation, had reacted the instant he'd sprung into action.

She had been forced to the edge of the grave by the man on her right, who was pulling her by the wrist, and the man on her left, who had a grip on her elbow. In response to Ki's barked command, she had applied *Tao Nien Hou*—the *T' ai-chi* maneuver that translates as "Step Back to Repulse the Monkey." She simply let her left elbow relax, dropping it into the man's grip— which, by removing all resistance, threw him immediately off balance, causing him to stumble. At the same moment, she placed all her weight in her left leg, extending her right palm in a forward thrust to the chest of the man holding her wrist. He had been pulling her, so the last thing he expected was for that hand suddenly to come toward him with lightning speed, as it now did. He also stumbled, and let go of her wrist.

Confused, the two men pounced for her again. Daphne barely had time to ward off one by striking his face with her left palm, when the other closed with a bear hug. She evaded his right arm by pushing it aside with her left forearm, and then, swiftly following through with the *Shih Tzǔ Shou* or "Cross Hands" movement, she simultaneously stabbed her right hand forward over her left forearm, her extended fingers rupturing the man's trachea just below the thyroid gland. The man clawed at his neck, strangling . . .

But his partner, swearing, was bearing down on Daphne with his Colt .44-40, squeezing the trigger before she could turn . . .

And Ki came launching across the pit again in a *tomoenage* whirl, caroming into him, sending the man sprawling on his back. Desperately the man tried straightening, aiming the pistol he still gripped tenaciously in his fist. Ki feinted with a kick, as if to knock the pistol away, and the man responded as Ki anticipated, rolling back to gain more space. Half through his roll and facedown, the man suddenly felt Ki jump on his back, and then he felt excruciating pain, and then nothing, as Ki grabbed both his ankles and pulled violently up and backward.

A scream, a dull cracking noise, and the man died, his back broken and his spinal cord severed.

Daphne rushed to Ki, almost collapsing with relief into his comforting arms. "Oh, I was so terrified," she whimpered, clinging tightly to him.

"You did beautifully," Ki soothed her, cradling her head to his chest. "You're a little rusty with your timing, but you did just fine."

"I know. I should practice more. My father would be ashamed." She drew away then, her eyes bright disks of fear and excitement. "Ki, we've got to get out of here, and fast!"

Before Ki could answer, other voices starting filtering from the clearing:

"Boss?"

"Hey, you all right?"

"Boss, what's going on there?"

Then came the noise of boots approaching through the brush.

A low word came from Daphne's lips. Ki touched her to warn her that silence was necessary, holding on to her right arm as he guided her out of the defile and into the sheltering woods. But he was aware that she was right. The very compactness of the pocket would make any possible refuge out of the question for long. Daylight would, of course, make them easy game for the remaining rustlers.

"Crap, looky here!"

"They got the boss!"

"They got everyone!"

Ki dropped low to the ground, Daphne stretching close beside him. "If we can, we should circle back to the shed," he whispered in her ear, "and try for our clothes. What there is of them."

"Goddammit, they've escaped!"

"Where?"

"They can't have gone far. They gotta still be in here someplace, so let's block the hole before they can get out it."

"Yeah, four of us can do that."

"Me an' Clyde, we'll stake out that shed."

"Good idea. Some of you help me build up the fire so we can see 'em, and then let's spread out, track 'em down."

So much for getting out the simple way, Ki thought glumly,

or for getting back to the shed for their clothes. "We'd better find a good place to hide," he said to Daphne.

In a crouching run, they wormed through the low scrub and trees toward the nearest slope of the pocket, ducking before they reached it and lying down prone, motionless, as four men trampled past, heading for the entrance hole.

The campfire was flaring briskly now, as kindling, brush, and tree limbs were tossed on it. Across the pocket, Ki and Daphne reached the steep, rocky wall, anxiously watching the growing flames brighten the encroaching night darkness. They moved along the slope, exploring the stone with their hands and bare feet, hoping, praying to locate enough rubble to hide in. The light was growing in the pocket, casting reflections almost to the walls. In a few more minutes it would be light everywhere. They must be undercover by then.

Cautiously they continued groping along. The pile played out, and for the space of a hundred feet, they encountered no more loose rock at all. Growing desperate, Ki went straight down the side wall and around to the one supporting the land-bridge that concealed the pocket. Daphne kept close beside him, touching him occasionally as if for support. Nothing. Nothing at all. Still they moved on, hurrying more, running out of time.

They almost bumped into a rough jumble of boulders that seemed to jut out of nowhere. Signaling Daphne to wait, Ki moved around it, searching its contours with his fingers. He came to a narrow crevice that angled in to the face of the wall like a wedge.

"I think we might have found a hiding place," he whispered to Daphne when he returned. "Maybe it won't last long, but it's something."

He also thought they must be so close to the land-bridge that any guard posted up on its rim would surely notice them when the fire rose full enough. That there would be a guard, or guards, was something Ki could almost certainly count on; Volpes couldn't have lasted as long as he had, if he hadn't taken elementary precautions like that. Yet by shifting some of the stones, Ki was able to fashion a place for them to lie flat. No part of the pile of stone was high, but it would conceal them from a distance.

The rustlers were already divided up into teams, and were impatiently scouring the pocket from one end to the other. One group, reaching the exit that led through the land-bridge, called out, "Hey, Johnson! McCully! What're you doin'—sleepin'?"

"Hell, no!" a loud bellow replied. "We're right here on this side of the hole, and Winnie and Sam are on t'other. A field mouse ain't gonna get by us. What's up? You lost 'em?"

"Naw, we just ain't found 'em yet, is all."

"We'll ride this pocket till we root 'em out," another of the group shouted, as the men turned and moved on through the brush.

The roaring blaze from the campfire was strong enough now to illuminate the entire area, even high up the walls of the pocket. Hidden in the rocks, Ki kept surveying the slope they were against, curious about a line of blackness along it. A slight crown cast shadows far above it, but something lower down, not ten feet over their heads, also drew his close scrutiny.

After a long study, Ki decided that what he was seeing was a fault line running up the wall, a thin slice of softer stone that had eroded, crumbling, forming the rubble they were lying in now, and leaving a depression in the otherwise sheer surface of the wall.

Ki wondered if it could be climbed. Probably not, but on the other hand, they couldn't stay where they were forever. A losing proposition, no matter how he chose. He chose to try.

Touching Daphne on the shoulder, Ki slipped from his bent-over crouch and began inching laborously ahead of her into the fault. She promptly, unquestioningly, followed his lead. Slowly they worked their way up the fault which was like a stovepipe cut lengthwise down the middle, bracing themselves against the thin sides of the depression with elbows and knees, exerting all their strength to retain a hold in what time-scalloped chinks they could find. They climbed and climbed some more, clawing with broken fingernails and tensed feet, realizing that if they should slip now, their height would guarantee a grisly death.

A second bunch of riders trotted up, and Ki and Daphne froze while the men exchanged a few words with the four guarding the hole. Then one of them stretched in his saddle to yell out, "Tait!"

When nobody responded, he shouted again, "Tait, damn your mangy hide, where the fuck are you up there? Answer me!"

Nobody did, and now another of the men said, "Ah, forget it, George. Tait's likely over watching the other side of the bridge, where Volpes told him to set tight this morning."

"Yeah, maybe, but I don't like—"

"Hell, Tait's a good egg. He'll nab 'em if'n they get up there. Which they can't, 'lessen they suddenly grow wings."

"Almost seems like they did."

"Can't find no sign of 'em in here, 'pears like."

"They've gotta be here!" George raged, wrenching his horse about. "They're lying out there laughing at us, I knows it!"

Ki and Daphne held their breaths; the men were so near the boulders below that it seemed impossible for them not to have noticed the two naked bodies clinging up in the fault. But the men all turned with the one named George, and rode back toward the clearing, where the others were gathering now, equally discouraged.

Ki surveyed the ridge above, and the surrounding cliffs, then glanced at the sky, pleased to see that the rainy overcast was blanketing the stars and moon. He craned to whisper down at Daphne, "There's a guard up there, but evidently he's posted way over by the trail leading in. There's a chance we can avoid him."

"There's a better chance I'm going to fall if you don't get moving again," she quavered.

Ki started the perilous climb again, Daphne moving right behind him with a sigh. They struggled higher as fast as they could, but the steepness and shallowness of the fault made their progress agonizingly slow.

Eventually they reached the overhang of the ridge. Ki caught the rim of the fault and flung himself over. Immediately he turned and helped Daphne over the edge. She fell forward, scrambling to her knees and then pitching forward a second time.

"Hurt?" Ki asked hoarsely.

"Out of breath. Let's get out of here."

They got three feet from the rim, when a shape loomed out of the trees directly ahead. It was a hard black outline against the softer black of the forest, and the most Ki could tell about it was that it was fat, it carried a rifle, and it was lurching toward them, babbling, "It's a trap! They think I'm helping, but—"

The shape stopped short, blurting, "You!" as Ki rushed toward it. "You again! You and that damned female!" the shape was ranting, leveling the rifle. "Least I'll pay one of you back!"

Ki didn't understand what the shape was saying, and he didn't care. He was simply assuming the shape was the guard named Tait, and that Tait would be able to shoot him before he could get the rifle.

"Here's lead in your guts!" the shape yelled.

And from behind Ki, Daphne threw a large rock, which beaned the shape smack in the middle of the forehead. The shape grunted in shock and pain, collapsing backward into the brush with a resounding crash, his nerveless trigger finger twitching just enough to discharge the rifle into the air.

And all hell broke loose.

Volleys of rifle fire poured down into the pocket from the surrounding cliffs, lances of flame sizzling from the blackness and raking the clearing. The rustlers below reacted with desperate swiftness. No more than three had fallen from where they'd been gathering around the huge campfire, before the others spurred their horses for the brush or dove for the cover of the shacks and rocks. And even while seeking shelter, the rustlers were managing to return the fire, scattering a few shots at first, then retaliating fully.

Shocked and baffled, Ki and Daphne leaped for the brush into which their mysterious assailant had fallen.

"Where did all that shooting come from?" Daphne asked, bewildered.

"I have no idea," Ki said, "but somehow you managed to knock out Deputy Oakes."

"A *lawman*? Oh, no!"

"Oh, yes. But beggars can't be choosers." Grabbing Oakes by one leg, Ki pulled him closer and then began to hurredly yank off his boots. "Quick, help me with his clothes," Ki told Daphne, unbuckling the gunbelt. "You get his shirt, I'll take his pants."

The deputy was stripped to his flannel underwear, while the gun battle raged around them. The hidden riflemen on the perimeter of the pocket were pumping bullet after bullet at the slightest glimpse of exposed flesh. And the rustlers were replying with a barrage of their own. From the shacks, rocks, and scrub, they were sending a shower of lead up into the cliffs. Some tried to bolt out through the entrance hole, but were blocked by bullets and forced back into the pocket.

There were other men on the floor of the pocket who were still out in the open. They were thrashing with wounds or dying in the muddy dirt. But for the most part, the rustlers were retaliating with withering brutality. Lead spanged and howled off the boulders and trees ringing the cliffs.

Impossible or not, Ki and Daphne had to brave it. Cursing, Ki began loping deeper into the brush, clasping Oakes's tentlike pants around his waist. Daphne, pausing on impulse to scoop up the deputy's rifle, then sprinted after him, the shirt flapping around her like some wide dress with too high a hemline.

There was no time for stealth. They ran toward the opposite side of the cliffs, veering diagonally to the left when they spotted a bouldered slope dipping down into the canyon, far enough away from the waterfall to miss most of the action centered there.

But some of the gunmen below turned from firing at the rustlers who were trying to get out the entry hole, and began blasting away at Ki and Daphne. Exposed on the steeply slanting hill and appearing to be running away—which they were— they were prime targets for the unknown attackers. Friend or foe, Ki had no way of knowing, and he wasn't about to try stopping to ask. Lead sang and ricocheted around the pair as they charged zigzagging down the slope. A bullet showered pieces of stone in his face, and he ducked reflexively, feeling a shard stab into his neck. He ignored it, seeing ahead where some horses stood tethered.

A handful of the gunmen broke from around the waterfall and came rushing forward with guns blazing to cut Ki and Daphne off. Clasping her hand, Ki fairly whipped Daphne off her feet as they raced for the horses, bullets buzzing around them. They only had time to grab one, Ki judged—the closest one, a moro with tan leggings.

Ki hoisted Daphne into the saddle, hurled himself at the

reins, then flung himself up in front of her. Fighting the spooked, rearing horse, he shouted, "Hang on!" and jabbed both heels into the moro's ribs.

The moro bolted straight down the creek as a barrage of shots pursued them. Just to keep the pursuing mob respectful, Daphne twisted around and, with one hand clutching the waist of the wide-bottomed pants Ki was wearing, fired the rifle. She fired only once, there being no way she could lever a new round and still keep her balance.

"Throw that thing away and keep down," Ki cautioned, feeling bullets clip past him. "All you're doing is making them madder."

Riding furiously, they galloped away from the hail of lead. Scattered shots chased them as they reached the mouth of the canyon and pounded into the hills beyond. The shots did not cease until they were long out of sight and range.

After another quarter-mile, Ki slowed the horse, which was lathered and panting under its double load. They rode on blindly, through canyons and across broken uplands, and the longer they went, the more like a labyrinth it became. They would emerge from one brush-clogged valley only to crown a barren crag that would lead into yet another canyon, with yet another bench stretching beyond that. Without the moon or stars, it was impossible to gauge their direction accurately. But by keeping the pocket and the canyon with the waterfall in a general line behind them, Ki sensed that they were heading generally eastward, and would eventually come out close to Eucher Butte.

He let the moro seek its own pace, feeling less concerned now about pursuit. Daphne squeezed tightly against him as she rode more or less on the rim of the cantle, her arms hugging Ki around his waist, her face pressed against his bare back.

"Who were those gunmen?" she asked after a while.

"I've been thinking about that. Ranchers, probably. Fed-up ranchers and their crews, who finally learned where the rustlers were camped, and decided to do something on their own about it."

"They sure are. They're finishing it for you."

"Finishing?"

"You told me in the shed you were staying because you

weren't finished. Well, you got to finish Volpes—and the ranchers, or whoever they are, are finishing his gang—so what else is there?"

"Volpes's boss, Ryker. I was hoping he'd show up personally, and maybe he would have later, except Volpes wasn't going to give us a later. And I was hoping to find out where the stolen cows are."

"Oh, I know where. In a bunch of box canyons way up in the hills of the Block-Two-Dot range. You should've asked me. I overheard Volpes and Ryker talking about brand-blotching all the cattle they were keeping there, so when Ryker bought out the other ranches, he could restock them with the ranchers' own herds."

"No wonder none of the stolen cows ever showed up."

"But Ki, about the ranchers—why're we running from them?"

"I only *think* they're ranchers, Daphne. They're certainly not the army, and for lawmen they're lousy shots, lucky for us. But, ranchers or not, they didn't know who we were, and didn't act inclined to find out while we were still breathing. And then there was that strange stuff Deputy Oakes was babbling . . ." Ki paused, then added, "Besides, did you want all those men to catch you naked?"

"No."

"The newspapers would have gobbled it up. 'Nude Queen of the Outlaws Captured in Shootout.' You have have had a hell of a time getting a fresh start, with that bandied about." Hastily, Ki amended, "Don't get me wrong, Daphne, I'm laying no claim to change you. Do exactly what suits you best. I'm only saying . . . well, maybe this way you've got a choice you didn't have before."

There was a giggle. "Your neck's turning red."

"No, it's not. Not me. Actually, the more I think about it, the more I'm changing my mind. I'm taking you in for charges."

Daphne gasped. "Me? You're having me arrested?"

"You bet. Serious offense too. They'll probably hang you for it. Stoning a law officer while he was performing his duties."

"I see. Is that worse than horse-thieving?"

"Hm, you've got a point. On third thought, you're too pretty and I'm too young to be strung up. Maybe by the time we've found our way to Eucher Butte, we'll have figured out an arrangement."

Daphne kissed him lightly on the spine, a purr to her voice. "I'm all for giving it a try." Her fingers coiled down from his waist and slithered inside the baggy top of Ki's borrowed pants, burrowing deep to touch his manhood. Gently she began stroking the fleshy shaft.

Ki felt himself responding, growing painfully rigid. And he realized that, whore or not, Daphne was not merely acting passionate now, she was genuinely aroused and eager. She simply loved making love! Obligingly, he leaned back slightly to allow her more room, her talented fondling driving him wild. She unbuttoned his fly.

Now Ki was open and exposed to Daphne's squeezing massage. Rarely had he felt so hard, so thick and throbbing, and he reined in sharply by a grassy knoll. "Daphne, at least let go of me long enough so we can get down, will you?"

Daphne had other notions. "Why dismount to mount?" she murmured, and with agile grace she hooked her left leg across his hips, and began sliding around from the cantle. Poised almost facing Ki by the front of the seat, she gently drew out his aching erection and cupped his sensitive scrotum with her other hand. "Now scrunch back. I've got the saddle horn in places I'd rather not."

Ki moved up onto the cantle, while Daphne balanced on her knees to rise over his thighs. Deputy Oakes's pants were so large on Ki that, despite being stretched by Ki straddling the horse, the open flaps of the front lay wide and unhindering. Rolling the tail of her shirt out of the way, Daphne looked down between their bellies at their coupling. Then, guiding him in with one hand, she slipped down the full length of her haunches to squat blissfully impaled upon his shaft. "Ahhh . . . !" she cooed, smiling rapturously.

The horse, misunderstanding the motions of her thighs and legs, began slowly trotting forward again. Head arched and mouth wide to emit sighs of raw pleasure, Daphne swiftly matched her pumping rhythm with the easy tempo of the horse's gait. She strained against Ki, her arms clutching him tightly around his back, while inside, Ki could feel his urgency burgeoning with every surge of her satiny sheath. He was hardly aware of anything but the incredible sensations of the thrusting, compounding movements as he held her upright, tonguing her breasts, hearing her whimpers.

And as the horse jogged through the meandering canyon, and they jogged along with it, Ki realized dimly, peripherally, that the slopes were broadening and the land ahead was widening. Glancing fleetingly over Daphne's heaving shoulders, he vaguely saw, beyond an intervening ridge, plumes of smoke lifting against the gray drizzly sky. Eucher Butte, it had to be.

"We're almost out," he whispered, tonguing her ear.

"You're in," she whimpered. "I can feel you, deep."

"Out of the hills. And what a way to go."

"Yes . . ." Again she whimpered.

"We're going out with a whimper *and* a bang."

Chapter 16

"How d'you expect me to go arrestin' properly," Deputy Oakes was complaining, "when I'm wearin' only my longjohns?"

"You'd better get to doing your duty right snappy," Daryl Melville retorted, "before you lose them too. Making us believe you were going to help, so we'd uncuff you! And give you a rifle! Then hightailing it away, sneaking around on your fat carcass!"

"Well, I was gonna fight!" Oakes rubbed the middle of his forehead, where clotted blood gave him the appearance of having a red third eye. "I did, too. Struggled somethin' fierce when that howling mob attacted me, but I was overpowered and knocked out."

"Howling mob!" Toby Melville scoffed. "You tripped."

"No such! And I didn't snitch m'own horse, neither."

They were standing in the front room of the outlaws' log cabin, feeling agitated and pumped up in the aftermath of their successful battle. A few men were with them, guarding a half-dozen wounded rustlers, who were slouched grimacing with pain and brooding over the fate they knew awaited them. The combined ranches' crews were still combing the pocket, remorselessly hunting the stubborn holdouts of Volpes's now shattered gang.

Jessica entered from the clearing, her arms filled with Ki's clothing. She placed the bundle on the table, alongside his daggers, his jammed *shuriken* devices, and his other weaponry, which she'd found in a rear room of the cabin. Then, stalking over to the nearest rustler, she demanded with cold fury, "What have you done with him?"

The rustler looked up with filmy eyes. "Who? The gent Volpes brung here?" Pink spittle drooled from his mouth. "Nothin'. He killed Volpes and vamoosed, just afore you laid into us."

Jessica sighed, relieved. "He's alive."

The man coughed. "With a gal."

"A girl?" Daryl blurted. "A lady was here too?"

"It figures," Jessica said, recalling the nightgown she'd found in the shed with Ki's clothing. "If there's a woman within a fifty miles, Ki will somehow get to her."

"Nekkid," the man said, coughing again.

Jessica nodded. "That figures too. He's safe, anyway."

"Safe? Jessie, your friend could be out there anywhere in those wild hills, lost, wandering, catching pneumonia!"

"Leave it lie, Daryl. If Ki's out there naked with a woman," Jessica said wearily, "he'll do fine. No, I'm not so worried about Ki right now. What I'm worried about is that we haven't much time left and we've got to act fast."

"Doing what?" Toby asked, his old face wrinkling with perplexity. "We done what we come for. We stomped these snakes good."

"We've only cut off one end of the snake," Jessica explained. "The rest of its body and head are still very much alive at the Block-Two-Dot. And it'll all wriggle away if we don't stop it."

Daryl gasped. "You mean another raid?"

"Yes, now, as quickly as we can, before Ryker gets wind of what's happened here. If we don't, if he and his men escape, then mark my words, that snake will soon grow another full-sized body."

Daryl grinned and touched his revolver. "You're right, Jessie, and I'm all for it. Let me round up the boys and we'll ride. But what about things here? There's still some mopping up."

"You hit leather, son," Toby said. "I reckon me an' a few Flying W hands can manage what's left."

"Good," Jessica said. "Let's waste no more time. Come on, Daryl. And you too, Oakes, you look in need of an education."

They trooped out the door, the deputy following glumly.

It didn't take long for the crews to be mustered, and voicing their support, they lined out toward the hole out of the pocket. Four of them remained behind to help Toby Melville track down and ride herd on the few surviving rustlers, one of them lending his Flying W mount to a reluctant and melancholy Deputy Oakes.

Once past the waterfall, the riders set a fast pace with Daryl leading the way, Jessica beside him. The miles flowed steadily by, and their unflagging persistence paid off; shortly before midnight, they reached the rugged barrier between the foothills and the flat range bordering the Block-Two-Dot ranch. Daryl now led them in a wide arc away from the direct trail, easing into the sloping, round-shouldered valley grassland in front of the ranch in such a manner as to avoid any Block-Two-Dot crewmen who might be out.

At last Daryl held up his hand as a signal to draw up. The men clustered around him as he explained, "We can't surround the ranch like we did the pocket, but we don't have to, either. The way those high cliffs enclose it on three sides, all we've got to do is spread out and strike all at once along the open front."

"We'll handle it like before," Jessica added. "Nobody make any move until you hear us fire one shot."

"Say," a crewman asked, "who gave the signal last time?"

Silence. Deputy Oakes sat like a stone in the saddle.

"Doesn't matter," Daryl said. "Just remember, when it comes, hit hard with all you've got. They'll be slinging a heap of lead, I imagine, but we've got surprise on our side. Understand?"

A low muttering of agreement answered him.

Jessica and Daryl veered toward the right, making sure the deputy was trailing close by. The crews spread out in an angular line, then advanced cautiously toward the ranch.

The Block-Two-Dot was not as quiet or dark as it had been the night Jessica had first seen it. Light glimmered from the bunkhouse and barn, and the main house windows were ablaze with lamps. A big freight wagon was in the yard, and men were carrying wooden crates out of the house and stacking them in the wagon bed. Another group was loafing next to the wagon, smoking cigarettes and watching the loading, while still other men were saddling horses in the corral.

Puzzled, Daryl turned to Jessica. "What're they doing?"

"Getting ready to pull out," Jessica said quietly. "I don't know how Ryker learned about our raid on the pocket—maybe one of the rustlers slipped through our trap, or one of his crewmen was riding there and saw what was happening—but that's got to be it. He's pulling up stakes, and we got here in the nick of time."

"Then let's hit 'em," Daryl said impatiently. He spurred his buckskin forward, triggering his revolver to signal the others.

Instantly the crewmen surged into action along their line facing the ranch. The long crescent of thundering guns swept in like an avenging tidal wave toward the Block-Two-Dot yard.

Ryker's renegade ranch hands, as vicious and callous an outlaw breed as the rustlers, were caught unawares. With yells of shock and pain, they turned to defend their exposed flanks, some digging in to fire a deadly answer to the riders' challenge, while others dove behind the wagon or into the buildings, blasting back against the onslaught of grimly determined men.

The line charged into the yard, turning the ranch into an inferno of pounding hoofs, rearing horses, roaring guns. Twice Ryker's crew recoiled in wild pandemonium. Twice it managed to rally in its frantic effort to bust out of this ring of death. The attack became a close-quarter melee of pistols and knives and hand-to-hand struggles with those caught out in the yard and grounds, while, with neither conscience nor mercy, volley after volley riddled those trapped inside the bunkhouse and other outbuildings.

The Block Two-Dot crew could only take so much of it. Suddenly they broke, leaping out of doors and windows in panicked retreat, fleeing headlong in every direction, scattering on foot toward the haven of dark hills. Only from one barn and the cookshack now came a few bullets, from remaining knots of desperate men.

Jessica focused her attention on the big ranch house. It had been strangely quiet all during the fight, no mad scrambling from within, no furious shooting from its windows. She wondered why. Maybe Ryker was cowering down in that torture chamber of his. And then she wondered how much of a defense he'd put up before he surrendered. Or died. She started moving toward the house, her revolver steady as she stepped out from the cover of the freight wagon. Then from the corner of her eye, she glimpsed a heavyset rider spurring out of the shadows of the barn, galloping off in the direction of the pass.

"Ryker's making a break for it!" she shouted to Daryl. "He's running out on his own men! Well, not if I can help it!"

She raced back around the freight wagon, where she'd dismounted from her horse. Perversely, the bay shied mincingly as she vaulted into the saddle, helping Ryker by causing Jessica to waste precious moments. Regaining control, she wrenched the horse about and set it into a fast pursuit, firing a slavo from her revolver at the retreating figure. But her aim was no better than anyone else's can be when shooting from the back of a frothingly galloping horse, and Ryker was hunched so low across his horse's neck that he was almost invisible.

Ryker swiveled around and fired back. His shots, too, flew wild. Jessica surged after him along the road to the pass, ignoring the bullets zinging past her. Ryker dove into the pass while he lashed his horse faster up the trail, and plunging in only moments behind, Jessica realized she was losing ground to him. His mount was fresh, rested, doubtless of thoroughbred quality, while hers was livery stable rental, of stout heart, but winded from long riding.

Ryker came in view momentarily as he crossed an open patch of the pass trail, and Jessica snapped a quick shot at him. The bullet struck rock near Ryker's head, making him hunch yet lower as he continued urging his horse onward.

Jessica still pursued him, even though her horse was panting with raspy, harsh breaths. She could feel the bay slowing under her, still game, but simply too fatigued to keep up the grueling pace. Yet she refused to give in, infuriated, recalling her own words about the head of a snake growing a new body. If Ryker escaped . . .

Abruptly, Ryker showed himself again, goading his horse frenziedly out of the pass, into the first draw of the foothills. Jessica raised her revolver to fire, but the hammer struck an empty chamber. She was out of ammunition.

The bay stumbled, recovered, lurched in an ungainly lope.

Jessica reined in, and patted her horse's heaving flank. There was no sense in killing the animal; Ryker had already vanished around the left-hand side of a long row of boulders.

"He got away," she said sourly to herself, quivering with frustration and wrath. "The bastard got away."

Chapter 17

Jessica walked slowly up the hotel stairs and turned down the corridor toward her room, feeling tired, haggard, and depressed.

Passing the door to Ki's room, she caught the faint sound of a woman's giggle, which only added to her pique. She backed a step to the door and, juggling the cumbersome load she was carrying in her hands, rapped smartly on the door. The giggling stopped. A moment later, Ki opened the door and grinned out at her, naked except for the towel clasped around his waist.

"Here," Jessica said, thrusting the bundle of his clothes and weapons at him, "I believe you left these behind in your haste."

"Thanks, Jessie, so I did. Wait a minute." He disappeared with the bundle, then returned, still clad in the towel, and eased out into the hallway, sliding the door shut behind him. "Shh," he said, handing Jessica a telegram, "A girl's resting inside."

"I just bet she is," Jessica replied as she opened the telegram and read:

PRELIMINARY INVESTIGATION OF H AND K SHOW MOST RECENT EMPLOYMENT BY SENATOR TRUMBULL AS CHAUFFEUR AND BODYGUARD RESPECTIVELY **STOP** BOTH WITH PRIOR PETTY RECORDS BUT SUSPICION OF INVOLVEMENT IN RECENT BANK ROBBERY IS REASON GIVEN FOR DISMISSAL FROM SERVICE **STOP** MORE LATER **STOP**

"The night clerk gave it to me," Ki was saying as she read. "The telegraph operator dropped it off when you didn't come to claim it yesterday."

"A lot of good it does now," Jessica said morosely, balling the flimsy yellow paper and tossing it aside. "We wiped out the rustlers and the Block-Two-Dot crew, but Ryker himself got away. I had him, Ki, I had him so close that I could've . . ." She sighed. "Well, I know he came in this direction, and I've been trailing him as best I could on that poor worn-out horse of mine, but he's long gone now."

"No, he's not," Ki said, shaking his head. "As I was coming into town, I saw Ryker heading into the Thundermug Saloon. I imagine he's still there."

"But that doesn't make sense. Why would he go there?"

"Greed. Panic. Halford and Kendrick may be rivals of Ryker, and they may hate each other like poison, but they're tied together by that." Ki indicated the telegram. "By Senator Trumbull."

"Trumbull . . . Dilworth Trumbull . . ." Jessica frowned in concentration, trying to remember what she knew of the senator, but he remained an enigmatic shadow in the back of her mind.

"Trumbull's their common connection, Jessie," Ki continued. "How, I don't know, but I suspect that since they're linked to the same scheme, Halford and Kendrick can't let Ryker fail, because that'd ruin it for them too. That's why Ryker must've gone there, to persuade them to lay their differences aside, at least long enough to save his skin and rescue the setup. And to remove us for good."

"The snake's already growing a new body," Jessica muttered to herself, and then to Ki she said, "I suddenly feel in the mood for a nightcap. At the Thundermug, to be precise."

"Hold still, I notice a thirst coming on myself." Ki went back into his room, and when he came out, he was fully dressed again.

"I trust the lady's not overly distressed about this," Jessica remarked, as they started back along the corridor to the stairs.

"Daphne accepted it in the line of duty, as she does most things," Ki replied. "No, I simply explained I had an urgent need to make a late-night visit. I didn't add that it's in repayment for the man Kendrick sent to visit you in your room."

"You knew?"

"You're quiet, Jessie, but not silent. After the man left, I followed him almost to the saloon. We had a little discussion." Ki smiled as if fond of the memory, but by the time they'd reached the lobby door, he was grim again. "I also didn't add that I wish to repay our second visitor, the one with the dynamite calling card."

"Oh, that wasn't Kendrick's doing," Jessica said as they stepped out into the street. "Daryl told me Kendrick and Halford have an option on the hotel. They would scarcely blow up their own building just to get us. And that's what those sticks would've done, if they'd exploded in my room. Thank Ryker for that trick."

"I hope to."

They moved along the boardwalk, walking slowly, noting that despite the late hour, the Thundermug was still open. It didn't appear to be doing much business; no loud voices or harsh laughter filtered out its batwings, and there were very few people around in the street.

When they were still about fifty feet from the saloon, Daryl rushed up out of the shadows and stopped them. "There you are," he said to Jessica. "That's twice now you've gone off on me."

"I did not. I said I was going after Ryker, and I am."

"Well, how could I know? When you didn't come back . . ." Daryl made a hapless little gesture, then grinned sheepishly. "You're all right, and that's what counts. Now, where's Ryker?"

"In the Thundermug," Ki answered. "Putting his head together with Halford and Kendrick. We thought we'd stick ours in, too."

Daryl's grin broadened.

Jessica, sensing what Daryl had in mind, shook her head firmly. "No, Daryl, I can't let you. Ryker's our game, always has been."

"Yeah, but whose ranch is in hock to what crooked gambler?" Daryl spoke with hard, vengeful relish in his voice. "If there're going to be heads knocked, Kendrick's all mine to butt. Period."

"You're getting in *over* your head, Daryl. Those are killers in there, desperate killers. This isn't going to be any picnic."

"After you, Jessie," Daryl said, opening a batwing.

"Picnic," Jessica repeated, standing there in the saloon entrance as if momentarily dazed. "Picnic . . ." And it was in that moment that the smoldering spark in the back of her mind burst into flame—the flame of rememberance. "That's it! I've got it!"

"Got what? Ki asked.

"Picnic in the park," Jessica replied, and walked in, now so wrapped up in the solution to the puzzling scheme that she wanted nothing more than to get it over with, fast.

The crowd was thin, and somber at the end of their drinking night. The same two white-aproned bartenders were at their stations, wiping down the counter and cleaning up the backbar. Halford was still under the painting of the nude, smoking another torpedo cigar, looking as if he were rooted to the spot. Seeing Jessica, Ki, and Daryl enter, his face turned pale and he sent a worried sidelong glance at his partner, Kendrick.

Kendrick was seated at a different gaming table, this one a bit closer to the front and to the bar. He was alone, and was idly riffling a deck of cards, a whiskey bottle and a glass next to his elbow. When he caught Halford's quick glance, he looked up and gave a slight wintry smile, placing the deck aside and moving a bottle and glass over to it.

"Ryker's not in here," Daryl said to Jessica, as they walked between the tables toward the gambler. "He must be in the back."

Jessica, glancing past Kendrick, saw what Daryl meant. There was a door set in the rear wall, which would undoubtedly open into the saloon's office and private quarters. "It'll be locked," she responded in a low voice. "We'll probably have to break it in."

"Once we get past these two," Daryl added.

Ki was not walking with them. He was edging parallel to them along the far side of the large room, keeping a very close eye on Halford. He skirted around a billiard table nobody was using—then hesitated and went back to it. A pair of cue sticks were resting on the baize, and billiard balls were scattered around the surface of the table. He picked up two of the balls, palming them as he swiftly moved on.

Jessica and Daryl stopped in front of Kendrick's table; Ki halting quite a few feet in back of them, still watching Halford.

"Evenin'," Kendrick said. "Care for a hand or two?"

"I care for Ryker," Jessica snapped. "Get him."

"The good Captain Ryker hasn't blessed our establishment in ages," Kendrick said blandly. "You must be mistaken, Miss Starbuck."

"He's here. You've got him hidden in back, so you three can try figuring out ways to salvage your plans for that parkland."

Kendrick jerked erect, staring at Jessica, while behind the bar, Halford gripped the counter, the cigar tipping from his mouth. And Daryl gasped at Jessica, completely baffled.

"Parkland? Jessica, there's no park hereabouts."

"Not yet," she replied in a short, clipped tone. "But think, Daryl, that huge block on Ryker's map could only represent an area the size of an Indian reservation—or a national park. Like Yellowstone. Bigger than Yellowstone! Ryker buys the land cheap, supposedly in the name of Acme Packers; then Acme merges with American Federated Development, while Senator Trumbull rams his bill through Congress establishing the area as a national park site. Then the government is forced to buy the land from American Federated at inflated prices."

"Gawd! A nation-sized swindle!"

"An *international* swindle, Daryl. There's only one gang, one international ring of criminals wealthy enough and unscrupulous enough to be able to rig such a conspiracy. I've known for some time that Ryker works for it; and now I know that through his complicity, Senator Trumbull is another of its corrupt tools. And I remembered as I was coming in here just exactly who Trumbull is—the chairman of the Senate Committee on Military Affairs."

Kendrick, having regained his composure, sank back in his chair. "Preposterous. Insane. You don't know what you're saying."

"Oh, but I do. I know this new park would be administered by the army, as Yellowstone is. I know the army's controlled by the War Department, and that the War Department is under the thumb of Congress. Through Trumbull's position, a powerful foreign cartel will not only reap a vast fortune, but will also be able to control a sizable chunk of America and our army garrisoned on it."

"Ryker, Trumbull, foreign conspirators . . ." Scoffing, Kendrick reached for his glass of whiskey. "Pipe dreams, Miss Starbuck. But even if your fantasies were true, they've nothing to do with me."

"You and Halford are up to your eyeballs in it," Jessica retorted. "You two learned of this scheme while doing Trumbull's minor dirty work in Washington. So you robbed that bank and rushed out here, spending your loot to buy and option as much of Encher Butte as you could, figuring to cheat Ryker and American Federated the way they and Trumbull are figuring to cheat our government—by squeezing them for all they're worth when they try to buy you out."

"But Jessica, Kendrick hasn't taken my ranch."

"Don't you see, Daryl?" Jessica cried. "He would have, as soon as it came time to sell it to Ryker or American Federated. Till then he doesn't need it, he doesn't want it. He'd let you keep running it, while making sure your father stayed strapped in his debt."

"Yeah, I see now, Jessica." Daryl leaned across the table, facing Kendrick. "I see it's more'n a swindle, it's treason." His dark eyes were icy and bright, and there was no concealing the hatred he felt for the gambler seated before him.

Kendrick pursed his pouty lips and flicked his gaze for an instant past Daryl to the bar. Halford eased closer along the counter, his hands now dipping below and out of sight. A deep hush held the room, as the few drinkers present hastily pressed back out of the line of fire. The silence held, growing, tensing like a wire on the verge of snapping . . .

Kendrick broke first. Cursing, he plunged his hand inside his coat for his stubby-barreled belly-gun. Daryl immediately dropped into a crouch, clawing for his old revolver, while Jessica swiveled aside and made to draw her custom .38. The customers and two bartenders dove for cover. Halford stayed where he was, his hands bringing up a sawed-off Ithaca double-barreled shotgun.

Kendrick, the first to break, was the first to fire. He misjudged in his haste, and the .32 slug from his Harrington & Richardson's Vest Pocket Self-Cocker plowed a furrow along the green felt of the table, a scant inch from Daryl's side. Daryl was still hauling out his Remington, ignoring the shot and heedless of another, his motions slow and methodical and virtually suicidal.

Yet the practiced speed of Kendrick's draw and fire was even too great for Jessica to match. She realized in that split second that she wouldn't be able to level and shoot before the gambler triggered a second time. And their backs were to Halford, and Halford was aiming his shotgun squarely at Jessica and Daryl, who were standing perfectly targeted for the two unchoked twelve-gauge shells in its breech. Unfortunately for him, Ki was already throwing one of the billiard balls. Ki had begun his pitch at the same moment he saw Kendrick twitch his arm toward his coat. The ball smacked Halford in the mouth, sending gold-filled teeth flying with the sound of snapping tree branches.

Halford started falling, taking the shotgun with him and accidentally discharging one of its barrels. The blast flew high, shattering one of the chandeliers hanging from the ceiling near Kendrick's card table, the spray of glass and kerosene distracting Kendrick for a second. And Daryl shot him between the eyes. The gambler lurched and slumped to the table, spilling the glass and bottle and deck of cards, his snub-nosed pistol hitting the floor.

Ki killed Halford with his second toss, a whiplashing overhand that hurled the ball like an arrow. It struck Halford, who was still crumpling from the first ball, in the forehead and crushed the frontal plate of his skull. Fitting, Ki thought as he watched Halford plummet out of sight; it seemed somehow right to repeat the stoning Daphne had given Deputy Oakes.

"The door!" Daryl shouted at Jessica, lunging past Kendrick toward the rear. He never slowed, but rammed into the back door with his left shoulder, tearing the door loose from its hinges and popping its lock. He surged into the room with Jessica on his heels, their revolvers braced in their fists.

Two burly men were in the room, neither of them Ryker. Daryl cracked the first man in the face with the barrel of his revolver, but couldn't reach Jessica in time to save her from being attacked.

The second man, partially concealed behind the opening

door, had leaped out and snagged Jessica by her gun arm, and was savagely attempting to wrestle her pistol away. She wrenched back, kicking and scratching, but was unable to break free or bring her Colt to bear. In their struggle, she stumbled back against a bureau, almost upsetting it. Frantically she fought for her balance, clawing the bureau with her other hand, her fingers closing around the handle of a china water jug teetering on the bureau's top. She scooped up the jug and bashed the man over the head with it.

It was enough to send the man staggering, and Daryl dropped him with a bullet through the knee, then grinned at Jessica, and sprang for the partially open window along the far wall.

"Ryker may've gotten out here," he said, raising the sash and poking his head out. But all he saw outside was Ki.

For Ki, back in the saloon, had had a different idea where Ryker might have gone. While Jessica and Daryl had run for the door, on the assumption that Ryker had locked himself in the rear quarters, Ki had the feeling that Ryker was already out and making his escape.

Sprinting in the opposite direction, out the front of the saloon, he veered around the side toward the weedy lot that abutted the rear of the building. He skirted a stack of beer kegs and jumped up onto a small loading platform, raised about four feet off the ground. Just past the platform were three horses, and Gurthied Ryker was mounting the middle one, while two other men stood cinching their saddles.

Ryker had his revolver out. "Damned Starbuck meddlers!" he snarled, and triggered his revolver three times, very fast.

Ki twisted in a low, rolling circle; the first of Ryker's bullets struck a beer keg, and the second splintered the platform deck between Ki's legs. The third went straight down into the earth next to Ryker's horse, because by then a thin, tapering dagger was protruding from Ryker's chest.

Ryker coughed, shaking from the impact of Ki's thrown dagger. He started mounting higher but couldn't quite make his saddle, and for a moment he clung with his hands grasping the horn, then slumped back.

The man on his left had danced away from the horses, and had dropped to his knee to sight his revolver. He was hunching like that, steadying his revolver, when a bullet from the rear window struck him in the side and toppled him over.

The third man fled out across the back lot, losing all interest in the confrontation.

Rising from the deck of the platform, Ki dropped off onto the ground and walked over to Ryker. The man remained in his strange position, a boot in one stirrup, both hands grasping the saddle horn, the index finger of his right hand curled around the trigger of his revolver, preventing the pistol from falling. His whole body had a soft, sagging appearance to it. When Ki loosened Ryker's hands, the man crumpled to the ground, as if deflating.

Ki removed his dagger, wiped its blade on Ryker's shirt, and slipped it back into its pocket on the inside of his vest. Then, from another pocket, Ki took out one of his *shuriken;* he'd purposely brought it along for just this occasion, having taken it from his jammed device before leaving his hotel room. Bending down, he stuck one star-pointed edge into the dagger wound as a memento, as a warning sign to other members of the cartel. Straightening then, he walked to the front of the saloon.

Jessica and Daryl were waiting for him outside the batwings. "Daryl pegged one from the window," Jessica said. "I didn't realize he could shoot that well at an angle."

"I didn't either," Daryl said. "Was it Ryker?"

"No, but Ryker's dead," Ki replied. "I'm glad you got the one you did, though, because the man was about set to peg me."

They started down the boardwalk toward the hotel, as Daryl ejected spent cartridges from his Remington. "I guess that takes care of that, then. You'll be leaving tomorrow, back to Texas?"

Ki didn't answer. Jessica also didn't respond for a long moment, but finally said, "Well, we might have to stay over for the inquest. There's sure to be one held, don't you think?"

"If not, there should be," Daryl answered, cheering.

"Plus the investigation," Ki added.

"Into the rustling and parkland swindle?"

"No, Daryl, I had more in mind into how Deputy Oakes's horse got from the canyon to the livery stable. Not to mention the disappearance of his clothes. I doubt he'll have forgotten that."

"Not much to fret over," Jessica said. "After tonight, the deputy's goose has been burnt to a frazzle." She turned to smile at Daryl. "Since we'll probably be staying in Eucher Butte a few more days, maybe we should spend it searching for your stock."

"I know where the stolen herds are. Up in some box canyons at the far end of Ryker's ranch," Ki said, then he let out a wearied sigh. "I'm not feeling up to it, I'm afraid. I need a rest."

"That is a shame," Jessica consoled. "Well, you just stay resting up in your room. But my, I do dislike riding alone."

Daryl moistened his lips. "Reckon I might be able to fill in. They are my cows, after all." He reflected a bit longer, then suggested, "How 'bout if I slept over the night at the hotel, and me and you take a ride over thataway after breakfast tomorrow?"

"Whatever you think best," Jessica said primly.

"Good," Ki remarked with a flicker of a smile as they stepped into the lobby of the hotel. "I can see everybody is going to get a hell of a rest."

GIANT-SIZED ADVENTURE FROM AVENGING ANGEL LONGARM.

BY TABOR EVANS

penguin.com/actionwesterns

M456AS0812

GIANT ACTION! GIANT ADVENTURE!

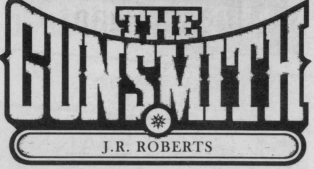

THE GUNSMITH

J.R. ROBERTS

penguin.com/actionwesterns

M455AS0812

DON'T MISS A YEAR OF

Slocum Giant
by
Jake Logan

Slocum Giant 2004:
Slocum in the Secret
Service

Slocum Giant 2005:
Slocum and the Larcenous
Lady

Slocum Giant 2006:
Slocum and the Hanging
Horse

Slocum Giant 2007:
Slocum and the Celestial
Bones

Slocum Giant 2008:
Slocum and the Town
Killers

Slocum Giant 2009:
Slocum's Great
Race

Slocum Giant 2010:
Slocum Along
Rotten Row

Slocum Giant 2013:
Slocum and the Silver
City Harlot

penguin.com/actionwesterns

M457AS0812

Jove Westerns put the "wild" back into the Wild West

LONGARM
by Tabor Evans

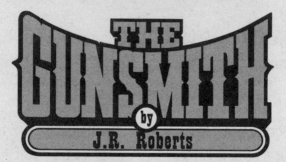

THE GUNSMITH
by J.R. Roberts

SLOCUM by JAKE LOGAN

Don't miss these exciting, all-action series!

penguin.com/actionwesterns

M11G0610